LOTTERY RAGE

A Novel By

Robert Lance

ISBN: 1983688290
ISBN 13: 9781983688294
Library of Congress Control Number: 2018900384
CreateSpace Independent Publishing Platform
North Charleston, South Carolina

CHAPTER ONE

Who goes to the Waffle House every morning and orders the same crap over and over again? Morons like me who live in an RV with a broken down microwave. I didn't have the money or motivation to fix the microwave, so I went to the Waffle House for the grease and to read the paper.

I didn't buy the paper because I was interested in reading about a team of overpaid, obese losers who called themselves football players. I didn't buy the paper to read about the dozen or so crime sprees going on at any one time unless I knew the victims. I could care less about the weather unless I had a concrete job. Sometimes I peeked at the society page to check in on what my celebrity buddies were doing, which pissed me off because I was never invited to the galas. So why did I buy the newspaper? I bought the paper to check the Tennessee lottery numbers.

I had a routine when I was home in Nashville. Every morning I marched down to the Waffle House, which was across the street from Hajji's liquor store, where I usually bought my lottery tickets. The Waffle House crew knew exactly where I sat, what

I wanted, and that I was a lousy tipper. I always had the same order, number six, coffee black. So why did I have to tell the waitress, Jolene, exactly what a number six was? I *knew* she knew. She never wrote it down, not one damned time.

"One or two biscuits?"

I held up one finger as always.

"Sausage or bacon?"

Jolene knew, so I tested her mental recall. "Guess."

"Bacon. You want your eggs over?"

I nodded.

"Hash browns?"

I nodded again. We did this every morning. "Jolene, what does it take to get a second cup of coffee around here?"

"You just walk your lazy redneck ass up here to get it. I ain't got no time givin' refills to lousy tippers."

"That's not true. I leave you the newspaper every morning."

Jolene waved her hands in front of her face like she was batting off a swarm of bees. "Hah! When have I got time to read the newspaper? Shit, Owen, you don't even read the newspaper. You just lookin' up lottery numbers. I seen ya all the time and it's always just lottery numbers." She laughed.

"If you ever brought me a refill, I'd split the winnings with you."

Jolene laughed again and said, "Sammy, did ya hear that? Redneck Owen said he'd split the lottery with me." Sammy Gonzales was another of her regulars and a day worker I sometimes hired. Why did everybody but me think that was funny?

Sammy said, "Owen, you got as much chance getting a refill as you do winning the lottery." My Waffle House friends thought Sammy was hilarious, including me. That's how my pungent friendship with Jolene muddled along. I respected Jolene who was a single mom struggling with the harshness of balancing her world. She was actually a very good waitress, except when it came to me. In a way we were friends, sorta. I was her one regular customer she didn't have to be nice to, and she enjoyed picking on me because she knew I was a good sport and enjoyed her annoying games.

There, in the Waffle House, just after six in the morning, I was perusing the winning lottery numbers of the previous day. People who buy lottery tickets, idiots like me, never read the small print, so the newspaper did us a favor and printed them in great big bold type. I looked at the numbers, then at my ticket. I looked again. Holy Shit! They all matched in the same order. It just wasn't possible. The chances the newspaper screwed up one of the digits had a higher probability than me actually winning the whole damned thing. I looked at the grand total of the lottery; sixty-four million and change. My hands were shaking so badly I could barely see the numbers again. That's why the type is bold and large.

The thoughts going through my mind were one gigantic squeal, like an overpowered amplifier at a rock concert. My day worker friends looked at me strangely, as if I had disintegrated right in front of them. Even Jolene waltzed her ass from behind the counter.

"Are you okay, Owen? You don't look so hot." She saw my lottery ticket and picked it up before I could stop her.

"Gimme that!" I snatched it out of her hand. Jolene was the first person who tried to steal my money, but she wouldn't be the last. I realized right then and there that I had better cover my ass.

"How many numbers did ya hit, Owen? Two?" She chuckled. You're carryin' on like you hit 'em all."

"Yeah, two," I lied.

"Lucky you," she huffed as she stormed off, not pouring a drop of coffee from the pot she carried in her hand. I realized all I had was a crappy piece of paper that meant nothing unless I could safely, and I emphasize safely, get it into the hands of the head cashier at the lottery office. If any of the working stiffs at the Waffle House had any inkling what was in my hands, I wouldn't make it to the front door. That point panicked me. I looked at the concerned stares coming from the regulars sitting in the restaurant. My imagination kicked into overdrive, and I backed out of my usual spot. I was trying to play it cool, trying my best not to show just how freaked-out I was. I joined in line to pay my tab. Two-Bags Ferguson, a husky construction worker, had a furrow on his forehead and a frown on his face.

"Man, you look like road kill. You want me to drive you to the morgue?"

Sammy chimed in. "Yeah, you really do. Jolene, did you piss on Owen's number six again?"

"Uh huh, honey, just like yesterday and the day before. Owen is carryin' on like he won the lottery. He hit a couple numbers is all, enough to buy tobacco spit and a bucket of minnows."

Two-Bags was more than curious, and his hand went to my breast pocket where I had my ticket. "Lemme see."

My hand went to cover my pocket, and I took a step backwards. Two-Bags showed his fangs and snarled. "Jesus, Owen, I just want to see your ticket. Not like I was goin' to steal it or nothing. You need to take the day off and go fishin'."

My hand was still shaking when I handed Jolene a ten. I told her to keep the change, so I did give her more than table change. You would have thought I had spit in her face by the nasty snarl on her lips. "Wow! I'm goin' to frame this and put it over the door. 'Jolene's first dollar tip from tight assed Owen Fletcher,' is how it's gonna read."

I walked quickly out of the Waffle House with a big urge to sprint home. Instead, I whizzed over to Hajji's place to see if he could verify the winning number, but he didn't open until ten. I bought most of my tickets from Hajji, a sorry assed, buck-toothed Iranian who owned the liquor store across the street. He always acted like I was stupid enough to split my winnings with him or something just as idiotic. He'd always say, "We win big this time, Mr. Owen," *We* were not partners. *I* bought the ticket and it should've ended there. Hajji always had his hand out. I didn't have a family to feed, and I didn't really care about the measly pay off, so *one* time, just one, I split with Hajji because he begged so well. Do not ever split your winnings. If you do, you'll find yourself setting a precedent that could potentially land you a lawsuit, as it did me. I didn't exactly know how it worked, because Hajji wasn't on easy street peddling lotto tickets.

I never signed the tickets since most of the time I didn't have a pen on me. I never expected to win either. Now that I had a time bomb in my hands, I hauled ass to my crappy RV.

I locked myself in and found my Smith and Wesson peashooter, but no pen. I knew I had a carpenters pencil in the truck and figured that would turn into an unreadable crappy signature and could be erased. "No goddamn pens. Shit!" Maybe I could borrow one from next door. I scurried over and knocked on the door. I waited and waited. I knocked hard enough to tip the single-wide on its side. I saw the curtains part and then heard the lock click. I heard the dog, old Jeff, and his owner, Kim, bark in unison. I couldn't understand old Jeff, but Kim I did understand. "Get the fuck off my porch or I'm callin' the cops!"

"What the hell?" I looked down and saw I was carrying the pistol. Shit! So there I was running around the trailer park, waving a pistol in one hand and a winning lottery ticket in the other. Screw it. I had to get my ticket turned in before someone shot me, called the cops, or robbed me.

CHAPTER TWO

I jumped in my pickup and joined the morning traffic rush without a single clue where I was headed. Have you ever looked on the back of a lottery ticket? The damned print is so small you'd have to be related to Superman to read it. I figured the people who ran the lottery assumed the chances of anyone winning were pretty slim, so they didn't waste a whole bunch of ink telling you how to collect your money.

I was bobbing in traffic while squinting at the damned fine print. I was going in the wrong direction, which cost me another agonizing hour dodging mindless bimbos whining on their cell phones, acting as if they weren't late for work. There was a loaded gun on the front seat, and I was tempted. I think that was my first encounter with road rage. Normally I didn't give a shit, but that day I was buzzed. Money brings out a lot of personality changes, and I found it out at the speed of sound.

The State Lottery office wasn't what I'd expected. Shouldn't the State Lottery office be a hole in the wall next to a pawn shop, with a CLOSED sign in the window? The lotto office was in an upscale downtown office tower. People came and went from the lobby, and I wasn't expecting anyone else to be there claiming prizes. No one was doing back-flips or yelling, "I won!" I concluded they must be all losers wanting their money back.

I looked for the teller window, or some kind of window with bars on it. All I saw was a nice looking young woman at a reception desk painting her fingernails black. The woman looked up at me with a pleasant enough smile and raised an eyebrow. I looked like Digger Dan with work boots, and I saw just a hint of disapproval on her face.

"How may I direct you?" She said with a slight frosty edge.

Bursting at the seams, I finally got the opportunity to blurt out what I had been dying to say all morning. "I won the lottery!"

She rolled her eyes, looked around as if she heard that all the time, and she said, "I hear that all the time." *Geez, Owen.*

"But I did! Here's my winning ticket." I pulled the ticket out of my jacket pocket. "Can I borrow your pen? I need to sign the fucker."

"Sir, take my advice. Calm down. You should always sign your lottery tickets when you buy them." She rolled a pen to me, and I signed the ticket with an explosion of relief drifting out of my lungs. "Please take a seat with the others; someone will be with you. Do not talk with anyone about your winnings."

"What others? Just how many winners could there be besides me?" I wondered how many pieces of my pie were going to be dished out to other lucky meatheads using my investment scheme.

Broom Hilda, with the black fingernails, escorted me to a waiting room. Holy shit, the room was nearly full. I sat down next to a young couple with a kid sitting on the mother's lap, giving her a breast examination. The adults were grinning like cats, whispering to themselves. I was dying to know what they won. Maybe I'd have to split the ticket with them. A middle-aged man with a cheshire grin on his face looked at me with interest.

"How much did you hit?" He asked, with a cheerful lilt to his voice.

"The lady said for me not to talk about it."

"Come on, tell us. The kids hit 'em for ten grand. I got eight out of them. That fellow over there with the cowboy hat won fifty grand."

"Yeah, can you believe it?" the husband said, rather than asked. "We've been saving for a house. This is going to do it for us. So how much did you win?"

What was I supposed to say to happy saps who are just upside down tickled with chump change? I wasn't going to screw up their day by telling them the truth, so I lied. "I won a couple of hundred."

Every eye in the room was on me. They knew I was snarking them, so I said, "How the hell should I know? I don't even know what the numbers are for sure. When they give me the check, I'll tell you."

The husband said, "That's easy enough to find out." He pointed to a promotional big screen that scrolled the winning numbers below gimmicky commercials promoting the lottery. I fished for my ticket and checked the numbers. I'm sorry, but I just about lost it right there.

I had to find the men's room really fast because I was about to unload my loose bowels with an explosion of shit. Fortunately, there was a men's room in the waiting area. The single stall had a customer, and I had to wait my turn, straining my butt cheeks to the limit. My bowels were screaming bloody murder when the other customer finally finished. I quickly shuffled through the stall door, feeling a horrible quaking down below. My belt came loose, the zipper went south, and the rumbling increased. My claws snatched at my drawers, and I squatted to hit the toilet seat. It was close, but I didn't make a clean launch. A cloud of shit splatters painted the walls inside the stall. What a fuckin' mess! Explosive and diarrhea are two words you don't want to use in the same sentence. As I sat on the pot filling the porcelain bowl, I thought to myself, this probably happened a lot in this office.

I finished my business, unstuck my ass from the toilet, and did an awkward battle damage inspection. Great, just fucking great. Now I had shit stains on my boots and my Levis. Normally I would just sneak out, go home and change, but I had a sixty-four million winning lottery ticket that I desperately needed to cash in. I did my best, but when you shit yourself, you're going to stink up the room, no matter what.

I went back to the waiting room and found myself alone in a matter of seconds. As a former rock star wannabe, I knew what it was to play to an empty room, but this was different. You want to clear a room and be first in line? Do what I did. I could hear the kid screaming his ass off in the distance. Hell, he shit his pants ten times a day and should be used to it.

The receptionist walked towards me and stopped, then backed up a few paces outside of the shit-smell-zone. Her hand went to cover her nose. She tentatively said, "We were just looking for you. Wait here and I'll have Gordon join you." I saw her back and heard her gag.

A plump, young gerbil danced into the room with an outstretched hand and a toothy smile. "Gordon Jenkins," he said just about the time his nasal senses picked up my scent.

I reached for his hand and said, "Owen Fletcher." It was a speed-greet, and his hand recoiled faster than a cobra strike, maybe the shortest handshake in recorded history.

"This way," he gasped. I followed at a respectable distance so he could get a breath of fresh air. He stopped at a door with his nameplate on it and put his hand out to stop me. "Would you mind coming back later, I mean, when it's more convenient for both of us?"

"Sorry, but no. Yeah, I had diarrhea in the men's room. I'll bet you get that a lot."

"This is going to take a little time, and there's no hurry. It would be best for both of us if you'd come back later."

"I'm not leaving before I get my ticket punched. There's just too much riding on it."

Knowing what I know now, I should have gone home, cleaned up, and taken the matter up later. I would pay dearly for that oversight. At least I could tell my grandchildren what I did when I claimed the lottery. I shit my pants.

What I got from Gordon was a much abbreviated set of instructions, with him standing in the door way and me sitting at his desk. Gordon placed a large stack of materials on his desk and said, "If you have any problems or questions, I'll be standing in the hall." I had forms to fill out with a bunch of options, ones I should have paid attention to as he rattled off what each meant. I barely understood the gerbil chatter echoing from the hallway.

I could have an attorney set up a blind trust so I didn't publicly identify myself. Lottery officials didn't like that because they wanted to use you later as advertisement for their money laundering scheme. We just brushed over that topic. I thought I was in a catch twenty-two anyway. Without the check, how would I pay an attorney to set up a blind trust? Dumbshit me never considered that any cockeyed attorney would advance his fees against the winnings, and Gordon never mentioned it, which he should have.

We breezed right along and before I knew it, I was done. It was time to cut the check. I should have known something was up as Gordon stood beyond the doorway, passing me goodwill marketing crap. Rather than argue about it, I signed up for all of it. *Now write the freakin' check.*

Gordon collected everything and stood in the doorway, when he said, "Mr. Fletcher, we have to validate all of this, and it could take a few weeks. In the meantime, we would ask that you not tell anyone about your claim. Our public relations counselor will be in contact with you."

"Whoa! I'm not leaving without the check."

"It's not that simple. We need to validate a few things first. I'm sure everything will check out."

"What are you talking about? I have the ticket. I signed it. How much simpler can it get?"

Gordon's look made me feel like I was in a criminal line up. "We need to verify the ticket's authenticity, where you bought it, a few details concerning your purchase, and other obligations that might pertain to it."

Gordon was questioning whether I had stolen or forged the ticket. "I told you I bought it from Hajji's liquor store. I've got better things to do than churn out counterfeit lottery tickets!"

"Settle down, Mr. Fletcher, we're just following standard protocols. You'll have your payout in a few weeks, if not days."

I was highly pissed off by the time I left the State Lottery office…without a check. The emotional experience of that morning captured all my experiences from the day I was born. I was scared five times, pissed off a dozen, paranoid a couple, and embarrassed three or four times. That was a lot to bank in the space of a few hours, particularly when I went six months without experiencing any of the just mentioned tantrums. Truth be known, I'd already learned a lot about being a millionaire. I couldn't endure this all by myself, so I decided to spend what little cash I had on one big bender with my best friend, Frank.

I was just about to the door when a very beautiful woman, about six years younger than me, shouted my name. Yeah, I did a double take. Who wouldn't? I needed to clear the building. Here she came, hell bent for my attention. *Please no, don't embarrass me.*

Her shining smile turned to a frown. "Mr. Fletcher, My name is Megan Marsh. I'm the director of Public Relations for the lottery. I'll be working with you on the promotion that you've been kind enough to help us out with."

I got why she was frowning, and I could feel my backbone wilt. I grumbled something as an acknowledgement, as my "totally fucking embarrassed" light flashed in my brain.

"Congratulations! You're one of the few privileged people who can claim they actually won the lottery."

Shit, I thought she was going to kiss me. I backed off a step or two. She must have misread my reaction.

She sniffed the air. "I grew up on a farm..." She swayed her head side to side, like it was supposed to mean something. She looked at her watch. "Can I buy you breakfast? I'd like to get to know you, the sooner the better."

If I couldn't sit through breakfast smelling the way I did, how did she expect to? "I've already had breakfast, and I've got chores waitin' on me."

"Can I call you tomorrow? I'd like to get started right away. Here is my business card. I'll be in touch."

How about that? I watched her tight buns swish across the lobby. I wasn't sure how our next conversation would work out, but I was definitely looking forward to concocting some lie about me being Farmer Brown with a herd of pigs.

CHAPTER THREE

I stopped by Hajji's liquor store. What a monumental mistake. He was being a prick as usual, so I laid into him. "Hajji, did you know you're required to have a pen for customers to sign their fucking lottery tickets at the point of sale?" He ignored me and wouldn't speak to me, like always. There I went, pissed off for no good reason. See what I mean? "I forgot, you dumb-fuck Iranians still use stone tablets and chisels, and you have no clue what an ink pen is." I slammed my palm to my head for effect.

Hajji and I were friends in a weird sort of way. I was a redneck, and he a towel head, but we kept it civil and generally showed some respect towards one another. I just crossed that line and Hajji exploded.

"Mr. Owen, go buy your lottery tickets somewhere else. It is my freedom to tell you so. I'm an American now, and I don't have to put up with your shit."

For once, Hajji defined how he felt about freedom and his adopted country. Good for him. "I've had a strange day so far. I'm sorry. I don't know why I said that to you." Yes I did, but there was no need to be as hateful as Hajji.

"You're a red-neck peckerwood. You don't know what a bad day is, Mr. Owen. You smell like shit, now fuck off. Go."

When you're going to shoot yourself in the foot, you should not have the gun pointed at your head when you pull the trigger. I couldn't contain myself, so I blurted out, and I was going to regret what I said, "I won the lottery, Hajji."

The one cardinal rule about winning the lottery is *don't* tell a soul. I mean not one freakin' living, breathing soul. Not your Siamese twin, your grandpa with Alzheimer's, and especially none of your low-life relatives. Guess who the first person I told when I won sixty-four million? Hajji! Shoot yourself in the head first, but I am warning you, just get the check, and head for the other end of the planet.

Hajji looked at me dumbfounded. It didn't sink in. "How much?" he asked.

"All of it, the whole nine yards."

I don't care how long Iranians live here; there are just some idioms of the English language they don't pick up on, so Hajji just blinked.

"Hajji, the jackpot was sixty-four million and change. I won it all."

Call it what you want, ape shit is a good start. Hajji went darting about his natty little liquor store like a chimpanzee with a four-week-old case of gonorrhea. He bellowed in babble, which if I understood a word of it, translated to "We Won! We Won!" I heard a few Allah's tossed about, which invited a suspicion there was another person to split my winnings with. Iranians hugging infidels was against their religion, and Hajji forgot his place. He was on me like a chimp in a peanut shop. Hajji had a pounding and tossing fit that lasted for freakin' ever.

He realized I hadn't paid for my liquor purchases yet, and settled down. I didn't have enough cash to pay for all the liquor I intended on consuming, so on that one rare occasion, Hajji made me write out an IOU. See what I mean about Iranians? They can produce an ink pen in the wink of an eye when there's something in it for them.

I left Hajji standing behind the register chanting, "*We* won the lottery."

Back at the RV I just needed to settle down and think through what I was going to do with all that money. Every postcard I had ever seen flashed through my mind. I could see my house in every one of them. My *real* home was an RV parked next to the dumpster station. I needed to calm down. I was exhausted, so I flopped on the bed beckoning dreams.

Maybe I could go to Colorado and get my ex-wife, Bonnie, back. Did I really want to live in Colorado? I could buy Colorado, at least a huge chunk of it. I couldn't linger on one thought long enough to make any sense as another one entered my brain.

Forget relaxing. I popped out of bed, found the pen I stole from Hajji, and sat down to write out a budget. I gave myself another fifty years of quality life, which I multiplied by twelve, then divided by the thirty-two million I was expecting after taxes. I did the math twice. Okay, I was now on a budget. I couldn't spend more than $53,000 per month. I laughed until tears came to my eyes.

I called my friend and loan officer at Planters Bank. "Hey Jerry, what's the annual pass book savings rate?"

"Geez, Owen, you're thinking about starting a pass book account?"

"Yeah. How much on a pass book?"

Jerry put me on hold. The loan manager didn't know the passbook savings return in his own bank? Jerry and I became friends when my band, 'Shylock' hit the music scene in Nashville. Jerry was something of a social kingpin in the music crowd. He knew all the hotshots and all the gossip on the circuit. He was also the non-offensive token homosexual whom everyone loved. Even after my music career tanked, Jerry was on the inside and always tried to get me back in the game. He's the only person who remembered my birthday, so that made him a real friend.

Jerry got back on the phone and told me, with a minimum balance of $5,000, I would have an annualized return of one half percent. I did the math. Damn, if I could squeak by on $40,000 per month, I could live for the next fifty years and never touch the principle.

"What are you doing, cutting lawns? Saving up for a bicycle?" he laughed.

"No. I have some extra cash coming my way."

"It's none of my business, but you should get caught up on some bills."

"I intend to. After I'm caught up, I should have some extra money lying around."

"Owen, who died?"

"What? Nobody died. Jerry, I said I have some extra cash coming my way."

"Bullshit. You're so far underwater that your fucking credit rating is measured in fathoms. Sorry about that construction loan you wanted. I did my best, pal, but when your credit score is double digits, there isn't much I can do to help you."

I had a surprise for my pal Jerry.

CHAPTER FOUR

Thirty minutes went by when I saw a dozen Iranians descend on the trailer park. People from their part of the world are easily excited to riot. They were going door to door, alarming the residents and looking for me. Even though they were singing in Farsi, or what ever shit language they speak in Iran, I picked my name out of the chanting drone. Allah was included in the chant, which I thought was a blasphemous translation that went, "Jesus Christ, where the fuck is Owen?" Raving lunatics took over the park. As my luck would have it, one of the bimbo drama queens ratted me out, and my RV was besieged by a growing mob of Iranians and unemployed park residents, which was just about everybody in the park.

A jubilant Hajji choked the living shit out of me with hugs and kisses. In English he chanted, "We won the lottery." Where had I heard that before?

I yelled into his ear, "*We* did not win the lottery. *I* won the lottery."

I thought Hajji was going to have to rely on his English-to-Farsi dictionary to catch the drift. While we tried to communicate, word must have traveled back to the Waffle House, as I saw Jolene in the growing crowd. She whacked Iranians around like bowling pins, pushing her way to me. She wrapped her beefy arms around me and started kissing me. Jolene was a big woman with a perpetual bad attitude. Then was not the time to piss her off. I let her dribble my ass around until I couldn't take it anymore.

I wrestled free of her and yelled, "Why are you here?"

"You promised you would split the winnings with me if you ever hit the jackpot."

Jolene and I had never had a civil conversation from day one. I distinctly told her I'd give her half the jackpot if she'd just pour me a refill, and I still didn't get that cup of coffee. Whatever I told her was out of duress. "Jolene, have you ever figured out why I leave you table change?"

"Owen, a promise is a promise. I got witnesses."

About that time, Hajji connected with the translation of "I and WE." He started rattling off in babble talk, and the mood suddenly turned ugly. It was all I could do to squeeze through my RV door. I hadn't even received the check, and there were already two borderline maniacs wanting half of the haul...each. Fortunately for me, a squad car pulled up, and the Iranians dispersed like cockroaches, leaving a pissed off Jolene howling at me from the street. The cops talked to her. Then they came for me.

"Afternoon officer, how can I help you?"

"Your girlfriend says you won the lottery. Is that true?"

"She's not my girlfriend. She's a hysterical waitress from the Waffle House with some kooky notion I won the lottery and that I promised her half."

"Did you?"

Why can't cops complete a sentence? "Did I ...what?"

"Win the lottery."

"If I had won the lottery, I'd be at the Ritz Carleton drinking champagne with a five hundred dollar hooker instead of sitting in this rattle trap listening to a completely whacko bitch, who I don't know shit about." I made the cop laugh. Actually, I had come up with a very good idea.

After a brief confabulation with the cops Jolene went on her sorry-assed way kicking the can down the alley. The cops left me to resolve my problems on my own. I was dead certain that my last known residence would be getting visitors night and day. I say it was my last known, because I put my 'ten minute' plan into action.

Living in an RV and having a P.O. Box address had its advantages. When screwing the trailer park queen got overbearing, or the IRS came looking for me, I could vacate with everything I owned in ten minutes flat. I had the routine down pat, as I've done it before, and what did I tell you about ten minutes? I was bogey down and gone. The RV belched blue smoke, and I was on my way to my temporary hide out, the state park out by Hickory Lake

Hickory Lake State Park was where I went when I needed to find temporary lodging for a couple of weeks or until I could find a new trailer park pad to rent. It cost me twelve bucks a day. I knew the park ranger, Frank. His home was a trailer at the park, and he lived there full time as the night watchman, which was ridiculous because Frank was too blind-drunk to see anything by the time the sun went down.

As I pulled to a dusty stop at the ranger shack, I heard old Frank bark at me from the dumpster site across the gravel road. "Yo, Owen, what did ya do this time?"

He wouldn't believe me if I told him, so I ignored him by asking, "Do you have any RV pads available?"

"Your usual hideout is taken. How long you figure you'll be staying this time?"

"Not sure, Frank. Two years tops." We had this same conversation every time I went there.

"You know the rules. Two weeks, then you gotta move."

I set up in the very back of the park, and it took just ten minutes. Frank came by to collect. I asked Frank if he could give me a ride into town so I could pick up my truck.

"I don't drink and drive, so it'll have to keep till mornin'."

I looked at my watch, and sure enough, it was five o'clock somewhere in the world, but not in Nashville. It was only just past two, and Frank looked like an unsteady boulder, swaying slightly, getting ready to roll down the mountainside.

I really needed to have an adult conversation with a human being, so I called my brother, Ron. Ron was not a human being. And not much of an adult either. He was a scientist who cared even less than I did outside of his invisible environmental sphere. Because of his peculiarities, I never knew if Ron would answer his cell phone. Step one, he picked up. So far, so good. Step two, I said, "Hey Ron!"

Long silence. Longer silence. "Hey Ron!"

"Owen! Hahahaha."

He lived in St. Louis and I lived in Nashville, but that laugh put us in the same room. "Guess what?"

"Don't start with that, Owen. I'm busy. What's up?"

"I won the lottery today. I shit you not. I won the whole fucking thing. What do you have to say about that?"

"Hahahaha! Did you hear from pops? He's retired, you know. He's back in Georgia, chasing pussy."

"Ron, I won the damn Tennessee lottery; sixty-four million dollars."

"That's cool, Owen. Did you hear about Lawson?"

Lawson was my other brother. "Ron, did you hear a fucking word I said?"

"Yeah, anyway, Lawson and his goofy girlfriend did a tandem parachute jump, and the main chute failed to open. The emergency chute was a fraction of a second early or they'd both be dead. Lawson's busted up pretty bad and his girlfriend, Tammy, is too. Lawson said he'll be out of work for awhile."

Ron and I talked about family and not one time did he ask me about the lottery.

So much for an adult conversation with a human being. Okay, I'd call Lawson. He was the oldest and most different of the three of us. His daredevil lifestyle and whacky opinions were why he was called 'Crazy Lawson.' He also hadn't held down a real job longer than two years. I decided to call him when I sneaked back to the RV and poured myself a stout scotch.

I had grown up in Indiana and was a child prodigy. I had a full ride scholarship to Purdue University. Inches away from an engineering degree, I threw it all away for a chance to strum guitars in the mountains of Colorado and screw ski bunnies until dawn. I had lived with Lawson for four years in Lafayette, Indiana, during my college years. Lawson went berserk when he found out I had quit Purdue and blew the scholarship. It was years before he would even speak to me after I pulled that stunt, and we were still not close.

Anytime I called Lawson, there was always an anticipated moment where I might say something that would set him off. With trepidation I dialed his number.

"Yo, Owen, you fuckin jack-off. What's up?" Lawson couldn't answer the phone like a normal person.

"Lawson, I just talked to Ron. He told me what happened. Why didn't you call me? How the hell are you doing?"

"Jesus, that was two months ago. I'm about all healed up. Got six more weeks of physical therapy and I'll be good as new. Tammy's a tough old broad, but it's going to be some time before she gets out of bed."

"Damn it, you should have called me. I have some good news."

"Yeah, I heard. Ron called and said something about you winning some cockeyed lottery."

"Yeah, I did. I seriously did."

"Take my advice. Take the money. Don't take the twenty-six year payout shit plan. They reel it out to you slowly, but you'll always be in the fifty percent tax bracket. The fuckin' government is going to get half, no matter if it takes twenty-six years. If you croak somewhere along the line, they clobber your ass with estate taxes and keep the rest. I heard about a case where a guy did that, and government snipers killed him so they wouldn't have to pay off the full amount."

What did I say about Lawson being a conspiracy nut?

"I've got it covered. I told them I wanted the cash out, and I volunteered to make it public. When I get the cash, I want to send some up your way to help out."

"Owen, don't do that. There *are* people watching. They track lottery winners and their *entire* families. They get everyone mad at you and then scam the living shit out of you. Do you have any idea how much danger you're in?"

Jesus Christ, I still hadn't had an adult conversation yet, and the day was wearing thin. What I would later learn was Lawson was spot on. I gave up and let whiskey carry me to my dreams.

CHAPTER FIVE

The public relations department did get in touch with me. Megan and I played phone tag. She was my handler. Those were her words, not mine. I made the connection immediately. She had the leash, and I was tethered to the other end of it. She was very helpful from the start and explained why I needed to keep my mouth shut until the validation was confirmed. Then she gave a preview of what to expect later. She already inked in a calendar for me; luncheons, presentations, speeches already written, photo and media spots. There would be damn billboards, three acres long, with me wearing a penguin suit, toasting the Tennessee Lottery. Megan scheduled sporting events, society bashes, and a homey, gosh shucks, rags to riches TV biography. I jumped the leash right then and there.

I liked Megan, so don't take this wrong. She was just doing her job, and I was doing mine. She treated me like a mongrel that she was cleaning up to take to a high society dog show. I was no mutt of the month candidate, no matter how many dog treats she fed me. I just wanted my life. If I hadn't shit my pants and signed off on all this bullshit, I'd be free and clear to do whatever I freakin' wanted to do.

Here's something I didn't know. Megan was not a state employee. She worked for a private firm which had signed contracts from me, and they'd sue my ass off if I should skate on them.

Cell phones are weapons and Megan used hers to barrage mine. I'd let it go to voice message, but in a moment of weakness I answered my phone. We got through the small talk in two seconds and she started in on me. "So let's start with your background. You're a farmer, right? I guessed it. You have a P.O. Box for an address, so where is your farm?"

"It's not actually *my* farm. I work for a friend that's from Borneo and when he goes there, I watch his herd."

"Borneo? Is that in Tennessee?"

"No, it's a big island in the Pacific, which is where I'm going when I get my money."

For a classy woman with a higher education, she was geographically challenged, which was good news. The bad news was her demand to know the GPS location of my RV.

"I'd like to come by and take some photos of you in your home."

What she was driving at was my 'humble home' under the sewer lid of the trailer park I lived in. "I'm homeless."

"That's even better. You live in a shelter? Under a bridge? God, this is great."

That's how PR people think. I was actually a step above being homeless. I owned rental properties, did odd jobs, and tuned guitars for rock stars. What was wrong with that? It's a piss-ant way of getting through life and we all do it. Life is tough, and I got by doing what I did. All this money wasn't going to change Owen. Nope. I'm Owen Fletcher, just your average citizen avoiding the intrusions of government, very content to fuck with the powers that rule my life.

Megan's pungent comment pissed me off. "Megan, I'm just a guy getting by and very uninteresting. Yeah, I live in a P.O. Box and it's none of your business. I'm a private citizen that pays his taxes," which was not exactly true "and I have privacy issues."

"You waived those rights. You belong to me. You have signed contracts with us and don't even think about breaking them."

That's exactly what I did. I lived at the state park, went on hikes with Frank, and took calls from Megan, day and night. I always thought about the lottery. My new house measured in square acreage, not in square footage. I could go places, real places, like the moon if I wanted. Hell, I'd buy Rhode Island and carpet the entire state just for grins.

How about dating classy women? Megan's vision played to my mind. She was uncomfortably in my subconscious, which sent a bolt of fear to my brain. Truth be known, I lived with an inferiority complex that I hadn't paid attention to for the last ten years. Being a millionaire with a center-fold hood ornament girlfriend had its appeal, but it also scared me. I hadn't been in a serious relationship since Bonnie walked out on me ten years ago, which, maybe wasn't serious enough.

My TV was at the mercy of sunspots or some ridiculous phenomena. I discovered mice had nibbled into my cable, and I helped Frank repair it. From then on, old Frank stopped by every morning for coffee to watch the hot Fox News dolly on my TV. Frank didn't have cable to his trailer, which I thought was odd because all he had to do was run a cable from one of the rental sites. Frank, meticulously honest, lived by a standard of rules, which I found annoying at times.

Over coffee one morning, Frank had something on his mind.

"Your time is up, Owen. Two weeks is max, that's the rules. How about you just move one spot over? Nobody's goin' to notice. However, you have to move. What with everyone lookin' for you, that's the smart thing."

"What do you mean by looking for me?"

"You were on the local TV this morning. You're the mystery man who won the lottery. I got that much figured out. It's in the paper too. Everyone wants to know who the mystery man is. They described him pretty good too."

"What did they say about me?"

"Said you looked like a scruffy hippie with a long pony tail and that you hauled ass from the trailer park. I sorta figured out you're hiding out from the media crowd."

I jumped up and ran to my truck to find my cell phone. My message log was full. Most of them were from Megan. She was a clever little minx and the very minute my ticket had been validated, she made it into a media event. Shouldn't someone from the lottery have notified me and given me my money before turning the hounds out? Megan violated my contract, which pissed me off.

I checked my message log again. Fat-assed Gordon called, asking me to stop by the office. When I went back to the RV, Frank told me he'd keep his mouth shut, but I still had to move. Rules were rules.

I found a secluded spot in the park and set up camp, just to get Frank off my back. The next order of business was to call Gordon. He told me to stop by his office to discuss 'matters.' Matters, my ass. I wanted my money and told him so. My rant blew his eardrums out, and the conversation ended with him hanging up.

Frank suggested I disguise myself, just in case of a media ambush at the lottery office.

"Good idea, Frank, but I quit dressing up for Halloween when I turned thirty and threw all my crappy costumes away. Got any ideas?"

"You look like Halloween year round, son. A good start would be cuttin' off that damned pony tail. You look like you escaped from the petting zoo across the road."

I supposed my ponytail was my trademark, but I didn't think it made me look like a Shetland pony. What the hell did I care? I said, "Cut it off Frank, light trim around the ears."

While he slashed my locks, he jabbered away about Owen joining the human race. Frank was not a barber, and I didn't expect to look GQ, but when I checked the mirror, my hair looked like a hilltop ravaged by a wildfire. It didn't cost me anything, and my hair would grow back in a generation or two.

Wearing a ball cap and sunglasses, I sneaked into the lottery office without being attacked. The same receptionist, with green fingernails, greeted me. I could tell by her turned-up nose and the sneer on her face that she recognized me. I thought she'd burst out laughing, but she contained herself and told me to have a seat to wait for Gordon.

A rather subdued Gordon stopped about half a football field away and tentatively called my name. I hopped up and he sorta jumped, as if someone had just butt fucked him. We got that all over with, and he took me to his office and made nice about me winning the lottery.

"Your lottery ticket has been verified. Normally, we would arrange to have the funds available to you in a day or two, but we need to clear up some matters before we can release any funds."

There he went with the 'matters' bullshit again. "What 'matters' are you talking about?"

"In the State of Tennessee, we are required to determine if you have any court ordered payments, arrears in child support, alimony, public fines, back taxes, property liens, that sorta thing. These must be resolved before we can release your winnings to you."

"I have a settlement with the IRS, and I still owe them about $8,000 dollars."

"The IRS claims you owe them $39,000 in fines, penalties, and delinquencies. It appears you were late on your last few payments, which the IRS claims, nullifies your settlement."

"What? I always make sure I pay those bastards on time."

"Your attorney needs to straighten this matter out. Now, Polk County has back tax issues with you, as does the city of Nashville.

The State of Colorado has an outstanding warrant for your arrest for your overdue tax issues."

"I just want my money. Can't we just take out what I owe from my winnings?"

"You should have your attorney check into these discrepancies. When a settlement is reached, you'll have to sign a waiver, allowing us to clear up your back debts."

"Just let me sign the waiver and let's finish our business. Can you believe it, my winnings are being stalled because of a few parking tickets?"

"We can do that, but there's just one more thing. Do you have your divorce decrees, Mr. Fletcher? It would certainly speed things up. We just need to check that you don't owe alimony or child support to either of your ex-wives. The county records in Colorado don't indicate that you were ever divorced."

When I was young, mother taught me to respect the sanctity of marriage. With mother's moral Catholic dogma concerning sex fixed in my mind, I did what she expected of me. Having regular sex with any woman, according to my mother, required a marriage certificate. I followed that advice twice. Both times, the women I married walked out on me. Given another opportunity, I will live in sin and suffer the moral consequences later.

My first year in the mountains I tripped over a hot Irish chick with a dance troupe, whose smoking hot ass and big tits jiggled better off stage than on. I went to Bernadette's shows and suffered through all the squeaky, ear-piercing, fingers down the chalkboard crap that the Irish call music. There are just so many stomping combinations one can come up with, and it gets as boring as the music after about thirty seconds. Well not exactly, I could watch tight butts wiggle and tits flop until I'm dead, but I got that form of entertainment from Bernadette, without having to listen to Irish music.

Bernadette was a light-hearted nymphomaniac right up to the day we married. After that day, she put out on national holidays, and if you count them, it's about a dozen. Halloween was not one of them. Thank God for Columbus Day. I suggested we include Irish holidays, but all I received was a frozen stare. We struggled along for a season, hitting half the holidays, but eventually, like the cold blowing snow, we just drifted apart. The divorce was like stopping the circulation of a weekly magazine. Make the call, sign the cancellation form, then call it a day. It was about that time I started buying lottery tickets.

Right after Bernadette left me, I hooked up with a ski instructor named Bonnie; she had moguls on her that would make your ski tips stand straight up. Yeah, I did. I married her. She put out on every national holiday and the holidays of all the countries in the United Nations, which was about everyday and sometimes three or four overlapping holidays. I still love her to this day.

Bonnie couldn't break away from Colorado. She tried Nashville, but when the snow fell in the mountains, Bonnie was back on the slopes, trying to forget about us. I guess it worked because I never heard from her again. That was a life changer for me.

My personal recollections were interrupted by Gordon turning up the volume. "Do you have divorce papers?"

"God almighty, I signed the papers years ago. Both times."

"You need to produce the divorce decrees or locate your ex-spouses and have them sign an affidavit to that effect."

Was Gordon serious, or was he just fucking with me? The only legal papers I kept were things like my birth certificate and social security card; everything else was junk mail. I know I signed the papers sent by both women. I didn't recall getting a divorce decree in the mail. As much as I moved around, it's possible they ended up in some dead letter file in the basement of the post office. What was I going to do? I was up shit creek and I needed to get some legal help.

CHAPTER SIX

After wishing I had set fire to Gordon's office, I almost made it to my ratty old pickup in the parking lot. Megan, the PR chick, jumped out at me from her Mercedes hotrod. She turned on her charm and rattled questions at me. I pretended she didn't exist. Megan grabbed my arm, tugged on it like a dog with a fresh bone. I could drag her around the parking lot all day and never tire of it. Out of courtesy, and courtesy only, I stopped.

She looked at me with puppy dog eyes and said, "Take me to lunch and let's talk about it."

I hadn't taken a woman to lunch in years, and I certainly didn't feel in the mood then. I wasn't exactly dead broke, but a lunch date didn't fit my budget.

"No way, Megan. Gordon didn't give me any lunch money."

"Come on, Owen, lighten up a little. You'll get your payout. It's just going to take a little time."

"We could drive through the Taco Bell, and I could buy you a ninety-nine cent taco."

"Okay, let's go."

That was *way* too easy. I looked her over. She wore one of those upscale safari business outfits. After a ride in my pickup, she'd pay hell getting the grease stains out of her ritzy suit, and I told her so. She offered to drive, so I hopped into the hotrod with her. She hadn't left her parking space before she started up with me.

"Who cut your hair?"

"It's an Einstein cut. Do you like the look?"

Megan smiled, showing an unusually glossy set of white choppers. "Actually, I do like it. You *are* kinda cute, you know."

I knew bullshit when I heard it, so I returned the compliment by saying, "Who cut your hair? Rasputin?" That wasn't a nice thing to say, but I wanted to change the tone of the conversation. "I know a park ranger who can straighten it out."

Megan looked at herself in the rear-view mirror and gave me a satisfied look of contempt. She switched gears and began yapping about herself, just in case I might be interested in a hot looking marketing graduate from Vanderbilt, between boyfriends, and a feminist with a thousand-horse power attitude. Megan wasn't my type, after all, she had a lot of class, which meant she also had plenty of goofy opinions. She tried them out on me as she whizzed through several slightly yellow-red lights.

Megan wheeled into an upscale Mexican joint. "This okay with you?"

"What happened to the ninety-nine cent tacos?"

"I'm buying," she said

I wasn't buying, not the tacos, not her slick come on, and certainly not what I knew was eventually coming next—a sales pitch. After we seated ourselves at a nice table with a miniature sombrero centerpiece, Megan said, "Why haven't you returned my calls?"

"I listen to my cell phone messages once a year and I always return both calls"

By now, Megan learned that I was sensitive, caring, and a total reclusive smart-ass, so she ignored my quip. "What happened with Gordon today?"

"I have to pay my parking tickets off before I get any cash from the pay out."

"That's normal. When you win a prize the size of yours, it's easy for the person to vanish to anywhere on the planet. It's happened before. The state wants to make sure that all public debts and a few personal ones are resolved."

"He wants me to produce my divorce decrees to determine if I have any alimony or child support judgments. My problem is I don't have any decrees."

Megan laughed. "You mean you have more than one ex-wife?"

"Why is that so funny?"

"I don't know. I wouldn't peg you for a guy who would commit to anything."

"Don't worry, it won't happen again." I gave Megan a brief explanation of the dilemma.

I wasn't telling dirty jokes at the bar. I told the woman my sad saga about women I once cared about. Megan was easily amused, which pissed me off.

"It sounds like you're a bigamist. Are you sure you were legally married to either of these women? You need to check the county records."

"Of course we were married. I went before a justice of the peace, both times, and we signed documents."

"You'd better check."

"Jesus, that sounds like I need to go back to Colorado."

"No, you can pull it up on the Internet."

"I don't have a computer."

Megan was a little more than just interested in my two exwives, which invited big whoppers from me.

"What caused your first marriage to fail?"

I was pissed that she had categorized my marriage as a failure and the innuendo that I was to blame. "It didn't fail, it just went away. Bernadette was as frigid as a polar bear's ass. We simply lost interest in each other. She went on her way, and I never heard from her until after she disappeared from the colorado mountains."

"Why did she contact you after leaving? I'll bet she wanted you back."

"Yeah. She said she had a tumor removed and that she had a whole new vaginal outlook on life. I was a better lover than the piccolo playing leprechaun she hooked up with, but I was already married to Bonnie.

"Was she pretty?"

"Who?"

"Your first wife, Bernadette."

"Yeah, in a flat chest, scrawny assed way." I lied about that. Bernadette was well built and a very intriguing looking woman. She was dark-Irish, had large blue eyes and contrasting locks of silky black hair. Bernadette had a button nose and a Cosmo cover girl face. I'd lie and said, "I'm not a tits and ass man." I tried to make Megan interested in the subject, and there was something else. I wanted her jealous of my exes.

"What happened to what's her name?"

"You mean Bonnie? Same thing. You ever watch kids at a park going up and down the sliding board until they can't take another ride? That's how good our sex life was. Our rides together down the sliding board weren't enough. She never told me why she left. I suppose she was as much into her skiing as I was into my music. When the snow fell in the mountains, she was gone."

"Why didn't you ever go find her?"

"I wake up every morning thinking I'll drive the RV back to Colorado."

"You have an RV?"

"Yeah, doesn't everyone?" For some reason I didn't tell Megan I lived in it. Every single time a woman, whose interest I had captured, discovered my bland lifestyle in the RV, and quickly moved on.

"Do you still love her?"

"Everyone who meets her loves her. It was a long time ago, and I suspect she's married and has a family. I leave it at that."

"What was Bonnie like?"

I had this lie pre-packaged. "She was a lawn dart with long legs. I'm a leg man," I said, because Megan had nice ones. "Bonnie was the typical athletic Nordic Snow Queen. In fact, she won the title once. Grace, beauty, charm, that was Bonnie, and I lost the whole package."

I accomplished my task of making Megan jealous. She cleared her throat and changed the subject. Megan told me she would research my problems for me. I gave her the marriage dates and the approximate dates of the divorces.

Megan said in a snobby, 'I'm so much smarter than you' cadence, "I've been in this business for awhile, and I can tell you I see some nasty things come out of the past. What if one of your wives or old girlfriends brings a paternity suit against you? You need to get yourself a lawyer. While you're at it, it might be a good idea to get a will drawn up."

She crossed her legs seductively and said, "We need to become friends. This public relations campaign would work much better if we did. When I get the info off the Internet, I'll stop by your place, and maybe we can go out for a drink."

Getting laid in my RV was a hygiene issue. No hard-working, five dollar whore would even consider setting foot in my cockroach mobile, let alone a high tone babe of Megan's caliber. I had an answer for her that I kept to myself. *Let me check with the Terminix guy, and I'll get back to you.*

My lunch date with Megan wised me up and left me with a sickening feeling in the pit of my stomach. The after-burner in my brain kicked in. I never had the opportunity to question the motives of a woman flirting with me. All my life, I had been Owen au natural, barren of attributes, and naked as a jaybird. I acquired a new luxurious set of clothes that was thirty-one big ones, which gave me another new brain-twist to deal with.

There was still the matter between us about outing me to the media, and I told her what I thought about it.

"Owen, we never make public announcements of any kind until well after the winnings are deposited into the proper custody. We would have a law suit from you and the State of Tennessee staring us in the face."

If I believed her, we could be friends. My problem? I didn't believe one word she said.

CHAPTER SEVEN

Three weeks had passed and I didn't wake up fresh and wide awake, as I've done for the last thirty years. I had "concerns" that kept me wide awake at night. I received a call just as I put the final touch to my morning ritual. It was Megan. "What! I'm busy."

Good morning, I tried to text you. Did you get it?"

"I'm sorry, I don't know what 'text' is. Send me a smoke signal. I know how to read those."

Megan laughed. "You're going to love this smoke signal, Tonto. The state finally finished conducting its search engine research, and there are no more outstanding domestic claims against you. You owe taxes, fines, and there are no civil actions at this time. I talked to Gordon earlier, and we're ready to do the premiere at the end of business today."

I knew it was still early and I was still in the ass scatchin' mode, but I didn't get it. "Huh? What's a search engine?" was all I could squeak out.

"It's like a credit report, only through different official sites. It takes awhile. Where are you?"

"Hiding out, enjoying a private and peaceful moment." I wasn't going to tell her that I was sitting in an out-house in Hickory State Park. I could just see the smirk on her face over the airwaves.

"I want to know where you are. Hiding out is a good idea, but you and I should meet before we go to the lottery office."

We didn't have any business until after the winnings were in my hands. I informed Miss Megan of that fact.

She yelled, "Today is Owen Fletcher Day! Pay day!"

Good news and a good shit, all at the same time. I did a Tarzan yell, followed by imitations of other wild beasts. I screamed, "Mother, Mary, and Jesus, I'm richer than you are, Frank!" I'm sure Frank heard me, as did everyone else in the park. I stomped the floor and banged on the walls, yelling bloody murder at the top of my lungs. I could only imagine what passers-by thought was going on in that out-house in the park.

I whooped it up for a bit before getting back to business.

I still had Megan on the phone and I could hear her laughing. "Owen, you there?"

"Yeah, I'm here, but I won't be for long!"

"Who's Frank?"

"He's a very good friend I owe money to. I have friends, and you don't need to know them all."

"Owen, this is your first hayride, and you need to be prepared for it. Lottery officials always throw a big bash when they announce the winner of the lottery. There'll be cameras, journalists, publicists, and hotshots wanting to capture the moment you sign for the payout. Do you want to handle this by yourself?"

I didn't. I also knew the transaction wasn't something I couldn't do over the phone. Megan was right, of course, and I wanted someone to be with me when the moment arrived. Frank would be great, but Frank's uniform would tip off my hideout to the media.

"Owen, are you still there? Your pay day is at four PM, and we really have to cover some ground before then."

"Yeah, I'm thinking about it. We should meet somewhere. How about that Mexican joint?"

"Meet me there for lunch. We have a few things to go over."

"The meeting isn't until four, why so early?"

"Owen, you don't even have a clue. Just promise me that you'll be there."

I shaved and showered at the communal bath at the park. At the RV, I searched for some decent clothing to wear. I had a wrinkled old polo shirt with a duck logo on the breast and a wadded up pair of Dockers that I hadn't worn in years. Both smelled of mold, so I made a quick trip to a Laundromat to make them wearable. I changed in the bathroom, then headed off to meet Megan. I was feeling all dressed up when I arrived ten minutes late to the Mexican joint. Megan saw me and rolled her eyes in disgust.

"What was that for?"

Megan was looking sharp, classy, and a bit overdressed. The first thing out of her trap was, "You can't go looking like that."

"Like what?"

She pointed a crooked finger at me and barked, "That! You look like a homeless rat with a bad haircut. You need to look GQ, or at least like a member of the human race. Your shirt has food stains on it, and I can't guess what those splotches on your pants are."

"Those splotches aren't mine. They belong to my girlfriend, and I'd like to remind you, she was on her period when she put them there." I was lying about that part.

Megan rolled her eyes again, not even amused one tiny bit. I looked down to see what she was talking about. The stains were very faded, and you'd have to look hard to see them. I didn't buy new pants just because I got a drop or two of squirrel blood on them.

She delicately skated around that line of talk and said, "We'll just have to go shopping after lunch."

"Megan, I haven't worked since this all started, and I don't have any money for a fancy wardrobe that I'll never wear again." I finally sat down to get out of the inspection line.

"Don't you have a credit card?"

"Yes, but it's tapped out, and I've made minimum payments for three months." There she went with those eyes again. If she kept that up much longer, her eyeballs would be permanently frozen in the top of her head.

"Look, you can't go looking like you just finished skinning a deer. I'll loan you the money, and you can pay me back." Her little unhappy pasty face told me that she was not really willing to spring for the tab. I avoided financial obligations, so I gave her an out. "Not one single time did anyone ever come up to me and say, 'Hey, Owen, you have crotch stains on your slacks.'"

Megan laughed and replied, "I need to take control here. We do it my way, and we're going to stop off at a barbershop to see if anything can be done about that nasty haircut."

We needed to rush through a fast lunch if my makeover was going to be finished by four. Megan made good time munching a Mexican salad, and I speed-mulched through a burrito.

Megan happened to mention, "Have you given any thought about the transaction? Do you have an estate planner lined up to manage your money?"

"Yes. When they hand me the check, I'll hop down to Planters Bank and deposit it into my savings account. I have a checking account there too, and it will be easy to transfer back and forth."

Megan thought my well laid out estate plan was over-the-top funny, especially when I told her that I made myself a budget, and I would try to keep my monthly bills below forty thousand. Tears of laughter were rolling down her cheeks, and she choked on her salad.

After her funny bone healed, she said, "I've never heard of anything so damn funny or ridiculous. I'm not a financial planner, but a passbook savings account? You can't be serious. You should let a professional manage your assets. Putting it all in a passbook account is like burying it in a can in your backyard."

"I would, but I don't have a backyard. This keeps it simple, and I know where my cash is. If anyone is going to steal my money, it's going to be me."

"Does the bank know that a large cash infusion is headed their way?"

"No. It's a big-assed bank, so why do I need to tell them shit?"

There she went with the eyes. "Do you have any idea how screwed up the transaction will be if you show up with a thirty-plus million dollar check at closing time for a passbook savings account? They'd laugh you off the property. Our first stop should be to meet with the bank president. We need to leave now. We're running out of time." Megan took out a twenty, plopped it on the table and headed for the door. I followed, and we took her car for obvious reasons.

We were in downtown Nashville in no time at all. We rolled through the bank door in a hurry. I've never figured out why the damn bank's doors have to be the size for the fifty-foot woman to walk through without bending over or why the door takes a linebacker to open it. We arrived in the lobby to hit the first roadblock. The bank president was tied up all day. We could make an appointment for sometime into the next ice age before we would get to see him, assuming he hadn't died with the rest of the human race. I had an ace up my sleeve. I knew Jerry, right? We used to party together. I took Megan by the arm, and we glided across the marbled floor to Jerry's office. His secretary looked up at us, or to be more specific, my blood-stained trousers. She pinched her nose and asked how she could help us leave.

I cheerily said, "Jerry and I are old buds. I stopped by to just say hi."

That earned me a cold stare and a question about my appointment, which I didn't have and wasn't likely to get. I could see Jerry loafing behind his desk pretending to be a banker. I shrugged my shoulders, stepped past the secretary, put my head around Jerry's open office door, and said, "Hey Jerry, it's me, Owen Fletcher! Got a minute?"

Jerry looked up from his desk and stared at me, blinking owl eyes. "Who?" he asked with a puzzled expression. I saw him glance to his secretary, who was probably calling the FBI.

I stepped in to show myself and said with glee, "Owen Fletcher. We talked a few weeks back."

"I know Owen Fletcher, so who are you?" He also looked at the splotches on my pants. Jerry squinted his eyes, and a glimmer of recognition showed in them. "What the hell happened to you, Owen?" he asked none too cordially. "You don't look even close to the same person with the long glossy pony tail."

I ignored the slur and said, "I need a minute of your time and it's important."

He looked around in all directions, hoping the Feds would show up and cart me off. "Look, Owen, I'm real busy and I don't have the time."

"Hey, Jerry, I just won the lottery, and I want to put the money in your bank."

He laughed and said, "Yeah, and I'm the queen of England."

Jerry was sure enough a queen, but not of England. "I *did* win the lottery, and I have someone with me to prove it."

He looked out his picture window and saw Megan. He nodded to his secretary, and she showed Megan into the office. She introduced herself and handed a business card to Jerry.

Less skeptical, Jerry asked Megan, "What portion of the lottery did ole Owen here win?"

"The mother lode. You're going to have upwards of thirty million dollars hit Owen's passbook account by the close of business today."

"Are you serious? Passbook account? Thirty million dollars?"

I was miffed and said rather indignantly. "No—Fuckin' Pesos, dickhead. We talked about it, remember?"

"Yeah, I do, but I thought you were talking about lawn mowing change. Nobody puts money into a passbook account but ten year olds saving for a bicycle."

Megan had my back. "Yes, sir. Don't ask me, but Owen insists on it. Your friend is a nut job."

"That he is," said a stunned Jerry. He tapped a few keys on his phone, picked up the receiver, and began speaking to presumably the bank president's secretary. "Mrs. Fogerty, can you interrupt Mr. Kline? Something important is happening down here." Jerry explained what had him so excited.

The bank president must have taken the express fireman's pole down, as he quickly appeared in Jerry's office, glad handing me. The minute that my thirty-plus mil hit the bank, I would have a line of credit, my credit card bill taken care of, and a vast offer of services the Planters Bank could provide. We had to cut it short, as we had an agenda, but Jerry was going with us to make sure the transaction was executed properly at the other end. There was no way he was going to let a thirty mil client out of his sight.

"Owen, I don't pay any attention to the lottery, so was that thirty mil before or after taxes?" Jerry asked.

"After."

The first stop was the barbershop and a thirty-dollar do-job, which didn't included a shave or manicure. We then hit a swanky upscale men's store called Henry's, or something along those lines. I didn't want Jerry's assistance picking out an outfit unless I wanted leather chaps with the butt cheeks cut out of them.

Megan had fun and so did I. She had her hands all over me, all in the interest of straightening out wrinkles. She was swelling with pride as she watched her creation take shape. I swelled too, but it didn't have a thing to do with my pride. I couldn't help it. Her face was close to me. I whiffed her scent while she was tugging on sleeves or her hand was pressing against wrinkles on the expensive jackets that I tried on. Her dry run disrobing me felt good, but not the way you'd think. I felt cared for, picked at in a nurturing way. At the end of my makeover, I didn't recognize myself in the mirror. I had to admit, it was a change for the better, and I felt pretty hot looking. Megan thought so too. Whatever Jerry gushed on about didn't impress me that much.

CHAPTER EIGHT

It was PAY-DAY. I hadn't had one of those in a very long time and was nervous about going to the state lottery office to collect. Gordon recognized Megan, and the media three ring circus began. Ten minutes into it, no one mentioned the reason I was there, which was to collect the loot and make the transfer. I posed with all sorts of big shots getting their pictures taken with me holding a phony check the size of a shower door. The check read sixty four million and change, which was a crock of shit, but I acted as if it was all mine. After taxes, thirty one million was nothing to sneeze at, so my grin was the real deal. We rehearsed my part receiving the check and signing for it, which was really a prop to fool the public. After more takes than a Vincent Price horror film, I was getting antsy and perturbed. I could understand why Howard Hughes was found wandering around in the desert in his underpants babbling like a moron. The freakin' camera crew pushed me around, this way and that.

I looked over at Megan and she was too busy—being busy—directing the photo op. I raised my voice and asked. "Would you tell Cecil B De-whoever to stop pushing me around? I don't screen test all that well, but I'm a damned good stunt man and I *will* kick his ass."

I got a menacing chuckle as though I had actually screwed up my acting debut. I replied, "Nobody pushes Howard Hughes around, so why am I different?" Silence.

Megan held up two fingers and gushed in a whisper, "Just two more takes honey."

So work this out. How much PR leverage can the Tennessee lottery get from a winner who is a borderline vagrant, anti-social, paranoid, and trending towards a Howard Hughes lunatic episode? I started laughing because in my mind I could visualize doing the next take in my underpants. Eventually the umbrella light screens were removed and the lights shut off. The camera crew packed up and took off in a hurry.

After thirty minutes of smooth speeches, hand shaking, and brown nosing, I was asked to say a few words. Megan had them written out for me, and I put on my most sincere Ward Cleaver accent and spilled out words as if I were on stage again. When asked what I was going to do with all the money, I said, "I'm going to Barnes and Noble, buy up every picture post card, then I am going to all the places and have my picture taken." I received a nice applause and a few laughs.

The deed was done and the flashy caterers brought out the champagne. But it wasn't done. I had yet to get a penny. Megan nuzzled my neck and cooed. "When was the last time you had this much fun?"

"When I played the part of Jesus on the cross and everyone forgot I was up there and closed the auditorium for the weekend. Speaking of Jesus Christ, when do I get my thirty silver coins?"

"Stop being sacrilegious. Enjoy the moment. Drink some champagne."

"Nope. How do I know it doesn't have hemlock in it? It's getting close to closing time, know what I mean?"

She pushed a flute at me anyway and patted my ass.

We dismissed the media and went into Gordon's office where Jerry sat down to make the money transfer with the head of the lottery. There was a stack of checks to pay off what I owed the Federal Government, student loans that I didn't remember or care about, nuisance public obligations, fines, fees, and just because. How the hell does a fourteen year old get six parking tickets in Orange County, California while residing on a farm outside of Lafayette, Indiana? I had an overdue bill from the public library that went back to my days in college. It took awhile to explain each check. *Would you please come on and give me mine?*

The lottery commissioner typed in his password and added a flourish of entries while mumbling under his breath. I could tell he didn't want to let go of that much money all at one time. Jerry said, "It's a good thing you had the forethought to give us a heads up, or this transaction would have been intercepted and put on hold well into the next century. Who the fuck deposits thirty one million into a pass book savings account?" He laughed. Jerry tapped a few key strokes and said, "Bingo, there it goes! You wanna see your account, Owen?"

Hell yes, I did. I also had a strong desire to see the cash in one big heaping pile, just for kicks, like the movies, when two suitcases are opened for some drug kingpin to examine. My pile would probably fill up a city trash truck, and I put that idea out of my mind. There was my bank balance on Gordon's computer screen;

Previous Balance: -$9.39 Current Balance: $31,876,249.62.

I howled and howled like a coyote with a hard dick. I'd been drinking champagne earlier, and I went on a romping rampage, making a royal mess of Gordon's office. No one seemed to care. I hugged Megan, and she hugged me back. Hugging Jerry was risky, but I did anyway. I hugged everyone, even the receptionist with the orange fingernails. My arms became wings, and I flapped my way through the lottery office like a hundred pound blind Canadian goose with no sense of direction. I was rich,

F-I-L-T-H-Y RICH! Hell, I was climbing on chairs, tap dancing on Gordon's desk, singing and squawking, barking and growling. I was having a Howard Hughes moment. Shit, I was Howard Hughes. Next thing I knew I was riding on Jerry's shoulders heading for the door. We were done and the three of us left the building with a train of media geeks waiting to follow us.

I asked a stupid question when we settled into Megan's hotrod. "Well Megan, what now?"

"You tell me, Daddy Warbucks." She wiggled her eyebrows and grinned, which caused me to laugh.

I said, "Pull over to an ATM; I owe you a few bucks. Then we can party. You up for that, Jerry?"

"Hell yes! You made me a hero today. Do you realize what you did for me? I *sooo* owe you big time!"

"I need to pay some bills. Can I get my hands on some of the green?"

Jerry said, "Forget it, Owen! It'll keep."

I said, "No. I owe my friends some money and I'm paying up before I party." I thought about Frank and Megan.

Megan reached over the console, stroked my upper thigh, and said, "It'll keep."

I saw a flash in those gray-blue-green eyes of hers. By then I knew her mood when her eye color changed. Most of the time they were gray-blue, but when she was flirting, the green light came on, and who knew what that meant?

Jerry giggled just a little too pitchy, "Hey, Owen, you have a platinum account, with a gold key pass, which means your daily limit is $5,000 at any ATM."

I owed Megan about $600 for the make over and Frank twice that for the short cash flow loans over the weeks. Owen Fletcher wanted to be debt free before another ounce of liquor passed my lips. We stopped at an ATM and I tested the gold key. It gave me $5,000 dollars in $600 dollar increments. That was more than I made in a month by a long shot. I was in shock, knowing I could do this twice, *every week,* for the rest of my life. I paid Megan and threw in a hundred dollar tip for the interest.

Megan smiled and said, "Where to?"

"Do you know where Lake Hickory State Park is? We need to stop off at a liquor store on the way. We're going to party with Ranger Frank, dance in the woods and howl at the moon. Frank's been dying to meet you."

"Seriously, you want to celebrate with tics and mosquitoes and a guy named Frank?"

"I'd rather be among tics and mosquitoes than my music pals who sucked my blood without me knowing it. I've been dancing under the starlight by myself for a very long time, Megan. I just want to go to the camp ground, play the songs I wrote, and dance with a beautiful woman in the woods. Just one dance, Megan. Just one. Then we can party any way you want."

"Owen, I have plans. It's all set."

Jerry, from the back seat, piped in, "Humor him, Megan. Owen owns his music, and it's a beautiful journey. I vote the state park. If anyone deserves a dance in the woods, it's Owen."

While Jerry and Frank unloaded the beer cooler, I went inside the RV, put on an old demo-tape I made ten years ago, and turned up the volume as high as it would go. Megan and I had that dance in the woods, to the music I wrote and recorded. The way she melted into my arms, I fell instantly in love with that moment. I'm sure she did too. My voice echoed among the pines, and we danced and danced, feeling the pulse of the music and the pulse of our rhythm. It was one of the happiest moments of my life. How could it get any better? I was carried away in the caressing woods of Tennessee. I needed for that thought to linger because that moment swept me away. I truly felt more than rich throughout my heart and soul.

It was not to last, as Megan looked at her watch. "It's time to really party. I have a surprise for you." She reached up on her tiptoes and kissed me, took my hand, and led me back to the campsite where Frank and Jerry were drinking beer under the canopy of my RV. Megan had one more thing on her mind. She wanted a tour of my RV. I showed her around and turned the music off.

"Leave the music on," she said.

My RV is spacious enough for me, but when Megan grabbed me, pulled me to her, and passionately kissed me, my world shrank around me. We held each other and kissed until the song ended. If we didn't have another stop to make, I would have sent Jerry home and christened my virgin RV.

"I'm just giving you a demonstration of what comes later," she teased.

I teased back, "How about later, right now?"

"No, later-later."

"What do you think of my camper?"

Megan gave me her opinion. "It's dated, that's for sure, but you keep it clean. May I use your restroom?"

"I always use the camp restroom when I'm not hooked to a dump site. It's a short walk."

"Please Owen! I need to go!"

"Just this one time." I went outside to wait on Megan. She came out and put her shoes back on, giving us a view of long shapely legs. Frank involuntarily crushed his half warm can of Old Dixie, and Jerry, he looked too.

"So, Owen, where do you really live?"

Frank *had* to butt in, "Owen lives all over town and sometimes out here when he's hidin' out. How long has that old RV been your home, eight years?"

Megan sported a curious sneer of disbelief, "Really? You live here full time?"

I shrugged and said, "I could live in one of my rentals, but when the morning sun rises, I have the freedom to be on my way to a different destination. It makes life simple and uncomplicated."

Megan's nose went an inch in the air and she wisecracked, "I didn't see any condoms in your medicine cabinet, which tells me that you don't have many overnight visitors."

I snapped right back, "I'll make an exception in your case, but you'll have to use the camp toilet."

"I'll pass, thank you. Let's go party."

Megan upped the ante by divulging her plan. "I have VIP privileges at a private and very exclusive club for times just like this one. Get your phones out, and call your friends."

My indecent proposal and Megan's high toned refusal put us at separate ends of the social staircase. I showed her my end, and she was going to show me her end. Jerry was busy calling my old rock star buddies whom I avoided for years.

I eavesdropped on Jerry and heard him say, "Clayton my man, you remember Owen Fletcher? Hung out with Fenton and Chase? Yeah, that Owen Fletcher." I saw Jerry's eye flicker in my direction. Whatever Clayton said was *not* complimentary. I saw it all over Jerry's face. "Anyway, Clayton, Owen won the lottery and there is a big bash that you don't want to miss."

Clayton Phillips, a well known production mogul, had slammed the music door in my face more than once. I sure as hell didn't want him at my party. Jerry was calling every joker who owned a guitar pick or a drum stick, putting the word out that Owen Fletcher was throwing a huge come-back party. Finally, I reached from across the front seat and batted Jerry's cell phone out of his hand.

"I'm not spending one red cent on the music business, so stop with the calls!"

"You have to, Owen! It's in your blood. You can afford your own fucking record label."

"The music world took all the blood I had, and that's the end of it."

I wasn't very convincing, even to myself. Jerry ignored me and picked up his cell phone.

CHAPTER NINE

We arrived at an estate overlooking the Cumberland River. There were no gate markings. Megan pulled up to the security booth at the gate and rolled down her window to talk with Fred who was a double for the bouncer at the Emerald Bar in the Star Wars movie. Fred sported a uniform almost as nice as Frank's. He looked like a game warden and I thought I should introduce them, and they could become drinking buddies. As it turned out, Megan had planned this impromptu gala well ahead of time. Fred let us through, and she sprung her trap.

There was a long driveway lined with tall oaks to give the place a distant-past atmosphere. The main house had the British mansion architecture of sandstone and slate, pillars and a fancy portico. Americans can't seem to keep their hands to themselves and screwed it up by installing oversized windows with purple awnings on the lower level. The whole business sat atop a high bluff and I got a glimpse of a large veranda add-on with a Sea World pool that backed to the edge of the bluff

One thing about me, I didn't party with people whom I haven't spilled beer on, so when I saw a group of strangers lined up to welcome me to my own party, my spine stiffened. I'd been rich all of a couple of hours. My quiet interlude of ten years was about to be thrown back in my face. I saw the garden party had started without me, and I was in no hurry to join in.

I recognized a few old party dogs right away. Bill Weathers had aged...badly. *Good.* The music circuit did that to a person who never missed the opportunity to get high on drugs and booze. Bill always used me as the butt of his jokes while he laughed all the way to the bank. I recognized other aged faces of famous musicians and insiders who never gave me the time of day once I had fallen off the musical planet. These assholes weren't here to celebrate my good fortune; they were here to spend it. That's the music business. It had nothing to do with musical notes, but bank notes were a different matter altogether.

The huge patio began to draw a decent crowd. I saw Gordon with a flute of champagne in his hand. The receptionist with the purple finger nails flitted around, sucking up to her boss. Just freakin' great! I also saw media scum I met earlier.

I looked over at Megan. She wore a smug look on her face. I yelled at her, "I hope you aren't expecting an ounce of civility out of me towards these turds!"

"Come on, Owen. It's a surprise party in your honor. Call your friends and let's party like rock stars."

"My friends *are* rock stars and we quit partying together a long time ago. I work as a roadie for 'Jackhammer' and not one time have I been invited to any of *their* parties."

"Well, Jackhammer is at yours, and they'll perform tonight."

"Who the hell is paying for all of this crap?" All I wanted to do was buy a thirty pack, go back to the park, play music, and dance.

Megan quipped, "You are."

"The hell I am! I'm on a budget and this is not in my budget!"

"I'm only kidding. 'Jackhammer' volunteered to play, and the lottery is picking up the rest of the tab as a PR venue."

"Hence the video production crew?" I slammed the palm of my hand on my forehead and said, "My earlier offer is withdrawn. I no longer want to sleep with you." As mad as I was at her, I didn't really mean what I said.

"Liar," she said. Megan looked at me solemnly, and yup, rolled her eyes. She said, "Get on your cell phone and call some people. Let's get this party rolling."

I walked to the edge of the bluff to look at the beautiful vista of the Cumberland River and the mellow sun gave the valley below a warm summer evening glow. I cooled down and thought about whom I should call. I could call Jolene and create a real drama, or better yet, Hajji and all of his Iranian sidekicks. I had a list of past acquaintances whom I could invite just for spite. This wasn't really my party, was it? Screw it.

I stood on the bluff alone for thirty minutes taking in loneliness I had never experienced before. I pretended to be on the phone so people would leave me alone. For the first time in my life, I understood the difference from 'being alone' and loneliness. See what money can buy you? A totally life changing shift to something entirely unexpected.

A stiff-necked waiter interrupted my quiet hiatus with a tray of champagne flutes. I looked at him and asked, "Can you bring me a Gomer Pyle?"

"Sir?"

"It's a water glass. Mix two parts lemonade, one part iced tea, and four parts moonshine. In my case, skip the iced tea and lemonade."

A few minutes passed, and I felt the tug of Megan's hand on my sleeve. She served me the water glass and said, "You really want this much alcohol?"

"Yeah, I do. Never eat on an empty stomach." I took a gulp and *geez*; I squinted and gritted my teeth, as the moonshine took its sweet time coating my esophagus with liquid fire. When I regained my composure, I said, "Moonshine has various pedigrees and this comes in under the category of rot gut." I took another gulp. "WOW, good shit!"

Megan knew where my head was. She made an apology, which I ignored by saying, "I called my buddy, Ranger Frank, who would rather jack-off watching Daisy Duke show her ass."

"I was only trying to give you a great celebration. You can have anyone you want to come to this party. This is your night! Please, Owen."

"No, Megan, this is *your* night. I came to this town to make music and a name for my band. I got caught up in the glitz of it, and ended up tuning guitars for a living instead of playing them. Do you really think there is anyone in Nashville who I want to share this charade with? I'll tell you what, I'll finish getting stupid drunk, and then I'll be your trick pony."

I kept my word to Megan. By the end of the evening, sloppy drunk described me in a favorable light. I became the centerpiece of the evening's entertainment. The questions were always the same. What was I going to do next and how was I going to spend all the money? In a drunken stupor, politically correctness, or even common decency, weren't in the same ballpark I was batting in. To Jerry's pals I said, "I'm buying an island and turning it into a gay leper colony where the inmates can exchange parts." To the media crowd I said, "I'm starting my own news network to chronicle how you bastards 'make up' the news."

To Clayton, who was trying to invite me to invest in a few of his projects, I said, pointing to Megan, "Get with my social secretary and we'll pencil you in, but in the meantime, get the fuck out of my face."

The only person who I didn't outrage was my boss, Duke Findley, of 'Jackhammer' fame. Duke let me play with the band for the first time...ever. I killed the spectators with my performance. Drunker than Cooter Jones, I belted out the songs as if I had never missed a day of practice. Redeeming my respect as a musician among my peers was the only thing good that came of the party. Had I *not* won the lottery that would never have happened.

Duke gave me that 'we'll talk later' speech, which made me paranoid about my performance. Megan attached herself to me tighter than a four day old tick. We danced and laughed, leaving no doubt the intense chemistry that overindulgence temporarily creates. When Megan let her hair down, she flirted heavily with anyone, becoming the diva party tramp.

Having thrown up in the flowerpot, and then using it as a pillow, I had no clue when the party was over. I woke up in a strange bed with a familiar woman glaring at me as the sun was well past the halfway point of the day. Megan was naked, straddling me, and I was naked as well. How I got from the flower pot to Megan's bed without any clothes on, was a mystery that didn't take a great imagination to figure out. My sundial popped up, and it was well after noon if the shadow was correct. The shadow went away as she mounted me and began a rhythmic motion which intensified to a point of recklessness. When we were both less than satisfied, we took a recess and started from the beginning. We had several time outs and in the interim, we actually spoke to each other.

"God, you're fantastic!" she roared over and over again.

"I know that. I have a five star rating in the lay category."

"No, well yes. I'm talking about last night. You were *sooo* hilarious and outrageous. No one wanted to leave. That performance with 'Jackhammer' was *amazing*. Owen, you're a PR dream. I'm serious. You can really go places!"

"Megan, can you put the coffee on? We can talk about it over some caffeine."

"I'll put the coffee on and then you can join me in the shower. After we shower we have to discuss our plans."

There it was. Megan had plans for me. I had a strong reaction to nice snooty chicks, like Megan. I was intimidated by their clever beguiling enticements to make me do things I didn't want to do. She hadn't done anything wrong and I loved our sex therapy romp. After our shower, we would visit her list of items for me to check off.

While she showered, I dressed, took a very long horse piss, and headed for the front door. My reason for taking a hike revolved around a new discovery…Megan…and an unnatural fear that I might be in over my head, or put another way, overly infatuated with her. Explained this way...three weeks ago, Megan would have turned her nose up at me if I opened a door for her. She'd strangle herself with a lamp cord before letting me touch her. I felt the inferiority welling in my chest. If I couldn't carry my half of the load at my end of the block, how could I possibly lift the load at her end? Failure, ineptness, rejection, and the list went on. It clouded out a light that I wanted to shine down on me, touch me.

From day one, Megan liked me. It didn't matter to her that I was sawdust on the floor. She couldn't get enough of me. I could insert gold digger here, but it wouldn't fit. She had an intense obsession to connect with my soul as much as it contrasted with hers. The fact that she oozed runway model, and I oozed sanitation worker, never seemed to bother her when people would look at us, not getting the connection. Any hint I may have harbored about her being stuck-up ended when I took her to meet Frank at the park. I couldn't see her attraction to me. The only thing different about me from three weeks ago, was thirty one million plus U.S. dollars. Was her motivation a career enhancement opportunity? Possibly. Anyway you cut it, it had to be the money after all.

I heard the shower hissing and that was my queue to hit the road. Once outside, I felt immediately unburdened. I looked around the nice upper class suburban neighborhood with manicured lawns and garden club landscapes. It was vaguely offensive to me. I didn't belong here. I took a look over my shoulder at Megan's mini-mansion. I had an urge to turn around but she was like one of those very expensive vacuum cleaners that door-to-door salesmen spring on you out of nowhere. I loved the demonstration of the suction to pull up wall paper, but there were just too many attachments that came with it and I swear to God I felt the suction. I kept walking.

I took any bus and found myself in downtown Nashville, where I hailed a cab and hauled ass back to the Mexican joint where I had parked my truck more than twenty four hours ago.

Back at the state park I met up with Frank. We talked and parted friends. I told him he could keep my pickup, and we did the title change on the picnic table. Mind you, my truck was a rattle trap, but Frank's truck was a road hazard.

Frank said, "I see yer not takin' the left turn I advised you to take. I got a real bad feeling that your next destination is goin' to make you wish you had. Good luck, Owen."

Ten minutes to the exact second, my RV was belching blue smoke as I left Tennessee for a destination unknown to me. It would turn out that Ranger Frank was dead on.

CHAPTER TEN

I had a house in disorder and I needed to start over from the beginning. My relationship with my father was as thin as dental floss because my antics as an adult were embarrassing to him. Of his three sons, I was his most dismal failure. My lifestyle versus his was a reason to declare war. I called him on holidays, but not one time did he call me, not even on my birthday. My father remained a gratuitous part of my life. I wanted more than that, even if I had to force it.

My father, Colonel Lawson Fletcher, was somewhere in western Georgia chasing pussy, if I believed anything my brother Ron said. Lawson Senior had earned the nickname 'Boots' long before Lawson Junior parachuted to earth. He set up headquarters in Wentzville, Georgia. Boots Fletcher was scandalizing Harris County while trying to make himself a pillar of the Republican Party and turning western Georgia into a police state. These activities were mutually unsynchronized, and pops was earning himself some good and bad notoriety.

My mom had passed on from breast cancer the year that I left for Colorado. Was it fourteen years ago? Boots was stoic about it and was reclusive in his treatment of his children. The wind in his sail had died, but Boots had a sandbag of testosterone as baggage and a sharp eye for the ladies. He sorta dissolved after the funeral and we seldom heard from him. He was a robust old rooster, spreading his feeble old wings over the chicken yard, making a fool of himself.

I turned up at Boots' command post, a nice three acre compound with a ranch house that was modest and just a bit above government housing. He had satellite dishes and a ham radio tower in the back yard. Boots could call in air strikes from his house.

I approached my father's house. I didn't see any sentries posted, but I saw a fairly new Cadillac sitting in the driveway. I knew Patton was in residence because he always drove an American made Cadillac. I pulled into the drive and realized I had never visited my dad's home. As far as I knew, this was his first house now that the Army was no longer a home to him. The sun was setting, and I saw lights through the window and stirring shadows. He probably had chambered a round in the "ma-duce" setup on the kitchen table. I should have called ahead, but it was too late now.

I heard the back door open, and Dad stepped out from behind the house. He hadn't changed much. He was tall and muscular for a man in his late fifties; skin-headed, clean-shaven, and wore crisp khaki slacks. General Patton himself. He didn't recognize me in the dimming light and demanded, "Who are you?"

"I'm Owen, your son."

"Owen? My Owen!" He fairly flew across the lawn, tripping on his feet to embrace me with a bear hug. That's how I would have pictured it, but that wasn't how it went at all. Not even close.

He just stood there sizing me up. He'd glanced at my RV, then back at me. It took awhile for him to decide what to do. "Come up on the porch so I can see you better." I did and he recognized me with a scowl on his face and a handshake. "What the hell happened to you? What happened to that fuckin' fly chaser you always sported?"

"Frank, the park ranger, caught me asleep on a picnic table and he butchered me."

"Gimme his address. I'll send him a check. Let's go inside."

The kitchen table had steaming plates of food on it, and there was a buxom redheaded woman about my age working over the electric range. She had a nice figure and big blue eyes. I felt a bit unsettled seeing my father with another woman who was young enough to be his daughter. Dad said, "Betty, this is my youngest son Owen. Owen, this is Betty."

I noticed he avoided laying claim to her or suggesting a relationship. The expression on both faces told me they were like two teenagers caught screwing in the high school gymnasium. I smiled at Betty and said, "So you're the bitch who wants to be my step-mom." Those weren't the words that actually came out of my mouth. It was more like, "Hi."

Betty stepped away from the stove, came up to me, thrust her big tits against my chest, and gave me a hug. She planted a big sisterly kiss on my cheek and stepped away. "Boots is always talking about you boys, and I finally get to meet you."

I knew better, and Betty had established that she was capable of making shit up on the fly. She went to where my father had already seated himself and put a tender hand on his shoulder to show who owned that relationship. Dad was always a wimp around women, and Betty was making the most of it.

"Betty, would you mind setting a place for Owen. Sit down, son, we have a lot of catching up to do."

Yes, we did, but not in front of Betty. I had already cut her out of my will. I sat down and said, "I have some good news for you, Dad."

Dad said, "Yeah, I heard from Lawson that you won some kind of lottery. It's a money laundering scheme run by the government over the backs of poor people who can't afford to be in the game."

That was a nice summation of his opinion, and I could understand where Lawson got his cynicism. I saw Betty's face perk up, and I knew Dad hadn't mentioned this detail to her. This could be a problem. "Now that you're rich, what do you intend to do?" he asked in a sarcastic tone.

I, too, was a sarcastic asshole when times like these presented themselves and dad knew it. "I was thinking I could park the RV in your back yard, and you and I could build a new high school. You know, improve the aesthetic educational background for the community."

Dad laughed and said, "I see you've been in town for awhile." He chuckled again and said, "We should build a few barracks, put some concertina wire around them, and get some decent books and teachers." Boots understood the roots of starting a police state began with the kids.

"I see you've embraced civilian life by taking the children close to your bosom. You're fitting right in." We went on like that until we both tired of the banter. Betty looked back and forth, not understanding that this was how Fletchers talked to each other.

"Now, son, what are you *really* going to do?"

"The first thing I am going to do is help Lawson out. I thought maybe you could tell me how bad off he is."

"He won't take any help. I tried, but you know how he is. I visited him right after he got out of the hospital. His insurance covers him. Since he and Tammy aren't married, he's been trying to get her insurance, but can't afford it. He's selling everything he owns-boat, bike, and tools. The farm is mortgaged to the hilt. Lawson didn't bitch about it one time. I'll tell you this; Tammy is going to need a few surgeries if she's going to have any kind of life."

"I'll see to it, Dad. I've always liked Tammy, and God help me understand why she's put up with Lawson all these years."

"Son, we haven't been very close, but it warms my heart to hear you speak the way you are. Good luck with Lawson."

"I plan on going for a visit. I'll go up there and I won't leave Indiana without knowing that Tammy gets the medical attention she needs, and there isn't shit Lawson can do about it."

Dad laughed and asked, "Then what?"

I shrugged my shoulders and said, "Two days ago I was overdrawn at the bank, then yesterday I had thirty-one million in my savings account. I haven't given much thought about what I'm going to do. I might try my hand at the music business again."

Dad thought that was funny. "Christ on a crutch, Owen! You fucked that up years ago. You're too old to become a rock star."

Tired of being ignored, Betty butted in, "Owen is good looking, in a Gary Cooper sort of way. How old are you, Owen?"

"Thirty-five."

"You're my age and still young enough for a comeback."

Betty reminded me that my dad was robbing the cradle. Dad was correct of course. To have a comeback, I needed to have gotten there, or somewhere, which I hadn't. Dad pointed out that inescapable fact to Betty. Boots editorialized all my failures thus far in life. A few weeks back I thought I was normal and content.

Now that I was scary rich, these remarks meant something to me. Here is how it works. When you just slide through life with your thumb up your ass, no one pays much attention. No one says to your face you're a low life bum. Instead you get other labels like, 'laid back, free spirit,' blah, blah. Win the lottery, and your past life is open season for nasty remarks that you're expected to whole-heartedly embrace. The truth is what it is. The shades get blurred and colored in. I would've never learned this lesson had I not won the lottery.

Boots' chronicles of my fucked up past, including two failed marriages, had Betty looking at me differently. Why did I care about that? Winning the lottery was beginning to really piss me off and nothing pissed me off.

We finished our dinner and Dad invited me into the living room so we could talk...about Betty. Betty, as it turned out, was not a native of Georgia. She had been a civilian employee, working at the headquarters at Boots' former duty station. Betty was married to an army sergeant who had conveniently been deployed overseas to avoid a divorce. My crazy dad got his dick too close to the flame and started screwing Betty. There were a lot of professional and ethical reasons to keep the zipper zipped, but not Boots. He got caught and that was the end of his career. Betty went with him into retirement. She was technically still married. Technically my ass. Technically, I was still married, but that issue remained my little secret.

I asked Dad to give me a hand setting up my RV out back under the pretence of getting him off to the side where I could tell the hypocritical bastard what I really thought. That was my intention until I gave it some more thought. Who really cared how Dad and Betty got it on? It wasn't my business or my problem. I chickened out and kept my mouth shut. He could have lied about why he retired, and I wouldn't have learned the truth, at least for awhile.

We set up my RV in the dark and went back into the house without me blowing my stack. I looked at Betty and her stack. I was a little envious of my dad when she playfully pawed at him. Harlot, I thought. My fault line with women was I couldn't tell good acting from real passion. Back in the day, which was twenty-four hours ago, I didn't care if women were acting or truly passionate, and I always gave them the benefit of the doubt. After I walked out of Megan's house, my perspective had changed one hundred eighty degrees. My impression was Betty put on a happy act to show me that she truly loved my dad.

Dad was at the table counting cards. It was a family ritual to play cards before turning in for the night. Bedtime came. Betty had made up the spare bedroom for me, but I declined as I was not ready to listen to Betty moaning in my father's bedroom. I smiled and said my best goodnight to both of them. *Good night, John Boy. Good night, Pa, fuck well.*

CHAPTER ELEVEN

At three in the morning, I woke to a gentle tapping on my RV door. I looked out my window and behold, there stood Betty in a short nightie. I watched her for a bit, hoping she would go away. The tapping became more urgent, and I was really conflicted. What should I do? My dad's girlfriend was standing at my door, half naked, at three in the morning, tapping lightly. I played it safe and pretended not to hear her.

Desperate, Betty opened the door and slipped into my RV. She whispered my name and tripped over my clutter. I quickly put on a pair of pants, and barely had my ass covered, when she burst into my berth. She was highly agitated as she wrapped her arms around my shoulders, and her breasts were hot on my naked back. When I quickly turned to face her, I could see through the thin lingerie, even in the dim light. I was embarrassed and felt compromised, expecting an ugly scene.

"Owen, someone's in the house." She shivered with fear. Something was terribly wrong.

"Betty, you shouldn't be here!"

"There's someone in the house. Boots sent me out here to warn you! He said for me to lock the door and stay out of sight and for you to do the same."

"What's going on?"

"We've been getting threats from my husband. He's promised to kill me. He's crazy, Owen."

"Is he in the house?"

"I-I can't say for sure, but Boots thinks so. He sent me out the bathroom window to warn you."

I fumbled in my closet for something to throw over Betty's nakedness. All of my long shirts were in storage as my closet was the size of a large envelope. I pulled a clean linen sheet from a storage bin and put it around her.

There was no way I was going to hide out with Betty while my father was facing a pissed off husband in the house. I sat the quaking woman on the couch, grabbed my pen light and forty-five, and headed for the door.

Betty whispered, "Where are you going? Boots said to stay here and lock the door."

"I don't care what he said. I'm not leaving him to face your psycho husband alone." I made a scoffing sound and bound out the door.

There was a full moon, and I could see the bathroom window standing open with the curtains shuttering in the breeze. In my haste, I forgot to put shoes on. My feet hurt from the yard debris as I stepped gingerly to the corner of the house listening for any sounds for a clue as to what was happening inside. I heard nothing but the rapid pounding of my heart.

As I tiptoed to the porch, I saw how the intruder had gotten in. The front door stood wide open. Had Boots been careless to forget locking it? I listened again for sounds and didn't hear a thing but the wind in the trees. The blue light of the moon invited me to the front door, but I decided to go through the bathroom window where I was certain my father was hiding.

I made noise as I tripped on the toilet directly below the window. I expected my father to shout for me to stay silent, but I heard nothing. I stayed frozen in front of the toilet bowl with my pistol ready. The internal noises within me were banging around like wind chimes. I took out my pen light and inspected the room hoping with a pounding heart I would find him safe in the bathtub. I pulled back the curtain. Nothing.

Dad's bedroom lay just beyond the closed door, so I quietly opened it. As soon as I did, a beam of light flashed in my face and I became a deer in the headlights.

"Shit!" a voice yelled. It wasn't my father's. I saw the frame of a handgun zeroing in on me, and I prayed I could pull my pistol up in time to save my life. The light quickly flashed off, and I fired blindly at where I thought the image had moved. A yelp told me I got the bastard, but the sound of feet on the floor meant I hadn't killed anyone. I turned on my pen light just in time to see a dark figure move beyond the door and into the living room. I fired another shot, but the man was gone by the passage he had used to gain entry. I accidentally dropped my pistol and urgently fumbled for it, giving the intruder time to get further away. I tried to follow him, but I wasn't fast enough. Now what?

Why didn't the intruder return fire or cap my ass when he had the chance? Where was Boots? I combed the whole house in the dark and never found him. He had disappeared. Vanished. Maybe he was in the RV with Betty. I went back to my home and knocked on the door. Betty was crying and I knocked louder. The terrified woman finally looked out the window, then opened the door. I entered and quickly locked up behind me. She clutched hold of me like a squirrel with a fresh acorn. Her hands, legs, and body tried to use mine as a shield, and her desperate sobs subsided a decibel. We made it to my sofa and crashed onto it with her monkey grip never letting up.

"I heard shots." She got out between sobs. "Where's Boots?"

"Dad's gone." Mistaking the meaning, her screeching pain and arching muscles were of an intensity which gripped my body. I yelled over and over that he wasn't in the house. He was fine. When the message soaked through, she went limp and collapsed in my arms. It was then I heard my cell phone ring. What the hell?

I found the damned thing and dad was calling me, or at least it was his cell phone. I tentatively pushed the talk button and got blasted.

"Tell Betty to stop screaming, God dammit! Well, you fucked that up royally! Did Betty tell you to stay put or not? I had the bastard. He was trapped in the house, you dumb fuck. Stay in the RV and take care of Betty. He's still out here."

"I'll call 911."

"No. I'm going to put an end to this shit, once and for all. I'll call you back and do what I tell you."

"Dad, be careful..."

The line went dead.

Betty was in the fetal position on my couch, terror stricken, covered in sweat. She was as helpless as a new-born fawn on the forest floor. Her hysteria was under control, but just barely. I went to the linen closet in the bathroom, dampened a cloth, and went back to Betty. I wiped off the sweat from her forehead and handed her the cloth. I sat with her and she curled up next to me.

What was taking Boots so long? Regardless of the present danger, I felt uncomfortable with the intimacy of Betty nuzzled next to me, so I took up watch from the driver's seat. Betty involuntarily whimpered, and my thoughts drifted. Yes, I was worried about Boots tracking down a would-be killer, but his girlfriend was lying on my couch, and I couldn't help envying him. Call it drama if you will, but I was there as a witness, experiencing the agony and pain of a woman mortified by a perceived loss. Sitting in silence, looking at the spent woman, I wondered if ever there would be a woman in my life who would agonize over me like Betty did over Dad.

Did I have the emotional depth to suffer that kind of pain? I answered my own question. I was an emotional coward. I had the litany of loss in front of me. I remember my mother's death and the absurd explanations that lessened the shocking impact. "It was her time"…"It's God's will"…"She wouldn't want you to grieve"…"Shit happens." All very mitigating and I bought the package.

I am ashamed to admit this, but at that moment, I was no longer envious of my father. I was jealous of him. To date, I had never given a woman a reason to shed a tear unless it was out of pure frustration. That's not to say I hadn't seen hysterical women in action. It was always about something else, never me. Betty's meltdown sensationally changed my attitude. There was depth below the skin, caring in her heart, and craving in her mind. To get to that place there had to be a bond of souls, which made me think of Megan. I knew I was having a weak moment as I nodded off, exploring the possibilities of Megan and me bonding the way Betty bonded with Boots. But Megan had her own hysterical moments that pushed me to Dad's house.

A sharp rap on the door startled me from my restless slumber. I jumped, but Betty didn't. It was Boots.

The first words out of Dad's mouth were, "How's Betty?"

"She's passed out on the couch."

Dad looked and I could see something in his eyes that didn't show any tenderness. Then he gave me a stern look, and I felt a burning guilt shiver through me. Dad didn't say anything, but I knew what was going through his head as he saw the sheet and towel laying on the seat back.

"Call 911. The son of a bitch got away."

I picked up my phone and edged to the door, with Dad's cold stare following me. "Where are you going?" he asked.

"I'm going to the house. Betty needs you. I'll leave you in private to see to your girlfriend."

It must have come out wrong as Dad said, "Don't use that tone of voice with me, and she's not my girlfriend."

"If she's not your girlfriend, what's she doing living with you and sleeping in your bed?"

"It's complicated. Call it a fringe benefit."

"Your fringe benefit comes with a psycho husband whom I shot a few moments ago. Correct me if I'm wrong, but that fringe benefit cost you your career. Is she really worth it?"

Betty was waking. Then was not the time for Boots and me to have this discussion. We stared each other down for a few tense seconds. Boots won the contest. I slammed the door and stomped off to the house.

CHAPTER TWELVE

The Harris County Sheriff sent a deputy out to the house. He treated the entire episode as a domestic spat. The pudgy possum cop took a few notes, some names. This goof was a real lazy bastard. I expected him to confiscate my weapon and arrest me. He winked at me, told me to get a permit, and reminded me not to discharge firearms in the city limits. We were at a crime scene, weren't we? He didn't bother to take the slug out of the door jam, dust for prints, take blood samples, or any of the other crap you see on TV when an intruder is shot in the act of attempted *something.*

Boots laid it out for the deputy. Sergeant Mike Harlan had been issuing death threats to his estranged wife. Boots played the death threats on Betty's cell phone. The deputy didn't seem interested in what could have been an attempted homicide. He took our written statements, perused them, and nodded thoughtfully. He stole a few lewd glances at Betty and the wheels spinning in his pea brain were in sync with mine. Psycho Mike had a perfect excuse to kill Boots for no other reason than the woman clinging to him for protection. Before cruising on down the road, Barney Fife advised us to call if anything else happened and assured us that the Harris County Sheriff's department would investigate further. We watched the deputy sheriff wobble out to his squad car, and Boots said, "The deputy is retired military. I know the type."

I said, "There's something very wrong with the way the preliminary investigation went. I've got the impression he was just going through the motions. We're on our own here."

Boots shrugged it off by saying, "Gotta remember where you are son. This is southwest Georgia and domestic violence usually involves firearms."

We sat in the kitchen talking about what had happened and speculated what would come next. I learned a lot about Sgt. Mike Harlan from Betty. He was a vindictive bastard, but we already knew that, didn't we? I had the impression that Boots and Betty had a long relationship and he had intervened in past marital scraps because he had been Harlan's commanding officer. By deduction, I assumed Boots was the shining knight and Betty polished his armor on a regular basis.

Mike Harlan had always been exceedingly jealous if any man even looked at Betty. Looking at Betty, I could forgive Mike for that minor flaw in his character. In fact, by some irrational logic, I could see myself taking his side of it. But, unlike Boots, taking sides in personal matters was not in my wheel house. Hell, I wasn't even a participant in my own train wrecks. Boots was quick to remind me that I already had my jersey and I knew which team I played on. No discussion. No equivocating.

It came as no surprise that Boots made a butt sandwich out of my ass for screwing up his ambush. I discovered something else; I had no qualms about shooting another human being. Was this a recent development, or was it in me all along?

All the talking did not solve one damned problem. Boots reassured Betty that Sgt. Harlan was a hardened killer who would try again and Betty agreed. Mike and Betty were way past the screaming and yelling stage, and a marriage counselor was out of the question. Boots was up and about, nervously looking through windows. He came back into the kitchen and announced, "Betty can't stay here. She's a sitting duck."

Hell, we were all sitting ducks. What was Boots thinking? It didn't take him long to come up with a marvelous solution which cast me as a central player in the drama.

"Owen, I want you to take Betty to Lawson's." Boots had yet to thank me for protecting his girlfriend, and that moot point was on my mind when he volunteered me to stand in as the get-away driver. Betty came to my rescue.

"Boots, I'm not leaving you here to face Mike by yourself."

"Don't argue with me. Leave with Owen tonight."

I piped up, "Betty, you should take this to the Army, file a complaint, and let them handle the problem." I saw the two exchange looks and their silence told me there was more involved than Betty getting her divorce papers signed by Psycho Mike. It wasn't my business, so I let it go. I said, "We should all pack up and leave until this blows over."

Boots said, "The Army isn't going to do shit. Harlan is off the post and beyond the jurisdiction of the provost marshal. That makes it a civilian matter and we know how that went."

I had a solution. "Why not offer him an incentive to sign the divorce papers. Enough to stay drunk for a couple months and enough to find a girlfriend."

Betty smirked. "It won't change anything because that's his normal behavior." She and Boots exchanged stoic glances. "Mike is OCD when it comes to me. He's outraged that I left him."

I expected Boots to be outraged by my proposal. "Harlan's a prideful soldier. It would take a lot of money to buy him off."

Betty cut him off. "Shut up. Giving Mike a dime would show a sign of weakness and he'd be back—over and over. You even start that and it would never end. Boots, you know him. Don't even go there."

I said, "Last night steps things up a notch. I shot him so that makes him immobile for awhile. He'll turn up at a hospital or a clinic. That gives us room to think this through and not fly off the handle and do something stupid."

"You know nothing about Mike," Boots said with a hint of pride. "The people in his unit can do brain surgery on the battlefield. You scratched him, but there is one other thing. He has a community and they have each other's backs, no matter what. He won't turn up at a clinic."

"What are you saying?"

"I'm saying we have to get Betty out of here because he's coming back. He *will* kill her and I'm not certain that he won't have help."

"I have to get back to Nashville. There's a problem I need to take care of," I said.

Boots' voice boomed, "What's this? I thought you were going to Lawson's to help him out? I'm not asking a big favor here. We've got a family problem, and just one time, could you stick to you guns and help us out?"

Last night was *not* a family problem. Last I heard, Betty and her psycho sick husband were not family members. To spare myself a guilt laden, long winded rant, I said, "Okay, I'll take Betty to Indiana with me."

"Thanks. Lawson's in no shape to take care of things, and I expect you to watch over things until I get there."

If I took Betty with me, I might not return her as soon as Boots would want, perhaps never. The temptation was overwhelming, but not a very good idea. I could end up with potentially two trained marksmen hunting for Betty and me.

He said, "I need to stay behind and clean this mess up. I have no intention of staying here waiting for him to come at me. I'm going hunting for him. I'll catch up to you at Lawson's in a few days."

"Boots, don't make us do this!" Betty whined.

"The matter is settled."

The matter was indeed settled. I felt the need to get in my RV, drive to the nearest welding shop, and get a couple layers of armored plating welded to my RV.

I went to my home to catch a nap before setting off for Lafayette, Indiana. A nap was all that I got. I was just too pumped up to sleep for very long, even though I was suffering from sleep deprivation.

Knowing I would be spending time with Dad's girlfriend was some irrational pleasure that I looked forward to. The events of last night had changed me, and I wasn't thinking straight. I'd had a few brief infatuations along the way, but this one growing in my brain was somehow different. *Stop it now, Owen.*

Maybe if I turned my thoughts to Megan, I could divert the weird guilt rattling my mind. I considered the prospect to redeem myself with Megan. Fearing I might miss an opportunity, I called Megan on my cell phone.

"Megan, I'm sorry I left without saying anything, but an urgent family matter suddenly came up." That sounded good to me.

"Owen, thank God! I've been trying to reach you for two days. Where are you?"

"It's rather complex. Let's just say I'm involved at the moment."

"Involved? As in–with another woman?"

"No, there is *not* another woman," I said testily. It wasn't exactly the truth, nor a complete lie. There was another woman, but we weren't involved ...yet. "I have a serious personal issue to deal with."

"Please, Owen, don't ignore me. *We* have issues to work out. Please, I've been thinking and it's my fault. Being fabulously wealthy takes a little getting used to. I just know I can help you."

"I don't want you within a mile of my checkbook." Did I really say that? Of course I didn't, but could have. "I can't talk right now, so I'll make you a deal. I'll call you once a day and I promise I'll meet up with you when I get back into town."

"You're out of town? Where are you ...Colorado?"

I wasn't married to Megan; even so, I wasn't crazy enough to tell her I was running off with my dad's girlfriend. "I can't tell you where I am. Trust me, I'll call you later."

"Owen ... are you in some kind of trouble?"

"No." At least not yet.

Megan had her 'Owen checklist' in front of her, and she let me have an ear full. The more she ranted, the less sure I was about making up with her. Normally I'd just hang up the phone, but for some reason I listened to her vent her spleen. What was I getting myself into?

The truth of the matter, I was looking forward to being in Betty's presence for a few days. I just needed the company, which was another first for me. Given her relationship to Boots, what possible harm could come from hanging out with a very intriguing woman?

CHAPTER THIRTEEN

We planned our escape down to the last detail. Boots picked that time of day when the sunlight was too dark to see objects at a distance but too light for night optics. Boots had a map laid out on a table, and we sat down together to plan a rendezvous. His property backed up to a state forest that belong to the Georgia Department of Natural Resources. Three miles from his property line was a maintenance road that meandered through the forest reserve. A seasonal creek intersected the road and there was a concrete spill way and a primitive campground there. The road was a loop and the closest public road was six miles away. To access it by car from Boot's house was a nineteen mile drive.

I would leave before sunset as though I was going towards Atlanta, driving up I-185 then switch back to a secondary road, and rendezvous at the spillway. Betty and Boots would go on foot to the rendezvous. I'd pick Betty up and finish the loop road, cross into Alabama at Bartlett's Lake Ferry, then west to Birmingham where we had a straight shot to Indiana.

We concluded that Psycho Mike would have to be on foot should Boots and Betty be discovered. Boots knew the terrain and he thought he could lose Mike in the darkness should he attempt to stalk them.

It was straight forward and simple enough. I had to be at the spillway no later than nine PM. The alternate pick up site would be the campground should something go wrong. What could go wrong? A lot of things, and we talked about it.

I took a nap on the couch in Boots' living room and was awakened by a nudge. I was staring at two large suitcases sitting on the floor, and I suddenly remembered where I was. I rubbed the sleep out of my eyes, looking up at my dad.

"It's time to go. Betty made dinner while I packed her things." I looked at the suitcases. My thought was Betty surely came with a lot of baggage for a few days at Lawson's, but I didn't say it out loud. I sneaked a peek into their bedroom as I carried the heavy luggage to the back porch. If my intuition was correct, Betty would be spending more than a couple of nights at Lawson's. So what did that mean for me?

Through dinner, we went over the plan one more time. I felt the tension between Boots and Betty, like a silent sadness. It was the same sadness I felt when Dad would leave our Indiana home for his next assignment. He was always very cool with my mother and left as though he worked nine to five. I knew that he was already a hundred miles away. I was so familiar with that callous stare.

The dimming light was upon us, and I carried Betty's suitcases to my RV and drove off as if the visit was over. I even honked the horn. I check the mirror as I drove down the lane.

For the next hour I drove with foreboding thoughts running through my head disrupted by my cell phone clacking. I couldn't very well turn it off just in case there was a change in plans.

Megan. She left urgent messages. I was into something more important and I couldn't be bothered.

I found the exit and a narrow two lane secondary road into the bowels of south Georgia. I was tense because my rig barely fit one lane and there were no shoulders. Pine forests growing out of red clay butted up next to the wavy patched asphalt. The map clearly showed it as an improved road. When was that? World WarII? I fell behind schedule and had to force myself to put the old RV through an endurance road test. I had a road test myself, but the damned phone kept ringing, and I had one hand on the wheel with the other holding the phone an inch from my eye, distracting me. Megan was really getting on my nerves.

I went right past the turn-off to the back side of Boots back lane to his place. I screeched to a halt looking for a place to turn the rig around. Nothing for the next mile and there was nothing to do but back up the goat path in the dark. The road was a giant red skid mark that went on forever. I looked at my watch. I was forty five minutes behind schedule. The cell phone rang again. I was tempted to turn it off, but I saw it was Boots, and I really wanted to throw it out the window. I hit the talk button and said. "I'm at the top of the road. I'll be there in ten minutes."

I heard Betty's voice. "I was beginning to think you left."

"Jesus, I'm sorry. Let me talk to Boots."

"He's not here. He had to go back to the house."

"What?"

"Yeah, he said he had to make it look like we were home."

"He left you by yourself?" I'm not a Delta Force guy, but that did not process well. Why would he leave her to fend for herself in the dark, in the middle of a forest, with a psychotic killer stalking her? My anxiety level ramped up. I was about to say something when she interrupted me with an urgent whisper. "Hurry Owen. I hear something moving in the trees."

"I'm six miles out. Stay hidden."

"Hurry! Please."

Thoughts were screaming in my mind. I was late, but what the hell was Boots thinking? What would it matter if he was home or not? Once Betty was aboard, Psycho Mike couldn't possibly get back to his truck and catch up to us. That's why we had her hike out in the first place. Betty was a tethered goat waiting for the tiger to attack. It didn't make any sense, unless Boots intentionally wanted Harlan to kill his estranged wife.

I slowed down as I saw the odometer less than a half mile from the rendezvous. Then I saw the road dip into the spillway. My lights caught a reflection of Betty scrambling up an embankment on the opposite side of the road. I slammed the brakes on sending a billow of red dust into the air. At the same time, I heard rifle shots which are quite different from pistol shots. Betty darted across the road in the dust cloud and disappeared around to my side of the RV. I had just come to a complete stop and my first reaction was to pick up my pistol and return fire.

It's a good thing I was thinking because a bullet hit the windshield in front of where I had been sitting. I fired into the darkness. Where the hell did Betty go? I fired a couple rounds off to make noise. Suddenly I heard the side door open and without looking I made a dive for the driver's seat. I did a quick head fake before slamming the shift in drive. Betty was on board and I hit the accelerator. My head was buried in the steering wheel and I could just see above the dash to keep the rig on the road. For good measure I stayed that way until well beyond rifle range.

I took side roads towards Birmingham, Alabama, where I'd pick up Interstate 65, which would take us all the way to Indianapolis. I was behind the wheel for ten minutes before Betty joined me. I made a quick assessment of her while she snuggled into the passenger seat. From all appearances, she looked unscathed. Her slight smile was a relief. I wasn't sure what her mental frame of mind was. Neither of us said a word. I was fishing for one when she suddenly stretched out of her seat and planted a kiss on my cheek. She was back in her place before I could react.

"Thank you, Owen."

I glanced at her. She was stoically looking out the front window. I asked, "Do you want to talk about it?"

She struggled to form a weak smile. "Not yet," was all she could muster. I needed her to talk to me, to tell me what the hell was really going on inside her head, but there was plenty of time for that. I needed her to navigate and that kept her busy.

Betty was streaked with dirt from her trek through some pretty rough country. She was vigorously scratching herself. She broke the silence by saying. "I can't wait to get these clothes off and take a shower. I have bug bites all over me."

"There's a shower in the back. I have only a five gallon water heater, but there's plenty of fresh water."

"Can I do it while we're moving?"

"Sure thing. But it would be easier if we pulled into a rest stop."

"I'm eaten up. I must've crawled through a nest of chiggers. Keep driving, I'll manage."

My RV was not spacious, and the bathroom was very compact. Betty wiggled out of the seat, squirming and scratching as she went. I shouted after her, telling her where to find a fresh towel, bite medication, and a bar of soap. I said, "It takes a few minutes to heat the water. The pump switch and heater switch is just above the sink. Make yourself at home."

She bobbed around and swayed in a dancing motion with the movement of the RV. She was getting the hang of it and I enjoyed watching her through the dash-mounted mirror. The door to the bathroom had a full-length mirror on it and when it was open I could see most of the shower stall. I shouldn't have been looking, and I think that moment started my troubles with Betty. As far as my memory bank of gorgeous naked women went, Betty was in my top drawer. I realized that I didn't know enough about her to justify my feelings towards her. I put it down to instant boner.

Later, Betty joined me, wearing jeans and a clean top, with her head wrapped in a towel. She handed me a hot cup of coffee.

I was surprised and asked. "Where did that come from?"

She blinked and looked at me queerly. "I made it in the microwave. It's instant coffee." She shrugged and took her seat.

"The microwave doesn't work."

"Yes it does. When was the last time you used it?"

"Ten years ago, two weeks after I bought the RV." I took a sip of coffee and said, "Damned that's hot."

She was having a fit of laughter and it was a nice laugh. I laughed for no other reason other than I was glad she was. Finally I asked what was so funny.

"Owen, all you had to do was hit the clear button. It works just fine."

We talked about our close call and I said, "I think he's just desperate, trying to wear you down, He's just trying to scare you."

"That's what Boots thinks. This time is different."

"What do mean this time?"

She glared at me, or to be more exact, studied me. "You're a nice man, Owen. You need to get clear of this. I'm very serious. This is a bad idea and you can drop me off at the bus station when we get to Montgomery. Please, Owen. Our problems don't involve you."

I actually thought about it and she was right. It didn't involve me and that's the avoidance mechanism that had always allowed me to walk around problems rather than face them head on. "As much as it doesn't involve me, I made a promise and I intend to see it through. This is as much between me and Boots as anything else."

She said, "You sound just like him."

"Who?"

"Boots. Tell me about you. Who you are."

"You really want to know?"

"I wouldn't ask if—"

I turned on the radio and pushed play. The demo of me from ten years ago began to fill the space with music. I said over the lead-in melody, "This is all you need to know."

CHAPTER FOURTEEN

We arrived at the Fletcher homestead, just west of Lafayette, Indiana, to be greeted by a swarm of savage beasts, barking, growling, and howling at us. Weeds were a foot high around the mail box, and I concluded that the mail person skipped the Fletcher house for a reason. I inched my way up the gravel driveway, which was lined by three acres of weeds that Lawson called wild flowers. I drove slowly, fearing I would run over one of Lawson's mutts, not that he would miss one or two from the horde. I stopped near the rickety old farmhouse.

The decades old two bedroom home hadn't been painted since Lawson had moved into it years ago. It needed a new roof, and the brick chimney was still leaning the way I remembered it when I lived there. The yard immediately around the house was lit up like a state penitentiary.

Lawson was out front, with his M-16 in hand, yelling orders at his excited pooches, who were attacking the tires of my RV. Something had to give because Betty and I weren't about to step out of the RV. Lawson kicked his way to the door and fired off a few rounds, which scattered the pack. Crazy Lawson was laughing his ass off. He wore cut-off jeans, an Oak Ridge Boys tee shirt, and work boots. Same uniform as always.

"Yo! Owen! Get your ass out here.! Ha! Ha! Ha!" Lawson and Ron had the same monster laugh that ricocheted to China and back.

I gingerly stepped out, looking for a rabid mongrel to leap from the darkness. Lawson clutched me and gave me his famous bear hug, which would crush the ribs of a sumo wrestler. That out of the way, he asked, "You got dad's honey pie with you?"

Betty stuck her head out of the door and descended the stairs. Shy Lawson, always tightly tuned into political correctness, yelped, "Holy shit! Whoa baby!" All the Fletchers are touchy-feely folks, but Lawson was *waaay* too touchy-feely as he embraced Betty. "You must be Betty, Boots' honey. Not what I was expecting, but dammit, Daddo always gets the best peach on the tree."

Obviously, Lawson was not what Betty expected either because she could barely sputter a single word after Lawson released her from his wrestling hold. "Let's get in the house," Lawson said as he took Betty by the hand, steering her clear of menacing hounds an inch from her knees.

We went through the clutter of the kitchen to the front room. Lawson and Tammy were what I'd call cursory housekeepers who never put anything away that they might use in the coming decade. The mess in the house was a salvage yard of filthy dishes, clothing, and broken furniture. Lawson had an infatuation with duct tape. The pillows, cushions, or any broken furniture had that familiar 3M gray patch.

A frail woman occupied a hospital bed in the middle of the room. I hardly recognized her. Tammy was sleeping and oblivious of our presence. By the looks of her, she belonged in a hospital, or at the very minimum, a constant care facility. I felt sorry for her as I took a moment to touch her forehead and whispered a respectful greeting in her ear. She needed a bath and her hair washed. I understood Lawson couldn't afford care for her, but he could at least see to her hygiene. Lawson wasn't that healthy, and he had neglected himself as well. I determined then that I would change all of that.

Lawson, all smiles, said, "Make yourselves at home. Beer's in the fridge."

Betty found a seat on a dust-covered couch. I grabbed a couple of cold ones and joined her on the couch. She said, "I need to call Boots and let him know we're in safe hands."

Betty was making an absurd assumption. Living under Lawson's roof was a hazard on a good day–and Lawson? Well, crazy Lawson was crazy, who owned every inch of his nickname. If he harbored any of the thoughts that I had, Betty needed to get the hell out of Indiana.

Betty made her call. While Betty cooed with Boots, Lawson asked me what was going on. I explained in detail what had transpired, but Lawson had questions that would be better answered by Betty.

When she finished the phone call, she said, "Mike is back from Afghanistan and has been for some time. He's stationed at Fort Benning, just a stone's throw from Wentzville. Mike signed out on leave last week and hasn't been seen since. He's taken thirty days local-area leave."

That answered a lot of questions, but didn't solve any problems. We now knew that a lunatic stalker was officially on the loose.

"I think we need to let law enforcement handle this," I said.

Lawson scoffed. "Nah. It's a domestic spat, and all that's going to happen is Boots will catch up to his ass and kick his tail. It'll blow over in a day or two. You're safe with us."

The chance of anyone sneaking up on us at Lawson's was nil, what with the brood of beasts prowling the farm.

"I shot a man at Dad's house."

"He! He! You shot an intruder at Dad's house, dummy."

"I hit him. He left blood all over the place."

"So?"

"It had to be Mike Harlan. He's still kicking because he's still making death threats to Betty. Here's the thing, Lawson. The bastard stalked Boots and Betty three miles through some pretty rough country and tried to kill both of us. How does a gunshot lunatic do that?"

"What did you hit him with?"

"A 45 slug, close range."

He seemed lost in deep thought, then nodded his head a couple of times. "Shit, that's gotta hurt and probably leave a mark. Where was Boots when this happened? He never said a word about it when I talked to him."

I immediately glanced at Betty. "What did Boots say when you told him we were ambushed?"

I could barely hear her reply. "You don't want to know what he said."

"He blamed me didn't he?"

She meekly nodded.

I was pissed and said, "This is getting out of hand. We should let the cops handle this."

Lawson shrugged, unconcerned. "So what? It ain't a federal case and nobody got hurt. No cop wants to enforce a protection order. If Psycho Mike runs a stoplight, they might bring him in, slap his wrist, then turn him over to the Army. Let Boots handle this. The boy has it coming."

There was one thing about Lawson, I could always depend on him to take Boots side of it. The way he looked at me I knew he thought I screwed up.

Betty and I had both reached the limit of physical endurance. Lawson offered Betty my old bedroom when I lived with him, and he offered to share his room with me. No matter how much I loved my brother, I knew bunking up with him was an invitation to sleep hell. I don't know which is louder, his snoring or his farts. I'd take my chances with the dogs in the yard and sleep in my ashtray in the RV. Lawson was just as relieved with my answer as I was.

My dash across the yard was a near run affair, as I was bowled over by a big monster with kinky hair. Had Lawson not been on hand with his M-16, I would have been devoured in a matter of minutes. As I mentioned, living under Lawson's roof was fraught with risks.

CHAPTER FIFTEEN

I slept in the following morning. An earthquake wouldn't have woken me, but Lawson's damn dogs did. A mentally deranged squirrel scampered on the roof, which provoked the frenzied melee outside my door. The squirrel and I were trapped.

I started the generator to get some electricity on line, to make the pump work, that supplied water to the heater, that sent hot water to the showerhead. To live in an RV you had to have patience and sing this song and its variations all the time. Clean-shaven and ready to meet the dawn of day, I headed for the door.

No man's land was in the hands of the enemy. The infernal beasts were strategically spaced across my route to Lawson's kitchen door, anticipating my next move. I saw the curly furred mastodon who had tackled me the night before, daring me to set foot out of the RV. I decided to shorten up the course by moving my RV within inches of Lawson's kitchen porch. Before I could move the RV, Lawson came out of the house with his M-16, fired a few rounds, and gave me the okay sign. Ammo was expensive, and it would cost Lawson about five bucks every time I ran the gauntlet. No wonder UPS and all other deliverers left their packages at the bottom of the long drive.

As I left the comfort of my friendly bunker, I heard Lawson laughing. "Come up on the porch."

"Something has to give here, Lawson."

He was completely comfortable with my anxiety attack. "Come sit on the porch and meet my dogs."

My older brother enjoyed torment, and I have plenty of stories about it being maliciously applied to me. I was welcomed to a chorus of growls, barks, and snarls. I testily inched my way across no-man's land to the porch. Every time a mongrel made a reach for me, Lawson would yell, and the dog would back off warily, anticipating another shot at me.

"They need to get used to you, then you'll be fine," he yelled above the din.

"Fine my ass!"

"Just don't make any sudden movement. Let them smell and get your scent."

"I don't have a scent. I bathe regularly." I could feel the nuzzles of dogs sniffing me and snarling. I moved very slowly when the big white mastodon made her move.

"Doodle! Doodle! Get back here!" Bang! Bang!

I stumbled off the ground after living through a short mauling, but otherwise unbitten. Lawson was laughing, which pissed me off.

"Te-freakin-he, Lawson."

"That one is Doodle. She's a labra-doodle. Part lab, part poodle." He pointed to a little dog mudded past his short legs. "This half dog is a dachs. You can call him Baron .... Baron von Dick-n-Draggin'. He's got a mean bite, and he's not people friendly. His brother, Jackson, is a real pussy and hides under the porch. The little bastard will back-bite you and run off. Jackson's a good night watchman. That one is Brody, an African lion dog. He doesn't bark but he *will* stalk you, so don't go out of the yard too far." Brody was one of the most regal dogs I've ever seen.

I spent an hour on Lawson's porch getting introduced to his extended canine family. The hair on my arm stood straight up the whole time. We went inside the house, and I saw that Betty had been busy cleaning and tidying up the place. I said hello to Tammy who was barely lucid. She recognized me and gave my hand a tight squeeze. Seeing the wreckage close up, I had feelings on the matter and recalled past conversations with Lawson. Lawson had been jumping out of airplanes for twenty years, had broken numerous bones, and seen his buddies splattered on the ground.

I know what sport is. Sport is an endeavor that if you practice long enough you eventually get better at whatever the shit you're trying to do. All this takes brains and/or brawn. When you jump out of an airplane, you become a rock, and the physics is simple. You accelerate at MxA squared until you hit terminal velocity. That formula is never going to change. You can't possibly get better at it no matter how hard you try. As a rock, you will always hit the ground every single time. Should you live, you are not a sportsman, you're a survivor. If you do it a second time, you're an idiot.

Lawson was an idiot a thousand times over, so I sort of blamed him for Tammy's fucked up future. I was a guest in his house, so I didn't say anything, and if you asked what I thought about it a month ago, I would have said, "Lawson's crazy. It's a free country and if that's his turn-on, so be it."

I visited that familiar dismissing litany that justified every plausible accident, as if it was meant to happen. Looking at pain-wracked Tammy, I put intentional irresponsibility in the back of my mind. Lawson and I stood looking over Tammy as if she were already dead and we were there to pull the sheet over her face for the last time. Lawson whispered, "Owen, I really fucked up, didn't I?" There was no reason for me to contribute to his misery.

Betty called us into the kitchen. She had prepared a late breakfast. She was in a melancholy mood but doing her best to remain connected. It wasn't working, so I asked, "What's wrong, Betty?"

"I'm worried about Boots. I talked to him this morning. He wouldn't tell me where he is or what he's doing. He said he'd call me right back, but that was hours ago."

Lawson was quick with an excuse. "Boots can take care of himself. I'm afraid what he'll do when he catches up with your husband."

We sat through a silent lunch when Betty's cell phone rang. It was dad, and Betty talked excitedly, wanting to know what was happening at his end of the line. I'm not good on the phone. If I haven't said what I want in five minutes, then I have miscommunicated or the other person over-communicated. I could tell by the expression on Betty's face that she was over-communicating, which I truly believe is a gender fault line.

Boots Fletcher was resourceful and had been all over Harris County with a makeshift wanted poster looking for Mike Harlan or anyone who looked like him. The sheriff was of no help, and the Army wasn't interested in what Mike Harlan was doing while he was on leave. He had disappeared. Boots wasn't giving up until this crisis was resolved. He told Betty that he was on his way to Wentzville to rest up to resume the search the following day. We were instructed to stay put.

My cell rang. I shouldn't have turned it on. It was Megan. Boots and I had something in common. We both had hysterical women trying to horn in on our routines. Betty could take lessons from Megan. A problem with highly educated women is that they have an expanded repartee and an infinite reservoir to extract unwarranted shit you don't want them to know; another reason to avoid an intellectual woman.

I was reprimanded for not calling her back as promised and for failing to mention when I was going to make good on my other promises. What other promises? It wasn't like we were an item and had set aside a date night. In fact, my initial reason for leaving Nashville was to put some distance between us. Cowardly me, shouldn't I have said something at the time? On top of that, I lied to her about our 'possibilities.' I couldn't fix the leaking boat by drilling a bigger hole, but that's what I did, again. "I do miss you." I shouldn't have said things I didn't mean, or had I said something that I desperately wished was true?

Lawson, who was eaves dropping, pointed his finger at me, knowing I was lying to the girl at the other end of the phone.

Megan asked, "When am I going to see you again? Just give me a timeline so that I can build you a new calendar. You told me a few days, and I've had a bad feeling all day."

I didn't remember saying any such thing, but never argue with a woman who is PMS stressed, has ESP, and is clairvoyant all at the same time. "It doesn't have anything to do with the lottery, and it's more complicated than I thought. I'll call you tomorrow."

Megan's five minutes were up, and it took another ten minutes to finish the conversation.

"Whoa!" said Lawson. "Owen's got a chic problem." He laughed again, pointing his finger at me accusingly. "The lottery bimbo?"

"I do not. She's not a lottery bimbo, and I'm avoiding her."

"Then you shouldn't have slept with her. I *so* know what 'I miss you' means."

Betty wrinkled her brow and asked, "You have a girlfriend, Owen? Why am I even asking? A man as handsome as you always does."

"We're not official boyfriend-girlfriend, but we're nudging in that direction."

Betty gave me a sly smile and a bump on the shoulder. "That's why you need to be in Nashville. Take off. Lawson and I can do just fine until Boots gets here."

Lawson agreed. "Yeah, Owen. Nobody's going to bother us here. I gotcha covered."

From a practical point of view, I had no reason to hang around. However, I promised I wouldn't leave Indiana without taking care of Lawson and Tammy's desperate situation. I promised Boots to look after Betty. Megan and I were doing better talking over the phone than face-to-face. My golden opportunity slipped through my fingers because I had grown a conscience. If I had left at that very moment, my life would have turned out differently.

I said, "Megan will keep. I made Dad a promise, and I can't let him down. Not this time."

We had more pressing issues to deal with. Lawson said he was low on supplies and needed to go into town to stock up and pick up some medications for Tammy at the pharmacy. He informed me that he wanted to be back by dark, just in case we had visitors. I volunteered to go with him, but he wanted me to stay in the house with Betty and Tammy. I knew the situation, and I gave him a wad of cash. "Get what we need for a long siege." He was in a spot and awkwardly took the money. He left us to go into Lafayette.

Betty, God bless her, made herself scarce. She helped Tammy with her urgent needs, gave her a bath, clipped her nails, washed her hair, and changed her bandages. I went through Lawson's financial wreck. I soon discovered he was just about to lose everything. That, I could fix with a few phone calls and some bank transfers. I'd deal with his long-term obligations later. Betty, who was coming back and forth, gave me a nod of approval, while I was busy on the phone. I said to her, "Not one word to Lawson or we'll be evicted."

CHAPTER SIXTEEN

A couple of days turned into a week. We knew that Boots was in Georgia looking for Mike Harlan. Harlan was making himself scarce. He wasn't anywhere near the Army post. He hadn't checked through any of the many ways onto the post. He was free to be at large. His apartment off post hadn't been used since he moved in, which meant he was most probably scouring the planet for Betty.

After dinner, Lawson and I retired to the front porch to drink beer while Betty cleaned up. When Lawson was drinking, his imagination got a kick start.

Lawson had mentioned he had the impression that Boots and Betty weren't a happy couple. He insinuated they were using each other. "Owen, something isn't adding up here."

"Betty loves dad. I witnessed her reaction when she thought he'd been killed."

"I'm not talking about Betty. I'm talking about Boots. Why are you here with her? Why isn't *he* here? He's a freakin' retired colonel, and he can cash in chips to pick Harlan up within the hour for Christ sakes. It's been seven days, and *nothing* has happened. I'll tell you another thing; Boots is going out on a limb for some girl that he intends to dump anyway, so how does that make any sense?"

"Lawson, that's crazy."

"There's more to this love triangle than either Betty or Boots is letting on. Trust me on that."

For whatever reason, I wanted to hear about intimate details of Boots' and Betty's private lives, so I'd let Lawson leak out what he was itching to tell me. I said, "You keep saying Boots is through with Betty. I know Betty loves him."

"Yeah, and I believe you, but Dad's in love with another woman. I wasn't going to tell you this, but I think you should know. I met the woman when he came to visit me. That's why I was surprised when you showed up with Betty. I thought she would've been long down the road by now. She's got something on Dad, and that's why he can't leave her."

We capped two more beers and looked out into the night sky. I was trying to think logically, and Lawson was thinking conspiratorially.

"You're saying Boots manufactured all this? Why?"

He looked at me sideways and asked, "You know Boots didn't exactly leave the Army without a lot of arm twisting. I've gotta a hunch about that."

Moments passed without either of us saying a word. Lawson eventually beat me to the punch. "That wasn't Harlan you shot. If it had been, you wouldn't be sittin' here drinkin' beer on my porch."

"If it wasn't Harlan, then who was it?"

"I'm just going to say this. You're the millionaire, which sorta makes you the paymaster. You don't shoot the paymaster."

"You think this has something to do with me winning the lottery?"

"I've been reading up on the Internet. Weird shit happens to lottery winners. Invariably, it almost always leads back to a family member. One lady in Florida had a granddaughter kidnapped. Turned out, her daughter and son-in-law faked the whole freakin' thing to shake her down. Another Florida case ...a man wins the lottery and doesn't share it with his family, so the brother hires a hit man to kill the winner."

Lawson took a long gulp of Coors and continued, "There are professionals out there who find most lottery winners easy marks. They use family members against each other. There's just too many unexplained suicides, deaths, threats of death, kidnappings, and extortion schemes to call it coincidence."

I'd learned not to interrupt Lawson when he worked on a classic theory to some devious plot spinning in his head.

"What are you trying to say?" I asked.

"You showed up at Dad's unexpected, right? This shooting happens in the middle of the night, right? The intruder happened to walk right through the front door...which was unlocked."

The insinuation put a needle in my spine and I put my hand up to stop him from saying the obvious. "Don't go there Lawson. Think about what you're saying."

"If you get knocked off, who gets your money? No wife. No kids. I bet you don't even have a will. Do you think it's a coincidence you were the only person in the house?"

"I wasn't supposed to be in the house. Dad gave Betty explicit instructions to stay put and lock the doors to the RV."

Lawson shrugged and sipped his beer. "I know you too well. Telling you to do anything is like a permission slip to do whatever comes to mind. Hell, he left the bathroom window open for you. He baited you. You foiled the plot. You have to ask yourself why Dad was so pissed at you for shooting the intruder. Then by noon the next day, it gets whitewashed."

"Lawson, you're really close to saying something that's going to piss me off. Don't tell me Dad is involved in this."

"You and Dad haven't seen each other in years. I'm not saying Dad set this up, but what if someone got to him? Maybe they have something on him, and they're using him to get to your money?"

"Now you've pissed me off."

"Flip the coin. What if it's Betty? Someone in that house set you up. For someone whom Boots doesn't care about, he's doing a lot of her dirty work. Could be they were both in on it."

My logic and Lawson's lunacy had a meeting point, and I hated to admit it, but there were some facts in Lawson's theory that were strong arguments against my logic. He pointed to my RV sitting at the end of the porch. "What does that hole in the windshield tell you?"

"It tells me Psycho Mike wants Betty dead. He tried to stop her escape."

"Come on, Owen. You were forty five minutes late. If it was Psycho Mike, he had plenty of time to bushwhack her. He wasn't shooting at her. He was shooting at you."

The old man had packed up everything Betty owned and dropped her in my lap like a used oil rag. What was the devious bastard up to? I bounced it off Lawson's whacko mind; after all, he knew the old man better than me.

"What if you're wrong?" I asked. "I promised dad. This is my chance to prove to him I'm worthy to be his son."

Lawson studied the top of his beer can before muttering. "Since when did Owen Fletcher ever seek redemption? You sorta blew that when mom came down with cancer. You and Dad have something in common after all."

I'd rather have taken a beating than hear the truth. It was bound to come up at some point. I wasn't angry with Lawson, but I was deeply hurt. "I made a promise, Lawson. It's the way we were raised."

He straightened slightly and smirked. "Dad didn't raise you. Mom did, and that's all there is to say about the old man."

"What am I suppose to do about Betty? This is all wrong. I should stay out of it."

"Now that sounds like the Owen I know. Get in your RV and roll your ass back to Nashville. I'll clean up Dad's mess."

He didn't mean it as a condemnation because it was a pattern of behavior expected of me. I'd always slink away from any meaningful confrontation in my life. I'd quit school, gave up on my marriages, ran away from my music career. Hell, I walked off from Megan at the first sign of commitment. On any given day, I'd be in my RV chugging my way back to the septic tank in Nashville, and the thought did enter my mind.

"I'm not leaving that woman in a crisis," I said. "This business could accelerate and someone could get hurt. I'm not sticking you with Boots' mess. You have enough to deal with."

He sucked in a surprised breath and laughed. "Gracious me. Moron having a midlife crisis? Who would have thunk it? Stick with what you know. I like you better that way."

I snapped back. "Betty's my problem now, and I'll take care of her, and I'll take care of Dad's bullshit drama. For once I'm in a position to make something stick."

"It's the money, isn't it? Boots is way ahead of you. I'll tell you this," he said, as he pointed a finger in my face. "The only reason he sent you here with his ex-girlfriend is to run her off, and you've got the money to make that happen. It's out of your hands, brother. You're a player and you don't know it. Don't trust a soul, no one, not Dad, not Betty, and not me. For all you know, we could all be in this together to get what you didn't *earn*, and to be truthful, you'd have it coming to you."

Winning an argument with Lawson was never an option. He'd painted a pretty good picture of me, and while he was at it, he'd painted me into a corner. It was a chicken shit double-dare if I'd ever heard one. He was in no condition to even minimally take care of Tammy. I suppose the reason I didn't take a hike was because I loved my brother more than I realized. Boots had royally screwed both of us. If Mike Harlan didn't shoot him, I would, and Father's Day would be the perfect day to do the deed.

I said, "I'm starting to like your dogs, so I'm staying put. What do you think Boots is doing in Georgia?"

Owen clamped his good arm around me and tussled me back and forth. Then he knuckle rubbed my head and laughed. "I've saved this for fourteen years...welcome home Owen."

I savored the awkward silence between us. Pride was choking my throat, and I had to change the subject before the silence killed me. "You didn't answer the question about Boots."

He sneered and said, "Boots is shacked up with his new honey, for all I know. He sure as hell isn't breaking a sweat trying to run down Betty's psycho husband. The smart thing for you to do is stop taking orders from him and think on your own two feet. My gut tells me this could get nasty real quick, what with the threatening calls. Mark my words."

"So you think Harlan intends to carry out his threat?"

"When I was in the Gulf war I saw what a cheating wife does to a soldier's head. I'm beginning to think Harlan is home to get a thirty caliber divorce and call it a day. The fucker won't stop until the job is over. You need to lay low and whatever you do, don't get yourself in his sight picture."

"We can't stay here forever."

"Yeah, and Boots can't stay shacked up forever, so he's got an end game. We just have to wait and see how it plays out. Hey, it's time for Tammy's meds. You shuffle the cards while Betty and I take care of her."

"Not tonight, Lawson. I'm going to have another beer and call it a day."

Lawson stood up, gave me a brotherly tap, and said, "I'll see you in the morning."

It was a beautiful summer night with a light breeze and night sounds that were soothing, or should have been. I looked out into the darkness, knowing that out there were plotters searching for

Betty and me. My dad was out there too. Had Lawson not put the thought in the air, I would have felt snug and safe. What father would shoot his offspring for a few million bucks? Given my past relationship with him, I couldn't rule out that noxious notion.

My infatuation with Betty had not diminished in spite of Lawson's crazy speculations about her character. Her caring tenderness with Tammy endeared her to me. She had been busy turning Lawson's dirty house inside out, and it was beginning to look like a home that was inhabitable. I looked at the stack of tools she had set out on the porch for Lawson to take down to the shed. It made me smile.

The night wind carried a sorrowful wave that drifted around me. I shuddered. Betty was caught up in a hopeless flight from oppression into the arms of deceitfulness. It was tragic and pathetic, and at the same time, I wondered how much of it was her fault. I reconciled it wasn't any of my business because when it was over, I'd let her go just like Boots. I had to get clear of her quickly or I might not get another chance. She had that kind of spell over me

Back to the problem. I could sit back and wait for Psycho Mike to kill Boots, or the other way around. Either way, it wouldn't be a happy ending for anyone, and I didn't want it to get that far and I certainly didn't want to be in the middle of it.

My windfall, which Lawson pointed out, was something that I didn't deserve and there was resentment. I promised myself that money wouldn't change me one bit, but it had. It was through the mirky lens of others that sent a tinge of guilt through me. I just couldn't get out of the way of myself. I was a hapless tycoon, a witless caged baboon. I felt artificial. Thinking on it, I had always been artificial and having money only amplified what was below the surface in my character.

Now, if money can't buy love, what's it good for? I've lived off clichés all my life, so let's try this one on, 'every man has his price.' I sat on the porch putting my plan together, and at the end I'd come up with a solution that was bullet proof. That's exactly what it was *not.*

CHAPTER SEVENTEEN

The next morning, Lawson was scheduled to take Tammy to the outpatient clinic for treatment. An ambulance pulled in early to transport her, leaving Betty and me to watch over things at the farm.

Betty seemed a bit off from her usual subdued manner. She seemed flushed, almost shy. Between you and me, I think she was reading my mind.

The ambulance pulled out on the road. We both waved and her hand found mine. A tingle went up my spine.

"What would you like for breakfast?" she asked. I wasn't thinking about breakfast. I was looking forward to being alone with her. Betty was uncomplicated. In her quiet way she made her presence felt and when she wasn't around I missed her. At times she was flirty with me in an unaffected way. When she got the response she wanted she'd quit. She laughed easily and didn't dwell on the problems facing her.

She had made herself indispensible around the farm. Tammy competed for her attention and I think Lawson was as smitten with her as I was. At least he cut back on the swearing in her presence. She worked hard, putting things in order, finding chores to do. She had put in a small garden behind the barn. The dogs were her escort when she left the yard. Lawson complained, "She stays on much longer she's going to ruin my hounds and they won't be worth spit."

As we shuffled to the kitchen door she asked, 'So what's it going to be? Cheerios, or eggs-over, biscuits and gravy, with hash browns and bacon."

"That sounds like a number six at the Waffle House."

She raised an eyebrow and laughed. "Along time ago I worked behind the counter at the Waffle House. It's a crappy job and the tips are table change. Let's go inside and I'll make you a number six." She continued to hold my hand. "You can help."

We were in the kitchen and by then Betty had it down pat. I was in charge of the Bisquick and stirred the dough. I decided to engage in small talk and get a handle on her personal history. "Where did you grow up?"

"I was a military brat and we moved around a lot."

"Me too. Only I didn't move around. Mom had a farm not far from here. I suppose it was the stability factor because Boots was always away playing at war or starting one."

She asked, "When did you start showing an interest in music?"

"I can't say that I remember. Mom always made sure our education was well rounded and I began playing the piano when I was maybe seven. It was my mother's gift to me."

"I got a gift from my mother. I can sing pretty good."

"No way. Sing something for me." It hadn't occurred to me that her piping around the yard was anything more than playful chirping to entertain the dogs.

Her eyes met mine, then she looked away too bashful to sing. Then she giggled. I egged her on. She composed herself, ducked her head a couple of times and belted out a solid old Betsy Kline tune. I was surprised and even more curious. I asked, "Why aren't you in Nashville?"

"That's what Boots used to ask, but to be honest I quit singing a long time ago."

That struck me as odd and I asked. "How long have you known Boots?"

Her faced dropped and she closed her eyes. "Long enough I suppose. Let's not talk about Boots. You want to help me in the garden?"

As sadness covered her like a fog shroud, I knew that she was wise to the reason Boots had dumped her with me. She found a fake smile and said, "You need to take the alternator off the tractor for Lawson first. Then I've got real man work for you digging furrows to plant potatoes."

She was suddenly in a hurry as she cleared the table and at the first opportunity she was out the kitchen door heading to the garden with dogs in tow. You just know when someone just wants to be left alone.

There went my day alone with Betty. I sulked for awhile then decided I could fix it by cleaning up the kitchen. I had an inspiring idea. I'd make a picnic basket and take it to her later in the day.

I heard her phone ring in the bedroom. If it was Boots I wanted to give him a piece of my mind. Then it could be Psycho Mike and I'd let it go to message. I found her phone in her dainties drawer. I looked at the ID. It was Mike with his poisonous rant.

I was pissed and answered her phone.

A distorted voice screamed, "Who the fuck is this! What the fuck are you doing on Betty's cell phone?"

I had his attention and it was a good time to present him with my plan. I knew how to bust his chops and I had constructed an elaborate ruse. "Take it easy, Mike. Betty and I go all the way back to Fort Pickett, that's a long time ago, isn't it? That's when you lost Betty, and don't say it ain't so. You fucked that up, and I picked up her pieces. We've been on again and off again ever since. It's not a pun asshole."

I wasn't expecting his response. He actually laughed. I continued. "I'll bet you don't remember me. You fuck over your buddies by screwing their wives while they were on deployments. Ring any bells with you?"

"What the fuck are you saying? Who the hell are you?"

"Figure this out, Mike. You and I didn't separate on friendly terms, which is just as well. It cost me a divorce and an opportunity to leave the Army and make some serious money."

"What are you doing with Betty?"

"I'm screwing her and have been for years. Are you that stupid?"

"You fucking bastard! I'll find you and cut your balls off!"

I laughed like Jack Nicholson. "She can stay with Sheriff Taylor out in the sticks and become the next Aunt Bee, married to an old geriatric has-been, or she can go back to you and your just above the poverty line level of living while you're having fun murdering 'America's Most Wanted' and gone for months at a time. Thing is, Betty isn't the Mayberry type, and she's left the old bastard. Check it out for yourself, but I suspect you already know she's gone."

I felt empty air around me and intuitively knew I'd tripped the wire in his brain. I heard heavy breathing on the line, and it caused a shiver to run up and down my spine.

His voice was a low growl. "You are in over your head, punk. She can't run from Boots any more than she can run from me. He's got as much reason to kill her as I've got."

That declaration caught me off guard and I ignored it. I said, "I've given her the option of an alternative lifestyle change, much different than anything you two bums can provide her."

"One of us will find her. And one of us will kill her."

"Good try, Mike. You don't have enough money for the air fare to find us. I have a solution that will make it easy for everyone."

I didn't hear the wail of tears coming from the other connection; instead, I heard a demonic laugh, and I said, "I can tell you're in a lot of pain, so I have an offer to help ease your suffering ... Five hundred thousand for old time's sake. You had divorce papers waiting for you when you check-in off of leave. You didn't sign them. It's worth a lot of money to me to see you out of Betty's life. Call it alimony if you like, and let's all just move on from there."

He started laughing. A horrifying laugh filled with irony. "You dumb prick, you think you can buy Betty from me? Who the hell are you anyway?"

I said, "In answer to your first question, I'm not buying Betty from you because you don't have the title anymore. I'm paying you so you can get some help and go on being a good soldier with a fat retirement. You know you can't stop the divorce or hold it up any longer, so why are you stalking and threatening Betty?"

"Listen asshole, if I wanted Betty dead, she'd be dead. She can wait until I finish with her lover. Put Betty on."

It was my turn to laugh, and I said, "Tell you what, think about my offer and get back to me." I hung up on him.

I was pleased with my spontaneous solution. Still, talking to a bona fide homicidal maniac with the skill set and a rack of citations as credentials, unnerved me. What he said about killing Betty was starting to add up. He was a pro who made a living killing enemy colonels and generals, why not one of ours? I concluded that Mike Harlan had been targeting Boots from the get go, but I was the game changer in all of this. With his jealous streak and his temperament, I'd just made myself a target.

I had a hunch about the voice at the other end of the line. The tenor of the conversation didn't sound at all like a hurting, troubled soul. I had missed something. Something Lawson had mentioned. Something Betty had on Boots, and that something threatened Harlan as well. This whole affair wasn't about a divorce, jealousy, or a cheating spouse. Harlan was right. I was in over my head.

I needed some help. Of all the people I knew, there was just one with the IQ to understand what needed done. That person was royally pissed with me at the moment. I called Megan anyway and spent ten minutes explaining the complexity of my personal problem, and I spent the next thirty minutes listening to Megan telling me what I needed to do.

"Owen, you did it all wrong. You've just put an added value tax on your dad's girlfriend's life. All he has to do is keep calling with his threats to kill what's-her-name. If this stalker calls back, and I believe he will, he will want to up the ante. You offer him less, and give him a deadline. The girlfriend, what's her name again?"

"Betty."

"Betty has, or should have, enough of Mike's personal information for Jerry to set up an account for him in a correspondent bank in Columbus, Georgia. You tell this Mike that as soon as the divorce is recorded in Muscogee County, the money will be deposited to the account."

"That's a brilliant solution, Megan. I knew I could depend on you to find an answer."

"It's not a solution. If this nut job takes the offer, then you know that it was never about Betty. I hope he'll go for the money. All we've done is bought some time for him to cool off, blow the money, and find someone who'll take Betty off his mind. If any of this doesn't happen, then you've got yourself a really huge-assed problem with an over obsessive freak."

"You're starting to scare me, Megan."

"You should be scared. Just get the information from Betty so we can get the mechanics in place to buy off her psycho husband. The next thing we're going to do is get you the hell out of Georgia. Don't go near your dad's house."

"I'm not at my dad's house."

"Good. Where are you?"

Megan was a quick study and had a better perspective than I did. She knew exactly where I was because she did the transfers to bail Lawson out of debt. "I'm in Indiana at my brother's farm."

"Really? That's nuts. Why are you in Indiana? Better yet, why aren't you in Nashville?"

Good question. For obvious and not so obvious reasons, we didn't want *anyone* to know where Betty was. When I told her *why,* I could feel her telephone cord wrapped around my neck. Once she unraveled, she wanted accountability. I briefly gave her the scenario. She gasped when I told her about the second ambush. She frequently broke into my narrative with pointed questions that I hadn't thought about. I finished and she ripped into me.

"Owen, this is not your usual hillbilly road show. What's with people like you? You have single handedly motivated every yokel you know to roost on your bank account and—"

"Stop it, Megan. I do not appreciate the way you characterize my family."

"Sorry. I will tell you this, what's in play has nothing to do with a lame divorce resolution. You need to fire up your RV and get down the road as quickly as you can."

"What about Betty?"

"What about her? What is she to you? She's a grown woman. Leave her at the farm. How long do you think it will take you to get to Nashville?"

"I'm not leaving her. We're by ourselves until Lawson and Tammy get home tonight...and besides, I made my father a promise to take care of her."

"Listen to you. Don't tell *me* you've never broken your word to a woman."

My problem was I couldn't remember the last time I'd kept my word to a woman. "I'm not leaving her. Someone is trying to kill her and I don't want that on my conscience."

"Let's make a distinction here. Someone is *threatening* to kill her and herding you into a corner, which is exactly where you are. You just opened your checkbook and how do you know it's not a setup? Get on the road, Owen…now. Shit, bring your dad's girlfriend with you. We'll figure out what to do with her later."

"What do I tell Psycho Mike when he calls back?"

"You're a moving target. Promise him anything he wants. Let's stop talking and start doing."

CHAPTER EIGHTEEN

I was of two minds. Megan made good sense but I couldn't elevate her somewhat hysterical paranoia to the crisis level. On the other hand, if I went on the road with Betty to another hiding place, Boots would be livid. Before I did something rash, I decided to call him and bring him up to date.

When he answered, his booming voice dished out a vile litany of profanity. At the end of it all, he wanted to know just one thing—where was Betty? I picked up on the nuance of the way the question was framed. It was void of concern for her. It was, more or less, a logistical question.

Dad and I had yet to breach the subject of his dick getting us all into this mess, and that he was still thinking with his dick. I didn't use those words, but the meaning was unmistakable. He got the message. The line was quiet for ten seconds as he pondered my criticism.

"Where are you, Owen?"

"I'm still with Lawson and Tammy. I'm leaving to someplace safe, and you don't need to know where. You don't have to worry.

Mike Harlan and I have a deal. He has ten days to sign the divorce papers waiting for him at the Judge Advocate's Office."

"Jesus Christ. You've financed his maniacal obsession to kill Betty. Shit!"

"The psycho had many chances to kill her, so why is she still alive?"

Boots couldn't answer my question. I told him I thought money was the game changer, but if that was true, why hadn't he killed her before he knew about the money? How many chances had he passed up? I didn't mention any of my bothering thoughts to Boots. Instead, I told him I thought Betty wasn't on the target list, at least not yet, but he was. "I think he's using her as bait to draw you out in the open. Betty's with me and his threats are useless at this point." What I didn't say was that I suspected Boots of using Betty for bait.

For once in his life, Dad agreed with me. Whether he really did or not, my plan was a lot better than his. I reasonably explained; Lawson and Tammy would be out of danger; Psycho Mike was headed back to Fort Benning to collect his money; and Betty was with me. That just left Boots in the cross hairs. I advised him to take the breathing space to pack up, sell the house, and relocate—with or without Betty.

"I'm not running from this. It's best that I don't know where Betty is. Keep her safe, Owen. I'm trusting you with her life, son. I'll call you when this is all over with."

"Dad, level with me. Lawson told me about the other woman."

The pause was so long that I thought I'd lost service. I could hear a sigh and he spoke, "I like Betty, but I don't love her. When this problem gets fixed I'm done with her."

"She loves you, Dad!"

"Yeah ...I know ...I'll have to figure out a different game plan. Promise me you'll look after Betty. She's a good person, and we have had a long history together. Too long. It has to end. She's more like a daughter to me, and none of this is her fault. Tell her goodbye for me. "

"Tell her yourself."

"Owen, I'm depending on you. I put her in a lot of danger, and it isn't Harlan."

"Jesus, Dad. If it isn't Harlan, then who took shots at her at the spillway and why?"

"It wasn't Harlan."

"You're sure."

"Positive. I know where Harlan was when the shots were fired because I've been watching him. That's not saying he isn't involved. There's more to this than I can tell you. Betty will tell you when the time comes, I'm sure."

"Does any of this have anything to do with me winning the lottery?"

"Not until you made it an issue. There are people other than Harlan who want Betty and I silenced forever. I can only hope your fuckin' money makes a difference." The connection terminated. Boots was gone.

I was conflicted and brooded over a mystery to which I was not privy to. All the lines of that mystery intersected with the woman weeding the garden. It was implausible to me that such a kind unassuming woman presented a danger to any living creature. The dots didn't connect.

I was in my RV deeply absorbed in contemplation when Betty's cell phone rang. I answered her cell in my usual polite and cordial voice, "Detective Sam Spade speaking."

"Very funny, champ. I was thinking over your proposition. I like the idea, but my pain doesn't come cheap. You ever hear people say, I'd give a million bucks for something? That's not too much to ask for a broken heart, now is it?"

The mood and tone of the voice changed dramatically. "I've thought it over too, Mike. I was rash, and I'm spending more money than my budget allows, so let's settle on one hundred thousand and call it a day. But there is a hitch, I'll give you ten working days to finish with the divorce and get it recorded at the county courthouse."

"You're the guy in the RV, aren't you?" When I didn't answer, he said, "Have you ever heard of the thousand yard shot, sport?" I still kept my mouth shut. "I can't get much closer because of the dogs, but a thousand yards separates you and me. Stick your head out the window and look to the east where I have you dialed in." He giggled. "Bang you're dead. Wake up, fucker!" Mike laughed in that maniac rhythm you hear in a horror flick. My heart rate went through the roof, and I about pissed my pants.

The side window of my RV shattered, followed by three seconds of silence before the sound of the bullet caught up. I dropped the phone. Laughter echoed from the phone on the floor.

Slowly, I recovered from the initial paralysis of shock and picked up the receiver. "You still there?" he asked.

The sniper fired another shot. The entire front salon of my RV was floating with debris in the air, like a feather pillow being ripped apart. "Yes," I said, with a trembling voice.

"Look out the window. Go ahead. Here comes Betty! She won't make it," he was singing the words playfully. "Wham!"

I jumped up and looked out the window. Betty had stopped halfway across the yard with a stunned expression on her face. I yelled, "Get down! Get on the ground and crawl to cover! We're being shot at!"

I picked up the cell phone and yelled, "Stop it, you crazy bastard."

"Fuck, I missed. Now how did that happen? Next time I won't. Just to show you, kiss the right side mirror goodbye." In a matter of seconds, the side mirror of my RV dissolved into mist and the loud wham followed.

I yelled into the phone, begging him to stop. I heard his murderous laugh. "Since she broke my heart, I should take her leg off so she won't have two of them to spread. That's a good idea. Hmmm, thinking here, champ. Leg for a heart, which one do you think? Left or right?"

"You harm her and the deal is off." I dialed 911 on my phone. "I've got the cops on the phone, Mike."

"On a scale of one to ten, how would you rate Mrs. Harlan?"

It was an odd question out of place with the dialogue so I didn't say anything.

"Answer the fucking question!"

"Ten."

"Ten it is. Check out those legs. Go ahead. Nice huh? Million dollar legs, don't you think? I'm going to take the right one and we can deduct that from the value."

I dropped the phone again and yelled at her. "Betty pull your legs up to your chest…now!"

I saw a dirt plume erupt around her lower limbs. She yelped and I saw her frantically clawing her way towards the barn."

Noise was coming from the cell phone. "Do you really think I'm going to let Betty get away with this without a scratch? Oh, I see she's crawled to the barn. Now that's not a problem because a 780 grain, 50 caliber bullet will slice through that timber like butter. Thing is, I can't guarantee Betty will live through it."

Three shots were fired. Wood splinters flew like saw dust at a lumber mill, followed by the report of the rifle. I could see Betty quaking behind Lawson's work table and dust falling all around her. Harlan's sharp voice made me jump. "We're done negotiating. Is it a million or not?"

"It's a million."

"Close the other line and come out of the RV where I can see you."

There was a huge thump that lifted the front wheels of the RV into the air, and the engine block was sitting where the console used to be. I knew how stupid it would be for me to stand out in the open with Betty's pissed off husband behind a sniper scope and told him so. He actually laughed, said I couldn't stay in the RV forever, particularly since it was being demolished chunk by huge chunk.

We were in a Mexican standoff. I told Mike how the transaction would work, and we were in the middle of discussing it when I heard him yell, "What the fuck! I told you…bring Betty out of the barn. I have a going away present for her."

"No!"

The rear of the RV exploded and the storage bins above my bunk shredded.

"Stop it, you asshole!"

"Bring-Betty-out-of-the-barn," he sang. "Now!"

"No. You'll kill her. We have a deal."

"I thought we talked about that? You can have her for a price, just not all in one piece." He laughed and took another shot. "Bring Betty out…" Growling and barking sounded over the phone *and* in the distance. "What the f—?" Then he screamed, and the roar of wild animals swarmed from the phone. Lawson's hounds had found Mike. I was certain that Lawson's mean-assed dogs were eating him alive, and I breathed a sigh of relief. I ran from the RV and found Betty cowering behind the work table. I grabbed her, forced her to the ground, and we crawled to the house while Mike was busy with the raging dogs. We reached the house and Lawson's M-16 in the kitchen. I gave Betty a brief sketch of what had just transpired. She started to cry. "I'll never be safe as long as Mike's on the loose."

"Don't worry," I said. "The dogs will have killed him before the cops can get to him. We're safe."

Why was it that my optimistic assumptions seldom worked out?

CHAPTER NINETEEN

Ten minutes went by before anything happened. The lion dog, Brody, wagged a happy tail, romping across the field, heading for the yard. He was splattered with blood. I suspected some of it was his, and hopefully the rest belonged to Mike. Since Brody didn't have a leg or arm for a trophy, I suspected Mike escaped.

Inspired by the brave dog, I back-tracked across the open field where Mike's sniper nest was set up. Blood was everywhere. Doodle lay at the base of Mike's shooting platform drawing her last breath. Other dog carcasses littered the killing ground.

The sniper nest wasn't a spontaneous selection. It had been there for who knew how long? Strewn about was military hardware, food and water canisters, and most telling, remnants of military K9 training pads. I examined them. An arm guard and shin guard had been torn off the shooter. It was evident that Lawson's dogs had overwhelmed Mike and it was equally evident that he was expecting them.

I collected a few weapons and went in search of a blood trail. I couldn't distinguish his from the dogs that he'd injured.

Secondly, it was stupid for me to track a killer armed with a fifty caliber sniper rifle who had a good five hundred yard buffer zone over me. I returned to the shooting platform and with a heavy heart used Lawson's M-16 to put Doodle out of her misery. I had a lot of pent up emotions, and shooting Doodle brought it all out in a gush of tears.

I surveyed my RV from a distance, and it would go into the scrap heap behind Lawson's barn. My next worry was putting distance between me and Lawson's farm as quickly as possible. Mike Harlan was indeed a persistent bastard. One thing was for certain; he would not stop until he inflicted severe injury to Betty or kill her. We had to leave the scene immediately, without calling the cops, or waiting for Lawson to return. I had the keys to his ratty pick-up and that would have to do.

We were on the last flight out of Indy to Nashville on a death tube commuter air service from hell. Packed like sardines, Betty spent most of it slumbering with her head on my shoulder.

It was a welcomed intimacy that I didn't object to, in spite of Lawson's warning. Above me was the last of my belongings stuffed in a gym bag. As a millionaire, I was now homeless, and Lawson could move my wrecked RV to the graveyard of dead dogs and old junk. I was going backwards; I virtually had nothing of any worth. My rigorous management of my $40,000 a month budget was off by three years. Over budget, homeless, and up to my ears with my dad's domestic situation, I wasn't bearing the fruits of my fortune.

Virtually living with Betty through these ordeals made us comfortable friends. In my mind, Betty and I shared too many close intimacies, and my feelings for her were becoming more complex. I rigidly avoided coming on to her. I thought my behavior was above board and proper. I knew Betty was fond of me, but for the most part, she kept me at arms length but was playfully flirty when Lawson wasn't around. Maybe there was a mutual infatuation. Lawson had seen through the veneer, hers and mine. He had warned me, "Do not get involved with Betty."

The flight out of Indy reminded me how fragile our relationship had become, and I had to get my head back on straight.

We arrived in Nashville, rented a car, and checked into the Hermitage Hotel with two adjoining suites under the name of Megan Marsh for an extended stay. The Hermitage is the only five-star hotel in the state of Tennessee. Old elegance doesn't give justice to the old barn. My suite had more square footage than my dad's suburban house.

Betty was so exhausted she didn't even check out the spa/salon in her suite. She flopped down on the king-sized bed and was out like a light. The large floral spray on the coffee table was a total waste. It wouldn't be right to properly put her to bed, so I closed the door and went to my suite next door.

My floral spray was a robed woman, about five ten in height, lushly sprayed in inspiring perfumes, and richly dunked in lust. After the kind of day I had, sex with Megan was not the first thing on my mind, but it was in the top ten.

She took me by the hand and led me to the bedroom. She soothingly said, "You look like you could use a hot shower, sailor." My shower was hot and steamy. The last time Megan took a shower in my presence, I had walked out on her, and she was having none of that. Naked, she joined me with only a bar of soap for cover. We made a fair share of suds, and someone dropped the soap, then the real fun began in earnest.

I finished toweling Megan's breasts for the tenth time, when she decided to dry her hair. She directed me to go into the lounge to fix us both a drink. I gulped down a stiff scotch and poured another when I heard the hair dryer stop whining. Megan came out of the bedroom in a robe. She had a snappy smile and a beautiful glow about her. She sat down in the recliner, and she suggested we could take our drinks to the other room. I took a sip and stayed parked. She informed me she was sleeping over, and she wasn't tired yet. We argued over the point, but I won the contest, which was uncommon with Megan from day one.

"Owen, I have been so worried over you. I felt like I was losing my mind."

I said, "I know that we've known each other just a little over a month, but ..."

"But what ...?

"I like you and here is the *but.* I have so many changes going on inside of my brain that I'm not sure where my head is going to be in the morning. I can't get involved until I find out what the final product is."

She flashed a fake smile, trying to take my rejection in stride. "I'm enjoying the trip. I've seen a complete dope step into a pair of men's shoes. What you did for your brother was so commendable and stepping up to the plate for your father was a selfless act. The finished product is getting polished and starting to sparkle. All I'm asking from you is to let me take the journey with you."

Suspicious, I asked, "How do you know what I did for Lawson?"

"I had drinks with Jerry, and all we talk about is you. Jerry is your biggest admirer. He loves to tell Owen stories. You're still very popular in his musical circle of friends, but you fell off the planet."

"When my musician friends shut the door in my face during the day and partied with me at night, I bought a new cell phone and lost interest."

"Since it's well known that you won the lottery, a ton of old friends have been looking for you to catch up on old times."

"I caught up on 'old times' at your party, remember?"

"You're being cynical. Eventually, you'll have to come out of hibernation, but for now you need to stay in your cave. "

"Hibernation? Isn't that when the bear goes to sleep for six months? Do bears get laid in their sleep?"

Megan laughed. "Close your eyes, Papa Bear, and see what happens next."

Megan and I talked around what form our relationship would take, and I should admit Megan's negotiating skills were much sharper than mine. We had a loose understanding that Megan and I were officially an item, and I would set aside a date night for her. That's how that ball got shoved to the cliff's edge.

Megan jumped up from her recliner and hopped into my lap. She gave me a tongue-down-the-throat kiss. I wasn't putting the expected enthusiasm into our sparking session. Suddenly her head jerked back. Her eyes narrowed. "What's the matter?" She batted her eyes, waiting for me to respond. "Owen ... what happened.?"

Since I didn't know myself, what could I tell her? I needed time to figure this out, and I needed help. "Megan, I have a feeling the business in Georgia is growing beyond a family matter into something criminal."

"Don't worry. I hired a personal protection company. They're expensive but very good."

"What?"

"Honey, I told you this morning I was hiring a private company. Don't you remember?"

I did remember, and it struck me odd that she brought it up before the lead started flying at Lawson's farm. Lawson's parting words came back to me. "Don't trust the lotto babe."

CHAPTER TWENTY

I had things to do the following morning and so did Megan. She dressed, and we agreed to meet up later in the day for lunch at the Capitol Grille in the hotel. It took ten minutes to peel my frisky new girlfriend off and get her out the door. I picked up my room before I tapped lightly on the connecting door to Betty's suite. She was wearing a robe and had her hair wrapped in a towel. She didn't get the scrubbing I got, but she was suspiciously bubbly as if she might have. "Owen, come in. This suite is *sooo* grand!" She skipped and twirled around like Shirley Temple on speed.

The fairy princess was giddy. She cooed and pranced until I laughed and found a chair to watch her show. She gasped. "Did you know I have my very own butler, and he sent up coffee in a fancy urn and a silver platter with the most delicious pastries I've *ever* tasted." She poured two cups of coffee and made a ballet out of serving me. "This is sooo heavenly. You can't possibly expect me to stay in this fantasy suite. I can't let you spend that kind of money."

She finally settled down and took a chair next to me. She cocked her head, and a serious wash replaced her girlish innocence. "What's the matter?" She asked.

How could I tell her that the man she'd lived with for the past three years had dumped her. Instead, I explained to Betty that we were getting our very own goon squad, and we were scheduled for a consultation.

She was concerned that she had nothing to wear but what she'd packed in a little travel duffel. Betty's wardrobe consisted of jeans, sneakers, and lively Wal-Mart tops. I'm sure she felt as out of place as I did. I wore cargo pants and a pull-over shirt that Megan made fun of. Betty eyed me and said, "We're a fine pair. We'll look like farmers on market day. All my nice clothes are back at the farm. We could have Lawson send them to Megan's office."

Boots had packed her up with every stitch she owned. I wasn't going to make it easy for him, and I didn't want Betty's stuff in Megan's possession.

I said, "We'll fix that later today. We'll go shopping after breakfast. How does that sound? Let's eat in my room, just knock when you're ready."

She was back in twenty minutes, wearing tight jeans and a blouse that I had seen her wear over and over again. Still, she looked very mouth wateringly attractive. Betty went about my suite on a self-guided tour, sniffing the air. She must've had a coon dog nose because she picked up Megan's perfume scent. Smugness didn't become Betty as she spit out, "The lottery chick?"

"Yes, we had a consultation."

"I know you did." Was there a twinge of sarcasm in her voice? You bet there was.

We had our private breakfast in my suite, talking about what was coming next. The subject of Megan came up, and Betty was a little more than curious about her, almost jealous if I didn't know better.

I usually felt relaxed and comfortable in Betty's presence, but Boots had put a game changer in the mix. Betty was her exuberant cheerful self through breakfast, and she talked optimistically about resolving the problems with her divorce. At the end of breakfast, she said she had heard from Boots and that I had news for her. The bastard. Iasked, "What did he tell you?"

Her blue eyes sparkled and she teased, "He told me I should trust you completely, and I would be safe with you. He said he thought it would be all over in a few days. Boots has a plan to force Mike to sign the papers, but he wouldn't tell me what it's about."

I ignored her question. "Did he tell you what he meant by 'all over.'"

"No, but I assume he told you. He said you'd explain."

I couldn't stand looking into those trusting blue eyes. That rotten bastard. He'd tossed Betty for some other woman, and he expected me to do what? Take care of a woman with a broken heart? I was so angry that my face turned red and my jaw tightened. There was just so much of Boots' women problems that I could handle. Telling Betty to move on wasn't one of them. I now understood where my evasive ducking of responsibility came from.

"What's wrong?"

I put my hand to my forehead, trying to construct bad news into a format that wouldn't be shocking, but how do I tell dad's girlfriend she's old history?

"Betty, you and Boots share a history that I'm not privy too. That aside, he believes you are in greater danger than we first thought and I gave him my word that I'll keep you from harm. That's as far as it goes."

"You've done more than anyone should expect. Thank you. I could get used to this, but is this necessary? It's costing a fortune. Couldn't we just find a fishing camp in Minnesota?"

"No. I have to be here to setup a transaction."

"I'm comfortable with the company, and you won't hear me bitch about the accommodations. I feel like a queen, if only for a day! Can I ask you what transaction you're talking about?"

Her mouth dropped open when she recalled my solution to her problem. "Oh, no. No, Owen. You didn't. How did you find the time to arrange that? Does Boots know about this?"

"Yeah, and I'm going to need your help. You have enough of Mike's personal information to set up a bank account for him. The account needs to be where he can quickly access it, preferably in Wentzville, Georgia."

"Tell me you didn't!"

"Yeah, I cut him a deal yesterday on your phone. He has two weeks to sign your divorce papers and move on."

"What? And you didn't consult me? Do you think money is going to change anything? For the love of God, you don't know anything. He would've killed us yesterday."

I said, "I believe you, but the only reason he didn't is because he needs me alive to make the payoff. There is no doubt he intended to cripple you regardless."

"We talked about this. Why didn't you tell the rest of it? Yesterday was his way of leveraging a bigger payoff." Betty grew angry and solemn. "How much?"

"A million."

It took Betty back as she rolled her eyes towards the ceiling. "Mike knows the extortion game. He's done it before, but this doesn't sound like him." Worry spread across her face. "Mike's not above extortion. It might work for awhile."

"The idea is to put him behind bars."

"For what? Shooting up your RV? You're so naive. You made him the offer, remember that. He can't avoid the divorce much longer, and he has to sign the papers eventually. The Army will make him. So what business is it of yours to push him to do something that he already knows he has to do? It's stupid." Betty folded her arms and turned her back on me.

"There's more. The shooter at Lawson's wasn't your husband. According to Boots, Mike was in Wentzville, Georgia, yesterday. He thinks Mike may have been involved, but he wasn't the man behind the trigger. Do you have any idea who may have been taking pot shots at us?"

Betty's knees gave way and her shoulders slumped. She slowly turned around and looked through me as if I wasn't in the room. Body language is telling, but not translatable. I immediately knew she had made a surprising discovery, and it shocked her. I watched Betty stiffen, then slump. I saw a vault door slam. She wasn't giving up anything to me. When I checked her eyes again, the clarity I had seen fogged over. She stretched her neck, raised her head, and with a stoic expression, walked to the window to stare out across the skyline of downtown Nashville. She stood there with her back to me.

I said, "You know something. Tell me."

The silence was deafening. It went on and on. Betty had a conversation with the window pane. She turned around, braced herself with her palms against the sash, and let out a low sigh. Her head sagged in defeat

"It's getting out of hand. Owen, you need to step clear of this. Break your deal with Mike because a million dollars isn't going to change the outcome."

"Say what you mean. There's a lot more to this than either of you are telling …isn't there?"

"Yes, and it goes back years. If I said anything it would make it worse for Boots. I love him too much, and I won't betray his secrets, no matter how I feel about him now."

"Can't you do anything to stop all of this?"

"Not without hurting your father." She turned her head and her jaw hardened and her eyes turned opaque. She gave me a quick smile. "Get clear of this, Owen. We both need to."

"What kind of trouble is Boots in? What are you holding over him?"

"What did your father say about his feelings towards me? Did he say he loved me like a daughter? Was that his words?"

She caught me off guard. I stuttered, "Yes, those were his words."

"I am a repository of all his sins. This 'arrangement' is his way out, and to be honest, I have a vision that makes it the best solution for both of us. Before you ask, I am the keeper of your father's soul, and I won't betray him, even to you."

"He seems to think that my deal with Mike is the game changer. What's he talking about and how does it involve me?"

"It doesn't and it won't."

"Betty, you're talking in circles. Tell me something that makes a lick of sense."

She flicked a quick smile. "So this is how it's to end?" She nodded several times. "He's found his way of ridding himself of me." There was something absent in her tone. "I suppose that makes you his legate, delivering my notice of exile." She spread her arms in supplication and closed her eyes.

What was I supposed to say? "He asked for my promise to protect you and to take care of you. He does love you Betty. As you may suspect he's asked me to say his goodbyes."

She said, "You see, I'm yours, like a family heirloom. You're his surrogate. How do you feel about that?"

"I'm not so sure I understand."

"Men like your father never give up ownership of the things they treasure. As long as I'm your possession he can reach out and reclaim me should he wish to. Your father is cruel in that way. Still, I love him." She looked at me with a fawning expression, assessing me, her eyes dancing up and down my frame.

In my day I've turned a few heads when I was on stage. I've seen the vibes that women can give off, but nothing like what I was experiencing. I would like to say desire and adoration, but there was something more meaningful; seasoned pride and approval, as if we'd been in love forever. Considering the subject of our conversation I had a hunch I could be in real trouble because my infatuation had just shifted gears.

My intentions were to address Betty with my personal situation over breakfast, but that was abruptly put on the back burner. The two of us were going to be in a close living relationship for the next two weeks and I had to let Betty know what the limits were, especially since I was involved with Megan. I' didn't need women problems, at least that was my thought at the time.

What's on your mind Owen?" she asked.

"Look, I like you very much. We're going to be together for the near term and we need to establish some limits. We're too close in age and we're friends. Some people might get other ideas."

She interrupted me. "Yeah, your brother didn't say anything, but I know what he thinks. We haven't done anything, but it's all about appearances, isn't it?"

"That and something else. I'm trying to get my arms around a relationship that's developing."

"The lotto babe? I can't wait to meet her." The sarcasm was swimming in the air.

"Look Betty, Megan got us out of a tight spot. You could show a little gratitude."

"You're right. I shouldn't meet her at all. She might draw the wrong conclusion about you and me."

"You think? Her new boyfriend walks out on her, picks up with a woman he's never met, who, by the way, is stunningly gorgeous, charming, and slightly flirty. 'Megan, meet my dad's girlfriend, Ha Ha.' You think she might draw the wrong conclusion?"

"I see your point."

"Betty, I haven't had a girlfriend in ten years. Megan is new territory and I really want to explore the landscape."

"You did that last night. Judging by the noise from next door, I think I heard you reach the mountain top."

"Were we that loud?"

Betty smiled devilishly, and said, "Woke me up and I couldn't go back to sleep. I'll stay out of your business."

"Thanks, Betty. Speaking of business, I have a lot of things to do this morning. Will you be alright by yourself?"

"I'll be fine. I think I'll spend the day spoiling myself."

I couldn't pinpoint any one trait, but Betty had changed, almost as if a load was lifted from her shoulders. A wall went up between us and I recalled her melancholy ramblings. There must have been something more to it. I tried not to read anything into it, but Betty possessed a mystery, and I could tell she was resolved to a new course in her life. I didn't know it at the time, but it had everything to do with me.

CHAPTER TWENTY-ONE

I didn't want Betty knowing about my personal business, so I went to see Jerry by myself. I looked across the bank lobby to see if he was picking his nose. He wasn't in his office, but someone else was. I asked Jerry's old secretary if he was available and got the same retarded, 'do you have an appointment' bullshit. She didn't recognize me.

"I'm Owen Fletcher," I said. That worked. She jumped in her chair and all but squirted her britches. It seemed Jerry was no longer a floor working stiff. He was now a vice president on another floor. Jerry would see me right away.

I took the glass cage up about ten stories to find Jerry at the elevator door. I hate it when he hugs me, I really do. He took me to his office and we sat down. I told him I needed more allowance money, and I was racking up the credit like the rectal temperature thermometer up a monkey's ass.

"The reason I stopped by was to rethink my investment portfolio."

Jerry displayed a wizened grin. "I'm way ahead of you. Got anything in mind?

"Yeah, stolen art collections, maybe some ivory. I'd buy Fort Knox, but Megan said we don't own the gold anymore. I've been out of the investment loop for a long time, so you tell me."

Jerry grinned. "Your account has government insurance, but not enough."

"You know how I feel about the government insuring anything. How much is not enough?"

"Two hundred thousand, the remainder is at risk, which is why I told you a passbook account was really fuckin' stupid."

"You're always telling me I'm fuckin' stupid. I could do something crazy stupid like investing in a 401K, where I could watch my money go down the shitter without the deduction. If I should live so long to actually spend my IRA, I'll be taxed out the ass on the pennies I earned. After I account for inflation, I'll still be in the losers' column."

"We're doing an IRA, sport, tax deferred investments, tax free bonds, safe shit. I have some very good mutuals and a few blue chips that pay dividends. There are some Asian rim stocks that are undervalued too. We'll load up on some of those. It's conservative, but very productive. It takes money to make money."

I was getting a mouthful of words right out of the IRS tax code book, and when you're as rich as I was, it's God awful embarrassing to pretend you have any idea how people are fucking with your money. I figured, what's good for Jerry, had to be good for me, so I just faked it because I didn't want him to repeat himself or try to explain what the hell an Asian rim was.

Jerry was only too glad to spread my dough around. He'd already done a little investigating on his end, and he whipped out what he thought was a rock solid plan. After reading through pages and pages of supposedly 'easy to understand' money schemes, I thought I was watching a roulette wheel spinning on Jerry's mahogany desk. Exasperated, I said, "Do whatever you think is best, but you lose one damned penny, you're freakin' fired."

Jerry's laugh was less confident than it should have been. We then turned to the problem of the extortion payoff I manufactured, only I didn't come right out and say I was under pressure, so I approached it in a casual, 'oh, did I mention,' kind of afterthought. Jerry had misgivings about it. Actually, misgivings is sorta soft. He pinged like a bird trying to fly through the window.

"What are you doing setting up a transfer account for one million dollars, Owen?"

"I'm expecting a divorce settlement."

Why did Jerry think that was so funny? "Owen, you just started dating her, and you're setting up a divorce settlement?"

Explaining something simple to Jerry, or any banker for that matter, was just not in the cards, so I danced gingerly on the outskirts of the problem.

"Wait. Wait. Owen, back up. You're telling me that your dad's girlfriend can't get her husband to sign divorce papers, and you're going to pony up a million bucks as a motivator? That's bribery. You'd be in a lot of trouble."

"I don't care about the divorce. I'm just trying to keep the guy from shooting at me and Betty."

"Who's Betty?"

"Betty is my dad's girlfriend. Her estranged husband is trying to kill her."

"So what's it to you? Happens all the time. The bitch probably deserves it for running off with your dad. This is a joke, right?"

"No, it isn't a joke. The psycho bastard shot up my RV with a fifty cal sniper's rifle. Moved the engine block two feet."

"Why would he be shooting at your RV?"

"Because I had Betty with me."

"Why is what's-her-name with you? Why isn't she with your dad?"

"Jesus Christ, you'd have to ask my dad. I made a deal with the asshole, and it's a million bucks for him to leave me alone."

"You're an idiot. That's extortion, and you should go to the police."

"That's not a good Idea."

"Why not?"

"He has more bullets. You sit behind an incoming fifty caliber bullet and tell me what you think of the experience."

"Jesus, Owen. You're not wanking me off. You're really scared."

"I need your help on this. I need you to set this up and keep your mouth shut."

"Back up. Not only would I be breaking a few laws assisting a psycho with the extortion, and/or murder of my friend and client, I would be violating banking regulations. Ethically speaking, we should be talking to the FBI right now."

"Dammit, Jerry! You want to take a chance on Psycho Mike finding me before the Feds find him. The Feds won't do shit until he fires the first shot and one is all the bastard needs."

"Let me see what I can do. Where can I find you?"

"I can't tell you. I'll call you. You can get word to me through Megan."

"Megan's a hot one. We hit it off. You banging her yet?"

Coming from Jerry, I wasn't offended, but maybe I should've been. Maybe he pitched in two ballparks. We parted with him not knowing where I stayed and a promise to meet for drinks at the end of the week.

As I walked out the door, I asked, "Know of any good used car lots?"

"Buy a new one, you cheap bastard."

Speaking of cars, that was next on my agenda. I've never owned anything new. Why start now? When I walked out of the bank, I was worried I was spending money too quickly and I'd run out. My past worries of where the next buck would come from spun through my mind. Now that I had too much, and saw how fast it went out the door, I was worried that plenty was not enough. I was pissed at myself for even thinking that way. My old habits died hard.

In all my life, I have never paid more than ten grand for a vehicle, including my old ratty RV. I've never owned anything but a truck and most of the time, a Chevy. I stepped out of my rental car to see the ride of my dreams, a cherry red Silverado 3500 extended cab, gas guzzling man-machine. This was my dream truck that I would never in a million years have expected to own...until now. I was all over it before the salesman could get to me. The truck was fully loaded, low miles, and a couple of years old. The sticker price was also a gas-guzzler. Just under my monthly allowance.

A thought went through my head. Why would a millionaire need a pick-up truck? Hell, what was I going to be hauling around? If I needed anything delivered, I'd hire someone. Shouldn't I be at the Mercedes dealership, buying a luxury set of wheels?

I had dreamed for so long about a Silverado 3500 that I just had to hang on to one old dream to the very end.

Clarence, the salesman, said, "Not a scratch on her. Wanna take her for a spin?"

"Don't really have the time." That's my way when I bought something. "Can we talk price?"

Car salesmen never just come right out and tell you the going price. We haggled back and forth, and Clarence had some worn out old trivia to throw my way. Yawn. When I asked if I could just pay cash, we talked seriously. I skipped all the add-on warranties and held the keys in thirty minutes. I asked Clarence if he could drop it off at the Hermitage Hotel under Megan's name. He was only too happy to.

I met up with Megan at the Capital Grille for lunch. She wanted a blow by blow run down of my day. I explained that Betty had a mental breakdown with all the pressure of a psycho husband trying to kill her.

Megan asked, "Is there anything I can do? Poor woman must be frightened out of her skull."

"She's on enough meds to put an elephant to sleep for a week. I'll check in on her after lunch." I needed to change the subject. I didn't want Megan digging around in Betty's business with Boots too deeply. "Did you come up with a security company?"

"Yes, I talked to Gordon this morning. Things like this happen too frequently, and he recommended Fox Securities, a firm which specializes in safeguarding high profile individuals. He said the company specializes in resolving special cases without bringing the attention of law enforcement or the media."

"You think I'm high profile?"

"Yes, and you do have a nice one. I took the initiative to have a private consultation with the company owner in your suite at one o'clock. Do you want me to be there?"

Hell no, I didn't. "I'll handle it, Megan. This should be all over within a couple of days, a week at most. Anything on Betty's divorce?"

"Not yet. I check twice a day. Would you like me to stop by later? We could have drinks and dinner, and then I could give you a full body massage in your room?"

"I already have a hysterical woman in the next room to deal with. I'm not sure I can deal with two. I promised to take Betty shopping. The clothes we have don't meet the dress code. Maybe tomorrow?"

"Owen, if she's on meds, she'll probably be out for a week. She won't suspect a thing."

"She already does. She picked up your scent this morning."

"What was she doing in your room?"

"She stopped by with a formal noise complaint. We had breakfast together because we had to talk over a few things."

Megan flashed a disapproving frown which I ignored. "You're a media sensation at the moment. There are a lot of rumors about you."

"It must be a slow news day."

"At least two people claim that you promised them half the jackpot. There's also a rumor that you stiffed a talent agency."

"It's all hype, I can assure you. Anything else?"

"Your wife, Bonnie, is in town."

That bit of news bothered me. I didn't have to use much of an imagination to guess what she was after. It had been ten years since I last saw her, and my memories of her drove me nuts. I wanted to see her one more time, but then I concluded that I would, and it would probably be at a civil hearing. "She's not my wife. It sounds like I need a lawyer. Got any ideas?"

"I'll ask Gordon for some advice as soon as I get back to the office. You might want to ask Mr. Fox if he has any suggestions. Just for your information, one date night a week isn't going to cut it. I'm horny all the time because of you. When your patient recovers, you're going to have another lunatic on your hands"

CHAPTER TWENTY-TWO

I checked in with Betty after I finished lunch with Megan. She had spent the morning grooming. She'd obviously visited the hair salon, the cosmetics shop, and the spa. Betty was a natural beauty, and I had never seen her with makeup. I wasn't even sure that I gazed upon the same woman. She had cut her long locks and tinted her auburn hair with highlights. The hair style was playfully full and flirty. Blue orbs shone under long lashes. The lips had a teasing touch of pink. Overall, she radiated majestic elegance and mischievous exuberance.

Her mood matched her looks. She all but danced as she showed me into her room. "What do you think?"

She was begging for a compliment, so I obliged. "The wart cream you bought worked."

She playfully tapped my shoulder and struck a seductive pose. "Come on. What do you think? Be nice."

"It's nice to see you come out of the broom closet."

"I spent all morning trying to make myself beautiful for you, and that's all you have to say?"

"You don't want to hear what I have to say."

"Try me. I need a man's opinion."

"We could start with shockingly exquisite and work our way up from there. If you get me started, I won't shut up."

Betty gave me a gentle hug and a kiss before hopping onto a sofa. "I haven't been to a beauty salon in years, except to get a trim. I always wore my hair long, straight, and drab to please Mike and Boots. Do you really like what I've done?"

"Yes. It gives your face definition and liveliness. You look younger, and you need to stop flirting with me."

In the space of a morning, Betty's mood and looks took on a dramatic change. There was something else that had changed about her. In one sense, I was happy for her, but in another, I thought something I had said to her had prompted her decision. Was there something in Boots' message that triggered her?

"Tell me about your morning," she said.

I sat down at the far end of the sofa and told her everything was set at the bank. I admitted that Jerry was extremely reluctant. I mentioned my new truck and skipped over lunch with Megan. Betty wasn't an idiot.

"How did lunch go with Megan?"

"How do you know I had lunch with Megan?"

"I finished at the salon and walked by the Capitol Grille. I could see you both from the lobby. How am I supposed to hide out from a woman I don't know if I haven't seen her?"

"Don't be doing that."

"She's quite pretty. What did you tell her about me?"

"I told her you carry the anthrax virus, and you're quarantined to your room for the duration."

"You did not."

"I told her you had a mental breakdown, and you're on meds most of the time."

"Do I look like I'm having a mental breakdown?"

"You did this morning when I left. Megan's arranged for us to have a security protection detail assigned to us. We're having a consultation in a few minutes in my suite. I think you need to be there. Are you up for that?"

"Is it absolutely necessary?"

"Yes. I absolutely love to breathe and walk around."

CHAPTER TWENTY-THREE

There was a knock on the door, and the goon squad stood outside as I inspected them through the peep hole. All three had badges up for me to inspect. I opened the door and allowed the three chipmunks to enter my suite.

The wiry little team leader thrust a tiny paw at me. "I'm Alvin Fox, team leader and your point of contact." Nothing about him reminded me of a fox, chipmunk perhaps. That said, Alvin fit his cartoon namesake to a tee, as he flashed me a Chicklet smile. I got through the introductions without snickering.

We settled into the business of personal protection, which is a slick name for all loss of freedom of movement and many other freedoms. Neither Betty nor I were allowed to leave the hotel without giving the team advanced notice as to where we were going and at what time. To complicate matters, Betty and I could not be away from the hotel at the same time in two different destinations. Alvin informed us we should confine ourselves to the nearest extent possible to the hotel proper. I felt like I was being handcuffed to the heat register.

Alvin set about interrogating us so that he could better identify the threat. When he learned that Betty was my father's girlfriend, there was a pause and a sly look of disbelief. I recounted what had occurred, and Betty provided pictures of Psycho Mike, which had me wondering why Betty was carrying around photos of a man that she had been estranged from for over three years. Alvin asked to borrow the photos, Alvin, the sharp little tick that he was, asked the same question. Betty said she didn't know why Boots put them in her overnight bag.

Alvin wanted to know to what depth law enforcement was involved. Betty told him she had a protection order and explained the situation with the Harris County Sheriff's department. He then asked how Psycho Mike could have tracked Betty to Lawson's. She said Psycho Mike had probably made a calculated guess that Boots would hide her with relatives.

I told him about the encounter with the sheriff of Tippecanoe County in Indiana. Alvin said I did the right thing. "I'll coordinate with the sheriff and keep him off your back. Still, you need to cooperate with their investigation."

Alvin the fox was not surprised by my plan to buy Mike off. "You can nail his ass for extortion as soon as he makes a withdrawal from the account, but you would have to explain why you deposited a million dollars into the account. Do you have any proof that he's a threat?"

"I have his threats recorded on my cell phone," Betty said.

Alvin asked, "Do you mind if I listen to them and record them? Mark is our tech expert. Can you let him borrow your phone for a few minutes while I talk to Owen?"

Betty led Mark to her room. When they were out of ear shot, Alvin asked, "Whose bright idea was it to buy the bastard off?"

"Mine. I thought it would solve the problem. Harlan gets his money. Betty gets her divorce."

"Normally I would agree. I'm not sure it's the answer, but it did save your life. It won't happen a second time. I'm curious how you struck the deal. What did you offer him?"

"I called him using Betty's cell phone, and I offered him $500,000."

"That's a nice divorce settlement when it isn't your divorce. How did you come up with that amount?"

"Shit, I don't know. It sounded rich enough to entice him. He laughed and I hung up on him."

"Let me ask you something. You talked to him a couple of times; were there any subtle differences, tone, attitude, voice, anything?"

"Now that you mention it, yeah, there was. The first conversation was with an angry bastard. The second time sounded like he was having fun, not in any hurry... resolved."

"What happened next?"

"I backed down the offer to $100,000, and he upped it to a million."

"He knew exactly who you were. You have plates on your RV, and all he had to do was run them through the DMV. It took him two hours to find out that you won the lottery, or someone found that information for him. Where's the million dollars?"

"I have it set up in a transfer account at my bank."

"Walk me through the details, account numbers, banks, the whole nine yards."

I read from my notes and rattled off the whole setup. Alvin was taking notes and asking the questions. When I finished, his face was a large question mark.

"You're telling me that ... you and Megan came up with all of this in the space of a couple of hours? I'm not buying it. Keep this to yourself. I need to think on it and get some answers." Alvin paused, then yelled, "Mark, we're done in here, bring Mrs. Harlan in."

My opinion of Alvin was growing by leaps and bounds. While Betty was out of the room, he informed me he was sending a team to investigate the shooting site, and I should call Lawson and ask for his cooperation. I discovered that Alvin was a retired detective, so I asked him if we could get Mike on attempted murder.

"Why would he want to kill the golden goose? You have to ask yourself how he knew you're good for a million bucks. Remember, you just won it the day before all of this started." Alvin gave a meaningful look in the direction of Betty's door. "How did he know he would be confronted by a pack of dogs?"

"You just said he probably ID'd the license plate, and he had a week to scout out the farm. Betty wanted to call the cops both times we were assaulted so we could build a case against Psycho Mike."

Alvin ignored my probing thoughts with a shrug. "But you did, which was smart. If this bastard has an inside to the DMV, what makes you think he doesn't have other law enforcement hook-ups? If the cops had provided you with protective custody, everyone in town would have known where the lottery winner is by the end of the first shift. It's a good thing you have us."

Betty sauntered back into the room and handed Alvin her cell phone. Alvin listened to the message log. "The gentleman seems to be stressed. Owen, does his voice sound familiar to you?"

"I couldn't say for sure. The guy I had talked to was a cool customer, but there are similarities to his speech pattern."

Alvin had one last business transaction. I had a contract to sign with a very stiff dollar sign attached to it. Fifteen-hundred bucks per day, plus expenses, and a huge retainer fee that took my breath away. I certainly didn't feel like a rock star, but the way Megan was spending my money, I should have.

Before Alvin left, I gave him my itinerary for the day. I had every intention of making Alvin and the chipmunks earn their keep. I told him I'd bought a truck, and I was taking Betty shopping, then we were going to dinner. I got the 'where and when' bullshit immediately.

"Whatever you do, keep a low profile, and don't draw attention to yourselves. Get your shopping done, and you should probably dine in. Make that your habit until the check at the bank clears. No calls, visitors, or public excursions."

"What about my date night with Megan?" I asked. "Well, it's up to two date nights as of lunch today."

"You're dating the lotto doll? You forgot to mention that. Rent a porn movie and send down for popcorn. Do *not* go partying."

"How long will all of this take?" Betty whined.

"You gave the bastard two weeks. It could take that long. You two should be well acquainted with each other by the time this is all over. Play solitaire or whatever; just don't piss each other off. Oh, and one other thing," Alvin took a leering look at Betty, "You need to make yourself scarce on date night."

Betty said, "We've already talked about that."

"Good. We wouldn't want to give the girlfriend a reason to be jealous."

The air filled with the suggestion of temptation. Betty was my dad's girlfriend. Then it dawned on me ... she was actually his ex-girlfriend. The two of us exchanged a look. We were both on the same page, and there wouldn't be a problem. Not one. I cleared that hurdle thinking I was home free. That would be the last time I'd have a clear conscience for a very long time to come.

We let Alvin go about his business, wiring the corridor with security monitoring gear. He assured us we would have complete protection and privacy. The Heritage staff would be alerted to not disclose our presence to anyone. I felt very secure and satisfied by the time the trio left us.

CHAPTER TWENTY-FOUR

Betty was jumping the leash to go on a shopping spree. There wasn't a Wal-Mart within miles of us. That left a trendy mall nearby where there were some swanky women's apparel shops. Betty made a list of items to get her through a couple of weeks. It was a short list, and we could be spending a couple of weeks together and one of anything wasn't enough.

Betty was the first person to ride in my new truck. Correct that. I was the first passenger in my new truck, which wasn't new. Betty loved my new ride. I wonder if Harlan's Silverado was as cool as mine. I could ask Betty, but I didn't want to distract her because she was burning rubber and we were still in the parking lot. It probably was, because she knew where everything was. I'd taken a tip from Alvin and didn't register the truck because I didn't want anyone in the DMV knowing what I was driving. The way Betty was hot-rodding about, my truck could soon be in the police municipal impound.

Betty and Megan had a couple of things in common, of which fast and reckless were two. I kept yelling at Betty to slow down and to look out the front window. If women drove their relationships as hard as they drove their vehicles, it's no surprise the divorce rate has zoomed through the roof. We arrived at the mall parking lot without injury, damage, or hitting a highway worker. As soon as the gear shift was in park, I said, "Keys, please," and held out my hand.

Betty, who had not stopped laughing since we left the hotel said, "What?"

"Keys. You're grounded, young lady."

"Why, and for how long?"

"Because your driving borders between homicidal and suicidal. You're grounded until you turn sixteen."

"What? I'm way past sixteen."

"I'm talking about your next life."

The one thing I'm good at is picking out women's clothes. Playing on stage, I'd seen some classy looking chicks. I know what looks good on a woman. It doesn't have to be sexy, tight, or extravagant, but it usually works out with that combination. We made a plan. Betty set off to find a few outfits to try on and so did I. I went to the high dollar rack and she went to the sales rack. She tried on bag lady garbs that were dull as coal lumps. I sent her back to the dressing room with my picks. She came out in a little dark blue dress that was just an inch from risqué. She blushed and I lusted. She looked at herself in the mirror, pleased with the radiant image. "It's a bit snug for me. Did you look at the price tag?" She waved her hand as if she had just touched a hot stove.

"Try the next one on."

She took it, looked at the price tag and said, "Take it back, Owen."

"Try it on. We're staying at the Hermitage, and you have to look like you belong there."

Betty had fun modeling dresses I picked out for her. She had a fit problem because she was top heavy, but that didn't prevent me from dragging more dresses off the rack. I finished bringing her the big bust, small waist dresses in the store. I pretended to show cavalier indifference, but Betty could see the saliva dripping off my chin. She gave me a few flirty poses and swished her hips seductively. I didn't mind taking Betty shopping, and we ran out of dresses for her to try on.

"Which one did you like the best, Owen?"

I liked them all, but I picked out three. She thought all three were too showy, too sheer, or too risqué, and all of them had a cleavage problem. We debated the issue and decided on a dress that was more or less regal. Just for kicks, I threw in my three choices.

"I'm buying only one dress. I've already spent too much on myself, and Boots is going to hit the roof when he sees the credit card bill."

Fuck him, since he threw her out, the least he could do was give her some decent clothes to wear. That tidbit of knowledge grated on my conscience. "You might be buying one, but I'm buying three, and I can't see myself wearing any of them. Don't make a scene. Now we need to find some day clothes."

We spent another hour shopping for her. The last stop was the lingerie department, and I hoped Betty would ask me to the fitting room, but I wasn't that lucky. I didn't see any of the chipmunks, so I assumed they were hiding out in the fitting room, waiting for Betty to strip down for them.

Next, it was my turn. Betty said my cargo pants had to go, and we reversed rolls. I remembered my makeover trip with Megan, and this trip was just as much fun. I finished up buying underwear and Betty said, "I know you're a briefs kind of guy. I did your laundry." We had a load of clothes to haul, but the sales staff offered to take the packages to my truck since I had inflated their commission checks.

We arrived back at the hotel just before dark. I dutifully called Alvin just to make sure he wasn't sleeping on the job. He wasn't there, but one of the other chipmunks answered, and I told him Betty and I would be dining at the Capitol Grille.

CHAPTER TWENTY-FIVE

The Capitol Grille at the Hermitage didn't have a dress code, but it was *the* Capitol Grille and neither Betty nor I were up to standards. I needed five seconds and a tie, but Betty needed an hour. I dressed and poured myself a scotch while I waited for Betty to get ready. Much to my delight, she was only thirty minutes. I opened the door for her and I thought my eyeballs were going to fly out of my eye sockets. WOW! Talk about put together. Betty was chin to the floor gorgeous.

I'd never spent time in a fancy place like the Capitol Grille, unless I was being paid to sing and dance for my food. With Betty on my arm, we, as a couple, created a buzz. That's not being fair to Betty. No one paid the least bit of attention to me. This millionaire business started to reap some benefits as we were escorted to the best table in the house. As we took a seat, Betty was chatty and wanted to walk me back through our shopping spree. I let her gush, but my mind was elsewhere. The joy of relaxing, spending money like pouring water down a rat hole, and having an intimate dinner with a Victoria Secret model was a bit dizzying. I hold that memory with reverence to this day.

The wine steward popped up before we ordered from the menu. What I knew about wine consisted of one word—nothing. I let Betty take on that duty, and she knew as much as I did, maybe less, so I said to the steward, "Red swill or white swill?" The steward sneered and made a recommendation. If I was to become a no-shit, serious millionaire, I would have to attend wine tasting school. Betty thought that was funny.

Most of the time, I eat with my hands, as most fast food comes in wrappers. Mother made sure I learned how to use eating utensils properly, but which ones to use was a mystery to me as I saw a line-up of cutlery by my plate, like the armory at the Tower of London. Armed to the teeth, I wondered aloud if there was a table setting school. When in doubt, ask. "This looks like the tool aisle at Home Depot. I'm clueless; help me out here."

Betty rattled off the names and uses of each of the fancy utensils, and I shot back with stupid questions that made her laugh. "Shouldn't the salad fork be a hay rake? How can I load up on veggies with that?"

"It's designed for portion control, silly. You're not supposed to cram your face like a Viking overlord at a Nordic feast. The point of fine dining is to converse and eat in polite and restrained company."

I informed Miss Manners that they had yet to make a Big Mac that I couldn't devour in two bites and still have a four way conversation at the same time. Betty defended the Western cultural traditions around the dining table, as I supplied her with ridiculous alternatives that kept her laughing.

Betty drained her glass, and I asked, "More wine? This selection is really quite good, isn't it?" Betty daintily held her glass to me.

We polished off a bottle of fine Piesporter before the salad serving arrived. She nibbled like a rabbit while I mowed the lawn in two swipes. The waiter explained the salad ingredients were fresh picked that very morning. We learned the chef was running his own subsistence farm operation, but the waiter spun it as a quality issue so we would think we were getting our money's worth. My palate wasn't that delicate, so I couldn't tell the difference, but Betty could. I kept my mouth shut.

The food at the Capitol Bar and Grille was rated four stars, and I had to admit, it lived up to that reputation. But what did I know? Three weeks ago, the Waffle House was five-star in my book. Betty and I sailed through dinner, making small talk and laughing like five-year olds on their first visit to Chuck E Cheese. Our table could have been sitting in the intersection in front of the hotel, and neither of us would have paid attention to the traffic. I learned something that I didn't know about wine. You can get drunk drinking wine. I found out as Betty and I polished off three bottles of very smooth Piesporter.

Betty and I were done for the day. At least that was my thought. She had never seen, or been to the Wild Horse Saloon, which was just down the street. She was in the mood to go, but I wasn't. I remembered we were supposed to lay low, and I told Betty we weren't on vacation. We stumbled to the front entry to leave the restaurant for our rooms.

Not so fast. We were just about to the door when a gentleman stood up and asked, "Aren't you the young man who won the latest lottery?" I saw the eager attack-chipmunk emerge from nowhere out of the corner of my eye. He stopped casually, just within earshot. The man went on to say, "I saw you on the six o'clock news. I just wanted to say congratulations." He extended his hand and I shook it. He sat back down. I looked back into the Grille and heard a murmuring and saw glasses raised in salute. I smiled and gave what I thought was a decent royal wave. Betty weaved and bobbed before catching on. Then I heard clicking. The paparazzi had caught up to us, and the flashing camera had perfectly timed my shiny smile and kingly wave.

This was my virgin solo flight to fame. I had mentally prepared for this moment, and I took Betty by the arm. We walked briskly out, and Mr. Chipmunk got between me and the cameraman. I had all but given up on becoming famous when my music career tanked. I had watched from a distance how Duke Findley and my other successful friends dealt with impromptu photo shoots. Now that I rated local celeb status, Owen Fletcher, glimmering in the limelight, felt disappointment. What made me famous? A freakin' lottery ticket. I couldn't put much stock in that. What a cheap way to instant notoriety. There was only one other way a washed-up musician like me could get that kind of attention. Climb up onto the freeway bridge over the Cumberland River and threaten to jump. Now that would get camera crews off their asses, but when my body hit the water, my fame would go down with it. Fame is short and not so glorious.

We went to my room, and I headed for the mini-bar. Betty wasn't done with her overly exuberant discovery of the grand life. She asked for a nightcap and slid into a recliner. We talked until Betty fell asleep, or more correctly, passed out. Betty was not a hard core drinker like me. If she ever had been, it stopped when she moved in with Boots. Anyway, she was in la-la land, halfway through the sissy drink I made for her.

I turned the tube on and watched my infomercial on the ten o'clock news. There I was pumping hands with big shots, signing for the bogus sixty-four million dollar check. I was introduced as a career musician and there was a bit of speculation about my history, since no one had ever heard of me. Even losers can win the lottery. A month ago, I felt like any other citizen trying to keep a roof over my head, suffering through the frustrations of life. There was nothing wrong with that. I was pissed off and for no good reason.

I turned off the TV and sat down to watch Betty sleep. She was breathing deeply, and I wondered what she was dreaming about. I thought about letting her sleep it off on my recliner and decided that would not be a good idea. I gently picked her up in my arms and carried her to her bed in the adjoining room. I stood there looking down on her, wishing she wasn't my dad's girlfriend. What did I do? Yup, I bent down to kiss her good night thinking she would never know.

Wouldn't you know, she woke up and pulled me on top of her. I didn't resist, and at first allowed myself to believe it was an accident. If that was the case, why did I allow her to roll on top of me? I felt the softness of her melt into me and the passion of her kiss draw the breath out of me. Her hand took mine and she guided it to her breast. As I began kneading, I felt her arch beneath me and heard a slight moan. I rolled on top of her, hanging onto her breast. With both hands free, she pinned me to her, and her wet lips moved to my neck as she put a new energy in her kisses. Both sets of hands were moving, and articles of clothing started to litter the floor around the bed. I helped with her cleavage problem by unsnapping her bra and buried my lips onto her ripe nipple. She helped me with my erection problem by stroking the business end of my brain. My other brain, completely useless, had shut down. After an hour of delicious impassioned lovemaking, I understood exactly why Boots had gotten into trouble. In that hour, Betty had taken me on a sensual lap around the universe, nothing like I had ever experienced in my life. Betty was nothing less than spectacular and knew how to use every part of her body and mine too. My big brain kicked in with Lawson's warning words, "Be careful around Betty." It was too late for that now.

I left Betty's room with a huge quandary and a huge erection that wouldn't go away. This should *not* have happened! What was I thinking about? Were we both drunk and careless. Did I use that as an excuse? You bet I did. I understood that Boots was finished with her, but my promise was to protect her, not screw her. The only thing to do was to take a shower and pretend it didn't happen. I made a note to self, Don't get Betty drunk.... ever...ever...again.

CHAPTER TWENTY-SIX

I was awakened early the next morning by a shifting weight on my mattress. Startled, I sat straight up, looking into the eyes of a very beautiful woman. Betty wore a negligee that served only as an ornament to tantalize. I was going to have to start locking my other door at night. Sober, I said, "We can't be doing this. We just can't."

"Please, Owen? Just one more time, please?"

"The answer is no. We were both drunk, and it shouldn't have happened."

"Yes, we were, and we still are." She thrust her big soft warm torpedoes in my face. "Make love to me one more time, and then we can pretend nothing happened." I had my own torpedo problems to deal with. My torpedo had its own self-adjusting mechanism, spring loaded in the upright and erect position, ready to fire. I was angry at myself for being coerced into doing something that I badly wanted to do. Betty settled the matter by sliding down my torso. The woman had total control over me, and I couldn't help it.

My experience to date with the pace of having sex was something between a mechanical bull ride and sixty seconds in the paint mixer at Home Depot. I thought that was what women expected, and my complaint file was empty. I had never had any woman tell me to slow it down until Betty came along.

The lovemaking that followed was a slow, churning passion that tingled my spine. We took deep pleasure from each other. Lustful sex and lovemaking are not the same by a long shot. What Betty and I were doing was lovemaking. Neither of us wanted it to end. We laid together stroking and caressing one another in silent bliss.

My perception concerning communication between partners is that women don't talk at all during sex. They might yell or scream, grunt, moan, or throw out someone's name other than mine, but they don't talk. Betty was different. She was talking to me like the fleet air boss on an aircraft carrier, directing me, talking me all the way to the deck. I bolted the wire a couple of times and had to go around. Her whispered instructions and flying lessons in my ear were a turn on I had never experienced.

I had to call a seventh inning stretch. Betty had gone to attend to female business as I sank in the ocean of guilt that could drown me. Then my cell phone rang and I was afraid to ignore it. I knew who called. I had a frightful feeling she was standing just outside the door. I answered tentatively, which tipped off Megan.

"And good morning to you too, Owen."

"Sorry, I wasn't expecting your call." Did I not mention that Megan was telepathic?

"What's up?" she asked. My dick was what was up. My guilty conscience went into overdrive. I was a no good son-of-a-bitch without a spine. I let my dad's ex-girlfriend seduce me a second time.

Megan chuckled and said, "If I didn't know better, I would think you had someone with you. I called to offer you a ride to the studio. We've got a nine o'clock session."

My disgust with myself had me on the verge of making a confession. Betty came back into the bedroom and shook her head vigorously, as she probably knew I was about to spill my guilt.

I didn't have a kamikaze death wish, so I said, "Thanks just the same, but I bought a set of wheels yesterday, and I'll meet you at the studio."

"I could stop by early, and we could have a morning therapy session."

"Thanks to you, I have a security detail on my ass twenty-four/seven. We wouldn't want anyone to get the wrong idea," I said. Betty's eyes widened and she had to clamp her hand over her mouth to keep from blurting out a squeal.

"You mean the right idea. Thanks to you, I'm constantly horny. Come on, Owen, make my day."

"What happened to date night?"

"Geez, I'm throwing myself at you, and I feel that maybe I should have my head examined. You make me feel cheap. I'll see you at the shoot." Click. Megan was throwing herself at me, and I wasn't ready to catch her. Not yet. She weighed too much for a man who had no experience in a serious relationship. I didn't know where the pain in my head came from as I unsuccessfully tried to separate my guilt to make it something lesser.

Betty had listened to the whole conversation. I was silent for several moments. She sat next to me and put her arm around me. A lingering silence hung in the air for the longest moment. There was nothing either of us could say to each other. Betty rose and pulled my head to her flat tummy. "Owen, don't make too much out of this. I planned to seduce you. Take a shower, and I'll see you for breakfast."

CHAPTER TWENTY-SEVEN

The knocking continued as Betty and I tried our best to make ourselves decent. I prayed that the caller was not a long-legged brunette with a million-dollar smile. Betty gathered her lingerie and headed for her room, running on tiptoes. I put on a robe, did a finger brush through my hair and went to see who was at the door.

It was an impatient Alvin with two suitcases and a numb expression on his face. I put a curious nonchalant expression on my mug before opening the door.

"Alvin, what brings the chipmunks out this early in the morning?" I got a smirk and a flash of anger before his dull expression returned. He didn't say anything as he slowly walked past me into the central salon of my suite. He had that cop swagger that told me he was taking everything in, like he was investigating a crime scene, which was unsettling.

"Owen, we need to rethink what we're doing. That episode last night was uncalled for."

Did he know that I screwed Betty? "Which episode?" I asked testily.

He took a seat in an overstuffed couch and said, "I see you've taken the liberty of having coffee and pastries sent up. We need to talk, the three of us. But before I wake Wonder Woman, we should chat."

"Is something wrong?"

Alvin scoffed. "Something wrong? Yeah, you reek of your dad's girlfriend's perfume. You want to have a Roman orgy in your room, it's your business, so let's not make fucking pretend."

Whatever the expression on my face gave away, it made him laugh.

"Your dinner date. I went out on a limb. I paid the freelancer more than the papers would have paid him for the pics." He tossed a set of photos of King Owen and Queen Betty across the coffee table. "You were celebrities caught in the headlights. By noon every barking dog in town would have had your scent."

"What's your thinking, Alvin?" I saw his eyes snap, and just as quickly he resumed his professional glare.

"Your other girlfriend is anxious to get you out there and up on the billboards, but that will have to wait."

"What are you implying?"

"She lined up an interview with a shock-jock for a prerecording. The problem is the guy isn't trustworthy and is syndicated all over the south. He's not going to miss the opportunity to showcase you before someone else. He'll put it on the air, and the Hermitage will be one big flytrap with media hanging all over by noon.

"We'll cancel the interview."

Alvin chuckled. "Consider it cancelled because you won't be here. We need time to reel your father in to keep him from doing something stupid, like killing Mike Harlan. We'll keep him out of jail, and then we'll have a chat with the FBI and let them deal with the sting you've set up for Harlan."

Alvin made perfectly good sense. "Find my dad. I'll tell Megan to put a lid on all this PR business."

Alvin's dead silence left me with a problem I didn't know about. What had I missed?

"The media is more than just a little bit curious about you. The hunt is on. Your PR handler has other plans for you, chum. If it's a slow news week in Nashville, what about the rest of the country? Any lottery winner caught doing some goofy stunt is news. By my count, you're at least four up on the rest. One photo of you and Betty together will hit the major broadcasts, and if Miss Marsh find outs, here's the news story, 'Tennessee's latest mystery millionaire seen wooing his dad's girlfriend, while dad is out trying to kill the mystery woman's husband, while the mystery husband is extorting our millionaire for a million bucks.' Do you see a problem developing here?"

No shit. I nodded my head north and south vigorously. Betty and I were caught up in our mutual infatuation, which we made very public. The sales staff in the mall were witnesses to a very flirty and playful couple spending money out the ass. Mega-millionaire Owen Fletcher, who used his credit card, provided the connection if anyone was interested in the story. While we were at it, we put on a nice display for everyone at the Capitol Grille, with an impromptu acknowledgement and a photo session. Millionaire Owen paid cash for a tricked out, high dollar truck, and the mysterious Betty's complete makeover was sizzling gossip in the making, if all the dots were connected.

"If your PR girlfriend learns any of this, your ass is grass."

"It was all innocent. Betty and I were friends having a quiet dinner."

"Are you kidding? You and Betty had your own fucking billboard. That sexy modeling show the two of you put on at the mall would make a monk jack off. You and your dinner date were having foreplay in a very public way. Betty dripped with sex, and I'll guarantee there wasn't a soft dick in the house. If the women come face to face, you're a dead man walking. If your father finds out, skip the walking part." Alvin rubbed his chin. "I know what's going on, and I'd give a fortune to be in your shoes. Someone tipped the photographer off last night. Got any ideas about that? The tip came from the only other person who knows where you are. She's got the hots for you in a serious way. Did you know she tried to get into your room last night, did you know that?"

"What?"

"Don't worry, my guys sent her packing. The thing is, you have women problems, plural, which is none of my business."

"What do you suggest?"

"Take Betty on a ten-day cruise and get cabins at opposing ends of the ship, or you could get one suite and get her out of your system. That's up to you. Snuggle up on the love boat and stay lost at sea for at least ten days. It'll be all over by the time you get back. We'll have someone with you, but just be a damned middle-class tourist, no fancy suites. Ten days should wrap this up."

"Why a cruise? Couldn't we just hang out at a fishing camp in Minnesota?"

"We don't know how Harlan found you in Indiana yet. I have my ideas, but we're not taking any chances. You can't get on a cruise ship with a gun, that's first. The ship is moving all over the Gulf of Mexico which gives us opportunities to move you two love birds around without suspicion. Next, we have tighter security control over who has access to your quarters. Think of it as a swanky jail on the high seas."

"What about Boots?"

"I'll send people down to Columbus to make sure he doesn't do anything crazy."

"What do I tell Megan?"

"Absolutely nothing. Think about it, she could be the cause of all your misery. We're moving your stuff out of the Hermitage, and you're out of here on the noon flight to Miami. Do you have your passport with you?"

"I don't have one."

"How about a birth certificate?"

"Shit, I left it in the RV."

"Not a problem. I'll get a certified copy faxed to the cruise line when you book."

"Where are we going?"

"Do I look like a fucking tour guide? Ten days at sea and I don't give a shit where. My agent will keep you appraised on developments here."

"Thank you."

"I'm not done. You have a couple of process servers waiting for you on behalf of namely, your wife, Bonnie Fletcher, and your nine-year-old daughter, whom you abandoned. There's another from a liquor store owner, who's laying claim to half of your winnings. This is the least of your problems for the moment. I specialize in this shit, so go have a nice voyage. You're leaving through the freight elevator."

"One of my former colleagues must have tipped Bonnie off about me winning the lottery. Is Bonnie downstairs?"

"She's in town, plotting with her attorney. No one knows where you're residing."

Bonnie was not here to open her blouse and take me to her bosom. Even so, I badly wanted to see her and get an explanation of why she left in the first place. The words clicked into place in my head. Wife? Little girl? Oh shit, I was in it now.

Reading my mind, Alvin said, "This isn't a time for a family reunion."

"Let me say goodbye to Megan. I really owe her. She said something like this might happen."

"No way. The one person you don't want to know is the PR representative of the Tennessee lottery. You're toast if she ever discovers Betty is the hot redheaded girlfriend. I've taken care of that. We have a photo of a fifties looking woman whom we morphed into the photo. I love digital technology."

"I thought the reason I had to be in Nashville was to trigger the money transfer."

"That would have made everything much cleaner, but you dicked that up, and we'll have to think of another way. Do you have any friends that you trust explicitly?"

"Jerry, my banker, but he's not on-board with any of this."

"That won't work. Anybody else in town?"

"Just Megan."

"Does Jerry know Megan?"

"Yes, they're recent friends."

"Well, it's this way. Since Megan seems to be pulling the strings, we'll make her power of attorney to act on your behalf while you're vacationing. We'll keep her busy. I know an attorney that she can set you up with to manage your other problems. We'll limit her power of attorney to the payoff, just in case."

"What do you mean, 'just in case?' Why can't I make you power of attorney?"

Alvin didn't answer the first question. "There's a conflict of interest, and I don't know your banker and don't want to. It would raise some suspicions on his part."

Over the brim of a steaming cup, I heard him say, "Bring sleeping beauty over. She's going to love hearing this."

CHAPTER TWENTY-EIGHT

Betty and I showed up at the Royal Nordic Cruise Line ticket counter, looking for the first ship out. We found a seven-day cruise leaving in a few hours, but Alvin said ten days. The next ten-day cruise left the following day, but its itinerary was the Mexican Riviera, which our new chipmunk chaperone found unacceptable. Simon came from the same gene pool as Alvin. They were cousins. He started bossing us around the minute we arrived in Miami, and he was already getting under my skin.

Luck favored us. The Nordic Breeze was departing for a fourteen-day excursion around the Caribbean. What were four more days? We checked at the desk to discover there were plenty of steerage class stalls called cabins. A cabin to me was a hideaway in the woods where bandits avoided the posse. We were the good guys hiding out from the bad guys.

The floor plan of the 'cabin' was just a tiny bit larger than a shipping crate. Alvin's advice to book two rooms as far apart from one another was not very appealing to me, considering the choices I had. These Chinese packing crates were going for bargain basement prices. I asked the cute ticket clerk if upgrades were still available. She frowned and said all the balcony cabins and suites were sold out.

The woman, seeing the frustration on my face, looked into the computer screen, and looked up as if she'd measured the thickness of my wallet. "We do have one royal suite and two 'owners' suites left. I can sell either one at a discount price. Would you care to look at the floor plans?"

I did, and I gasped when I saw the layout. It was a huge, four room suite, with a fantail cocktail balcony and a private hot tub, the most luxurious flop pad on the boat. It came with all kinds of personal services, and I held my breath waiting to hear what I was going to have to pay. My chin dropped when the clerk whispered the price. It was less by half than staying at the Hermitage for two weeks.

I was indeed tempted to take the royal suite. In fact, Betty was hinting that would be her preference too. "Who's going to know?" she cooed.

"One of Alvin's attack chipmunks. We'll go submarine class and take shifts sleeping."

"Nobody is going to know."

Megan? She'd dig around and learn the truth, of that I was certain, so I said, "I'll take both suites." So much for laying low and blending in with the masses. Betty hit my arm and made a nasty face.

The layout was perfect. Betty's suite was next to mine, and Alvin's pal lived down the corridor in a utility-closet-sized stateroom without any windows. We were on the very top deck of the ship with a splendid view. The royal suite was laid out spaciously, with a small dining room off the foyer, which could open up to a grand salon with a great view of the balcony. The bedroom had a king-sized playpen and a workout station. The designer thought of everything by putting in a computer work station, big screen TV, and tastefully decorated the suite with old world charm.

I paced around the suite, snacking on lobster bits, drinking champagne and marveling at the ice carving on the dining room table. The suite came with a grand piano and I sat down to play. Krebs, the steward, be-bopped to my music ditty while he unpacked the few things I had brought onboard. Although Betty was next door, she couldn't get to me unless she gnawed her way through the partition.

Then my cell phone rang. Megan, mad as hell and particularly with me, vented her disappointment and frustration. Put another way, she ranted insanely.

I ignored her ranting, but I did want to talk to her about Bonnie. "Megan, why did Bonnie suddenly show up?"

"I told you. I knew something like this would happen, and you lied to me."

Which lie was she going off about? I had the dumb idea to ask.

"You told me you aren't a tit and ass man. Bonnie has a dolly Parton rack on her. She's gorgeous."

They weren't that big, so I replied, "They must be store bought because she wasn't big-breasted when I was married to her." Yes she was, but how would Megan know?

"According to her, you're still married to her. She claims you abandoned her when you found out she was pregnant...before she left for Colorado. You can bet it's going to be a battle when it hits the court, and she has the media gushing. One other thing, stud, what's with you and women whose first names start with the capital letter B? Bernadette, Bonnie, and Betty. Give me a freakin' break."

"It's a minor alphabetic quirk of mine. I don't know, Megan."

"Alvin suggested that you hire an attorney and have the sheriff deliver his summons to his law office. You want me to handle it for you? Alvin stopped by with the power of attorney and explained everything, but where are you? Why did you suddenly up and leave...again?"

Megan had clawed her way under my skin, literally and figuratively, and I didn't want her washing my dirty laundry. I would be at sea for the next fourteen days, or next fourteen years for all I cared, and I said, "I'm hiding out on Alvin's advice. I don't have the luxury of shopping around for an attorney."

My run-ins with lawyers involved me standing in front of a judge, which prejudiced my attitude towards that vocation. I said as much to Megan. "The only attorneys I know deal with taxes, or they're working in the district attorney's office. Therefore, I'm just going to hunker down and stay lost until this all blows over. If they can't find me, they can't serve me."

"Don't be stupid. Running will only give Bonnie's claim legs to stand on. I've already talked to Jerry. He's a bit jumpy, but I don't think he'll be a problem. Alvin explained why you and Betty had to leave town, but he wouldn't tell me where you went. Where are you anyway?"

"Megan, you should know better than to even ask." Just as I made my remark, the ship's horn made a debarkation blast. There was a long pause on the line. Megan mentally connected with the sound.

"You're on a freakin' cruise ship?"

"No, that's the noon whistle at a munitions factory. Betty and I have been pressed into making B-52 bombers."

Megan laughed and asked, "Is Betty with you? How long is the cruise?"

"Betty is with me, and we'll be lost at sea for the next fourteen years."

Megan's wheels turned. "Owen, I miss you already. Two weeks is too long. Tell me your first port of call, and I'll catch up with you. We could have a real holiday."

I could picture Megan, Betty, and me drifting around the Gulf of Mexico, tanning in the nude together on the balcony. One of us would be thrown overboard. Any guesses?

"Who's going to fix me up with an attorney?" I asked.

"It's only two weeks, and it can wait. Come on, Owen, let's do it. Do you really want to spend two whole weeks with your dad's old frumpy girlfriend as company?"

Frumpy girlfriend? The air raid horn just went off in my head. Yes, I would love to take a fantasy trip with Betty, even if it was two weeks, and no, it was just too fucking wrong. My temptations and my conflicts were getting the better of me. If I had been thinking straight, I should have listened to Megan's plan and everything would have been out in the open. Megan would take ownership of my ass, and my affair with Betty would have ended, whether I liked it or not. I do outsmart myself by half most of the time. I didn't want Megan taking my title just yet, and I thought I could get by with it. I could never have been more wrong. I shifted the blame on Alvin Fox.

"Alvin gave me explicit orders. Not even you are supposed to know where I am, and he wouldn't even let me say goodbye to you this morning. Find me a competent attorney, and I'll call you tonight. We can have phone sex. I'll see you in fourteen days."

"Owen, please, pretty please. I'll shovel coal into the boilers as long as I can be with you at night. I'm going to be honest with you; I've never needed any man in my life, and I can't explain it over the phone. I want to tell you in person. This is our opportunity."

Megan had mentioned the critical word, need. That scary word, when used to describe our relationship, threw up a huge red flag. "*need*" sounded too obsessive, which presented visions of jealousy, control, dominance, and a ton of other possessive negatives to an unhappy relationship. It was a done deal for me, and I had to formulate a good lie. "Let me talk to Alvin and think about it." I knew Alvin's thoughts on the matter...definitely not.

"Thank you, Owen. Call me back, and I'll be on the next flight out of Nashville."

Why did I have a sinking foreboding?

CHAPTER TWENTY-NINE

Betty and I were on the promenade deck, arm in arm, with flutes of champagne, and enjoying the contrast of the bon voyage partying full swing around us and the view of the serene emptiness of the sea stretching ahead of us. Betty exuded calmness. The sea breeze, cool and strong, whipped through the locks of her auburn mane, dancing flirtatiously around her face. Her blue eyes dazzled with happiness and inspired tranquility, and her soft, gentle mood highlighted the spectacle of a serene setting sun. If this wasn't a lover's moment, I couldn't come up with a better one. The gentle vibration of the engines began to move the ship on a journey to many unknown discoveries. Alone and yet together, we were content with our fate, if only for that moment.

As the ship gained speed, I felt her grip tighten on my arm. We steadied ourselves as my arm slipped around her waist, and hers encircled mine. We both experienced a new sensation together as we watched Miami slip off into the distance. The froth of the sea, one hundred feet below us, churned a spectacle as exciting as standing above the Grand Canyon or Niagara Falls. I'm sure that we talked to each other, but our souls were having a deeper conversation. If there was a moment that needed a frame, this was it.

A loud blare of monkey music disrupted our splendor. Betty's hips started to sway, and her hands moved rhythmically until they were above her head, swinging in harmony with her hips. She started an enticing, and wholly seductive dance as she explored the promenade deck. I followed, with less enthusiasm.

I have a musical ear, and nothing in the genre of Caribbean music inspires anything other than spontaneous anarchy. It's all high tempo and low talent. It's like being stuck in a traffic jam in New York City on the hottest day in August without an air conditioner. There is honking, beeping, and annoying bedlam that can't be turned off. Betty, caught up with the spontaneous malaise of the moment and went on a drinking binge. We'd been there before and I grabbed her arm to haul her off to her quarters. It was time for dinner.

We were supposed to be low-profile so we mutually agreed we should take our meals with the steerage class at the early seating. Simon, our personal chipmunk, advised us to take our meals in our rooms and if he had his way, it would be a tray slipped through a slot in the door.

I discovered that when you are at a communal feast with seating for twelve, you might wish you were at an AA meeting confessing all your sins to a jury of peers. Everyone had a tale to tell, and they jumped into it with far too much detail.

Bill and Mattie, from Iowa, swindled their son into buying the family dairy farm, which was close to receivership, and they were celebrating. Max and Ethel, New Yorkers', were celebrating their fifth anniversary of their third divorce from each other, and they argued incessantly, trying to get us on their respective sides. Jack and Erin, a couple of nice kids from Atlanta, had multicultural issues. Sam and Pearle were two old people hoping that one or the other would die at sea. This was a business trip for Sandy and Irene; they canvassed the ship for converts to their evangelistic cult. This was what I had to look forward to for the next fourteen days?

Then there were the two of us. I admitted I worked for the IRS, and Betty worked as a bank auditor. No one wants to draw attention to themselves by befriending federal sniff dogs so we were given plenty of space at our end of the table. We let the assumption that we were married form a silent halo around our heads.

After dinner, we took in an abbreviated broadway play in the theatre. I went to sleep five minutes into it. For an instant, I thought I saw my banker buddy, Jerry, in purple tights waltzing around the stage. The brief show, threatened to bore me to an early grave, provided a badly needed cat nap. The cheering applause roused me from my slumber and I caught my second wind. It was, as I was later told, a very good drama, with musicality. Betty's first outing as a critic and her summation failed to convince me.

The lottery was my singular vice with gambling. I found out that Betty's gambling vice was slot machines. On a cruise ship, playing the slots was like surgically opening an artery and slowly bleeding to death. It should take fourteen days, if the machines were rigged properly.

CHAPTER THIRTY

The door to the penthouse had barely closed when Betty's paws turned into a wood chipper. She disrobed me so fast I thought I was in a magic show. My belt, zipper, and buttons went flying to the universe and the next thing I felt were Betty's lips on my neck and then slowly sliding south. She had a grip on my butt cheeks pressing me against the door. Anyone walking outside in the corridor would think that my suite was where they kept the circus animals. She wouldn't let go until I reached climax or the door broke down.

"How was that?"

"That put a Bill Clinton smile on my face."

"Okay, it's my turn," and she sprawled out on the hand-woven Persian rug in the foyer. What a photo op, but I was afraid to take the picture in fear that it might turn up later.

I took a nose dive into the oasis like a dehydrated camel who hadn't had a drop in a month of Sunday's and had her howling like a banshee. This went on for some time until my neck started to cramp and I had a bad rug burn on my chin, which would be hard to explain to anyone who might notice it.

We hadn't gotten past the front foyer yet, and there were four other rooms and the balcony that needed christening. Betty and I finally made it to the balcony at one in the morning. I learned a little secret about Betty while we flailed around like fresh caught flounder on a trawler deck. Betty was definitely a screamer. If I could have edited out all of the sounds at sea, I'll bet Betty would be in the top three of orgasmic vocalists of the night's orgy going on elsewhere on the love boat. We spent the night indulging in unforgettable, and unforgivable, passionate lust, pure and simple.

I helped her put her clothes back on, while she was taking them off again, trying to get into my bed. It was early in the morning, so I put a robe on her and carried her to her suite. This pleasant habit had to stop at some point. She wanted me to climb into the rack with her, but I used better judgment and waited for her to pass out before I crawled in with her.

The smell of fresh brewed coffee woke me up the following morning. The cabin steward had sneaked into Betty's suite with a cart filled with delicacies and a big urn of coffee. It was very early, and the movement of the boat had stopped without me knowing it. I rose from her bed and walked out onto her balcony completely naked. The sight of the upper knuckle of a dockside crane made me flinch. I had been told that I had complete privacy on her private balcony; still I felt odd. I made a fast retreat to the bedroom to put a robe over me. I returned to the balcony with coffee and sat down to enjoy the view of the docks of San Juan, Puerto Rico. My head jerked involuntarily when Betty sneaked up on me. She looked as fresh as she acted. Her slow cat walk wasn't meant to be seductive, but I whistled just in case.

She sat down in a lounge chair with a cup of coffee and I could sense a quiet tone developing. We'd spend the morning doting on each other. I was swept away by her. Loving her was easy and natural, not forced like my relationship with Megan. I was lost in a surreal contentment.

I had come to a critical moment that awaited a decision and a commitment on my part. I had two girlfriends and a strong desire to love them both, but one of them had to go. I couldn't go on treading water. No matter what I did, someone was going to get hurt. Betty knew exactly where I resided and didn't seem the least bit conflicted by it. Megan, on the other hand, made work out of seducing me. She dedicated her waking hours to making my life and hers a transition with a lot of expectations. No two women could be more opposite than Betty and Megan.

One of the reasons for the cruise was to get Betty out of my system. We were into our second day, and the opposite was taking place. If I had to make a choice at that very minute, Betty won hands down. Betty came without complications; Megan didn't.

Table fifty seven had a full compliment after we arrived for breakfast. Max and Ethel were head to head, like doves, well not like doves, because one of them was about to take the head off the other. Bill and Matte had signed on the cruise to eat their weight in food. Both had a stack of dishes brimming with dairy products. Jack and Erin didn't need nourishment as they were too much in love to be bothered. Erin was playfully hand feeding Jack a sliver of bacon. Sam and Pearle had both survived yet another night at sea. Sandy and Irene were busy going over their strategy to bring Jesus to the next heathen outpost on the itinerary.

They all looked up and clapped warmly as we joined table fifty seven. Betty's binge at the slots had gotten out, which made her something of a princess. Betty's natural sway and grace made more heads turn and there was a low murmur in the dining room that became a dull buzz. We tried to blend in like any married couple, but it didn't work. Betty had to repeat the same story over and over while we ate breakfast, or tried to.

I failed to mention that Betty hit the big jackpot for a million because I'm pretty sure it was rigged. If you're running an offshore casino with a captive audience for two weeks, drop a million on a classy PR chick with a profile to fill up the gaming tables. The photos taken of her shoveling coins into a bucket were worth a million bucks. The gimmick was something I was familiar with and Megan taught me the value of maximizing on contrived opportunities.

Old Sam used up his daily calorie reserves to get to his feet and strike his water glass with a spoon. He made a short congratulatory speech and we all toasted Betty's windfall. Ethel had photos of Betty riding on my shoulders while she tossed casino chips to the crowd. She passed the photos around.

Sam had a piece of paper in his hand and no glasses to read from his notes. He felt around in his pocket, but Pearle had his specks out trying to put them on his nose. By this time I would have thought they'd have that routine down pat, but they danced and wobbled like fledglings. Finally, Sam pushed his glasses further on his nose and stretched his arm out as though he was Tommy Dorsey playing the trombone.

He cleared his throat and announced, "There's a talent show at the end of the cruise. What do you say kids? Anyone interested in joining Pearle and me?" Singing Bugle Boy of Company B with Sam and Pearle on the last night of a romantic cruise didn't raise a storm of takers, and everyone did a head dip to avoid the topic altogether.

Sam said, "Don't tell me there's no talent at this table? I'll put fifty bucks on Pearle and me."

I looked around. Sandy and Irene, who had been doing evangelistic sing-alongs for thirty years had to have some talent.

Surely. By the look on their faces, maybe they worked the back of the tent and massaged the collection plate. I saw Erin's eyes twinkle, as she did a dare jab in Jack's ribs.

I felt a sting to my ribs and heard a throaty whisper in my ear. "Come on Owen. You used to sing. Let's do it."

"If they pay musicians' scale I might think about it."

"Come on, we have nothing else to do," Betty persisted.

"You do it."

"Think I won't?" Before I could say anything, Betty chimed in. "You can count on us."

Sam gave us a grand tour of his dentures and Pearle giggled. Sam started conducting the orchestra with his hands as Pearle began to sing, hoping to induce others to enlist. Pearle was good, as she started into 'Somewhere Over the Rainbow.'

Erin joined in, then Jack because he was pussy-whipped into doing it. Betty tugged my shirt collar, but I wasn't Jack. Betty got to her feet, and the sound coming out of her was fingers up and down my spine. I knew she had a set of pipes and a high voice register, but I never expected to hear an actual melody come out of her.

When Sandy and Irene finally capitulated, that song echoed through the dining room and when it was finished, the room rocked with applause. Table fifty-seven had unknowingly reenergized my interest in music, even if it was just for an amateur contest.

CHAPTER THIRTY-ONE

After breakfast and Sam's Shanghai job, it was agreed that we'd all meet up in my suite after everyone had explored the port and got sunstrokes. Betty and I were under house arrest by Simon, so we wouldn't be taking any shore excursions. Instead, we'd visit with Sam and Pearle until it was time for their nap.

That's when I found out Pearle had been a cabaret singer. While reminiscing about her career, she leaned over to Betty, her tone one of hushed confidentiality, and said, "Something told me you have an outrageous voice."

Damned straight she did, but how did Pearle know unless she was up all night listening to Betty warble on the deck? Pearle's wicked wink had Betty and me looking at each other while Sam and Pearle looked at both of us.

Sam had been a media mogul and knew the ins and outs of promotion and advertising production. The old couple had melted away a hundred years between them and seemed enthused to be day-tripping into times forgotten. They were on a mission.

Sam made notes while Pearle played voice coach with Betty. I was busy arranging music in my head, day-tripping into my times forgotten.

Nap time approached … our nap time, not Sam and Pearle's. We broke loose and went to my suite. Behind closed doors, I went directly to the piano bench and began pounding out music. Betty slipped onto the bench beside me. Her head would nod in time with the music as she tried to find the words to the song I played. Then she belted out a smoky bluesy rendition of Cry Me a River.' She sang it in different scales and played with every lyric as if she were fitting it on for the hundredth time. She took me on a vocal journey that made me stop playing the piano.

"Did I do something wrong?"

"No. No. I just can't believe my ears," I stammered. "You never mentioned you're a hell of a singer."

"I'm not." She chuckled. "I only sing when I'm happy, and that was a long time ago."

"With your voice? You're telling me you've never entertained the idea of singing professionally?"

She shrugged. "When I was a little girl, I used to sing for …" She skipped over who she sang for and continued. "Sometimes when I'm doing laundry and no one is around, I pretend I'm Faith Hill. Do you think I'm good?"

"Good? How about smokin' hot."

"Really?" She giggled.

I did an exaggerated head roll and said, "Can you sing any Whitney Houston stuff?"

"I can try."

I spent the rest of the afternoon test-driving her voice through every genre known to God, and I was in the choir of angels as Betty sang. She finally begged me to stop my fanatical search to find something she couldn't sing. With some coaching and coaxing, practice and patience, I could have her ready to frontline with the pros providing entertainment on the ship in a day or two.

By late afternoon, the shipmates of table fifty-seven began to filter into my suite for band practice. Bill and Mattie were the first to arrive and the first to leave after they had polished off the shrimp and lobster appetizers I had ordered. The rest were there as much out of curiosity as enthusiasm for Sam's vaudeville Show. After the wow factor wore off, we convened on the deck to discuss our talents and how we could incorporate them into the show.

Sandy had a few tricks up his sleeve, which sort of went with his occupation as an evangelist. He wasn't going to turn water to wine, nor was he going to walk on water, but he could do magic and miraculously cure people. He had it all worked out and gave us the layout. He and Irene would work the front of the stage, and the rest of us would be 'testifiers' and the heavenly choir.

I had to stop him before he got any further into his fanatical conspiracy to cure sea-sickness. "Why don't you cut Irene in half and put her back together," I suggested.

Sandy laughed. "We don't have the props to pull that off, otherwise we could do it."

I said, "No, I mean really saw her in half. That's much better than curing sea-sickness."

I was all for sawing Irene in half and didn't care one way or the other how it turned out. We couldn't make a whole show around a saw dripping blood, so we went on to Jack and Erin. Erin was as lithe as a snake and as seductive as Bathsheba. The two together were pretty good dancers. Pearle had a hunch about Erin, the way she had a hunch about Betty and asked, "Erin, have you ever done any singing?"

Erin looked at Jack and blushed. Erin mumbled, "I sang in the church choir, but not much since."

"Oh, dear, I don't believe that for a moment." That Pearle, she was a sweet old peach with a dirty mind. She asked me to hit a few cords on the piano. Erin's voice was weak but consistently spot on. Pearle nudged me from the piano bench and went to work on the keys. In no time at all, she had Erin howling like a white BillieHoliday.

It didn't take me long to figure out what those two old geezers were up to, and I was happily along for the ride. Betty had already passed her audition, and Sam inquired about my dubious talents. Before I could modestly claim that I played the guitar, Betty announced that I was one of the original members of the fabulous Shylocks. I was surprised that Sam knew who they were.

Sam had a wizened, curious look on his face and said, "Then you know, "You Can Kiss My Bass."

"You Can Kiss My Bass" was a sharp-witted red-neck tune that takes little explanation and yeah, I wrote it, scored it, played lead, and sang the damned thing. Shylock remastered it and made millions off dumb asses with IQ's of...bass. I said, "That was released after I left the band."

By the twinkle in Sam's eyes, I knew that he knew better. "What do you think, Owen?" he asked. "There're some good vocals. What do you think about Betty and Erin out front, with Jack, Sandy, and Pearle as backup? We can pipe in the surround."

Sam knew what he was talking about, but Sandy had to prove that he didn't. When he said, "For a gospel theme to work, we need a strong male and female lead, which is where Irene and I can make a contribution." It was obvious that Sandy saw the opportunity to hijack the idea and make it an extension of his world evangelistic tour.

"Who said anything about a gospel theme?" Pearle asked with more than a hint of sarcasm. "In case you haven't noticed, Brother Sandy, this ain't the Mayflower, and these folks ain't pilgrims seeking redemption for sins they're paying big bucks to enjoy on this cruise. Let's do something current, up tempo, and contemporary."

Sam had already done his homework. "The demographics of this cruise are fortyish, urban, and upper middle class, so Sinatra, Ella Fitzgerald, or Doris Day isn't going to work. What do you think, Owen?"

I didn't care if we sang Dixie. I was just glad to be doing something I used to love. I shrugged and looked over Sam's shoulders and saw Sandy and Irene retreat from the suite. Maybe we'd see Irene in a box at the competition. I sat down at the piano and played a Julian Lennon arrangement of 'Too Late for Goodbye's' to set the mood. With my eyes closed, I was surrounded with old and odd visions, retracing my musical footsteps from Colorado to Nashville. My song choice was appropriate. I opened my eyes, as if the adoration radiating from Betty would fix that problem. In a way it did. Could I possibly rekindle my love of music? Without a word from her I knew she fit into my lost dream. Despite the mystery of her, new channels opened to me and I couldn't wait to explore them.

We had the beginnings of a garage band, and all of us toasted the fact, more times than necessary, and started to click in gear as we sang favorites that everyone knew. We had yet to name our little group, but Sam was ahead of us. He'd already made up a flyer to pass around and tentatively called us Table Fifty-Seven. Sam was a promoter. The way he brushed Sandy aside, I had a vision of Sam standing in front of the coliseum handing out leaflets depicting lions eating Christians. The old bastard never stopped, ever.

Since we had sung and drank past the official dining hours, we had dinner at the private restaurant reserved for high rollers, like me. I had my reasons for being overly excited about a stupid amateur talent contest. Why Jack and Erin were even on board was a mystery to me. Those two had better things to do than hang out with has-beens. Since Betty and Erin were the headliners they got close, and with Pearle's interference, they began matching up their tastes in music.

Jack and Sam wanted to know about King Midas and why I was spending money faster than the government could print it. When I told them I won the lottery, they laughed…and laughed. They tried to pin me down, but I was vague to the point of being rude. When the subject of my music career came up, I was just as vague and a bit less rude.

All through dinner and drinks afterwards, Betty was a constant presence even as she was engaged elsewhere. Her hand found my neck to stroke, a touch to my collar, a quick glance and smile, and a warm smugness at every opportunity. I wouldn't exactly call it possessive, more like reassuring. I could get used to being subconsciously stroked. Betty was in love with me, and I knew it without a word being said.

In deference to two elder codgers in need of a full night's rest, Betty and I retired early. As soon as the door closed, we melted into each other as if we were one living being sharing the same breath, the same heart beats. I had finally found the gates to heaven, and I could see every day of the rest of my life just like the day I finished.

CHAPTER THIRTY-TWO

The following day, and the one after that, were the happiest I'd ever had in my entire life. For all practical purposes, I had never known such a feeling existed. I was constantly energized, full of empowerment, and bullet proof. Even my fingers and toes danced and tingled freely with a light-hearted life of their own. My face hurt from smiling constantly. I was even nice to Simon, who seemed content to brood and hovered over Betty and me wherever we went on the ship.

We docked in Martinique, a French possession with a rich mix of French and Creole culture. We weren't allowed ashore, so we lounged at the poolside on the upper deck. We had it to ourselves, and took a time-out from arranging music to work on tan lines. Her skin was settling into a deeper shade of pink that gave her a healthy looking hue. I marveled at the voluptuous curves of her body that had softness and at the same time toned dimensions of a super model. She had her auburn locks pulled away from her face, fastened with combs. There were light freckles on her cheeks that I hadn't paid much attention to. Somehow it added wholesomeness to her persona.

She caught me gawking and put a floppy hat on her head. "You're looking at my freckles," she grumped.

"Why would I be looking at freckles when I can inspect your tan lines? They're kinda sexy."

Her lip curled. "Which, my tan lines or my freckles?"

"Both."

Betty brought up an observation about Simon. "Why is that when we're in port, Simon disappears? Isn't that when he should be on the job?"

I thought about it and said, "No. The ship's almost empty and it's his chance to take a breather."

"From what? Where is he anyway?"

"We're always in our state rooms, so it doesn't matter. As long as we don't go ashore, we're safe."

"Why does Simon go ashore?"

"He does?"

"Yeah, he left around nine. I watched him go into Fort-de-France."

"Betty, he's a detective doing detective stuff. Stop making a big deal about it. Hey, I've got the scoop on Sam and Pearle. Did you know they actually live on cruise ships? No shit. Rather than spend their retirement in a fancy constant care facility, they hop from cruise to cruise. They have all their meals prepared, never have to carry their own luggage, clean up after themselves, or make the freakin' bed. There's always a doctor and a pharmacy in case of a medical emergency. I bet they even have their social security checks sent to the cruise line."

"That's clever. How did you find out?"

"Everyone on the crew knows them. They've been on this ship for the last three cruises and guess what? They always enter the talent contest. Yeah, they really do."

Betty laughed. "No wonder Sam has the run of the ship and was able to recruit a drummer, base player, and sax player from the crew complement. You don't suppose the contest is rigged do you?"

I slapped my chest in mock indignation. "Hell, no. Sam and Pearle have a leg up, but it's up to the passengers to pick the winner."

"Yeah, there's just no way to cheat, but it doesn't prevent Sam from handing out flyers with our glam shots to everyone coming up the gang way. I sorta feel sorry for them."

"I don't. It beats sitting in a dayroom, watching Oprah day in and day out."

She pulled her dangling leg out of the pool, rose and did a cat stretch that made me purr. She said, "I've had enough sun. I'm going to get ready for band practice. You coming?"

"I will be if you don't stop posing." My smart remark went over her head, and I watched her put on a wrap and swish towards the stairwell. I began picking up, when a sleek woman in a white jacket blocked out the sun.

She was the ship's purser, and she stiffly announced, "Mr. Fletcher, you have an urgent call from a Miss Megan Marsh. Would you care to take it?"

Megan was busy directing my traffic back in Tennessee. She ticked off all the outstanding items on her to-do list. She'd exercised her power of attorney, and everything at the bank was set up. I now had a lawyer to handle all the nuisance lawsuits popping up. All of my engagements, appointments, and cover story had been buttoned down. In fact, there was little for her to do. Why did I have the feeling she was standing in line at the airport waiting to board the next flight to Caracas, Venezuela?

"Guess where I am?" She gushed.

"No, Megan. Please tell me you're not at the airport."

"Not yet, but I'm on my way. I can't wait to meet you in Caracas."

"Did you clear this with Alvin?"

"He's a dick. I'm not telling him and neither are you. We can take turns pushing Betty's wheel chair around the promenade deck. Come on, Owen, whose thighs would you rather be rubbing with sun blocker, mine or Betty's?" She laughed. "It makes me hot just thinking about it."

She'd be really hot if she knew who won that contest hands down. I'd pretty much made my mind up, and I was an inch from telling Megan the truth, but I wasn't absolutely sure where Betty stood with our expiration date. "Megan, I'm not able to talk right now. Can I call you back?"

"Is Betty with you?"

I lied. "Yeah, we need to talk privately."

"Hurry up, honey. My hormones have left the building."

Aside from being a giant chicken shit, I'd never had to break it off with any woman. They always left me. That's not entirely true either. More than once I'd simply walked off, like I did to Megan after the party. I didn't see it as breaking up. Since I didn't have emotional chips on the table, it never occurred to me that anyone got hurt. That's how dark my tunnel had been, up to now.

I handed the phone to the purser and decided I needed to tell Betty that I was ready to share my life with her. Tell her I loved her. Tell her Megan was no longer a conflict in my mind. We'd proclaim our love for each other and that was that. That was my simple plan. I'd have a clear conscience, and I'd make that call to Megan. It would be difficult, but with Betty's reassurance, I'd get through it.

I found Betty in the bath stroking her shimmering hair. Her bare back was slightly pink and I had the presence of mind to ask her if she wanted me to put lotion on her. I'd caught her by surprise, and I saw a wickedly gleaming smile in the mirror. It faded quickly as her eyes caught my reflection. She spun around and said, "What's wrong, Owen?"

"Nothing is wrong. Quite the opposite and I think it's time we talked."

The quick tilt of her head framed a questioning expression.

I said, "We need to talk about us … now."

"Why now? I thought we had a deal. Fourteen days. No strings, no attachments. Our love affair has an expiration date. That's the deal."

"Megan called. She's on her way to Caracas."

All emotion drained from her face. Her expression became rigid, almost stone. She said, "I see. Make us drinks and I'll join you on the deck." She passed the brush through her hair once more and slammed it on the dressing table. I hadn't moved from my spot, hating the way her eyes wouldn't meet mine. "Please go. Give me a minute to compose myself," she whispered.

I made a pitcher of mint mimosas to quench our thirst. Betty's lack of composure disturbed me. Perhaps she feared rejection. The knot in my stomach suggested there was more to it than that. I was fumbling, dropping stuff when Betty slipped up on me from behind and put her arms around me. She rested her head on my back, and the touch and the smell of her made me weak. We lingered like that for a few minutes, not saying a word. Then she released me and walked to a deck chair and sat down. I still recall how regal she looked at that moment.

I poured drinks, carried a tray to the deck and joined her. I had no idea how to start this kind of conversation, so I decided to make it anti-climatic and a foregone conclusion that we needed to be together. I sat down.

"Betty, we need to talk about our expiration date—."

She interrupted me. "All I asked for was fourteen days. That's all, but I understand."

I shrugged. "That's been pushed up. Megan will be here tomorrow unless I call her and tell her the truth."

"Don't do that. Just tell her you'll see her when we get back."

"You know she'll come anyway. She won't make it past the foyer before our relationship is thrown in her face. She'll kill both of us, and Simon can't save us. "

"I can't say I'd blame her. I knew it would have to come to an end …it's just that …never mind." She brushed away a tear.

I said, "I'm not sure how our expiration dates work when I'm in love. Fourteen days isn't going to work for me. I've discovered greed and it's not money. I'm no longer on this planet by myself, and I need *you* to walk me through whatever is in front of me. I love you."

She began shaking her head vigorously and tears sprang from her eyes. She kept repeating herself. "Oh, Owen, it's impossible."

Finally I shook her. "Baby, stop it. You love me and don't say you don't. We'll get through this together. As bad as it is, this will all end and we can take it one step at a time. I just don't see myself taking one step without you. I promise to make you happy."

"You already have, more than you'll ever know." She pushed me away and broke free, distancing herself from me. She wiped her face with the back of her hand. "Before I say anything else, I'll tell you I do love you, and it's the reason I have to give you back to Megan. I'm damaged goods, and when I say damaged, I mean it can't be fixed. Your father and I have a bond that we must live with until we're dead."

"Are you still in love with him?"

"I've loved him all of my life, and I'll always be in love with him. Always."

I shook my head. "No, he won't come back for you. I think there is another woman involved."

"There's always another woman involved."

I detected a deep sadness, and the insinuation wasn't missed on me. It entered my mind that Boots and Harlan were obsessed with her as much as I was. Something bothered me. This drama had happened before and more than once? I should have stopped her from playing it out for me. I knew it then, but I could no longer pretend the mystery of their relationship was history. It was like I'd hit a piñata filled with spiders and they were crawling all over me. "You're going to tell me what you have on Boots. He doesn't come back to you. You force him to, don't you?"

I'd caught her in an indecisive moment and she was slow to respond. "You'll find out anyway, so you might as well hear this from me. After I tell you, you'll understand, and I just hope that you won't hate me."

The beating of my heart overtook the fear residing in my skull, and the old Owen surfaced.

"Never mind. I don't want to know about it. My father's sins belong to him. Let's just step away from this and get clear of this mess." I stood up with every intention of ending my curious need to know what she had on Boots. Whatever he'd been doing since my mother died was behind enemy lines, and it could stay that way.

"Where are you going, honey?" Betty asked.

"I'm going to call Megan, and I'm going to call Boots. My father's shadow belongs to him and he's not going to block our sunshine. This is not a rebound romance, Honey. I don't need to know how many times he broke your heart and I don't care how many times he has deserted you. I've always been free of him and you will be too. This will be over in a couple of weeks, and we'll go our own way. Fourteen days is not enough. I need at least fourteen years."

"You can't have that. Neither can I. I have damaged him and I won't damage you. We need to stop. You need to stop. I wasn't expecting to fall in love with you. I don't even know what it is like to be loved. It's as new to me as it is to you, but circumstances of my past makes it impossible. We both need to get clear of your father, but not together. I have indulged in a selfish need of you. It ends now, Owen. It has to."

"There is nothing in this world that can stop us. We can work through whatever is bothering you. Hell, we already have. I'm staking my claim to you…now. Boots and Harlan can kiss and make up because I'm not letting either one of them interfere with our happiness together. Get over it Betty. Stop living in the past."

She rose to her feet and towered over me. She bent to talk to me as though I were a pet that she couldn't communicate with. She said, "Owen…you are so naive and I love that about you. Our timing is all wrong. I told you going in that we should have no expectations from each other. None." Her head swung to the door and I suspected she was about to bolt. Instead she turned to me and blew me a kiss. Her departing words were, "I'll leave the ship when we arrive in Caracas. I truly hope you and Megan find happiness." She wanted to say more, but she choked up and swiftly left me in a complete and total quandary.

I didn't see it coming. I had yet another new experience. Desperation and an emotional amputation of sorts. I could blame God for taking love from me, but I suspected it was much closer to home than that. I could feel my father's hands around my neck. What mystical powers did he possess to cause Betty to walk away from what I supposed was a happiness that had eluded her. Sitting there, I knew in my deepest depths that she loved me, yet there was some circumstance, some pervasive evil ripping her apart. What was she protecting me from?

I slid sideways into anger. Maybe it had to do with what she had done to my father. He lost his career over her, yet he stood over her, protecting her from her psycho husband. I had first hand experience of the spell she cast. I could not fault the old bastard for that. I knew all that so there had to be a much deeper root cause to trigger her abdication of the cravings within her.

I could fix it. I knew I could. I had to head off a disaster, so my first call went to Alvin. He had to keep Megan off the boat so I could get to the bottom of the mystery plaguing my life.

Not much surprises Alvin. He's a wise old bird and my immediate dilemma required a simple fix from the ship's security. Megan would not be allowed to board. Period. He had to know what was going on in my state room and Alvin is the kind of guy that acts intuitive as though he's the seeing eye and he smugly said, "You need to get your dad's girlfriend squared away. She's not getting off the boat in Caracas. Simon will see to that."

"How do you know she's planning on leaving?"

"She called down to the purser to inform them there would be a vacancy and made arrangements to vacate the holiday cruise, including her winnings at the casino. What tripped her ticket?"

I said, "It's all about her history with Boots."

"No shit. She's been a millstone around his neck for decades."

Alvin had said something he shouldn't have and I picked up on it immediately. "What do you mean by decades."

He tried to back crawl. "You'd have to ask him."

"Why don't I ask her?"

"That's ill advised. Getting a straight story from a scorned woman is highly unlikely. Too much drama. You know what I mean?"

"No–I don't. Maybe you should tell me and save me the agony."

"It's all gossip for all I know. Officer's wives talk without much substance. It's no surprise to you that your old man has a reputation as a womanizer. Word is your father likes his women young, like real young. Who doesn't? What else is news?"

It was all news to me. Alvin had lifted a shroud of Boots' character that was disturbing. Infuriating. Not even remotely believable.

He said, "You there? Owen, what did I tell you about laying low? You and Mrs. Harland need to stay out of the casino and public areas. You're not on your honeymoon and you need to get it in your head that Mrs. Harland is a married woman and your dad's mistress. She's damaged goods. Slut, if you ask me. Have fun with her, but don't even think about getting serious."

That's exactly what I was thinking. Alvin was giving me the wake-up call that Betty had already given me.

He continued. "Go along with the program. She knows her place and you need to keep her there. Screw your brains out, but remember you have another girlfriend that happens to be covering your tracks. Don't worry, We've got Caracas covered. Have a nice cruise."

Alvin had thoroughly impugned the character of my father and Mrs. Harlan. His advice was sound and I should have followed it. I didn't. Alvin had misjudged my character and assumed Betty had ratted out Boots. I was owed an explanation, so my next call went to the slut next door.

CHAPTER THIRTY-THREE

Betty showed up at my door dressed in denim shorts and a Wal-mart top, the clothes she wore when I first met her. It was a visual message of sorts–her humble way of rejecting the expense I went to clothe her. Her eyes danced around, finding anything to look at but me. Without a word she walked past me and out to the deck.

It dawned on me the reason we were on the cruise in the first place and I had been making light of the fact that some one tried to kill her…and maybe me. My weak legs allowed me to shuffle to the chaise where I flopped down like a sack of potatoes. My mouth must have been hanging open as Betty pushed my slacked jaw shut with her fingertips. She searched my eyes as if she would die if I blinked. She kissed me lightly and let it linger as if it was her last. Slowly she resumed her place on her chaise and wilted into a woman overwhelmed with loss.

I said, "People want *us* dead. There's an underlying reason that everyone but me knows. I'm owed an explanation because you're mysteriously at the epicenter."

She had a long stare over the rail and out to sea. She whispered, ghost like. "Boots has solved his problem by making you his surrogate. He's rid himself of me. It's unfair of me to pain you with sins of the past that your father and I equally share. Damn him."

She assumed I had talked to him. I jolted her with my next statement. "You've been my father's mistress for decades. Before your marriage to Harlan, before the death of my mother. You had to be in your teens, Betty. Please tell me my information is wrong."

I watched her dissolve as though she had been electrocuted. Without a word I let the accusation stand. She gasped for air and began to calm. She suddenly looked up. "He told you this?"

I said nothing.

She said to herself. "Why Boots? Why? Why do this to your son? Oh my God!" She shook her head and then looked at me. "It's his punishment for both of us. It's his way to make sure our love for each other never has a chance. This is not the first time he's done this to me."

It was all enough to confirm Alvin's allegations about her, but I felt a need to probe the confession for the salacious details. I needed solid reasons to hate her for her sins and absolve Boots of his. "You owe me. We have unfinished business before we can call *us* finished," I mildly said.

She nodded several times. "I've known your father all of my life. He used to come to the house when my father and he served together. I developed a childhood crush on him and it simmered. I was just a kid out of control, chasing after a much older married man. When I was thirteen, it was cute, but when I turned seventeen, it was shameless. I was embarrassing him. Everyone saw what I was doing, and it was humiliating to him.

"He came to the house one afternoon after school. My parents weren't home. He was angry and upset by my antics to get his attention. He lectured me and ordered me to stop. He took me to my bedroom and spanked me. I began crying because of the humiliation of his rejection of me. I threw myself at him. I was strong-willed and bursting with hormones. It was as much my fault as it was his. Then he showed me what happened to little girls chasing after mature married men–

"Are you saying my father raped a seventeen year old girl?"

"I didn't know it was rape because I wanted him. What started out as a little girl's fantasy turned into a woman's obsession."

"Bullshit. I'm not that stupid." I could feel my jaw tighten and anger roil within me. "That's not possible. My father was dedicated to my mother."

"Oh Owen, you really don't have a clue. Boots and I did not stop with just that one time. It went on until my parents found out and sent me away. Your father has a weakness and it is young girls. I wasn't his first victim and definitely not–." She stopped short of completing her thought.

It took awhile for my brain to digest her dubious tale. I was never remotely interested in what my father accomplished, as much as he didn't give a shit what I hadn't. Should I be surprised that he was a criminal? Then I thought about mom. She was just seventeen when she became pregnant with Lawson. Boots was a senior in college, an ROTC honor grad from Purdue on his way to a career in the Army–but not with a felony rape charge hanging over his head. If I was to believe anything Betty was saying, Boots' first victim was my mother and my fucked-up childhood began to make sense.

When you discover something like that it's going to rock your head no matter how distant you are from the epicenter of the upheaval. My entire frame of reference was displaced by twenty years. Somewhere in my past there had to be plausible denial of what I now knew was the truth. Dad had been screwing around on mom long before she passed on. It might have explained why we grew up in Indiana, and why we didn't chase after my father from one post to another. Boots had made a career chasing women, while my mom made a career covering it up. I suddenly hated them both for it.

"Why are you telling me this? Is this some cruel way of inflicting pain on me? You're getting even with Boots for kicking you out. I *do not* believe a word of it. Come off it, Betty. You planned this. You seduced me just like you did him."

She played with an answer in her head, and she would start and then quit. Finally, she said, "You'd be the last man I would seduce. If I could get by with stealing you from Megan, I would. Don't think I wouldn't. Do you know why I can't? Why I won't?"

I pretended indifference by shrugging.

She answered her own question. "Because this is not the first time this has happened to me. I've never been free of Boots, even when I married Mike. I am the convenient mistress, his damsel in distress, keeper of his conscience and his only reliable friend. He has manipulated my life as though he owns it. He has been as much obsessed with me as I have been with him. When you hear the rest of it, you'll understand."

Betty continued. "After college, I went home to live with my parents at Fort Leavenworth, where my father and yours taught at the war college. It did not take long for Boots and me to resume our secret affair. When he transferred to Fort Pickett, Virginia, I followed him. I became a chain around his neck. Your father tried to keep our affair secret, but Army wives love to gossip. I fueled the fire and publicly flaunted our relationship. As a married officer moving into the senior ranks, Boots had to do something about me if he ever expected to be promoted, so he passed me off to a soldier in his command."

"What do you mean 'passed you off?'"

"Just that. He needed to get his mistress out of the way. Mike Harlan was a soldier easily intimidated by his commanding officer. I was a fairy princess in Mike's eyes and I swept him off his feet."

"Why Mike Harlan? Why not another officer?"

"He encouraged me to move on and I tried, but I was marked as private stock. I was still his mistress, but I refused to be his whore. In Boots defense, he never treated me that way."

"That doesn't explain your marriage to Harlan."

She sighed and paused. "Mike was charming right up to the day we wed. He was courteous and doted on my every whim, but he became obsessive as soon as he took title to me. I was the trophy he had stolen from Boots' fire place mantel. It got perverse as time went on. I couldn't collect the paper off the porch without being decked out like a street walker and with Mike watching me through the blinds. He constructed all kinds of bizarre conspiracies with respect to my fidelity and particularly when it came to my former relationship to your father."

I shrugged and looked at her with a dubious smirk. "You still haven't answered the question. What is Harlan to Boots?"

Betty's eyes found the railing and the sea beyond. She was on the brink of clamming up. I yelled at her. "You can end this by telling me the truth. Alvin Fox knows, but he isn't telling me, and he expects *you* to tell me." I calmed a bit and said, "I will find out. You gotta know that."

She blurted out, "Mike is Boots' illegitimate son from another officer's wife, whom he had an affair with many years ago. You've seen photos of Mike. He has too many of Boots features and he has the famous Fletcher smile."

Her words were a stun gun dart in my spine. I was speechless and I let her continue.

"Boots thought he was doing us both a favor. I didn't learn of their relationship until after I married Mike. When Mike learned who his father was, the marriage hit the bricks."

The significance of her words caused me to knock my coffee cup over. Betty said, "We need to stop this." She pulled her arms around herself into a protective barrier as though I might suddenly strike out and hit her.

It was tempting, but I yelled at her instead, "Are you telling me Mike Harlan is my half-brother?"

She nodded solemnly and looked away.

"Damn you! Finish!"

She sucked in a shaking breath before continuing. "Mike began abusing me. At that time, he thought he was getting even with Boots."

"You were married to Mike, screwing our father, and now you're screwing me. That makes you an heirloom because you *do* keep it in the family. You're a slut. You have to be making this up because it's too bizarre."

"Am I? Do you see the scar at the base of my spine? That's from being thrown on the coffee table as punishment for having been Boots' lover. I've paid a terrible price for loving him."

I was too dumbfounded, so I let Betty talk, hating every word she spoke.

"Boots watched my marriage disintegrate right from the beginning. I'd run away from time to time, but if Mike didn't come for me, Boots did. He knew what he'd done to me. He knew how I suffered at the hands of his son. Boots is the last person to admit he made a mistake and he'd mediate my marriage. Each time he'd send me back to Mike and the beatings would start again."

She raised her head and looked me in the eye as though there was defiance brewing within her. "The violence intensified and the frequency increased. Mike was obsessively suspicious of my fidelity, and he'd invent tests to challenge my loyalty. I told you about his sickness but it didn't stop him from doing it again and again and again. I can't count the times Boots patched me up.

"It got so bad that the Army brought him up on charges of domestic violence and spousal abuse. They forced him into a remedial program and marked his record. The next time, Boots got him sent to Afghanistan and I filed for divorce."

Betty's saga of abuse was somehow fascinating, and I would normally have fallen for it, but I wasn't buying it. For all I knew, Mike's fabricated exploits might *not* have been fabrications at all. By her own admission, she and Boots had something going on, and I wondered how much patching up they did together.

It's like that moment when your girlfriend suddenly suggests that "maybe we should start seeing other people." You suddenly know she's screwing everyone in town, because that lame line doesn't blend with anything. Nothing she says after that gets any credibility because you're too busy trying to figure out the who, why, and when, of her slutty deceit. Whatever you had built together in your relationship gets crumpled and tossed on the bonfire of regret, vaporized, and everyone is watching. That had to be Mike's point of view and now it was mine. My mind was busy with the who, why, and when, side of things, so I wasn't paying that much attention to her whining mitigation of her part of her epic saga.

I said, "Look, your revolving door affair with Mike and Boots stinks, and I don't care about it. It's pretty damned sick if you ask me, and I don't feel sorry for you because you're the home wrecker that fucked up my family. You knew my mother, didn't you? You had to meet her at some point. When was that, Betty?"

Then I remembered. A distant childhood memory came to light. We'd spent half of a summer with dad at the fort when I was about thirteen. There was this little girl who'd come into the yard and sing sweet little songs almost every morning. Mom would invite her in and dad would insist that she sing to my mom for her breakfast. Now I knew who Betty used to sing for, and I knew why she wouldn't tell me who it was. I also knew why she was in my dad's house singing for my mother.

I recalled that summer very well, and how could I forget it. I had discovered girls and erections and made the connection between the two. The girl standing in the yard was Elizabeth Stiles, Colonel Stiles' daughter. Elizabeth was seriously cute, big blue innocent eyes, a wicked smile, and with the makings of little bumps on her skinny chest. I got so many boners looking at her I couldn't count them all. I was instantly in love with her and consumed by her. I was whacking off all the time.

She didn't know that I existed, and she shunned me completely. Dad would have her sit on his lap and he called her Betty Boop. She was the little girl he never had and mom would joke about Elisabeth who declared that when she grew up she'd marry my dad. Mom always chided her and said she should concentrate on becoming a singing star. Elisabeth was a part of our family that summer and it took a long time for me to forget about her after we left for Indiana.

My flashback memory took me by surprise because for the longest time I had a fantasy of one day finding her and carrying her off to paradise as my bride. Army families move on and so do childhood fancies. The irony of it all blew me away. The cruel realization was that the princess of my youthful dreams had materialized as the vamp from hell.

Off balance, I said, "I remember you now." What else was there to say? I didn't want to give her the pleasure of knowing what was driving me nuts so many years ago.

"I remember you too." She smiled. "You scared me back then. The sad fate was that I missed the tail end of that comet. Don't you think I died inside wishing that I could wave a wand and recapture my innocence? If you had stayed a little longer things may have turned out differently."

My jaws tightened and I ground my teeth listening to her lament. "I see how you repaid my mother's kindness. There's nothing on this earth to cleanse that kind of sin. Stop acting like a victim."

I could see a flash of anger streak across her face. Whatever torment she suffered was deserved and her self pity was laughable.

I heard her say, "Haven't you heard a word I'm saying? Boots and Mike have always had their other women, but I'm property traded like an annual sports trophy and nothing more. None of this has a thing to do with your mother, Owen. Not one damned thing. It's punishment."

I had been listening and I could understand Harlan's motives. Boots, on the other hand, was in a hurry to transfer his title to her, so that didn't coincide with her sob story. I wanted to bolt right then, but there had to be more coming my way and I wanted to find the whole truth.

I said, "I know what this is. You're getting your revenge. You're late to the party and no one is going to care what happened to you. For that matter, no one is going to care what happened to my mother. Just tell me what else you have on Boots and we'll call it a day."

There was a stoic resolve about her and she toiled with her response. "He didn't tell you? That sounds like Boots. Always someone to blame. He's made sure that I will always be burden with our mutual shame, and I am not deserving of forgiveness in this life or the next, but I will not make treachery and deceit something more to atone for."

I scoffed. "It's a little late to take the moral high ground."

She tilted her head in thought. She asked herself aloud, "Why would Boots destroy his legacy and pride and not tell you the rest of it…Oh, my God, You didn't talk to him, did you. Did you?" Her eyes opened wide as she studied my face. She rolled her eyes to heaven. "God, what have I done? Merriam, please forgive me."

I had to get up, shake off the horror story, find a path to sanity. Betty seemed locked into her own torture cell. She gripped the chaise so tight her knuckles turned white. She was shaking and her face was distorted with fear and anguish. I stood at the rail and looked at my hands upon the rail. My knuckles had turned white and who knew what was written on my face? I could have thrown her overboard at that moment. She was praying to God and muttering my mother's name, which pissed me off even more. "Stop using my mother's name in your prayers, you slut. My mother was a saint."

"Yes. Your mother *knew. She knew about me.* She could have sent him to prison when he raped her, but she didn't, so don't be judgmental."

"How dare you!"

"Owen, your mother had sons to raise. She had a place to take her boys. What kind of life would you have had with your father in prison? What choice did she have? I do *not* fault that brave woman. What happened to me is small by comparison. She did nothing to prevent what happened to me and ignored it, almost approving it. I forgive her and the best I could hope for is that she found forgiveness. It haunts me."

"It should. What's changed? You could stop this vendetta any time you want. All you have to do is burn the evidence."

She snorted. "My entire adult life has been vacant. I don't know what it's like to feel loved. I know what it's like to be desired, lusted after, fawned upon and forced into compromising positions to provoke a rescue, a fight, an offense resolved. Do you know how empowering it is to have the envy of your peers, making them jealous because of the women you possess? Having the adoration of a consort half your age covers for a lot of insecurities and emasculates weak character. That's all I know about the love of a man.

"What Boots didn't plan on was that I would fall in love with his surrogate. You're nothing like your father. All I wanted was to be loved by you. Two weeks. Is that asking for too much? I know I'm being selfish and now it has to end."

I nodded. "That goes without saying. Let me ask you one last question. When did you decide on this course of action?"

"You don't know? The minute you told me the shooter at Lawson's wasn't Mike. Someone else wants me silenced."

"Who?"

"You'd have to ask Mike or Boots. You have your work cut out for you. I'm not the gate keeper of Boots' soul anymore. You just earned that job."

She stood, made a half turn, looked over her shoulder like a frightened child fearing the unknown. Her lips moved but there was no sound. She tried again. "I love you. I will not leave you with a single lie between us. I will wait as long as it takes and the expiration date for my love for you is forever. You'll always know where to find me."

"I don't own a suit of armor so don't hold your breath."

Betty walked off the balcony and my coffee cup followed, showering the foyer with shards of glass. Bitter, I asked myself why I let her tell me things about my father that I didn't need or want to know. The complex reason brought a sweltering anger to my soul, and I would hate her for a long time afterward and there was no expiration date on that.

CHAPTER THIRTY-FOUR

I was too mortified to leave my spot on the deck. My first thoughts rejected everything that Betty had said. That didn't last long, as she had filled in gaps of a secret history that always simmered below the surface. Not that my father was incarnate evil, quite the opposite. He could sell ice cubes to Eskimos, then sell them refrigerators to keep them from melting. Black is merely another shade of white; just ask boots. He was relentless in acquiring things and just as easily lost interest after putting his brand upon it. It explained Betty and my mother's mesmeric captivity and unreasonable defense of his character. Charm, served with an open hand can be more destructive than a fist with brass knuckles. That explains Boots. It doesn't explain the reckless trail of pain inflicted upon his victims.

The bitch next door had finally gotten her revenge. I was out of glasses to throw, so I picked up the pitcher and hurled it at Betty, who wasn't standing in the door laughing at me, but she might as well have been. She absolutely broke my heart. I was the village idiot, docilely prancing behind the princess unaware of the heckling laughter I left in my wake.

What did winning the lottery have to do with anything? Nothing and everything. I started out hiding out in the state park, changing my appearance and avoiding the hot lotto chick who had designs and a "to do" list of things I don't want to do. That didn't work out. I paid a visit to my father, who made a butt sandwich out of me and put me in the middle of a domestic situation that shouldn't involve him or me. I'm coerced into getting his hysterical girlfriend out of town and get shot at in the process, only to find myself living with her at my nutty brother's farm, who has at least six conspiracy theories involving my lottery winnings. I allow myself to be manipulated to throw a million bucks to resolve a vendetta between my father and a half brother that I didn't know about and go on the run with my dad's girlfriend…again. I allow myself to be seduced by the woman who I'm on the run with, while the hot lotto babe made me promise her date nights. It's too much and a fourteen day cruise is the ticket to get my head back on straight, but I get my heart broken in the bargain. To top it off, I find out my old man is a serial rapist and pedophile.

What did I leave out? If I hadn't won the lottery, none of the above incidents would have ever happened. Not ever. Odds were in my favor that I'd win the lottery again before any of the crap I had endured would repeat itself. Is it any wonder that my mind was a paranoid weed garden?

My disgust and anger was interrupted by the phone ringing. I almost didn't answer it because I knew who was at the other end of the line. I snatched the receiver off the cradle and tried to pretend that everything was peachy.

"Hello?"

"Hey, stud, you were supposed to call me back. What happened with that?"

"Sorry, Megan. I was completely distracted and I forgot."

"Forgot? You have six fantastic sex fantasies coming your way, and you forgot? Did you have a fight with Betty?"

"More or less. I found out stuff I didn't need to know and I'm pretty pissed off."

"Hang tight, lover boy. I'm on my way, and we'll keel haul that bitch when I get there."

"Where are you?" I asked.

"Where do you think? I'm in Miami, waiting for my connecting flight to Caracas. I have thirty minutes before we board, and you can talk dirty to me until then."

"Megan, I'm getting off the ship. I won't be in Caracas."

"What? You can't. Does Alvin know?"

"No, and you're not going to tell him. Go home. I'll see you in Nashville."

"Owen, throw Betty off the boat. I'm all worked up about taking this cruise with you. Please, make it happen. Please?"

"No. It's not that simple, Betty."

"You just called me *Betty*. What's going on?"

"Hell if I know. I'm just so pissed off I don't know what I'm saying. I'm getting off this ship right after we hang up. I'll call you when I know more."

"Why don't you meet me here in Miami? I'll make your reservation."

I screamed at her. "Would you just stop? I can't think. I said I'll call you."

I slammed the phone down, pissed off at Megan for complicating my life. I hadn't really planned on leaving the ship before I talked to her, but that's exactly what I did.

From the balcony of my hotel room in Fort-de-France, I could see the plume of smoke from the Nordic Breeze as she put to sea. All of my newly acquired burdens were on board, my father's sins, his lies, his deceit, my mother's pain, the complete history of my past. All of it was manifested in my memory of Betty. If only the Nordic Breeze would sink and take Betty with her to a sealed tomb on the ocean floor, all my troubles would be over. A part of me would go down with her, for I had given her my heart. If only it were that simple.

So this was what heartache was? How I'd gone through life without ever experiencing something so wretched was beyond me. I'd always ridiculed people who tanked into depression over such trivial self-indulgences.

I missed my mother. If only I could flip the page back, I'd take control, turn her life around, and make her happy. I'd start by killing my father. All of her suffering vicariously slipped into my awareness of her. She was a strong woman, not bitter, not unhappy, but resigned to her reality that she shared with God. Her short life was vested in her sons, and I suppose it was enough for her … but what did I know? I'd rarely paid her a visit after I left the farm. All of my adult conversations with her were impatient superficialities and were more or less a dull obligation. I had sent that ship to the ocean floor a long time ago, and there was no way to salvage that wreck. Her truth belonged to me now. To this day I carry the guilt of my ambivalence regarding her memory, thanks to Betty.

The Nordic Breeze was silhouetted by a beautiful setting sun as she slid behind the lee of the harbor. There was nothing more to look at. I'd move on. Maybe I'd chase down Betty's lies to see if there was any merit to them. Deep down, I knew there wasn't a single lie to uncover. I'd been living with them all of my life, plain as fucking day, and I'd never seen them for what they were. Maybe I'd have a confrontation with Boots. But then both of his sons would be gunning for him.

I was restless as hell. I needed a man-break from women and going back to Nashville wasn't in the cards. Call it paranoia, or whatever, but Megan's motives didn't stack well. It was completely out of character for me to feel like I had to do something.

What would my mother want me to do? I'd made promises and I'd keep them. I got that from her, or rather from her soft voice whispering in my ear.

The smart thing for me to do was to head for Borneo and hang out with cannibals while this whole thing with my dad blew over.

Since when did I get a sense of family obligation? Genetically, I owed my father something, maybe a lab sample of love that I never got from him. If there was a shining moment of honesty, I recognized it then. I wasn't doing it for Dad. I was doing it for myself and a sense of duty that I had been AWOL from since mom died. Honesty had delusional qualities to hide behind and I always picked the most obvious. I wanted to save dad from screwing up his life, but deep down I knew it was way past midnight on that clock. Honestly? I had my own clock and the hands were stuck on high noon.

I called Alvin, the head chipmunk, and let him chirp into my ear. "Hey Alvin, Simon has a nice cruise for fourteen days with a hot chic and a few days at the beach. Just tell him to get her drunk."

"Yeah, I heard. So you got her out of your system?"

His tone was callous and I can't say that I blamed him. "Yeah, it's a done deal."

"Must have been pretty bad. You fuckin' literally went overboard on that deal, son. Where are you? Owen, you're off the reservation."

"I'm not an Indian, Alvin. My dad is, and he's been off the reservation for over a week, and you simpletons can't seem to find him. Call me when you find Cochise."

"Don't hang up. We think Colonel Fletcher is laying low. We haven't found Harlan. Don't screw this up."

"Boots is shacked up with some teeny-bopper down the road from Wentzville. Go get him."

"What makes you think so? Who told you? Betty?"

"No, it's his MO, and you know that. You know what I think? I think he's waiting for my check to clear, and he's not going to kill Harlan. You figure that out yet?"

"What are you talking about? Harlan and his accomplice are dangerous people, and he *will* kill Betty, then he'll come for you."

"Bullshit, Alvin. What were you going to do with her after the cruise, put her in the witness protection program? Fuck no. I'm her witness protection program. I'm her sugar daddy, and I have to keep you salaried because there's always Harlan out there, right? I've got this all figured out."

"You're dead wrong, and you will be if you don't listen. There is a third party that wants revenge on Colonel Fletcher. We'll talk about it when you get back to Nashville."

I'm not coming back to Nashville." My usual passive 'take it down the road' attitude had changed. I directed Alvin to get off his ass and check out some of Betty's story. I just wanted to fact-check a few dates, places, the who, why, and how, of Betty's past.

I was halfway into it when I got that weird feeling I was telling him something he already knew. I said, "You don't seem all that surprised, Alvin. What exactly do you know about Boots?"

"Not much. The Army JAG slammed a lid on our inquiries and is doing everything to freeze us out. But we did ask around and the silence speaks volumes."

"Then what are those soft-shoed puds of yours doing in Georgia?"

"It's better you don't have a working knowledge of my field investigative techniques. Like I said, we'll talk about it when you get back to Nashville."

"I told you…I'm not coming back to Nashville."

"What about Megan?"

"What about her?"

"I don't know. That broad has your back, but she's left a lot of scratch marks. You need to cut her some slack or rein her in."

"Deal with it. I'll see you when I see you." I hung up on him, sorry that I wasted a call to him.

My original plan was to drive to Columbus, Georgia, go to an Army surplus store, and gear up like Rambo. Then I'd find Psycho Mike, and the two of us together would murder our father. I had a night to think it over, and it took two calls the following morning to talk me out of it. Megan reminded me I'd already been in the crosshairs once, and I should let Alvin and the chipmunks take care of it. On second thought, I'd stop in Atlanta and from there find a way to Borneo.

CHAPTER THIRTY-FIVE

I arrived in Atlanta and discovered there were no flights to Borneo, but there were flight to just about everywhere else on the planet. The world was very big at that moment and at the same time very small. I could fly to Denver, rent a car, and check in on my not-so-ex wife and her daughter. Not a smart idea, Owen. What did I do? I flew to Seattle, rented an RV, and went on a tour of the Great Northwest while waiting out the saga taking place in my life. I always ran, didn't I? How many women pushed my start button and how many times did I shift gears? There just was no end in sight.

Four days into my tour, I arrived in Portland, Oregon and realized I hadn't seen a damned thing out the window, so I reversed my course and headed back to Seattle. There's not much you can accomplish while running through a cycle of pouting, then brooding, then sulking. What I had to grapple with was my own sense of moral propriety.

Essentially, Betty had delivered Boots' fate into my hands. I could phone the FBI, and in fifteen minutes, I could wash my hands of the bastard. I equivocated on that decision. Hell, I wouldn't waste the gas to drive out to Leavenworth to visit him in prison, but there were repercussions beyond a jail cell.

If I made the phone call, my mother's legacy would come crashing down and there were plenty of detractors who would mock her delusions. The family legend would be disgraced, and by association, so too his children. I couldn't do that to Lawson and Ron. The other thing was that it mattered to me, to my reputation, my new place in the social order. Betty's warning about my conscience roared in my head.

My tour of the great outdoors was consumed with indecision. I teetered back and forth. At times I thought I should just let it play out, and at others, I was an inch away from calling the FBI. I called Alvin a few times to remind him that it was his job to extract Boots and I was pissed that he hadn't. He complained that his hands were tied and the Army wasn't cooperating. He rubbed it in by saying, "You just need to cool your heels and stay put. By the way, Simon's having a great time with your girlfriend. He's moved into her old digs."

"Where's Betty?"

He laughed. "She's a real Celene Dion and spends all her time gearing up for the talent show. She's real broke up that you jumped ship." He snickered. "I've got a lead that I need to check out. It seems Harlan was being investigated for extortion by the local JAG. Does the name Colonel James Thomas ring any bells?"

"No. Ask Betty, she'd know."

"The OSI was about to launch a sting to catch Harlan taking a pay off from the colonel, but it got canceled, stamped PI, and planted. We know that Betty was implicated in the coercion so we can't ask her jack-shit."

"Why not?"

Jesus, Owen, let us do our job. We got it from a former OSI agent who is practicing law in Atlanta. He can't tell us much because of prosecutorial integrity. We did find out it had something to do with Thomas' ding-bat wife fucking the HQ staff. It's not much to go on, but we're onto her."

'That's all you have?"

"For now. It would be real helpful if you'd turn in that RV you rented and get your ass back here. My three guys keeping tabs on you have caught their limit in salmon so let's find something else for them to do."

"Hey Alvin, tell them to get a trout license. I'm not going anywhere."

"Suit yourself. You're paying for it. One more thing—Megan hired an attorney on your behalf," he said. "They had a casting couch session the other day and my guess is she did take him on."

If he hadn't chuckled, I wouldn't have slammed the phone down. I take that back. If it were physically possible, I would've crawled through the phone, met him on the other side of the conversation and beat him to death with his phone receiver.

Betty was almost through with her fourteen-day goodwill trip to third world crappy islands. I wondered how much time Simon spent jacking-off to videos of Betty in various stages of disrobing. I remembered her piety concerning never letting a lie stand between us. There are all sorts of lies. The one that goes over most everyone's head is the lying by omission. She forgot to tell me she was being investigated as a part of an extortion ring. God, I hated her.

I was just rolling into Seattle when Megan called me with good news. Betty's divorce had been recorded at the Muskogee Court House. It was time for me to cough up a million bucks for Mike Harlan's account, which I wasn't happy about. I didn't owe my dad, Betty, Thomas, or Harlan a damned thing. There I was, steamed about a million dollars that I would never get around to spending. I had acquired the logic of a stingy tycoon, and it just slipped up on me from nowhere. A million bucks is a million bucks, and all it took was a ten dollar, seven-hundred-fifty grain bullet at Lawson's farm to motivate my business decision. If I backed out, the shooter and his accomplice had plenty of ammo to bring me back to the table.

"Betty's divorce decree popped up today in the public records," she said.

"Yeah? Call Jerry. You need to make the transfer."

"There is something very wrong with it, Owen. Harlan signed the divorce papers at the judge advocates office the day he checked into Fort Benning, *before* he went on leave."

"What are you saying?"

"I'm saying it was two weeks before the payout to you. I called the JAG's office and discovered that the Army delayed the filing as they were waiting on a return receipt notification to the plaintiff."

"I don't get the connection."

"Who collects the mail at your dad's house?"

"Betty worked eight to five in an insurance office, so it would have to be Boots."

"Did your dad run interference for Betty with the JAG's office?"

"Why would the JAG's office have anything to do with a civil case, like divorces?"

"The way it was explained to me was the Army learned the hard way during Viet Nam when GI's got dear John letters out of the blue and decided to check out on the battle field and a lot of innocent bystanders got killed. So the family service division and the JAG's office always try to get permissive notification authority for soldiers deployed in combat assignments. It allows field commanders to pull back unreliable assets from complex team dynamics."

"You sounded like you're reading it from a script."

"I am. Alvin e-mailed it to me."

I knew one thing about Boots. He was used to running an Army, and there was no question in my mind that he was running Betty's legal problems. "He knows a lot of people, and he's got some pull inside the JAG's office. Why do you ask?"

"Think about it. Boots knew that Betty's divorce was over well before you entered the picture. Why would he not tell Betty about it?"

Megan didn't know about General Thomas and his wife. The Army was being obstructive in their notification obligation and I saw General Thomas in the chain of obstruction. He let Boots obstruct the facts. Why? Alvin Fox had to know what I knew. He could have stopped the vendetta, but sent Betty and me on a luxury cruise instead. Perhaps there was more to it than I thought, but something wasn't making any sense.

Megan read my mind. "I hate to say this. Can you think of any reason why your father kept that poor woman in mortal fear for her life? Why would a distraught husband sign divorce papers and then go on a rampage? Nothing is making any sense. Harlan's actions and his emotional outbursts don't come together."

I was ahead of Megan. I read between the lines. General Thomas was Boots' commanding officer. Betty's rendition was becoming more plausible. Was Boots forced into retirement because of his relationship with Betty or because he was screwing the general's wife? In either case, it was a court martial offense, so Boots' dismissal was a slap on the wrist. General Thomas certainly set himself up for blackmail, but having a loose wife on the prowl didn't meet the bar. Having a loose mistress running for her life, is, in so many ways, a God-send. The motive for murder has to run to the core of sanity, but nothing thus far rose to the occasion.

What did I know? I'm rather passive and not a seasoned killer, like my male counter-parts. There was one thing I was certain of, my million dollars was essentially extortion. It also met the criteria for the motive for murder.

Megan continued, "That poor woman is on hooks of horror every day, every minute of every day. No wonder she's on meds."

That wasn't exactly the case. Two things I had heard independently: Boots said there were people who wanted them dead, and Betty said pretty much the same thing. Harlan had to be in the middle because that's where my investment was headed. I said, "Maybe, it's Betty. "Something isn't adding up. I should go to the FBI."

"Alvin warned you not to talk to the FBI."

"Alvin knows more than he's telling."

"What else hasn't Alvin told yu? Think about that. We need to go to the FBI. I have a gut feeling that this three-way love triangle has more to it than meets the eye."

Actually it was a four-way, but I wasn't going to correct Megan's assumption.

She said, "All this started before money entered the picture."

Alvin Fox specialized in protecting lottery winners from scams, keeping it out of the press and more importantly, away from the cops. If I went to the cops, Boots would do time. "Just make the transfer. Harlan gets his money and that's the end of it."

"Are you sure? I have a bad feeling about this. Where are you, Owen?"

"Dancing by myself in the forest, Megan. I'm ready to come home."

CHAPTER THIRTY-SIX

Megan would make a very good personal assistant. She had my flight double-booked to Nashville and would be at the airport to pick me up. She also made up the spare bedroom at her place. I had been to Megan's house once. I knew where the spare bedroom was that I never slept in. I needed my space and not much of it, so I told her to book me a room at the Motel 6 out by the airport. Megan suggested the Hermitage, and she volunteered to come over and help me change the linens. We compromised. I wasn't staying in the presidential suite, and I could do just fine in a regular suite, which was larger than most apartments in New York City. Since Megan was snooty about getting laid in a Motel 6, I accepted her linen service over at the Hermitage.

I'd been gone…what?…Just over two weeks? Here I went dashing through the TSA cattle sorting pen like I had just been branded on the ass by the TSA goons. Megan, parked at the hold line, jumped up and down like a teenager at a Michael Jackson concert. The wart hog that passed for a TSA agent had to hold her back when she saw me. Like I said, it had only been a little more than two weeks. Megan had a tendency to overdo exuberance. Still, I never had a greeting, ever, like the one Megan gave me, and that felt very good.

I'm sure our collision sucked the air out of the airport like a massive decompression, creating a fog. Megan was on me beyond the sterile zone, and wart hog was yelling at her. "Miss! Get behind the line!"

"Fuck you, fatso!" is what Miss Public Relations blurted out. She gave me a body pat-down that made the TSA agent's dick hard.

"You're blocking traffic, miss."

I had heard rumors that TSA twerps took their jobs harassing the public seriously, and I said, "We better get moving, or we'll both end up receiving a cavity search."

Some irritated, squared jawed, passenger, huffily blurted his opinion as he passed, "Get a freakin' room."

"Did that, asshole." That wasn't me. Little Miss 'well spoken' said it. She made a quick scan of other people around us, and I wasn't sure what would come out of her mouth.

"Hey, I have a surprise for you. Let's go pick up your luggage," Megan said, flashing me a beaming smile. I blew out a sigh of relief.

"I don't have any luggage. It'll catch up to me in a day or two, but in the meantime, I need to stop off and pick up a few things."

"I'm taking you to my house, and you won't need any clothes."

"We've been over this before. The answer's still no."

"Why not? Just until you find a permanent place. What's wrong with that?"

"Because I'm not looking for anything permanent. I'm not sure how long I'll be staying in Nashville."

That stopped Megan in her tracks. "What? You're running out on me again?"

That's exactly what my original intentions were. "It's not what you think. When this mess with Boots is over, I'm going to have to start my life over again, and as much as I love this town, it's a giant reminder of my past failures. I'm not sure I want to stick around for the memories."

Megan fell silent. She understood, and I could almost see wheels spinning in her head. "Where will you go?"

"I'm not sure. I liked Washington and Oregon. Maybe I can make a home there."

"Would I have visitation rights?"

"We'll speak to the warden about it. I'm sure we'll work something out."

My intention was to make a clean break from the feminine gender entirely. Megan was a nice girl, well a bit more than that, and her motives didn't have a clean bill of health. I didn't want to be a prick, so I thought I'd lay the landscape where I could just melt into her past tense.

Megan's not stupid, and she saw through the first salvo. Her driving reflected her anger as she barged through traffic. I couldn't think of anything to cover my intentions, and the silence spoke for itself.

She had a firm grip on the wheel, and her head locked like she was in a neck brace. She certainly wasn't looking at me. "What the hell happened on the cruise?"

"Nothing happened on the cruise," I lied.

"Yes, something happened on the cruise. You said so, remember? It has something to do with your dad's girlfriend. You can tell me."

No I couldn't, not in a million years. I'd been taken in by a very seductive woman, and I couldn't quite get it in my mind that it was a fling that went horribly wrong. I said, "Betty's a bitch."

"You're just now figuring that out? Owen, she's a married woman living with another man. She's been living off your dad for three years. I can't for the life of me see what either man sees in her. Mark my words; she's got something on your dad. She's a slut, and you shouldn't let her get to you."

I had covered all that ground with Betty before jumping ship. "Yeah, you're right," I said with remorse and guilt.

"Then let's get back to being us, okay? We'll get through this mess together. Deal?"

She took her hand off the wheel and patted my thigh reassuringly.

In hindsight, I should've had her pull into a Starbucks, sat her down, and told her about Betty. At the time I thought I was in the passing lane with Megan, and we could drive on down the road when it suited us. That was my plan.

CHAPTER THIRTY-SEVEN

What are good friends for if they can't bring misery into your complicated life? Jerry wasn't at the elevator, but he did get off his fat ass and walk around the desk to throw an arm around me.

When Jerry was in a good mood, it was infectious. When he was in a bad mood, you were a bowling pin at the end of the alley. He all but shoved me into a chair and parked himself on his desk. Every muscle on his face was southbound. He pointed his finger in my face. "Do you have any fucking idea how much trouble your best friends are in? Huh? Huh, do you? We are so screwed because of your dad's girlfriend's divorce settlement." He slammed his palm on the desk just in case I wasn't paying attention.

"My friends aren't in any trouble, Jerry. I am."

"No *you* aren't—yet. Your financial advisor, me …and your power of attorney…Megan, both of whom were acting on your behalf, are facing criminal charges. You weren't exactly Huckleberry Finn, riding a raft down the Mississippi with Becky Thatcher, which reminds me, when is Becky due back?"

"It's Betty, and she's scheduled to return three days from now."

"Whatever. In the meantime, your money sits in her ex-husband's account. I have a hunch it'll move when Becky hits the docks. Your transaction with Harlan went public, dude."

"What do you mean by 'public'? Whatever happened to private banking laws?"

"Public, as in your plaintiff's' counsel exercised their right of discovery. This ain't Switzerland. Your assets are frozen. I'm meeting with the dick weed attorney Fox Security set up for you this afternoon. He fucked up the hearing, big time." He waved his hand as if he'd said something trivial.

He rasped, nearly spitting in my face. "You remember Bonnie Fletcher? Yeah, that Bonnie. The one you treated like shit. The one that left you. Mrs. Owen Fletcher, that Bonnie? Her attorney wants a full accounting of where your million dollar transfer went and why. See …half of it is hers unless you can prove otherwise." He emphasized his point by slamming his fist on the desk. "Her attorney will turn up on the FBI's doorsteps by lunch time, and when he does, your friends, not you, have to explain why you wired one million dollars into an account in Georgia."

"Settle down, Jerry. It's very simple. I was just helping my dad out with legal issues. That's not against the law."

"Let's recap that legal problem, which isn't your father's problem. Sergeant Harlan is in the Army, and all he has to his name is a truck and camping gear. Mrs. Harlan is either destitute or a prostitute. Take your pick. Between them, their marital assets wouldn't buy groceries for a week." Jerry gave me that 'you-following-me' look. "Prince Charming just happens to show up with a million dollars so Sergeant Harlan can go on his happy way. A million fucking dollars, Owen? That's extortion, and we both know it, or …it's bribery. Either way, the feds will sniff that out in a nano-second. Bonnie's high-dollar attorney will see to it."

"So what? Stupidity isn't illegal. I was merely facilitating a transaction to produce a legal settlement. Fox said it was entirely legal. He checked it out with his attorney."

Jerry's laugh was dry and humorless. "If it's the same guy that let them freeze your assets, get used to wearing orange. Look dude, you need to get on the right side of this. You have to take this to the FBI."

Jerry wasn't going out on a limb for me like I asked him to. No. He did just the opposite. He called the FBI, which hit me solidly. The short of it, I had an appointment with an FBI agent for a consultation. I was advised to be prompt and to bring Megan with me. I could bring an attorney, but I was told that the meeting would be informal. Never listen to crap like that...ever.

I called Megan and told her to meet me in the lobby of the federal building. Oddly, she sounded relieved, almost like she'd made the appointment herself.

Joyce Houseman met us in the lobby of the federal building. Joyce was tall, reed thin, and flat-chested. She had an undertaker's smile that showed that her parents had neglected her dental health. Agent Houseman made quick business of the introduction and led Megan and me off to a private room.

It wasn't a white-washed interrogation room that I expected, and I could see the clutter of personal effects. As I breathed a sigh of relief, the first thing she told us was that we could end up with cuffs on and she could read us our rights. Where had I heard that line before?

Joyce played with a pencil between her fingers and studied both of us. She made several facial expressions that were scornful, curious, or amused. I didn't like what she might be thinking and waited pensively.

"Before we get started, let me tell you what brings us together for this little chat. An informant has brought an interesting allegation to this office."

Fuckin' Jerry.

"I spent a little time researching your predicament. Law enforcement in Georgia is not keen to cooperate in an investigation, but Indiana is. As far as I know, you haven't broken any federal laws. Neither of you are accused of a serious crime, but you, Mr. Fletcher, are a material witness, and you, Miss Marsh abetted Mr. Fletcher's flight across state lines. The state of Indiana would like to get their hands on both of you."

"Have I done something wrong?" I asked.

"Not yet, but like I said, you are a material witness to an investigation in the state of Indiana. You don't want to be charged with obstruction of justice, so your cooperation is required."

"Someone was trying to kill me and my dad's girlfriend."

"Don't interrupt me. I understand you were under duress and remain so. The perpetrator at your brother's farm has multiple charges to face at every level of law enforcement jurisdiction. We can clear that up as far as your involvement, but what interests me is a million dollar transfer waiting at Planter's Bank, payable to the prime suspect. That's what we're here to talk about. Who wants to go first?"

Joyce tapped her pencil on her yellow note pad as Megan and I looked at each other. I launched into the saga, giving Miss Houseman an outline of what had transpired and what I knew or what I wanted her to know. Megan came behind me and filled in the details, as I used a very wide brush in the telling of my woes.

"Congratulations on winning the lottery," said Miss Houseman. Her sarcasm was becoming cliché. "It looks like you're way over your head, Mr. Fletcher. It's a good thing you stopped by this office or you would have both been looking at conspiracy charges. If your story checks out, it could be mitigated as coerced, and since you are the victim of your own conspiracy, I think we can overlook your error." The bitch laughed.

"My security advisor advised against talking with the authorities. He said he would be in touch with you."

"What? Why would he do that?"

"He said he wanted to wait until the trap was sprung at the other end of the transaction." I told her about Alvin and our relationship.

Joyce Houseman rolled here eyes and shook her head. "Look, we haven't heard from Alvin Fox or his company. Did he happen to mention what law enforcement division is handling the intercept? It sure as hell isn't the state of Georgia. I need to run this up the flagpole, and I have a lot of calls to make."

"Are you sure Alvin Fox hasn't been in touch with the FBI, maybe a different office?"

"I'll find out. You've been given a tremendous volume of bad advice. This may come as a surprise to you, but your advisor is a nut job. The only federal laws involved with this case are wire fraud, bank fraud, and other banking regulations that I won't go into. Fortunately, none of this has occurred yet. Since you had the good sense to run this past us, I don't see a problem with us taking over your sting operation."

"We're talking about bullets as big as coke bottles aimed at me," I said.

"It is not a federal crime to threaten the life of another individual. That comes under state statues, as does stalking, extortion, and attempted murder. All the ex-husband has done was violate laws residing in local jurisdictions."

"Are you telling me that this Mike Harlan hasn't broken any laws? He's threatened to kill his wife, and he took multiple shots at her. He's extorted a million dollars from me, and he gets a slap on the hand?"

"I'm referring to federal laws, but I need to run it by my superiors. Can you come back at two-thirty?"

Agent Houseman stood up to indicate that our interview was over for the time being. Her grim smile was more like a flash-light-face in the dark, and a shiver ran up my spine.

Megan and I shared a sigh of relief. We weren't going to the can–not yet. I told Miss Houseman we'd keep the appointment.

"Okay then. In the meantime, do nothing nor speak with any-one else."

CHAPTER THIRTY-EIGHT

We went back to the federal building early, just in case Joyce had answers for us. She was choking down the last morsel of a fast food burger, so her life expectancy was extended until dinner time. Watching Joyce swallow her lunch was like watching an anaconda swallow a live pig. A bulging lump slowly slid down her skinny throat. She batted her hooded eyes at us, and I could tell she was trying to suppress a burp. She simply waved us into her office.

"Mr. Fletcher, how do you feel about standing in front of this case? Are you willing to go through with it? Don't worry, we've already flagged the account and tagged any transactions."

"I just want to get my dad out of trouble."

"That's a completely different issue. What we have is a conspiracy case. Any individual and another individual conspiring across state lines to cause harm or loss of life of a third individual is covered under federal law as conspiracy to commit murder."

Joyce went on, "Since it's believed the shooter has an accomplice to the crime, the public is doubly in danger of the crime being committed. The stated threat is murder, and the overt act has been acted upon at your brother's farm. That's what makes it a conspiracy to commit murder."

"That doesn't sound very harsh. Looks like Psycho Mike will get a month of community service at most."

Joyce made an O with her mouth and raised her eyebrows. "That's not true. The act of *attempted* murder with a firearm has a maximum penalty of twenty-five years in most states. Conspiring to commit murder, whether it is successfully executed or not, brings a penalty as though it was, *which* means life in prison. It's a very serious crime." We have to make the case that the elements for committing the crime are materially present and that the intention was acted upon." Joyce shuffled her notes and continued. "We need to collect the evidence before we can proceed with an investigation."

Megan asked, "The death threats on Betty's phone, aren't they material?"

"Yes, they would be, if we had the actual recording."

"We have the phone," I said.

Joyce crinkled her brows. "Where is the phone now?"

"I have it," I said. I got the eyebrow thing again.

She played the voicemail threats a couple of times. Her forehead was stuck in furrowed ruts the whole time.

"Is something wrong?" Megan asked.

"I'm not sure. Something isn't right. Are you sure this is Harlan's voice?"

"Pretty sure. Betty went into fits every time her phone rang."

"And she believes it's her husband?"

I shrugged. "Who else would it be?"

Joyce set the phone aside and said, "I'll send this to the lab and let the voice recognition folks examine it." She sat back in her chair, crossed her vine-like legs, and began twirling her pencil as if it was a helicopter blade. Her face was a slideshow of different expressions and not one of them was friendly. "I'm interested in investigating this case because there are lives at risk, particularly Mrs. Harlan's. I'm having a problem here. Miss Marsh, you're the PR director on behalf of the lottery. Can you explain why you're micro-managing this problem Owen has with his windfall? How did you get involved? Why did you hire his security company, his lawyer, and happen to be his power of attorney? What were you doing in Miami last week? Why were Mrs. Harlan and Mr. Fletcher registered in the Hermitage Hotel under your name?" The helicopter stopped and her hard stare fixed on Megan.

Megan seemed to grow a foot taller as her spine stiffened. The intimidation factor was so high that for once Megan was speechless. I watched her roast for a few tense seconds, and then I jumped in to bail her out. "Megan is my girlfriend. My other friend snitched me out to you, so I dumped it all on Megan."

The pencil helicopter started up. If she didn't slow it down, she'd be asking her questions from the ceiling. "The coincidence of your relationship with Miss Marsh isn't missed by me. Are you paying Miss Marsh for any of these 'services' she performs for you, or is it all off the books?"

The cork came out of my bottle and ricocheted around the room. I was off my ass and bent over her desk like an attack monkey. "Look, bitch, we're done here." I snatched the pencil out of her fingers, broke it in half and threw it at her. She didn't even flinch. I spun around and said, "Let's go, Megan."

Megan stood her ground. "It's a legitimate question, Owen, even though it was poorly worded." She raised her chin and said, "I'm not an employee of Mr. Fletcher and acted purely out of personal concern, which doesn't involve the company I work for, the State of Tennessee, or any professional services under contract. What you really want to know is if we have a date night set aside and the answer is I own all seven."

I did a head jerk. My understanding was we were up to two nights and maybe we fudged a little, but seven? Megan pulled me back to my seat.

Joyce gave a nod and a muted chuckle. "You work fast, Miss Marsh. Now that we've got that out of the way, I'm advising you to put distance between your personal relationship and this investigation. It will be important during the prosecution phase of this case when we get to that point. I want a straight shot at the perpetrator without the defense mudding the waters."

In girl talk, Agent Houseman was telling Megan to back off and stay out of the way. Megan's body language wore talons. She composed herself as Agent Houseman had backed her into a corner. She quietly reached for my hand and squeezed it.

I thought I knew what that was about and I said, "The FBI needs to confine its investigation to the investigation. Stay out of my personal business."

Agent Houseman nodded thoughtfully and said, "Miss Marsh, I have to discuss other matters with Mr. Fletcher. We'll call on you if we need further information. Would you excuse us?"

Megan huffed. "Owen, I think you need to call your attorney before you say another word."

Did I see a victory grin on Agent Houseman's ugly mug? "Miss Marsh, please?" She pointed to the door. "We won't be long."

Megan all but stormed out of the small office, while agent Houseman found another pencil to twirl in her fingers.

Pissed, I said, "I think I need an attorney present."

She responded a little too cheerfully. "Fine, I can't ask you another question, but I can show you why that's not advisable." She pulled out two photos from her desk and pushed them both across the table. "One of these is Mrs. Elisabeth Harlan. I could ask Miss Marsh which is which?"

"I can explain—"

"I'm sure you can. I understand why your people went to the trouble to substitute the photo of her that was published in the paper. I have the impression that Miss Marsh would pick the photo on the left." She picked up the photo on the right and held it up to my face. "Betty is seriously hot, even if it is a DMV photo. Says here she's your age, thirty-five. This is your dad's girlfriend?"

"What do you expect me to say?"

"You can start with 'thank you, Joyce.' Were you really fucking your dad's girlfriend?" she turned the photo of Betty around and said, "I can see how that could happen. She dumped you, didn't she?"

"No, and I wasn't fucking my dad's girlfriend."

"If you say so. I'm being sensitive to your personal problem, so from here on, Miss Marsh doesn't get a recap about anything we talk about. Are we clear on that point?"

"I prefer it that way."

"Good. Let's talk about Betty. Something doesn't add up right from the start. I have a hunch there's more to this than a rooster fight."

Not only did I hate this woman, I was in mortal fear of her. She was a dark raven parked on my shoulder pecking at my brain.

I stopped by Jerry's office with a heads up, and he gave me one. Get this; because of the lawsuits against my estate, most of my assets were frozen. That's why he couldn't make the transfer on the same day the divorce was recorded. I had to take out a loan from the bank to get my own money to send to Harlan, and had the FBI not been involved, I wouldn't have received the loan. That was just too fucked up. Bankers! The son of a bitch made me take out a life insurance policy, just in case I got sniped. Before we finished our chat, I verbally clubbed Jerry for ratting me out to Agent Houseman.

My next call went to Boots. He must have been on an inspection tour of the battlements, as he wasn't answering his phone. I left a message telling him everything was now in the hands of the FBI, and Mike Harlan would be picked up very soon. He needed to stand down and stay out of the way.

I could have called Betty next, but I didn't. I wanted her to sweat every drop of fear that was in her. I wanted her to suffer for not only what she had set in motion, but because she made me fall in love with her. That part of my pain was all her fault.

CHAPTER THIRTY-NINE

The following morning, I had a meeting with an attorney who supposedly had experience taking on messes that goofy lottery winners got themselves into. I had other legal problems from people who felt entitled to my money. Hajji for starters, then Jolene behind him, another person I'd never heard of, and then there was Bonnie. There was also a suit against me by my former agent at Tarzan Talent for breach of contract.

Why is it that attorneys and doctors are the only professionals who expect me to be on time for my appointment, but are never on time for theirs? When I have a one hour appointment, and I stick around for ten minutes, I'm going to pay for the full hour. My first experience with my attorney was like passing the differential of a Cadillac out my ass.

Kenny Scales reeked of sap. The dapper bastard wore cuff links that cost as much as my truck. He extended a manicured set of fingers adorned with a class ring and a wedding band wide enough for a four lane highway. His voice was high toned, southern syrup, and his language was versed like the Gettysburg

Address. A minute into his spiel, I wished he was at Gettysburg under the Tennessee monument. Alvin said the guy was good, so I stuck around to hear him tell me why he was gouging my ass.

We finally got to the meat of the conversation, which was framed like, "Let's hurry up, I don't have all day.' Kenny checked his watch and asked, "Have you been served yet?"

"No, I haven't seen the menu."

It went way over Kenny's head by a mile. He said, "Have you been met by an officer of the court, and did he give you any papers?" He quickly learned he was working with a simpleton. Finally, I understood the question. If Kenny and I were going to have future conversations, I would have to dissuade him of his initial opinion of me.

"I was told that process servers have me on their most wanted list and they're scouring the city, but I skipped town."

"That was probably best. As attorney of record, I'll have the summons delivered to my office, and you won't be bothered. Once that's done, I'll have consultations with the opposing attorneys." I would later learn that these consultations took place at the country club golf course, and I would be billed for attorney fees *and* green fees. One thing about attorneys, they don't even talk to their children unless it's billable.

I told Kenny about Jolene, Hajji, my ex-wife, and Tarzan Talent Agency. Wouldn't you think that would provoke a few questions? Here is what I got from Kenny Scales, Attorney at Law, "Let me read the complaints, meet with the attorneys, and we can go from there. I don't think we have much to worry about." Did I hear him say *we*? *I* had plenty to worry about. Kenny and his concerns were all about his golf handicap.

We were done, five minutes short of the thirty minutes he had allotted to my one-hour consultation. He looked at his watch … Ca-ching!

I talked to Agent Houseman frequently on the phone. We usually met at the Oak Bar, without Megan or Kenny Scales providing me scripts to read from. I think Agent Houseman liked me because she started using my first name, and she seemed less restrained when Megan wasn't around. I was curious what the feds had learned from Betty, and I didn't want Megan to hear any of it, so I asked Joyce if our scheduled meetings could be confidential.

The Oak Bar is a cozy hideaway in the basement of the hotel. It's small, quiet, and private, perfect for a meeting place to plot sedition. Joyce was already sitting at a table by the fireplace when I arrived.

"Owen, I have a few questions, but before we get to that, Betty Harlan has been picked up at the port of Miami and put into protective custody for questioning, which I would like to remind you was where she belonged from the beginning. Fox barged in, and without a lot of convincing, made off with her. You need to call off Fox and let us handle the woman. He has her lawyered up."

Fox was doing exactly what I wanted him to do. Betty and I were the only two people on our side of the investigation that knew what would put Boots behind bars. Fox was my smoke screen. I said, "Alvin's paid to make sure Mrs. Harlan is out of harm's way and not subject to harassment, which includes the federal government."

"If he gets in my way, I'll have him for obstruction of justice."

"That's Alvin's problem, not mine."

Joyce's wry grin announced that she knew more than she was letting on. "You really were fucking her." My nose went south bound and my eyes closed. Joyce continued. "And Megan doesn't know a thing about it? Geez, Owen."

I lifted my nose from my chest and said, "That chapter is closed."

Joyce raised her eyebrows. "Not according to Betty. She cried like a baby when she told our people she ended the affair. She says she loves you but won't say a word against Boots. Woman's got a screw loose. That's your personal issue and I'm just telling you to watch out. Why did she break it off?"

"She didn't, I did. We're both involved and it was wrong. One of those things."

Joyce's wicked snicker pissed me off.

I said "Look…I have a girlfriend for the first time in ten years, and I'm not throwing that away because I was seduced by my dad's girlfriend."

"So tell me, why did you really get off the love boat?"

"It's none of your fucking business, Joyce."

Her eyebrows worked their way up to the top of her forehead. "I'm just saying, I can understand why you're not leveling with Megan, but not leveling with me is a bad idea. What happened on the cruise? What did she tell you?"

"Dad had dumped her, and she seduced me to get back at him."

She said, "Shoot the messenger? Not today. My opinion, Betty was covering her own tracks. Did you know she and her husband were implicated in an extortion scheme a few years ago? Does the name General James and Susan Thomas ring a bell with you?"

"Should it?"

"The Army dropped an extortion investigation in midstream. We don't know why, but we'll find out. Owen, you could save us a lot of leg work and tell us what Betty told you. I *sooo* freakin' know why you left the ship."

My rational mind seized up. I couldn't open the watershed to my father's crimes, and I have to say this for Betty, she didn't either. I said, "What happened fifteen years ago doesn't have any bearing on why Harlan's trying to kill Betty and my father."

Joyce quickly grasped my gaff. "The extortion incident was dropped *five* years ago. Tell me what's significant about *fifteen* years ago?"

I clammed up. She put her elbows on the table and parked her chin in her palms, studying me as though I was a lab rat.

"What?" I asked.

"You're a nice guy, but you're so fucked in the head. You don't owe Betty a damn thing and your father even less for getting you into this mess. As much as I'd hate to do it, I'm an inch from slapping bracelets on you. Don't for a minute think I won't."

How was I going to respond to something like that? "I can't very well tell you something I don't know, Joyce."

"I have a bunch of questions to ask you, but we'll just stop because if I asked you, you'd lie to me, then I'd have to put you behind bars." She got up on her pencil legs, put her knuckles on the table and leaned close enough for me to smell her breath. "Here's one for you to think about. Harlan has no idea that he's got a million dollars in his bank account."

Joyce sat back down, crossed her arms and slid her chair back to wait for a response from me. She acted like she had all the time in the world. Wheels were spinning and she helped me out by saying, "You don't have to scroll down too far to figure out who else knows about the account. Who set it up? And who has access to it?"

I blurted out, "It's Betty, has to be."

Joyce scratched her neck as if I'd given her cooties. "It's too convenient that all the fingers are pointing to Betty. You have to remember the threats started *before...* a few weeks before it was publicly announced that you won the lottery. Betty's right, this is about revenge and not your million bucks. At least it didn't start out that way."

If I hadn't stuck my nose into it by putting up a million bucks there wouldn't be an investigation. No father or son was going to kill each other over a tainted woman. Thomas had to know his wife was a loose woman and he had plenty of time to either get over it or get rid of her. I thought it would all blow over and the feds should just stay out of it. "It would be a domestic issue if I hadn't entered the picture. Why not let it go? Isn't this turning into entrapment?"

She guffawed. "Extortion, fraud, and conspiracy to commit murder aren't misdemeanor crimes. The Harlan's were extorting money from the Thomas's. The Army investigation either didn't get far enough into the leverage used by the Harlan's, or the records have been expunged. By deduction, we can go through the sordid mess." She had her pencil out. She was making dots on a blank piece of paper. "I can't seem to connect these, but you can." She handed me the pencil.

Joyce was critically close to the truth as I understood it from Betty. I couldn't possibly drop a hint one way or other. She said, "Betty has something on all three men. One, or all of them want her dead. You might be able to help your dad by telling us what it is."

I acted innocent and dumb. "Who is Colonel Thomas to my dad, or for that matter to Harlan? Maybe Thomas was having an affair with Betty?"

"Thomas pins on his star in a month. To your point, it's all chain of command issues. Boots was his direct subordinate and likely to replace him. But your father resigned without any prior notice and it's said Thomas forced him into retirement because Mike Harlan filed a timely complaint. Any commanding officer sleeping with one of his enlisted men's wife is grounds for court martial." She laughed. "It's considered undue use of authority, prejudicial to good order and bad for morale. The charges are a matter of record. That's the connection, but there's more to it than that, isn't there? What did the Harlan's have on Thomas?" She placed her arms behind her head, plastered a complacent smile on her face and waited for my response.

"I'm as baffled as you are, Joyce. Are you sure the gunman at Lawson's was Thomas?" I'd sum it up as indifference and my shrug of the shoulders caused Joyce to raise her eyebrows.

Yeah, we know it's Thomas because we have all the evidence picked up at the shooter's campsite on Lawson's farm, and we've traced it back to Fort Benning. It doesn't take a genius to figure out who has the bones to requisition a hit squad. We can't get the Army JAG to give us squat, but we'll get there eventually. That's where you come in ..."

"Hey, I did my part. The money's in Harlan's account. Isn't that enough? He's not going to let it sit there forever."

"That's the reason I stopped by. The technicians found something interesting from the voicemail recording we took from Mrs. Harlan's phone. The threat messages are all pre-recorded, looped, and grafted. We can't pinpoint who the voice belongs to, but it's probably Mike's."

"Joyce, we know Mike's been threatening Betty. How does this change anything?"

"What dumb ass is going to issue death threats over a voicemail from his cell phone? Maybe in a fit of anger, but routinely? Come on. The fucker is reading from a café menu and who gets the same message right, word for word, in a fit of rage? The voice tapes are fakes, and anyone could send that message, including Boots, General Thomas, or his wife, Susan."

"Now you're defending Harlan." More to the point, she was understating an accusation that led to Boots.

Joyce rattled her fingernails on the table, her expression thoughtful. "Someone has fabricated this to payback the Harlans and is using your father as their instrument. The Thomas's shift into the suspect column, but there's one thing that bothers me. Why would Thomas agree to have the money deposited into Harlan's account unless he has access to it, which he doesn't?"

"Like you said, maybe it's not about money."

She said, "Betty said that, not me. Don't kid yourself. No one is going to leave a million dollars on the table."

I had an epiphany, and I was excited about it. "Joyce, I've got it. What happens to the money should something happen to Harlan?"

"It would go to the next of kin."

"Yeah, the widow, Betty Harlan. She wouldn't have to go to the bank; they'd send her the check. She's one hell of a seductress, and I have another million that says she and Thomas are the masterminds."

"That's good, Owen, but Harlan's divorce is on record, and Betty wouldn't be the widow."

The spool of string was quickly unraveling in my mind. "I have a question. Would the divorce make any difference if the beneficiary of Harlan's estate still lists Betty?"

There was a faint sparkle in her dark brown eyes. She said, "Damn…you're right. There's one person who would know. General Thomas has access to Harlan's personnel files. He'd know if Harlan changed his next of kin status. If he hasn't, Betty would still be the beneficiary. Thomas and Betty split the proceeds."

I took it one step beyond. "Boots was motivated and what if he were to get his revenge on Thomas and shoot the Bastard. Betty would get it all." Another thought chased up the flagpole. I said, "You might be onto something. "

It was all crystal clear. Betty had maneuvered Boots and her husband into a deadly confrontation, and one of them would likely kill the other. It didn't matter which way it worked out because both men would be disposed of. She would likely collect the Servicemen's Guaranteed Life Insurance on either one or both.

"Owen, we have to reach your father. We need to bring him in as quickly as possible. If you have any idea where he is or how to get in touch with him, you'd better let me know right now. I think you're on to something and I'll call my guys to pick up Betty and put her on ice."

All I had was Boots' cell phone number. It would take some gumption to make the call to the bastard. I pulled out my cell phone and bounced it around in my hand trying to construct something decent to say to the man. It took awhile, but eventually I punched in the numbers.

"Dad! Where are you?"

"What did I tell you about calling? How's Betty?"

"She's...she's under protection by the FBI —

"I got that message," he growled, and off he went on a tirade. I had to interrupt him.

"Dad, Betty and I talked."

"Yeah? She's a crazy bitch and you gotta know that. What's she saying to the feds?"

His reaction was a fist to my gut. His big concern was what Betty might say to the FBI. A moment of truth begged a question and I asked it. "Is there any grain of truth in anything she might have said?"

It got real quiet and I waited for his answer. What I got was a backhanded confirmation. "Did she tell her story to the feds?"

"I'm sitting in front of a Fed right now. She's asked me to tell her what Betty hasn't. Maybe you could tell me, and I'll pass it along."

"Keep your fucking mouth shut. That's water under the bridge. Betty is up to her ass in all this. Just take care of her and don't let anything happen to her. Just fucking do something I ask for change."

Not so much as 'I'm sorry' out of his mouth. So there it was, a diary of sins floating underneath a bridge of forgotten deeds. Pages of ink diluted by the watered down passage of time. Not one fucking denial. Not one fucking apology. Boots Fletcher passed under that bridge for the last time for me.

"Owen, are you still there? Hey, it's not like Betty tells it."

Probably not, probably much worse. It didn't matter as it was substantively true, and the degree didn't count. I had a message to deliver, and I just wanted to get it over with. I'd stricken "dad" from my vocabulary and simply said, "We think Thomas has set you and Harlan up, and we believe that he'll attempt to kill one of you. You need to turn yourself over to the FBI before something happens. I mean now. You hear me, you rotten bastard?"

He actually laughed. He said, "I figured it out back at the house. The assholes pushed my buttons and Mike's buttons, but it didn't work. I'm with Mike, and they're not going to get by with it. Your million dollars flushed all the players out."

"Dad, you're not making sense. The FBI is looking for you and Harlan."

"Yeah, I know. This will all be over in a couple of days."

"What are you talking about?"

"I've got to tell you. The bitch got by with it once before. She's a real smooth operator, and she's had years to plan this."

"Where are you now?"

"Hell, I'm in the great outdoors, camping and fishing. I think the fish will take the bait pretty soon, son. Keep your promise and take care of Betty. She doesn't deserve this shit. We'll talk when this is all over."

"You're contradicting yourself. I'm telling you, Betty and Thomas have this all planned out. She's not looking for a divorce, she's anxious to become a widow."

Joyce snatched the phone from my hand. "Colonel Fletcher, this is special agent Joyce—" She jerked her head in frustration. "He hung up. Call him back."

Boots must have tossed his cell phone in the tackle box because he wasn't taking any calls.

Joyce had a nervous tension fit, while I tried to reach him. She asked leading questions that went nowhere.

"Can you give me an idea where he might be camped?"

"He's fishing."

"So there can be only so many fishing camps. Where does he usually go?"

"Canada, for all I know. I never went fishing with him one damned time. Boots makes his own camp, so you've got your work cut out for you."

Joyce had a complacent frown that made her look better. "What was all the hushed talk concerning Betty about? I overheard some of it."

She overheard all of it. "You'd have to ask her, but I don't think you'll find her to talk to. She's making her move."

CHAPTER FORTY

After I finished with Joyce, I went back to my room to bask in my gloom. Little things gnawed at me. Shouldn't I be working, trying to eke out a living? I recalled sitting on my ass in my old RV, doing jack-shit. I'd give anything to have my RV back and be at the state park with Frank drinking beer. Living like a lord and not working up a sweat wore on my provincial conscience. I was bored by it and felt a twinge of guilt that I did nothing to earn my keep in this new world I found myself.

I was going crazy trying not to worry about Boots. That's not true either. I was more worried that his dirty little secrets would get back to my brothers and Megan. The evil bastard deserved to go to jail for life. The Bastard would skate...again. The Feds didn't have a thing on him.

I'd pace for a while, then flip on daytime news, scroll through channels, turn off the TV, and paced some more, trying to think of something to take my mind off of my problems.

I picked up a local 'About Town' rag and I saw that Spam had a gig in town. My mood changed instantly. I wanted Megan to check out my old friend Stevie Sievers. Stevie and I were from the same mold and we'd been together starting back in Colorado and all the way to my dead end in Nashville. Man, I really wanted to see him.

Stevie and his new band, Spam, were playing at the popular Blue Notes road house. I reserved a table where we could really get the tone of the whole performance.

When Megan did her afternoon room check, I told her what I had in mind. It didn't matter to her where we were going. She'd stand by me and watch paint dry if I asked her to.

We arrived at Blue Notes and Megan was giggly and excited to meet someone from my past. When Spam took the stage, the standing room only crowd started cheering. Megan poked me in the ribs and asked me to point out Stevie. I pointed at the long haired adolescent in tight leather pants out to her. He was still skinny as a rail, and the slick leather pants and the big belt buckle didn't go together. He wore a buccaneer's shirt, unbuttoned almost to his navel, and his little bird chest didn't come close to being sexy, but the girls screamed anyway.

"That's Stevie? He's beautiful!" Stevie had just acquired a new groupie, but I was unconcerned because Megan was over eighteen.

"He doesn't look a day over twenty-four. Oh, that hair! Owen, the two of you go back ten years. How young was he back then?"

Hell, Stevie was my age. "He hadn't reached puberty yet. Stevie went through tubes of Clearasil quicker than you go through KY jelly."

I got a jab for that comment. Spam went to work with their most popular hits, some of which I helped write. I brooded, feeling the nostalgia and jealousy. I was happy for Stevie and glum about me. I should have been on that stage with him. Spam had an edge in their genre, bluesy rock that belonged in both genres. They wailed magic from the stage. Megan was on her feet after the end of each song set. The band took a break, and she gushed like a teenager with wet panties, wanting to know everything about Stevie.

In all the time that I partied with Stevie, he never once had a grown-up as a date. It was always young girls, all underage. My recent troubles put a new light on his peculiar dating habits, and for that reason, I suddenly hated him.

Megan asked, "You know him. Has he ever been married? What's he really like?"

"He's a little too sweet if you know what I mean."

Megan's hand went to her mouth and her eyes were big. "No. Don't tell me he's gay."

"I can't say for sure, but he's strange in a Michael Jackson kind of way." There were a lot of nice things I could have said, but I wasn't in the mood, and her idol-ogling ticked me off.

During the second set, Stevie had been looking at our table with intensity. Suddenly, he stopped singing, and the band looked confused by what was going on. Stevie dramatically pointed straight at me and yelped. "Owen Fletcher!"

He told the audience how we got our start, wrote music together, formed Shylock, and my sudden demise from the music world. "Owen, get off your ass and get up here."

Before I knew it, I had a guitar thrust in my hands, and he asked, "Do you remember 'Advice on Vice'?" Yes I did, I wrote it. Stevie gave the audience the history of the song and why he had never recorded it. It was mine, and he couldn't find me. Stevie and I debuted "Advice on Vice."

My girl, Megan, wept. She knew my past, and it hurt her to see how far I had fallen and how fast I was back in it as if I hadn't been gone at all. My dick was as hard as the guitar neck in my hand. That song had as many runs in it as an ant colony, and my voice found every one of them. We finished with me taking a bow to the screaming crowd. From behind me, I heard the accolades from Stevie, "That was Owen Fletcher, inspiration for Shylock and my idol for life."

I found our table and Megan bawled like a newly branded calf. "Oh Owen, I feel *sooo* bad for you. All these years. That song. It was so moving, and I saw you in it as if it was a self-prophesy. You wrote that?"

"Yeah, I did." It filled me with melancholy, and I didn't want to talk about it. Megan sensed my mood and moved closer to me, squeezing my thigh. We listened to the second set as Spam jammed. During the break, Stevie flew off the stage and joined our table.

It was a good reunion apart from the fact that Megan spent too much time embracing my borderline gay buddy from the past.

"Geez, Owen, you were partying with us one day and fell off the map the next. I've been looking all over for you."

That was a lie and I knew it. I had a small ad in the yellow pages advertising my handyman business. If the zombies from the IRS could find me, so too could Stevie. I wasn't about to tell him I had been living by the septic tank of every damned trailer park in Nashville for the last ten years. "You know what it was like, Stevie. You were there when it happened. I got murdered by the politics of the music business." I felt Megan's grip tighten on my thigh.

"So, Owen, would you consider a cameo to cut 'Advice on Vice'? I'd buy it from you and pay royalties."

Short fuckin' reunion. Stevie was in the music *business.* He wanted my song, but I had to give it to Stevie; he didn't steal another artist's work. Shylock had stolen all of our songs and churned them out as if they owned them. "Forget it, Stevie. I'm not selling my music to anyone."

His shrug wasn't friendly, and he moved on to something else. "Hey, Owen, we're doing a gig over at the Wild Horse tomorrow, very informal. I'll make sure you have seats."

I noticed he wasn't talking to me or even looking at me. Megan, always up for a good time at my expense, said, "Let's do it, Owen." Then she looked at Stevie and asked, "Would you let me sing a song?" I knew Megan had a serious set of pipes. I've heard her moaning and shrieking at the top of her lungs. She certainly had a vocal range, but nothing I could put music to.

Stevie came to my aid, "Megan, there are music critics out there looking for any opportunity to see me screw up. They would make karaoke fodder out of you, and we would be laughed at for letting you do it." What did I tell you about Stevie being in the music business? I told Megan she had to be in the union and that's why I never filled in for Jackhammer.

"But you just went on stage and nobody objected. Why can't I?"

That come-back pissed me off ...royally. "Because I wrote the song, I own it, and I fucking performed it. Okay? And one more thing, it's not for sale."

Stevie wore a look of disappointment, and he asked, "Are you sure?"

"Even if you asked me six months ago, you'd have gotten the same answer. That's the only song I still own."

"Gotta get back to work. Don't be a stranger." End of not a so friendly reunion. I was mad at myself for going off like that, but seeing Stevie brought back so many memories of what could have been and the reality of what wasn't.

My next meeting with Kenny Scales went to the sewer in about two minutes. He explained he was in constant negotiation with the litigants' attorneys, racking up fees, and bickering about settlements. I paid for Kenny's dreams while he slept. Kenny assured me he would get the best settlement amounts possible. Get this; my assets were frozen except for a living expense allowance meted out by the court jurisdiction. Kenny thought that was a cool end-run, and I had ten grand to play with every month until we settled each case.

The court ordered a DNA test, and Kenny had a plan for that too. The complaint against me was filed by my wife, Bonnie, who was not exactly my ex because of a technicality. The complaint was on behalf of Carole Ann Fletcher, age nine. Kenny said that having my last name didn't matter. I wasn't so sure. He said, "Stall the results; wait the woman out. She'll run out of patience and settle for less. It could be a year or two."

I balked. "If I have a daughter, I want to know, Kenny."

"It doesn't work that way. We want to drag this one out so it's favorable to us. We're going to ask for liberal custody and everything else, whether you want it or not. It's a negotiating tool to mitigate their position. We'll even hit her with an unfit mother suit, if it comes to that."

"Have you even talked to Bonnie at all?"

"Aaaah. You mean Mrs. Fletcher. She left the climes of Nashville for her abode in Colorado."

I knew that two weeks ago.

He said, "I've been in communication with her attorney."

See what I mean? Kenny had a snippy tone about him. He rattled off the filing that was presented to him by Bonnie's attorney. Here was where my attorney scared the shit out of me, and I was supposed to be quaking in my boots. When I was sufficiently cowed, he said he found a miraculous glitch that might get me off the hook. No guarantees, of course, but if there was anyone to trust, it's him. When I swallowed it, that's when he told me just how deep I had to dig into my pockets in exchange for the rabbit he'd just pulled out of the legal hat. Always make sure to find out if the rabbit has a pulse.

Here came the rabbit. "The reason your inquiries in Colorado haven't produced results is because divorce filings must be in the resident county of the defendant, not the plaintiff. My legal assistant discovered the filing. All you had to do was sign the decree and return it to her attorney; instead, you sent it back to Mrs. Fletcher, who had time to ponder her decision."

So it was my fault? Kenny made me feel like a dumb ass and he drew on the pain of my anguish, lecturing me, "Legally, you and Mrs. Fletcher are still married," he explained. Then came the hook. "However, we will make the case that Mrs. Fletcher abandoned the marriage, and I believe I can prevail in that distinction. About your alleged daughter ..."

"What about my alleged daughter?"

"We need to confirm the exact date that Mrs. Fletcher left Tennessee for Colorado. We'll hire a private detective to find out what kind of mother she is. In the meantime we'll determine if the length of pregnancy coincides with her departure to Colorado. Was she screwing anyone in the band? I know what you musicians are like."

"Why don't we just wait on the DNA test results?"

"Mr. Fletcher, we're going to put off the test for as long as possible and dispute the DNA test should it not be in our favor."

Kenny's wry smile left the foregone conclusion that I was a dead-beat dad, and he was just the guy to pull it off. My head was throbbing, my mood was somber, and I had one of those high-dollar headaches that only rich people get. Well, I was rich, so I had it coming.

Normally, when I thought about being a father, visions of a lifetime of confinement with a perpetual three-year old screaming endlessly, sent a wave of panic through me. Fatherhood was the worst man-trap in the universe, and I had a natural fear that sent me running at the mere mention of the word "child." Actually, now that I was being accused of fathering a child, the way it was being handled was offensive to me. It was as if it was an immoral sneaky secret to be denied and hidden away. I despised the legal cauldron that Kenny was building, which could turn into a humiliating scene, tainting everyone involved. I wasn't going to do that to a child. My head was very clear on the matter. "We're doing the freakin' DNA test, Kenny, and that's my last word on that."

"Okay, but it's your loss. I'm just warning you that you're interfering with my defense."

When he said, "my defense," I lost it. "It's not your defense, Kenny." I ordered him to set up the test and stomped out of my high dollar solicitor's office...very pissed off.

CHAPTER FORTY-ONE

Megan came up with a bright idea. Her parents were Tennessee farmers who would love to meet me. I balked. When it came to parents, I was pretty transparent. Meeting the pastor usually followed meeting the parents and I wasn't quite ready to drop the hammer on that idea quite yet. I was getting there, or pretended to be. A quiet weekend in the country would do me some good. I could get away from all the media curiosity that was still in circulation.

Now that I think back on it, it was the smart thing to do. Flattered, I accepted on the condition that I would be allowed to sleep under the porch with the hounds. Megan was delighted, and I knew we were notching it up a step. A big step for Megan, since I had a tendency to fly under the bridge.

"Momma's going to love you." I could have taken that comment either way, but I wasn't crass enough to ask for a clarification.

We had a thirty mile drive down the Murfreesboro Pike. Megan gave me the low down on her parents. The Marsh family had always been farmers as far back as Megan could remember.

She warned me they were straight laced and just a tad set in their ways, like the couple in the famous painting with the guy holding the pitchfork. I was looking forward to a "Walton" weekend.

Walton Mountain, and everything within two miles, belonged to the Marshes. The Marsh farm was not a farm. It was a plantation with what looked like old, but recently occupied slave quarters. We drove by miles of fields, pastures, and forest land. Farmers my ass, the Marsh's were plantation barons. The white fence that edged the road to the main house started a mile before we even saw the house. There was enough room on the front lawn to build a championship golf course.

Megan drove my beast of a truck, and she turned into the lane beeping the horn while I gawked at the beauty of her childhood home. The mansion was an old antebellum style that had been impeccably maintained. Her parents came rushing out of the house, waving madly.

The wheels of my truck had barely stopped rotating when Megan slammed the gears to park and turned off the engine. She flew out of the truck and into her father's arms. The scene reminded me of my airport welcome home, and I involuntarily smiled. Mrs. Marsh was a duplicate copy of Megan, a gorgeous woman who had hardly aged. Mother and daughter hugged and danced. I watched with mild amusement.

Megan motioned for me to join them. I opened the truck door and slid towards Mom and Dad Marsh.

As I approached, I could see the parents go rigid in a formal dignified firing squad stance. Would the prisoner prefer a blind fold? I was nervous as hell. Megan made the presentation. "Mother, Father, I would like to introduce you to Owen Fletcher, who has been tearing up my G-spot for the past month." Let me rephrase part of that, "who I have spoken to you about."

Mrs. Marsh extended her arm like a southern debutante, with a bent wrist and fingers pointing to the ground, like it was broken. I wasn't sure whether to kiss her hand or try to straighten it out and put a splint on it. Starting out awkwardly, I touched her genteel fingers with mine. I'd watched Eddy Haskell on 'Leave It To Beaver' all my life, and I sorta knew what to say. "Geez Mrs. Cleaver, you sure look swell in tight jeans and skin tight spandex." I took the more cautious approach and said, "It is a pleasure to meet you, Mrs. Marsh."

"Thank you, Owen. It's not often we meet Megan's acquaintances from the city." She referred to me as an acquaintance? She had to know I was banging her daughter regularly and that I was acquainted with every inch of her.

My next presentation was to her father. He wasn't a big man, but by the look of him, he could split fence rails with his fingernails. I could see his farmer's tan as he extended his claw. He had that 'meet-the-boyfriend' drill down pat, and he kept cool and quiet, forcing me to speak first.

"Mr. Marsh, I'm glad to meet you." Nobody believes that lie, but I showed the respect and manners demanded by southern custom.

He had no illusions about our relationship, and I saw it in his eyes for a glint of a second, which was why the bones in my hand had been rearranged by his handshake. He suddenly brightened and said, "I'll bet you could use a stiff drink. Let's go in the house." I learned which side of the family Megan's clairvoyance came from. Jubilant Megan bounced over to me, and jumped up on my back, piggy-back style. I was shocked by the change of behavior, and I looked at both parents.

Mrs. Marsh gave a dismissive smile and said, "Megan usually rides on her daddy's back into the house when she comes for a visit. You get the honor, Mr. Fletcher."

The formalities disappeared as we trotted into the mansion. We stopped in the front parlor, which was decorated with the flair that belonged in 'Southern Living' magazine. Megan dismounted and showed me to the chair of inquisition. She trotted off to take her place with the jurors. When Mr. Marsh brought me a tumbler of sour mash whiskey, I held it in my hand because I didn't want to set it on any of the intricate hand-woven dollies that were scattered around like snowflakes.

Southern royals are genteel, congenial, courteous to a fault, and deeply suspicious of intruders. They also wield words that are brush strokes of verbal art. Mrs. Marsh could have handed me a questionnaire asking straight forward questions like; occupation; references; and religious affiliation. She started off with, "Mr. Fletcher, how do you pass the time of day in Nashville?"

The correct answer would have been, I'm a gentleman of leisure, contemplating a greater calling by housing poor, indigent unfortunates, which translated to slum lord.

Megan answered for me. "Owen was the inspiration of Shylock. He preformed for me on stage, night before last. He's a very gifted musician."

Mrs. Marsh's pencil eyebrows went upwards. "A troubadour then?" Which was another way of saying street trash.

Walt gruffed. "Shylock–never heard of them. Do they play our music? What kind of name is Shylock?"

"Dad, Shylock is a crossover band."

Walt looked at me as if Megan had said cross-dresser. "Crossed over to what?"

I said, "Mostly country, but they occasionally dip into R and B and contemporary rock." He still didn't get it, so I confused him even more by saying, "Country rock."

Mrs. Marsh was devious and asked, "Owen, would it be too much to ask for you to favor us with one of your songs?"

Megan ganged in and said, "Owen, sing Momma that ballad you sang for me."

I wasn't about to groan out the slightly bawdy 'Advice On Vice,' so I sang 'Life in Memories,' a reflective tear-jerker country loser song.

The Marshes seemed moved and appropriately clapped when I finished. Mrs. Marsh said, "Owen, that was truly inspirational. I hear that song on the radio when I'm driving the car, and so help me, it blurs my vision. It's very popular, isn't it?"

"Momma, Owen wrote it."

I was *in* ...sorta. We had yet to compare pedigrees, and Megan handled that department. My father being a real Colonel in the Army, and not some honorary Kentucky fried Colonel, automatically made me a rock solid man of virtue. I let that slide. Lawson being a "farmer," gave me humble dignity, and Ron being a lab rat scientist signified a strand of genius in my genetics. Megan was very good in the public relations department, and all I had to do was politely fill in the blanks, smile, and nod.

Mr. Marsh said, "Let's go out on the porch while Megan and Peggy fix up some supper."

We sat out in two old rockers that had been restored and made small talk. When the moment was right, Mr. Marsh laid it out for me. "I know my daughter pretty well, Owen. She's smart and a good judge of character, so you start off on a level playing field. She's excited over you, and I think you know what I have to say about that. We're glad to have you in our home, but I don't want you and her to disrespect our generosity, or at least not where Peggy might stumble onto something she shouldn't."

"Yes sir, Mr. Marsh."

"Call me Walt, and Mrs. Marsh, Peggy."

I loosened up over supper and Megan's parents entertained me with quaint stories about their children. I talked farm-talk, but nothing close to family. I could get it over in one sentence. My mother is dead and my dad will be next time I see him. I said, "Mom passed from cancer years ago and my father and I aren't close, before or after. The army interferes with a home life and there never was much of a spark from him, so it was just Mom and us."

The Marsh's exchanged glances and wisely moved on. Peggy said, "Owen, we fill out the evening after dinner, by turning on music, going out on the porch and dancing. How do you finish your evenings?"

I was polite enough not to tell her Megan and I screwed our brains out, so I settled for the next best thing. "I turn on music, close my eyes, and pretend I'm dancing on pine needles in the woods of Tennessee." I heard Megan squeak and Walt said, "That sounds like the start for a good country song, son."

Megan grabbed her father's arm and pulled him towards the porch door. "Daddy's the best dancer in all of Tennessee. Let's show him, Daddy."

Peggy placed her hand on my arm and whispered, "Walt is without a doubt the best dancer in these parts because he follows so well. Shall we?"

Walt and Peggy were some of the kindest people I'd ever met. Their love of each other was so open and honest it gave me goose bumps. Megan was open and honest in her treatment of me. She picked at me like I was a new puppy in the house. I knew she wanted more, but I think she got the same speech from her mother that I got from Walt.

I had my own guesthouse in the wing of the mansion. Relaxed and happy, sleep was hard to come by. My mind was clear of all problems for once. I was with family, her family, simple, normal, and without complications. Who lives like that? My cravings expanded beyond Megan. I was desperate to live that kind of life.

CHAPTER FORTY-TWO

Meeting the parents was one thing. Meeting the entire Marsh family tree was another. They all stopped by for breakfast. That chance coincidence didn't fool me one bit. They were all in a county fair mood and I was the prize bull they came to judge. Halfway through breakfast Walt asked, "Owen, do you ride horses?"

"I can get on them and off of them, but that's about it." Since I was a Yankee, there was no reason to expect anything other than that, but I'd grown up with horses and saw the trap coming.

"Megan, why don't you saddle up Traitor and take Owen up to Jackson Mountain after breakfast?"

"Stop it, Dad! You know Traitor is a man killer."

Peggy chided, "Walt, you've had enough fun at Owen's expense for one day."

This made me question what tomorrow would bring.

Peggy said, "Spring's a good horse, Owen. You should ride him."

"Maybe we should take the truck," I said.

Walt, still a bit proud of vanquished southern pride in his genes, lazily tossed out the challenge, "Any young man courtin' our Megan is going to have to get used to Traitor."

"Dad, stop it!"

"In that case, traitor it is," I said.

The children all had eyes as big as goose eggs, the brothers had shit eatin' possum grins, and their wives had a worried look on their faces. Now Walt had a pleasing smugness as he nodded his head. It was show time at the Marsh barn.

Everyone fell in line behind Peggy like turkeys as we headed for the horse barn. Megan was pleading, and at the same time giving me advice. "Don't even let on you're scared. Traitor will sense it and there ain't no tellin' what that jackass will do. Honey, their just playin' with you. Don't give them reason to make you a laughin' stock. They'll make it a Sunday topic for the next ten years if you let em."

"You sure went south in the mouth, Megan. I like the accent."

"You damn fool, you're playin' into their hands, and I'll be mocked all day long. Traitor is dangerous and mean as hell. I mean it."

The Marsh herd found places in the barn to observe my duel with Traitor. Girls hid in their mother's dress folds, boys found seats in the rafters, and the men leaned against the horse stalls with their feet propped up.

"Which one is Traitor?" I asked.

Pete said, "The big black at the back of the barn." He nodded into the darkness.

At first I didn't see a horse. Then I saw the whites of Traitor's eyes. I was looking at a caged panther and not a horse. I might have bitten off more than I could chew.

"You need help saddling up?" Pete asked.

"Let me see if I remember how this is done first. I might call on you if I need help."

I heard murmurs and laughs. I went into the dark stall, and there was a sonic boom as Traitor tried to take out the heavy timbered stall gate. I know something about horse sense, but not much else, so my arm went up over his neck, and my feet went off the ground. I held on for dear life as I was eye to eye with that big black stud. After a few neck tosses, Traitor showed some horse sense and let me bridle him while he thought about his next trick.

When I brought him out of the stall there was a collective sigh in the barn. The next thing was to get a saddle on him. Traitor turned and looked at me with mischievous black eyes that danced with confidence. It was sorta the same look Walt had on his face at breakfast.

About the time I was ready to throw the saddle, he'd cartwheel around and I'd chase after him and tried again. After entertaining the children for a few minutes, I'd had enough, and put all my weight into a gut check instead of tossing the saddle. "We can do this all day," I said to my panther. That horse understood English and I tossed the saddle. A roar of laughter rocked the barn. I put my hands in the air in victory. The laughing didn't die down, and I looked over my shoulder. The saddle was on the horse, but it was backwards with the saddle horn facing the ass end. I started over, and I had to listen to every last Marsh defile my horsemanship.

Walt pushed off a stall wall and inspected my job. He nodded approvingly. He said, "Folks down here ride lookin' between a couple of ears. I think you'll find it easier than lookin' at the animal's ass. The easy part is over. You ready to ride?"

Megan had to yell over the giggles. "Owen, we don't have to do this."

"You don't, but I do." I grabbed the reins and started to mount Traitor, but Walt stopped me. "We've had our fun. Take Spring."

I was dead set, and I began to mount my pony, but Walt pulled me back again. "Wait. We just repaired this roof from the last time Megan brought her beau to meet the family. Take him out into the lot. Let the kids get out of the way before you get on."

I thought he was joking, but maybe not. While I waited for act two, I had a real close conversation with the man-killer beast.

Traitor did his sidestep and bucked when I went for the stirrup. I didn't put up with it and check him smartly, then quickly went for the stirrup again. My leg was mid swing over the top when he turned and dropped his head and over I went. It wasn't a hard fall, but it was embarrassing in front of toddlers. We did this a couple of times, but I stuck saddle and Traitor blew like a scatter gun.

He was fast out the gate where he had room to gallop. We disappeared out of sight behind the barn. I won't say we hit it off right away, but we came to an understanding that I was sitting on top, and he was carrying me where I wanted to go. I rode back to the barn like I was Robert E Lee mounted on Traveler.

There were some oohs and aahs, and I saw money being exchanged, but what really got my heart to bounce was the look of pride on Megan's face. She rode up to me and parked a big kiss on me in front of toddlers and all the grownups. The show was over, and we left the lot to the sound of polite applause.

The view from Jackson Mountain awed me. I saw the valley below for miles into the distance. Low clinging fog hung along the fields and forests, making an ethereal perch for the two of us to take in. Sitting on the back of Traitor, I could feel the remoteness of the moment. I looked over at Megan and her green eyes dazzled. We were both thinking the same thing. "You know we have to, Owen."

The horses were tethered, straps flew, saddles came off, and we had horse blankets on the ground in record 'Rodeo Hall of Fame,' time. We rolled around like woodchucks in heat up there on Jackson Mountain. I had never been nuzzled by a horse during intercourse. It was irritating, but Megan took it all in stride. I thought she might have done this before.

My weekend at the Marsh farm turned out to be that 'Walton moment' I had hoped for. The enriched casual love of family was so touching and effortless, I wanted it for myself. It was another reason to crave Megan. If I had any reservations about her before, they dissolved in those two days. I'd finally surrendered my independence and she could take title of me whenever she wanted.

CHAPTER FORTY-THREE

Five days after my million dollar transfer, and one day after my wonderful weekend with the Marshes, I got the call from Joyce. She sounded distraught and wanted to meet privately. She told me to stay put in my room and she'd meet me there. I had a hunch what had happened, and I was putting together a list of questions and answers in my mind, when she knocked on the door.

The first words out of my mouth were, "Did they catch the bastard?"

She shook her head. "Owen, you need to be sitting down for this one."

My heart stopped, and I found a nearby chair. "What's the news?"

"There's been a development at Fort Benning. General Thomas, and his wife Susan, were found shot dead in their quarters on the post this morning … murder-suicide for now.

"What? The Thomases? Both of them?"

Joyce confirmed my questions with a simple head nod. "The Army let our guys in after the MPs ran over the crime scene. At the end of the day, this will end up as a double homicide. There's a lot of spin going on at the fort, and I'm glad I'm not there." I saw her looking around the room.

I said, "You want a coffee?"

"Coffee works."

I knew by then how she took her caffeine fix. She found a convenient chair with a side table next to it and flopped down. My heart pounded and I was profoundly sad. The first suspect that came to my mind was Boots. One look at Joyce, I knew she thought so too.

"The JAG on post is crawling up his own ass. He's out of a job when it goes double homicide," she said.

"Why are you so sure it's not murder-suicide?"

"Because it isn't, and you know it. You know why the Harlans were extorting the Thomases. We had to dig, but we found out your father was having an affair with Susan over a period of years. You also knew the Harlans got wind of it and purportedly there were photos. What pisses me off is if we'd had knowledge of it, we could have bowled past the JAG and solved this damn thing before we ended up with two corpses. You listening to any of this, Owen?"

I didn't know the Thomases. I had mixed feelings about their deaths. Regardless, people were dead. I couldn't deny that if my father had been an officer and a gentleman, none of this would have happened. I was making an assumption, the same one Joyce was making. "What if it was murder-suicide?"

Joyce rolled her head to the side and gave me a 'stupid you' look.

"What if General Thomas blew his cork? Things like that happen all the time. He was under a lot of pressure," I said.

Joyce's head went deeper to the side and her stupid look deepened. She shook her head derisively. "Look, Owen, Thomas laid the ground work. He's had five years to exact his revenge. Why now? What went on inside of that household to prompt Susan to murder her husband? If she knew he was on the verge of collecting a million dollars, which I'm sure she did, why kill the golden goose and then herself?"

You just said Mrs. Thomas murdered her husband so why wouldn't that be murder-suicide?"

"There is something I haven't told you, but I will now. Thomas has a solid alibi when you were ambushed at your brother's farm. It wasn't Boots. This is going to go double homicide in the next few hours and when it does, warrants will be issued for the two likely suspects."

"How do you know?"

"Depending how my conversation with you goes, I'm issuing the warrants. You can stop this, right now."

I had selfish reasons and really wanted the murderer to be Betty. I knew at the time it couldn't be, but I pushed ahead to deflect the blame away from Boots. "What if Betty discovered what was behind the threats? What if the co-conspirator is Betty's accomplice?"

Joyce sipped her coffee, thinking about that connection. I watched her face contort with different expressions, and I could tell she was dismissing the ideas as they entered her head. My deductive reasoning wasn't resonating with Joyce, and I said, "Come on. Betty has motive. I'll admit she didn't start it, but when you think about it, the plot plays right into her hands. Her accomplice murders the Thomases and Boots or Harlan takes the fall. Think about the shoot-out at the farm. She didn't get hurt, did she? In fact, that whole episode screwed with Boots' plan when she and I went into hiding."

"You're missing the entire scope of the motive factor. Betty's sitting on top of something that has accumulated over fifteen years. You told me as much. If she wanted to destroy her husband, the Thomases, or Boots, she could have at anytime in the last five years. She could end this right now. You could end this right now."

I could have. All I had to do was tell Joyce that my father was a serial rapist.

She said, "It's pretty much cut and dry. Susan Thomas was screwing Boots. Harlan had evidence and he used it to blackmail Colonel Thomas. What kind of evidence? Had to be photos. So ask yourself who took the pictures? Had to be Harlan, right? So ask yourself how did Harlan get the opportunity and access to take the shots? Follow me on this. Why would the colonel cave to extortion over the affair and then suddenly block the inquiry? Got any thoughts?"

I did, but I kept them to myself. I knew Betty had the photos in a safe deposit box.

Joyce was impatient with me and answered for me. "Maybe Colonel Thomas wasn't squeaky clean. Maybe he was doing Mrs. Harlan? Maybe she took the pictures? If that's the case, all three men have a motive to murder Mrs. Harlan. She could destroy all three men."

She was almost right, but I jumped at her assumption. "That's what I think too."

Joyce pinched her nose and shook her head. She was talking to herself as much as she was talking to me. I've been around a few double homicides, vendettas, and passion murders and none of this strikes me as hitting the bar. You know why? These types of crimes resolve themselves rather quickly. It's been five years, so this dog don't hunt in my opinion."

For once I had to agree with Joyce. Even what I knew, or thought I knew, I was baffled by the chronology of events. If Joyce was correct and someone had killed the Thomases it had to be over something more involved than a cover up of an affair five years ago.

Joyce frowned and said, "Well, we know Mrs. Harlan isn't the murderer because she's under the glass in Atlanta."

I said, "Maybe her accomplice isn't in Atlanta. Maybe he's in Georgia."

"You might be right. There is one fact we can't ignore. There are more players out there who we don't know about."

We took a break and ordered room service. Joyce needed nutrients, and I needed a sedative. I had adrenalin high and was pinging off the walls. Joyce took the opportunity to walk to the window to sightsee and make discrete phone calls. I could see her shoulders heave, even though I couldn't hear what was being said. Something was happening. I went to relieve myself, and when I came back she was waving her arms at the window. I heard some piercing swear words followed by guttural murmurs. She hung up, punched at the numbers on her phone, and the cycle started again.

I was worried. If ever I needed to call Boots, it was then. I went back to the bathroom, sat down on the toilet and dialed his number.

He answered on the first ring and was already speaking, not yelling, speaking and crying. "They killed Mike, Owen, They killed my boy. It was her. I know it." Boots was inconsolable.

"Stay where you are, Dad. Help is on the way."

"Too late for that. We were ambushed. I'm going to kill that bastard." I heard the distant crack of a rifle reverberate through our connection, and I yelled at him. There was no answer. I waited for an eternity when I heard another explosive discharge, this time louder. I heard the phone being fumbled, followed by his rasping voice. "Got the bastard."

His words were crumbling as he spoke them. The tinge of agony that followed each word made it clear that Boots had been wounded.

"Dad ….are you hit?" No answer. "Dad! Stay where you are. Help is on the way."

His answer was barely audible and was mixed with sarcasm and resolve. "Only one way…for this to end. I owe it…Owen, take care of Betty. Take good care of her."

The connection drifted into static and then nothing. I was stunned and scared. What had I just heard? The phone picked up a distant voice and the words were ones I had often repeated when I was a kid. It was the "Act of Contrition," the prayer said prior to confession. I screamed at the top of my lungs, "Dad. Don't!" I heard the sharp report of a rifle coming out of the receiver just as Joyce ran into the bathroom.

"Owen, we know where your father is. Tell him to hold on. We're on the way."

"It's too late." I numbly said. "It's too fucking late." I threw the phone as hard as I could, and it shattered the glass stall of the shower.

"We'll find him, Owen. I promise."

"He won't be there. He'll be gone, his way."

Joyce did her best to talk me down and give me reassurance. She made me a drink from the bar. I wasn't listening to a single word she said. I slammed back the drink and immediately tossed it back up along with everything inside of me. With my head between my knees, I wanted to cry, but no matter how hard I tried, tears wouldn't come.

Joyce rubbed my shoulders and chirped over and over, "Everything will work out," Her phone rang and she stopped rubbing. Suddenly, her fingers bit into my tendons. She didn't have to say a word. She went to her knees, put her arms around me, and pulled my head to her shoulder. "I'm sorry, Owen," she whispered.

There was an empty hole in my heart that had already been filled. What had been tenuous was final. I would never know my father, and that's what finally brought tears to my eyes. My friend Joyce gave me a kiss on the forehead and left me to my grief. I was left with thoughts of my father, the ones I dreamed about as a little boy, and the ones I had recently come to know the truth about. The paradox of the man that my mother painted as a fantasy and the illusive shadow that had crept across my life with a sip of fatherhood ... was dead.

I walked out of the hotel. As I roamed the streets of Nashville, I could only ask if I was my father's son. His last words to me were to take care of Betty. He didn't say I love you son, or even say goodbye, just take care of Betty. I felt miniscule, cheated, and outraged. I wanted more, deserved more. Boots had dashed through life so quickly; I barely got a glimpse of him, like a shadow in fast moving traffic.

It was raining, and I put my face skyward, as if the splashes would act as a catalyst to bring out bitter tears. I'd had my brief cry back at the hotel. All my fond memories of him would get me around the block, but I walked miles as my other memories trumped what was there. I walked and walked, talking in my own head, planning the next day, the day after that, and the one following. Each day counted. I reached December 31st by the time I found the hotel.

CHAPTER FORTY-FOUR

Boots' battlefields were his legends, and the Army let us know that during the funeral. From the first Gulf War to the siege of Tora Bora in Afghanistan, Boots Fletcher left a legacy. As a field commander in the Unites States Army, Colonel Boots Fletcher was one of the best, as attested to by the men who had followed him in combat and to his funeral. The chapel filled to over capacity and soldiers stood silently on the lawn. I noticed that aside from being a somber occasion, it wasn't particularly mournful.

Meagan had been by my side every minute for the last three days. She did all the crying for me, especially when Lawson spit in my face at the funeral home. He held me responsible for the massacre at Fort Benning. As far as he was concerned, I might as well have pulled the trigger when I dialed the FBI. He was quick to find blame in all the wrong places. He rejected the notion that Boots would take his own life, certain that the gloss put out by the government was a government cover up. Since I was in cahoots with the FBI, Boots' death was entirely my burden to carry around for life. It was pointless to offer up the truth because the truth bore down on my shoulders. Anyway, what part of the truth did I actually know? At the time, it didn't matter. I had opened the family bible, put the date next to mom's and slammed the cover closed.

I could understand Lawson's point of view because the entire massacre was laid to blame on the accomplice, who had been wounded by Boots' shot. He'd slipped off after killing an FBI agent responding to the shooting. He was still at large. The suspect's identity wasn't known, and it was presumed he was a soldier who had served under the three dead soldiers. Nothing was mentioned about Boots' suicide or the history between the victims. Our father's death was exactly what it looked like…a sham and a cover-up.

Ron and Lawson deliberately sat on the other side of the church. I knew things that they didn't. I allowed them to blame me for Boots' death, grieve the loss of their father, and I'd endured their enmity in silence. It was just as well because Lawson was holding Betty's arm. The woman had the audacity to show up to Boots' funeral. I couldn't look across the church. I churned with anger through the ceremony. The service at the chapel was brief because there were other services behind ours.

Boots was laid to rest at the soldiers' cemetery at Fort Benning. There were over 6,000 soldiers interned there, and it was likely the only place on the planet where his ghost would be among friends. There was a second grave site being prepared in another section of the cemetery. I instinctively knew whom it was for, as Megan and I drove past it. Owen and Ron would never know that two family members were being laid to rest, in the same place, on the same day.

At the graveside service, there was ...Betty, dressed in black dress, black hat and veil, with large sunglasses covering a tear stained face. She was sitting in the front row with Lawson and

Ron. We were forced to sit together. It's odd what the mind will come up with on short notice. As the honor guard fired shots into the air over Boots' grave, I thought, had he not killed himself, they would have been firing their shots into him. Twenty-one shots were fired at the grave site, and not one hit Betty. We all stood while "Taps" was played. Betty fainted and fell to the ground. Megan saw it and immediately went to her. I just stood there, hoping she'd been hit by a stray bullet. Megan struggled to help Betty to her feet, and a couple of soldiers helped her to her seat where she could recover. When Megan returned, she had a question mark on her face.

"Do you know her?"

"Yes, that's Betty."

"Your dad's girlfriend?"

I bobbed my head.

Megan's expression begged an explanation, and I'd get grilled later. "She's so stunning, Owen. I never imagined her being so beautiful."

Neither had I. I was angry for her being at my father's funeral, but of anyone present, she knew him best. My involvement with her haunted my conscience. In a way, it was my funeral, and all the souls were heckling me to leave hallowed ground. When the graveside service was concluded, I took one final look at my brothers and saw hatred simmering behind tearful eyes. I took Megan by the hand, and we walked away in a sad stroll through the grave markers, knowing my family was dead to me, and I to them.

Megan and I sat in our rental car as the immediate family stoically met the mourners and paid their last respects to Colonel Lawson Fletcher. Megan held back as long as she could, but she couldn't tolerate my distant behavior any longer. "Owen, for God's sake, will you please show some respect and compassion. It's your flesh and blood. Don't do this to your brothers."

Lawson and Ron didn't know that the woman they were fawning over was Boots' mistress while our mother battled cancer alone. As much as I would've liked to expose her, I would've tarnished Boots' well-prepared legend. Rather than say something revealing to Megan, I started the car and backed out of the line of vehicles parked along the lane of fallen soldiers. The tears that streamed down my face weren't for Boots. They were for my brothers, all three of them.

CHAPTER FORTY-FIVE

Megan and I stopped off at Walt and Peggy's on our way back. It was awkward. As hard as the Marshes tried to console me, my conscience couldn't be soothed. My soul was in a distant place, and Walt got the read of that. When we were alone, he took me to the side of the house. Traitor was saddled and hitched to a down spout.

Walt said, "Traitor's a good listener. Stay gone as long as need be." He gave me a hug, patted my shoulder, and walked away.

Traitor was just a high-spirited horse, and I didn't expect an animal to have a sense of my mood. The snap in his step was missing and his gait was forced. It was as though the added weight of my troubled mind was as much as he could carry. He knew where we were going, and I didn't have to touch a rein. When I dismounted up on Jackson Mountain, his legs folded under him, and he lay close to me. I put my arm around the shiny jet black hairs in his mane. I began to talk, and damned if he didn't listen. I swear to God he did. When I was all talked out, he took me back to the house.

We stayed for supper and were invited to stay over, but I had important things to do the following day in Nashville. It was as good of an excuse as any. Walt and Peggy's sincerity made me feel the absence of mine. I was eager to be on my way and they sensed it, so it was a quick departure. I was to the end of the lane wishing I could turn around and spend the rest of my days at Walt and Peggy's farm.

Megan and I sorta argued on the dark drive to the city. She couldn't leave it alone and trumpeted Boots' legacy. I knew what she was trying to do. She was reading a lot of presumed history into my dicked-up childhood.

She said, "Owen, your father was a career soldier, and that's a hard life for any woman to follow. It's even harder to raise children in that kind of environment. They did the right thing by giving you a stable environment away from the constant upheavals of a military life."

"Millions of military wives manage it, and that's a cheap excuse," I said.

"I'm just saying your parents made a sacrifice for their children. They had a strong marriage. They were married, what, twenty years? That says a lot about their love doesn't it?"

My mother was a devout Catholic, so divorce wasn't an option. Running a farm kept our heads above water, and it was a struggle for her. Boots provided adequately in name only, and our family reunions were a series of theatrics. Mother would make a fuss with preparations for Boots' arrival, and for weeks before, we'd be coached how to act, and what to say. It was a forced show of adoration over a man who was a stranger to us. The visits were always disappointing. They were, more or less, inspection tours.

"Megan, you weren't there, and neither was my father. At mom's funeral, he was antsy the whole time. He had a war that he just couldn't wait to get back to."

"All I'm saying is don't let this come between you and your brothers. It wasn't your fault."

"Yes it was and you know it. We should have gone to the FBI right from the beginning."

"Honey, what happened was driven by your father. He died trying to protect his honor."

"He died because he lost his honor a long time ago."

"You don't know what you're saying. Please, let it rest."

She accused me of holding back and suggested that I should stay over at her place. I was more than holding back. I was painting the canvass of my life black, but the paint kept sliding off. She didn't need to see any part of that exposed canvas.

My voice was belligerent when I said, "Drop me at the hotel. I'll call you, okay?"

She was stung by it, and she remained quiet the rest of the way into town. I think when I kissed her, I left the tension suspended, and I'm sure she was crying when she drove off. I went straight to the Oak Bar and sipped my way to oblivion.

The following morning I was up early and CNN was spouting the official version of another angry GI slipping through the crack to do what he was trained to do: kill all enemies, foreign and domestic...and some personal. I saw clips of the Thomases double burial, followed by a shot of the guns blazing over Boots' bier, and another of Harlan's pitiful funeral. The cameras weren't focused on me, but there I was in the background, trudging through grave markers. I pushed the off button fifteen times more than necessary and slammed the remote on the nightstand. I spent the next two days in lethargic fog.

A couple of mornings later I was ritually doing my thing with the TV remote, when the phone rang. It was Jerry at the bank. I looked at my watch, and it wasn't even close to bankers' hours. Jerry's only acquaintance with a rising sun was when he partied late on Saturdays, and it was only Wednesday. I tentatively put the phone to my ear to hear Jerry sputtering.

"Owen, you need to get down here, boy. Something is terribly wrong with that divorce settlement."

How could a million dollars here or there slip my mind? Hell if I know, but it did and I didn't really care. "The Feds have a tarp over it. Let them handle it."

"That's why I called you before I called Joyce. Did you do anything to alter the wire instructions? I mean anything at all?"

"No. Hell no! What happened, Jerry?"

"It blew up, dude, it's like freakin' confetti at a Super Bowl victory parade. It's gone and the international auditors haven't a clue where it went. You're sure you didn't mess with it?"

"What did I just tell you? No!"

"Get your ass down here …pronto. I'm calling Joyce. Go to the service door off Pine Street. I'll let security know you're on the way."

I looked out the window to the street level. I saw two local news vans parked further down the narrow street. "There's a lot of media downstairs. You'd think Charlie Manson was showing up for an arraignment."

"Let me think, Owen."

It dawned on me. The four people who might have been in line at the cashier's window were dead. I let the silence whisper a name in my ear …Betty.

Jerry was back. "You there, Owen?"

"I know who did it."

"No, you don't. Listen up. Haul your ass down to the mezzanine level and go all the way to the back. There's a door that leads to a stairwell that will take you down to street level behind the stage in the main ballroom. Cross the ballroom to the emergency exit. I'll be waiting outside. You got that?"

"Jerry, it was Betty, it had to be."

"Whatever you say, Owen. Now move your ass."

Joyce looked horrible. Her face and neck had broken out in red splotches, and her eyes had a 'hundred yard stare' quality about them. Her nose was red and swollen from either drinking too much or blowing it too often, probably both. She'd had a rough time of it. I wanted to hug her, but she pushed off in a dignified manner, nodded curtly, and flicked a professional smile that was as empty as her heart. She sighed and addressed Jerry. "We're aware of what happened. May I sit down?"

He couldn't hide his disgust. She had no make-up on and looked like she was just coming around from an all-night bender. Jerry didn't look much better. Without any particular guidance, the three of us pulled up chairs as though we were in for the long haul.

Jerry, always the master of ceremonies, said, "The bank president and the IT director asked to sit in on this meeting." He looked pointedly at me, and said, "Owen, I've called your attorney, and he's advised me to tell you not to say anything until he gets here."

I said, with a tinge of aggravation, "We all know what happened and who did it. Somebody screwed up, but that's not the issue." I looked at Joyce. "I assume you have a warrant for Betty's arrest." I shrugged my shoulders. "Case solved."

Joyce said, "It's not that simple. Fox has her sequestered. He's in our Atlanta office, and I have to ask you why is he in Atlanta?"

"He's looking for another job for all I know. Firing that bastard is on my 'to-do' list today."

"Whoa up there, Owen," Jerry said. "It's more complicated than that. The million dollars is a loan from this bank, which is insured, and the condition of insurance requires you to have a personal protection service engaged. You can't fire Fox—yet, besides, the problem is bigger than we thought."

"Are you telling me the money; which is mine in the first place; which I've borrowed back from the bank; which I'm paying interest out the ass on; which I had to take out life insurance to get; which is now missing because the company I hired to prevent that from happening fucked up—and I can't fire them? Really, Jerry? Where were they this morning when I needed to get out of the hotel?" I asked.

Jerry had the answer. "Two Fox clowns are drinking coffee downstairs, so they're a least aware that we gave them the slip this morning. That's a minor fuck up, but what I want to know from you, Agent Houseman, is how the FBI let a million bucks slide south. Who fucked that up?"

"Mr. Davis—"

"Jerry," He corrected.

"Jerry, we couldn't freeze the account without tipping off the perpetrators. We needed actionable cause of a crime being committed; therefore, there were no safeguards to prevent the transfer going through. We could however, tag the transfer and intercept it at the point of deposit. We're working on that."

Jerry slapped his desk with the flat of his hand. "We can save you the trouble. Your tagged wire transfer went to a bank in the Caymans, and the Cayman bank authorities have seized it, according to international banking statutes. They have a grand total of $2,200, just under the amount necessary to bring racketeering charges. Congratulations! The remaining $997,800 went into cyber safe havens all over the Gulf of Mexico."

I sat on the edge of my chair. "Who was the account holder in the Caymans?" I asked.

Jerry sneered. "We don't know. Ask Agatha Christie here."

"Do you have to ask?" Joyce said. "Elizabeth Harlan is the registered holder."

"I knew it!" I looked at both of them. I saw dismissive frowns as they exchanged glances. A cloud of doubt permeated the air.

What had I missed? It was obvious who triggered the transfer and why.

When the bank manager and the IT director arrived, I found out what I missed, and it was a lot more than a million dollars. Computer logic gates swing both ways and my central account had been hack. Everything that wasn't nailed down was loose change to the tune of five million and counting and all of it went into the cosmos.

Jerry and the IT guy were fired on the spot. There would be a lengthy audit and an investigation. He'd never be allowed to handle money for the rest of his life, assuming he'd be let out on good behavior. Now he knew how I felt when I lost my place in the music business. Security had him out the door before I could say goodbye.

Losing a good friend was worse than loosing the money. I said as much to Joyce, but she advised me to let it go. The bank didn't have a choice in the matter because if they didn't cooperate, the FBI would conduct their own investigation. There was a masked warning in her delivery and with it an accusation. It was my fault.

So there I was under the naked light bulb staring into angry faces chirping questions faster than an auctioneer. Megan showed up with Kenny Scales and I can't say that went well. Scales taped my mouth closed by over-talking me and I lost another friend. Joyce just sorta fogged over. She gathered her things, handed me a business card and whispered. "Don't make this cost you anymore than it already has." Her looked said it all: contempt and pity, both at the same time. She took her skinny frame out the door and now I had a hostile FBI chick gunning for me.

Kenny Scales buttoned everything up with legal jabber and I'm sure I heard "lawsuit" come out of his mouth more than once. Megan was acting like someone had stolen her money and she was just a tad too enthusiastic in her deference to poor ole Owen who got ripped off by his bank.

I did my usual, excused myself to take a piss, and head for the door.

Back in my hotel room I moved all the pieces on the situation board. I cleared the situation table and sent it under the bridge with all of Boots' sins. My only regret was that Lawson was right—almost. The unintended consequence of winning the lottery and my abrupt decision to visit my estranged father was the catalyst that eventually killed him. I neatly wrapped and locked that part of my life away. That's what the old Owen would do, and I needed some of him back.

CHAPTER FORTY-SIX

In spite of all of my troubles, I was getting my personal life together and humming along. Megan and I put it all behind us and we were attached at the hip. We didn't cohabitate mainly because of her parents, but I was a public figure since I was the latest instant red-neck millionaire and the son of the man murdered in the media sensation of the summer's reality news. Megan had completely taken over my life, and I was surprised that I was thankful—no—that's not even close. I was exhilarated beyond comprehension. She ran interference for me and handled the daily minutia that I regularly ignored or put off. She'd even talked to Kenny Scales and my banker buddy, Jerry, when it was my intention to avoid them. She had my social calendar under control and paid all my bills and parking tickets that I still seemed to accumulate. I was on easy street and enjoying every minute of it. She was like an obsessive pet owner, and I was the two-hundred pound pedigree Great Dane dropping turds in the park whenever I felt like it.

I spent a lot of time commuting back and forth to the Marsh homestead. I needed the exercise, needed to use my hands, work up a sweat, and I needed to get my arms around that big black man-killer's neck. I'd bunk up in the guest house after a hard day's work getting in the June cutting, but often as not, you could find me racked out in the barn so I could be close to Traitor. That horse loved me and I loved him. I'd be off raking furrows, and Traitor would show up on his own, stand at the end of the field, and watch me all day long.

I was careful not to overstay my welcome. Walt and Jenny treated me better than the boys, but still, I wasn't family. It was good therapy, good for my body and spirit. I was getting buff, which Megan noticed. I'd spend three days being a farm day-worker and four playing tycoon in Nashville. There's only so much tycooning to be done, and I was starting to look for a gentleman's farm to retire to.

Megan fashioned a social circle that I didn't fit into because I knew some of them *before* I had money. The music crowd was a closed community, and having money didn't get you a seat at the table. Stevie Sievers managed to open a few doors for us. We went to the parties. I won't say that I didn't have a good time because I did. I just couldn't see myself in twenty years, sporting a face lift, a silver wig, wearing skintight blue jeans with rhinestone studs on my ass, partying with the same people as though we'd just met. Now Megan was a different story. This was her dream world, and it should have been mine.

We rubbed up against some really nice people. We attended a pig roast given by my old boss. Stevie was there with his rent-a-bimbo hanging off his arm and steered Megan away to meet music tarts milling around with clown masks. I was glad to escape the superficial conversations that all started and ended with non-stop ass kissing. I went to the bar where I could always find a tumbler of good local hooch. I heard a sappy voice that grated on me like number nine sand paper. It had to be Kenny Scales.

"I see Sievers is making the rounds with Miss Marsh on his arm. I swear to gawd that boy squats to pee. I also see you're getting out, at least as far as the liquor stash."

I didn't even have to look. It was Mr. Smooth Talker, Kenny Scales. I said, "Who let your kind in here. Ha Ha." But not Ha Ha.

He tipped his glass at me and said, "When my clients are out singing about lawmen, I'm the other lawman, making sure their interests are protected."

I tipped back. "My friends wear snake skins as hat bands and boots. Watch yourself, Kenny; snakes are an endangered species around here."

He laughed. "Country singers aren't Harvard grads. What is it that they say about a fool and his money? I'm welcome because I make sure they don't get skinned."

"Yeah, I can see you working both sides of that equation."

"Good to see you out and about, Owen. You need to make an appointment. We have things to discuss."

If I said another word I'd be billed for it, so I nodded and moved on to find Megan.

She was deep in conversation and had captured the attention of a small audience. I stopped short when I heard the tail end of a woeful tale coming out of her mouth. She was giving a very skewed version of the Fort Benning Massacre to an enthralled audience. There was a country song in the making as she lionized the legacy of Colonel Boots Fletcher. The clutter of partiers all looked past her and their faces drained when they saw me.

She was caught unawares and spun around. She recovered quickly and was quick to jump my bones. "Honey, are you okay? We were just talking about…the tragedy."

I had to shake that one off. Megan was playing drama queen at my expense, and it seemed to be working for her. I simply walked off.

I heard her whisper, "Poor man, he puts on a good face, but it's hard for me to watch what he goes through."

Maybe that's how she saw it, but I saw something else. Our invites to parties were in part due to the notoriety by being close to the top headline on all the talk TV bullshit around the unsolved crime of the summer. I stopped going to parties and she went by herself.

The investigation churned like butter on a hot day and Megan suggested that I take matters into my own hands. I visited my bank and had a sit down with the bank president. I reminded him, "Jerry did you a favor. Whether you like it our not, he took most of my winnings out of your bank and put it into third party hands. If I'd had it my way, you would have lost it all. How much of the loss did your insurance cover?"

"Mr. Fletcher, I hate to say this but the FDIC doesn't cover that much of the net loss—

"I'm not talking about my insurance. I'm talking about yours and the negligence cap coverage. You do have negligence insurance, right?"

"Well Ah."

"Well, there you go. Hire Jerry back and we'll forego the lawsuit."

He stammered. "I don't think I can."

"Sure you can because you were looking over Jerry's shoulder and you could be that guy, *the* guy that had my account number, my password, Jerry's password and *please* don't even tell me this wasn't an inside job. We'll just keep this between us."

I was guessing, but that joker didn't know and it showed. "There's the investigation and we must—

"You can knock that shit off. If Jerry isn't my account manager by the end of the day, I'll close it and mumble a few words to my FBI pal. Did I tell you we're on speaking terms again?"

Yes, it was all bullshit, and no, he didn't have anything to do with it, but perception is everything in the highly competitive business of finance. His insurer had to eat the loss and it was nothing off his back. So Jerry was reinstated, but put on paid leave until the investigation was completed.

My next stop was a visit to Miss Houseman of the FBI. I did a walk-in. Her big brown eyes popped open and her mouth twisted into a wry grin. She quickly got over it and motioned for me to take a seat. I grabbed every pencil on her desk before sitting down.

She laughed. "I take it Scales doesn't know you're here. Let me just warn you; everything you say is admissible."

I was not without motive. I wanted to make sure that Betty would get her justice. "I want to know where you are with the investigation," I said, as if I was entitled to an explanation.

"Alvin Fox has a legal blanket over Miss Stiles, so she's *not* helping us out."

"She did it, so what would you expect."

She sat back in her chair, scrutinized my attitude and said, "We'll get to that in a minute. I'm hoping you'll confirm or deny a few questions."

I said, "There's a limit and I'll let you know when you're crossing the line."

"Fair enough. What was she holding over your father that would drive him to suicide?"

"You're crossing the line."

She blinked a couple of times, so I said, "It had to do with his reputation, honor, and his legacy. It's her side of the story and I won't repeat it. Out with it, Joyce."

"Have you told Megan about your tryst with Betty?" Her undertaker smile was absolutely evil.

"Fuck no. Do you think I'm completely insane?"

"Megan hates me, doesn't she?"

"Joyce, you're a cop. Everybody hates you."

"You don't."

"How do you know that I don't?"

"I just do, and I did you a big favor."

"Did I ask you for favors?"

"For no other reason than I like you, I put a gag order and an injunction out to prevent the investigation from becoming a freakin' scandal series on the summer daytime news dramas."

"What do you want, Joyce?"

"Tell me about Roxanne Thomas."

"I don't know Roxanne Thomas. Who is she?"

She placed a picture of a young woman in front of me to examine. The photo wasn't a DMV photo, but rather a mug shot. The girl was horribly emaciated. I asked, "The Thomases' daughter?"

Joyce nodded. "She's gone from one rehab center to the next, and her brain is completely fried. She's a vegetable in a wheelchair or so we thought. She's missing, Owen."

"Why would she be in a wheelchair?"

Joyce sighed. "The institution she resided in states she was violent and vicious. She had to be forcibly restrained and medicated to the point of immobility. It's a cover for institutional abuse, but that's not the point."

"How hard is it to find a kid in a wheel chair?"

"I'll get to that. Let's just say that the Thomas' fabricated a reasonable explanation why they were estranged from their daughter. She's an exotic dancer, junkie, and prostitute. You don't see many acts with wheelchairs as stage props."

She passed another photo for me to examine. Roxanne had been a pretty girl. I could tell that. No amount of air brushing could hide the premature hard edges on her promotional flyer. Under dark mascara, the eyes of a seriously troubled woman glared hatred back at me. "Should I know her?"

"Are you going to tell me about her or not?"

Hedging, I said, "Why would I know anything about Thomas' daughter?"

"Oh, you do, alright. If you don't, your hired gun, Alvin Fox, definitely does. She disappeared." She snapped her fingers and blew into them. "Poof, thin air."

"I'm under the assumption she was a troubled teen who had been institutionalized."

"People get well, believe it or not." Joyce flipped a photo on the table and stabbed it with her finger. "That's Roxanne Thomas today …well, six months ago."

I shrugged my shoulders as if it didn't matter and frankly it didn't.

She said, "That's strange. What did Betty tell you?"

"Nothing. This is the first time I'm hearing of it. Why would she tell you anything? Why would she bring up a damned thing about the Thomas family?"

You're lying to me. Help me out, Owen. The girl might be in danger."

Joyce finally tripped me up. I truly didn't know a thing about the Thomases' daughter.

"Did you know Roxanne had an abortion about the same time that Thomas dropped the extortion investigation. She was institutionalized in upstate New York shortly after."

This was all news to me. I shrugged and said, "Joyce, I don't know anymore than what I'm telling you. Why don't you check with Alvin? Didn't you say he was snooping into her background?"

"Your thug-in-a-rug isn't telling us anything either. What has he told you?"

"Why would he tell me anything?"

"According to him you hired him to check up on Roxanne Thomas."

"What? That's a lie."

"If you have any idea what has happened to that girl, I'd better hear from you right this very minute or you'll be charged with being an accessory to any foul play that might come her way and I think there's a pretty good chance that we're walking down that alley as we speak."

It clicked. Dad's last few words hit me. "The bitch got by with it once before. She's had years to plan this." He wasn't talking about Betty. He was talking about Roxanne Thomas. Boots had an affair with Susan Thomas. I recalled my last conversation with Betty and if any of it was true, Boots was also raping the daughter. Roxanne took advantage of the situation, took the photos and conspired with Harlan to extort money from her parents. That also explained why the investigation dead ended. The whole nightmare must have sent Roxanne over the edge and to the dregs of a runaway child preyed upon. She became a predator herself.

It was clear in an instance. Roxanne had no trouble getting into the family home and she killed both parents, then set about to kill the man who sent her to hell. My father.

How would Roxanne know about the extortion plot? How would she know about Harlan's involvement when he didn't? Of course! Betty and she had a common history with all three men. Betty was just one of her accomplices.

I said, "Roxanne and her accomplice killed all of them. Make no mistake about it, and make no mistake Betty Harlan was deeply involved." I was very circumspect how I doled out Betty's incentive to join the conspiracy. I left out Betty's longstanding history of abuse by two of the victims.

CHAPTER FORTY-SEVEN

After my terse meeting with Joyce, I had miserable moments grasping the consequences of Boots' debauchery. I lapsed into periods of stone cold bewilderment. My involvement in it sickened me. Two weeks went by and I was tiring of the cool 'interviews' I had with Agent Houseman. She, like me, was sure that Roxanne's killing spree was connected to the money trail. For the umpteenth time, I put forward the theory that Betty stood to gain the most and she just happened to be in all the places that five million bucks drifted downstream. Simple. Arrest the bitch.

It infuriated me that Joyce was soft on Betty's alibi. She asked, "How is Betty connected to Roxanne? Better yet, how is Betty connected with the Thomases? The logic of any of it doesn't conform to the time line." Her facial expressions compressed into a hallow mask that was frightening. "Roxanne's history mirrors a normal seventeen year old girl, but there is a persistent undercurrent that there were problems in the household. Then she snapped around the same time the Thomases quit their cooperation in the extortion case against Harlan. This departure also coincided with the date of her abortion. Are you following this, Owen?"

Obviously she had read something from my reaction. I made a pretense of ignorance.

She smirked and said, "Roxanne's motive to murder was revenge and it didn't solely extend to her parents. We have no way to determine the paternity of her unborn child, but you connect the dots. By deduction, Mike Harlan had impregnated Roxanne, which put him on her kill list. How your father got there is purely speculative at this time."

I didn't dare take a breath. I knew better. Joyce was very close to the truth so I steered her in another direction. "What did Betty say about your theory?"

Her eyes narrowed and she stalled, waiting for me to reveal more. I didn't and I waited. She rolled her eyes which told me the "good cop" had left the room. A knot formed in my stomach. I bluffed past her and said the obvious. "Boots was having an affair with Mrs. Thomas."

Joyce chuckled. "Mrs. Thomas was screwing half of her husband's staff. That reasoning won't fly, Owen. You tell me Roxanne's motive to murder your father."

The persistent banging of the truth in my head hurt. At that moment it was clear that whether I liked it or not, I needed to talk to Betty…soon.

Days flew by and eventually I made accommodation with a bad chapter. Megan was writing me a new chapter. She knew me well enough to bring me out of my funk. Let the chips lie where they fell, I had a bright future ahead of me and I just needed to make it so.

I met Megan and Jerry for lunch at a shopping center outdoor restaurant where the patrons could inhale the sweet mix of fresh air mixed with automotive pollutants.

They arrived together and I said to Jerry, "If it isn't my very best pal, Benedict Arnold," I said.

"First off, you're not my best pal. Second, you were asking your best pal to stick his neck out for you by committing a felony. And third, your chipmunk pal, Alvin, doesn't know shit, and I don't trust him to have your back."

"Don't you think you should have called me before you turned informer? Joyce was on my ass like stink on shit this morning. You could have given me a heads up. I know she questioned you again."

Jerry shrugged his shoulders. "So? We talked and not about you. You should fire the chipmunks, and while you're at it, fire Kenny Scales. He screwed you royally at another hearing the other day."

I said, "You screwed me royally the other day when you had your financial advisor conference with the feds."

Jerry didn't know about my conference with the bank president. As I suspected his boss put him as the front guy to respond to FBI inquiries.

I said, "You know, Agent Houseman needs to get out. I really think she's got the hots for me. Megan, help me out here. Don't you know of some compatible scarecrow down on the farm to take the heat off me?"

She didn't like Joyce and said, "She'd scare the scarecrows. Do you really think it would be a good idea to fire Fox?"

Jerry looked at Megan, then me. "I hate to bring this up, Megan, but why did you bring Fox in?"

The question took her completely by surprise. She flinched, then stalled for an answer. We both looked at her in anticipation, and she said, "Five state lotteries use Fox Securities when issues come up. They have a good track record."

Jerry said, "Megan, has it ever occurred to you that the reason issues come up is because Fox securities is involved?" He leaned in a little closer as if he was going to tell us who shot Kennedy. "Here's what I'm getting at my end. You *do* know that you're footing the bill for Betty's attorney, right? I talk to the scum bag from time to time and he has his hand over Betty's mouth. I know this, he's tight with Scales and what's common about that? Yeah, figure it out, Alvin Fox."

Megan said, "That's not so uncommon is it?"

Jerry said, "Shut up Megan. I've been snooping and one thing is barking at me. The kind of attack done on us was very technical, skilled, and expensive. It's well beyond Betty's comprehension and you have to know someone who really knows a *someone* who works in the dark. Owen, you tell me why it has to be Betty and not Fox?"

"It's obvious, Jerry. The Feds have traced the paper trail to every stop on the cruise." I shrugged my shoulders.

"Did it ever occur to you that Fox had his goof ball gangster tagging along for a reason? He could have had the moxie to open those accounts. Before you even start on me, it's illegal to misrepresent account holders, but in that part of the world you can open an account in a zoo animal's name. Owen, you would know if Betty got off the boat, right?"

He scared me with his insight, not because he was coming close to solving the mystery, because he was coming close to exposing what I was doing with Betty when we were in port. I said, "I slept in a lot. Maybe they went together."

Jerry twisted a brow. "Maybe. Follow me on this. Whoever set this in motion knew there'd be a tripwire so it's damned clever to send Betty down the rabbit path first and then deadfall the account after she cleared all the gates. I'm saying Fox is the guy who stole your money."

Megan's eyes widened and her hand went to her mouth. "Oh my God! What have I done?"

Jerry continued, looking distinctly smug. "Fox knew the setup from top to bottom. He had to know what I know, yet he let it happen. Correct that— made it happen."

"I need to fire the bastard."

"You'd better check with Joyce first. She might have a bigger picture than the rest of us." He looked beyond our table and straightened up. "Okay, here comes the waiter. Let's have lunch."

I felt uneasy and saw the making of unintentional entrapment. I stood up and said, "Jerry can you make sure Megan gets back to work."

"Oh, just sit down. I'm pretty sure Joyce has her finger on that pulse."

That was the problem and I needed to do damage control before it got out of hand.

I took Joyce to a late lunch. Actually we made it bar snacks and cocktails at the Oak Bar. She wanted to know where I was getting my information and I told her.

She said, "I really like Jerry. He needs to stop playing Sherlock Holmes. He could end up getting hurt. I haven't bothered to bring you up to speed to avoid putting Fox on the scent. We've been on to him for a long time and we're hoping to trip him up. We also think he had inside help at the bank. Owen, it's coming together, but it's a slow process."

"Do you really think we're in any danger?"

"Are you kidding? We found Roxanne Thomas in Denver. She's OD and DOA. Roxanne was a Jane Doe for a couple weeks before we found her. To answer your question, she had enough shit in her to kill several people. Where did she get the money to buy that much heroine? Yes, someone is attempting to drop a lid on this and the bodies just keep stacking up."

I was shocked. "What should I do?"

She sighed. "With you being suspicious he's going to know you've got bad breath. You'll reek, so we need to find a way to put distance between you. Damned if that doesn't screw everything up, just when we finally got a wire tap warrant." She shook her head in disgust. "Fire the bastard and let's see what he does."

"What excuse am I going to use?"

"Let us script it. You going to the farm this week?"

"Yeah, but there's something I need to do before I go."

"Check in with me before you go. You've just earned yourself a protection detail, courtesy of the FBI.

CHAPTER FORTY-EIGHT

My physical therapist arrived right on time as she always did after getting off work. After a particularly vigorous workout, we both had the munchies and decided to return where we had left off at lunch. It was a short walk to Friday's and the waiter showed us to the same table.

Megan was overly worked up about the debacle with Alvin Fox and her part in bringing him onboard. I relieved her angst when I told her Joyce was working on a script to fire the bastard.

She was worried by something else. "Look, Owen, you should not meet with her without having a witness present. I'm a woman and I know her interest in you isn't strictly professional. She's a whore."

"If she's a hooker, then it's professional. Megan, I like Joyce. Her life is the FBI and her every waking hour is professional. The woman never takes a vacation, takes a weekend off, or for that matter, doesn't even own a cat for company. I feel sorry for her, so leave it be."

"She's way below your class and you're not doing her any favors humoring her lonely existence."

I could remind her that it wasn't that long ago that I shared that existence with Joyce and she was *way* above my class. I avoided the nagging lecture about female intruders nibbling for my attention by saying. "You have nothing to worry about."

Never, ever, say something that stupid. It is a precursor to draw out the specifics of your commitment to the relationship and more importantly, it's a platform to challenge you to prove it. The whole jabbering about Joyce was a mechanism to put me at a tipping point.

Since I was reckless, spontaneous, and a moron, I wanted to test the water. "Megan, when this horrific fiasco is over, I want to plan a future, put solid ground under our feet and map out a life together. I'm desperately in love with you."

Megan was quaking. She reached for my hands, and her tremors traveled up my arm to my heart. "Owen, why don't you just come out and ask me to marry you? You know I'll say yes."

See what I'm saying? Did I mention I was testing the waters?

"Why don't you just ask the right question? Come on, Owen."

My habitual force of habit to commit to anything extended no further than renting space from Frank at the park for two weeks. I could end up like Frank if I lost my resolve. I hesitated for a breathless second, and then took the plunge. "Megan, will you marry me?" The pile of prettiness melted in front of me. Sobbing and laughing at the same time, Megan went limp. Then she had a seizure that spun out of control.

"Do you mean it?"

"Yes, I mean it."

"Prove it!"

For once, I was ahead of Megan. I'd known that I was going to ask her to marry me at some point, and one afternoon I passed Shultz's jewelry gallery when the idea struck me. Shultz sold diamonds by the pound, not carat weight, and I bought the biggest stone they could find. I never had enough money to buy my other wives an engagement ring, and I overcompensated when it came to Megan. I carried it in my pocket, waiting for the right opportunity.

Megan's eyes widened when she saw me digging around in my pocket. The ring that I produced in the bright sunlight lit up with rays of rainbow colors that were blinding.

Did Megan scream? You bet— loud enough to crack foundations a mile away. "Owen! Oh, Owen!"

She held it in front of her face, mesmerized by the size and brilliance. I had given her a primitive fire starter. "You need to put this on before the table cloth catches on fire."

I was a bit embarrassed by it all. Babies were crying at other tables in the open air restaurant. I wasn't performing an impromptu field amputation. I just asked the woman to marry me. Finally, Megan went into post-op, and she stared at the Star of India diamond that I put on her finger.

"Well?"

Megan was speechless as she waved her hand around looking at the stone from different angles.

"Stop that. You're drawing attention to yourself."

"What?"

"It's a museum piece and I think it's stolen, so you shouldn't be waving it around. So answer the question. Will you marry me?"

"Huh?"

"I said, will you marry me?"

"I told you I would before you asked me."

"Make it official, or I'm taking the ring back."

Her tapered hand disappeared below the table quicker than a cobra snake's strike. "Yes, and yes, a thousand times over! Oh, Owen, you've made a princess' dream come true. Let's do it right now."

I was used to Megan's spontaneity, and I was all for it, but technically I was still married, so I circumvented the issue by telling Megan to call her mom. Megan was now in my lap, chatting it up with her mother, and the way they were talking, the wedding would be bigger than Lincoln's funeral.

CHAPTER FORTY-NINE

July was zipping along and I had put most of my troubles on the back burner. I'd finished my advertising gig with the Lottery management firm so I spent more time at the Marsh homestead. At first I was smothered in family planning sessions of the big day and constantly urged to reveal the date. That was pretty much up to a judge in Nashville and I danced around the subject. A couple weeks passed and I suppose the new wore off and there was a distinct change of moods from her parents. Not that they had stiffened up and were having second thoughts. In fact they doted on me more than usual. I couldn't put my finger on anything but I gave myself a bit of elbow room and spent more time with Traitor. I was happier than any moment in my life, and I thought about venturing back into the music business. Traitor helped me write a ballad or two and I'd sing them for Peggy. Life was good.

I saw my life in transition. I had a loathing of who I once was. The minute I ducked out on a free engineering degree and took the low road and the easy way out, I'd abandoned the dreams that my mother had for a talented son. I accepted the passing of life in an inverted fog of ambivalence. A shrink would tell me it was an avoidance mechanism.

The reason I failed at my musical career was because I didn't have the backbone to fight for what was rightfully mine. It wasn't so much as what was stolen from me. It was my lack of commitment to reach my hand over the curb and engage in a worthy enterprise. Being a fucked-up rock star requires hard work and effort. I let it all fall down around me because the depth of my character was so shallow I'd rather fail than make an effort to meet the expectations and responsibilities that came with the territory. I'd spent the next ten years in an endless free-fall to oblivion. I felt the pain of my skin tearing through the long fall. During the fall I briefly felt the passion of a woman's love for the first time and I can still hear Betty's derisive laughter as I zipped past her on my journey to anonymity.

Had I not won the lottery and had I not met Megan I'd still be in free-fall and the lottery rage inside of me would surely kill me before I killed myself. I'll admit that at first I was in the relationship because I wanted a superior woman well beyond my grasp to fill a ten year void. I was an empty vessel and she made repeated trips to the well to fill my soul. She worked as tirelessly as a robin building a nest. My fears began to diminish, the pain was a faint regret and my entire perspective changed. I wasn't free-falling… I was soaring. I was becoming a whole other person. My entire focus was to make her as happy as she made me, and I had my work cut out for me. I had complete independence so long as my fingers touched hers.

I was alive with a strong awareness of the smallest sense of my new universe. The smell of fresh cut clover, the sound of Traitor swishing his tail, the feel of hot winds blowing up the valley and the sight of it all thrilled me as if I was experiencing it for the first time. The irony of it was that I was indifferent to the ambivalence of my previous existence.

I ventured back to Nashville routinely just to be pampered and tampered with by Megan. We usually had lunch at Friday's. It was a cozy place with outdoor seating, a good sandwich menu, and freezing cold beer. We had a lot to discuss. I take that back; she had been OCD about our wedding, which was tentatively four months off. I vaguely listened to all of it. At first it was cute, and I was flattered that she shared the details and whispered all sorts of kinky stuff in my ear.

One irritating thing about Megan bothered me. She couldn't leave the future alone. She had our kids enrolled in Vanderbilt, the house plans for our summer home in the Keys, and the details of my musical comeback. I stoically sat through all the crap, but I had no plans for a come back because I had nothing to come back to.

A degree of separation had sprung up between us and it was beginning to arc to a point of collision. I honestly didn't see it coming. I badly want to be back in the music business, but I had issues. To be honest, I was being a prick, and I was giving the industry the finger because I could afford to. There were a lot of losers on Second Street doing the same thing and that just makes a shitty comeback that much more difficult. Somebody has to like you for that to happen and I was doing my best not to be liked.

Megan was a relentless hysterical stage mom, advancing my musical comeback. So there I was with hat in hand while the bastards would have theirs in my pockets if I'd just roll over. The best way to get to me was through my future wife and I saw the dynamics and listened to the bull shit. I was getting all kinds of offers to back their label, their new artist, their concert tours and on and on, but not one invitation to thump a single guitar string.

Hanging out in Nashville on hot summer days without something to do drove me ape-shit-crazy. I spent a lot of time drifting from bar to bar, listening to kids belt out songs to tourist. Some of the talent didn't belong on Second Street and I played with the idea of becoming a manager and producer. Everyone was on my case for hanging out with the wrong crowd, but I couldn't resist the tapping of my toes to great music in the making.

My routine was to show up at the Oak Bar and meet Megan after she got off work. That's as far as my day planning went. One afternoon I slipped into my regular chair at the bar and Brent had a drink in front of me before the weight of my ass settled in.

"How goes it, Owen? Discover any Grammy winners today?"

"Yeah, a kid who sounds just like Roy Clark." Brent and I had the same discussion everyday and I'd pick a name out of the hat to talk about. We'd sing the praises of Nashville's legends until Megan showed up. Brent always had the timing down pat and had a chilled tonic waiting for her. That afternoon the ice melted and Megan hadn't put in her appearance. Brent pulled the drink down and replaced it with another.

Megan was idiotic about time management and if she was going to be two seconds late she'd call me. We'd talked Roy Clark to death and still no Megan and no call. I was getting tense and I was relieved when my phone rang.

I was tickled to tell her something and I said, "Hey Baby, did you know Roy Clark was a boxer before becoming a music star?" I heard the chuckle of a male voice and quickly glimpsed the caller ID. It was Megan's ID.

The droll voice said, "It's a hot one today. Were we expecting Miss Marsh?"

It was Alvin Fox. "Hey, what are you doing on Megan's phone asshole? Put Megan on."

"I would, but at the moment she's too hysterical to talk. She's very unhappy with you."

"What the hell have you done?"

I heard his raspy voice hissing, "Owen …Owen ….never double-cross your friends. There's always a cost, you know? Nashville Today will explain." The line went dead.

I looked at my watch, then at Brent. I asked, "Brent could you turn the channel to Nashville Today?"

"Sure thing. When did you start watching garden club crap?" He laughed because he knew I detested the local soft news program, which was mostly about old farts gardening.

As soon as he flipped the channel, there I was, bigger than the billboard my face was pasted on. "Hey, Owen it's you. You want me to turn it up?"

There were three tables of customers oblivious to what was on the screen. I moved further down the bar to be next to the TV. The windblown hair of Erika Hamm swirled in a stiff breeze in front of a highway billboard. She had a mike in her face and she was pointing over her shoulder at my goofy billboard. I got close so I could listen.

"Owen Fletcher is a symbol of humility with a mysticism that's captivated our viewers. Like so many musicians that migrate to Music City, Owen was no stranger to failure. He was just another average workingman, making a living on the fringe of the music industry" There were snap shots of my RV, Frank and me at the park, an old promotion photo of Shylock and me in cargo pants, sporting my trademark pony tail. *"Owen became something of a folk hero when he won the lottery and became an instant tycoon. Nashville loves the genesis of a sad country song, and following Owen Fletcher was just that. Legal problems crept up on him, creating a suspenseful saga."* The screen showed photos of Hajji and Jolene and lots of photos of Bonnie at the court house. *"His troubles were followed by tragedy with the death of his father at the Fort Benning massacre. Both stories have caught the attention of the national media, and it seems winning the lottery isn't all it's cracked up to be. There's been an outpouring of sympathy for our unlucky lottery winner, until this woman entered the picture. "*

The screen filled with Betty's gorgeous smiling face. Her freckled dimples, seductive lips, and sparkling eyes created a vision of temptation, and no one had to guess where this story was leading. Erika quickly did the overview of Betty's involvement with two of the victims of the massacre. The mystery woman was the recent wife of one, girlfriend of the other; then the story nose-dived into the dirt. Alvin had provided the news station with a slide show of Betty and me dining, wining, dancing, shopping, kissing; holding hands, and then came the cruise pictures. One after the other, all hot and intimate photos of Betty and me. There were even photos of me carrying her, wearing nothing but Victoria Secret, into my suite on the ship.

By the look on Brent's face, the sordid piece accomplished it's purpose. His jaw was slack, and his eyes were riveted to the screen. He was lapping it up, and it wasn't the gardening fare he was expecting. The final slide show made his eyes pop and a guttural growl rose from his throat. Then there was a series of pictures of Megan and me, all about town, and the last one made him gasp. It was of me putting the rock on Megan's finger.

Erika did a nice job splattering a steamy speculation about my sleazy character. A male voice interrupted her. *"Erika, isn't Owen still married to a woman in Colorado?"*

"Yes, Bill. According to earlier statements by Mr. Fletcher's attorney, the marriage is in default by abandonment. This is going to be a very hot summer as we see this epic saga unfold."

"Keep us informed, Erika. Now onto less intriguing happenings about town ..."

Darkness blinded me. Anger and rage blinded me. My door to oblivion was standing wide open, and Alvin had tossed me across the threshold.

CHAPTER FIFTY

A light tap on my door forced me to drag my sorry ass out of my puddle of self loathing. By the time I got around to answering the door, the caller had disappeared. I looked down and saw envelopes lying on the carpet. There were three, and I knew the contents would destroy me. I picked them up and tossed them on the coffee table. The engagement ring that Megan flashed about at every opportunity spilled onto the table, then rolled to the carpet. My knees buckled. Clear photos of Betty and me making passionate love also spilled from a second envelope. I couldn't bring myself to read the contents of the third envelope, so I put it in my pocket.

Alvin Fox had not only witnessed my sins, but photographed them. That vile bastard was the most vindictive son of a bitch known to man. I deserved punishment and so did Betty, but Megan was innocent in all this. Alvin didn't care about that, not one damned bit. The bastard just broke the woman I loved into tiny pieces of shattered glass. The scream that came out of my lungs wasn't human.

I was frantic. I had to get Megan back. But how? Plead insanity? I had to act fast and with demonstrated remorse. I grabbed my truck keys and flew out the door.

Driving blindly, my thoughts were on cruise control. I couldn't claim to be the victim in all of this because of my complicity in what happened. All the same, I felt like a victim. I had lost two women who loved me. I lost the love of my family, such as it was, and I was completely alone, filled with panicked guilt and sadness. I was just trying to help my dad, wasn't I? If I hadn't gotten involved, I might have had a shot with Megan. Then I remembered—the reason I was at my father's in the first place was to get away from her. I had grown to love her because she taught me what love was. She didn't deserve someone like me.

Alvin Fox had exacted his revenge on me. There were some people on the planet that I didn't particularly like, but no one I would truly wish to kill. Alvin Fox was the first to make that list. I resolved to find him one day and crush him completely.

I drove to Megan's house. She wasn't home, but media vans were parked in her driveway. I did a quick drive by and picked up a tail.

I drove out of Nashville hoping I could hide from the media in some backwater dive. I had been on autopilot and had driven down the Murfreesboro Pike, ten miles short of the Marsh homestead. I turned around, knowing what a bad idea it would be to turn up there. I drove aimlessly because it gave me something to do, but every road, lane, or highway led to empty destinations. I finally stopped when I arrived at Frank's outpost at the park. Frank wasn't there, so I let myself into his trailer. I had a letter that I hadn't opened yet, and I waited until I'd put a few shots of scotch down before I dared to open Megan's envelope. I was expecting a scathing blast of flame to leap off the pages.

Dearest Owen,

The man I met, what seems in another life, was a simple uncomplicated bum who touched me. He charmed me without knowing it. He made me laugh. His simple demeanor was so endearing. I was smitten, and I wanted him around me always. Then he walked out on me because I was too complicated for him. The only way I could get him back was to try to be like him, be a soul mate, and be modest in spirit. I went headlong into that pursuit with a passion and with both eyes open. It was a daring departure for me, and I loved the journey and I thank you for that.

I had to put the letter down at that point. I knew what was sure to come, and I needed liquid courage to face it. I poured a tall one before resuming.

Had I known what an impossible predicament I put a naive soul like you into, I would never have done it. You became another man. A man that I loathe. What kind of man takes his father's girlfriend to his bed? Had you confessed to temporary insanity, I would have been extremely upset. But you went on with your affair with Betty, lying and cheating, while I trusted in your moral fidelity. You failed yourself, Owen. You failed any trust that I would ever have for you.

That trust is forever gone. It's like dirt settling to the bottom of my heart, never to find a way out. It remains a filthy pit in my heart that displaces the space needed for love. Your loss of self-respect belongs to you. You earned it, you bastard.

I hope somewhere in your new life, you find that bum once again. Even if you do, I'm done with both of you. Thanks for the pain. I will cherish it forever, which is as long as I will hate you.

Megan

Megan had a way with words. I accepted defeat and the rage began again. That letter from Megan filled my brain with a vault of regret that I didn't want to open. There are some mistakes in life that you can make and forget about. And then there are mistakes you can never forget and live with forever. Guess which mistake I made? The bridge over the Cumberland River had an inviting allure.

Frank didn't try to wake me. Frank's bad habits woke me. The smell of squirrel gravy, burnt biscuits, and Dolly Parton warbling on about 'Hillbilly Holler' made me pinch my nose with one hand and cover an ear with the other. The temperature was soaring outside and boiling inside. Frank didn't believe in running more than one appliance at a time. The stove was going, so the air conditioning was off.

I tried to delay getting off his couch until I couldn't endure it any longer. Painfully, I stood up, shook out the cobwebs and scratched the bug bites I'd acquired overnight. Frank was in the kitchen, whistling Dolly's snappy song, stirring gravy while the biscuits burned. Without looking up, he said, "Make yourself at home, if you haven't already...you owe me a fifth of scotch."

"I needed to get away."

"I'm sure you did, judging from that 'Dear John.' Next time bring your own rot gut."

I looked at the coffee table and saw Megan's letter with glass ring stains on it. "Jesus, Frank, that was personal. I didn't intend for you to read it."

"Well it damned sure got read. Coulda bashed your head in with my tackle box. Didn't figure you for the slick bastard type. You know I'm partial to Megan, and by all rights, I shoulda tanned your hide and delivered it to Miss Megan. What the hell did you do, boy?"

"I got mixed up with another woman before Megan and I got serious, and it didn't last long, but Megan found out—

"Everybody found out about it." He squinted at me and shook his spatula. "You mean to tell me that was your pa's girlfriend?

Damn, boy, your ole man musta been hung like Jake's mule. Makes me envious in my old age."

"It was a mistake. I have to get Megan back. Frank, I need your advice."

"You want to go back thirty years and help me get Molly Sears back? Thing is, Owen, I've had all this time to figure out a way to fix that mistake with Molly and some things don't get fixed. They stay broke, and you just spend a lot of time walking around it, like a dry well in the yard. Just don't fall in the well cause when you've done something that bad, nobody is gonna throw you a rope."

"It's killing me Frank. I gotta do something."

He put down the spatula, fixed two heaping plates of biscuits and gravy and motioned for me to grabbed one. "Let's eat outside. It too damned hot in here." He walked out the screen door and let it bang behind him. I followed.

Frank was sitting on the picnic table and halfway through his breakfast before I could park next to him. He said to himself, "Lord, why do I have to talk this coon down out of the tree he's got himself up in?"

I started off with an inane schoolboy promise. "I made a mistake and I'll make it up to her. I just need for her to understand."

Frank laughed. "That's a lot of understanding to swallow all at once. You ran off from her once before, and we talked about it, remember? She ain't over that and she's been dragging you through a knot hole ever since, making you go places you don't belong. Put some ice on that pecker of yours and then ask yourself if this isn't about you trying to live up to expectations that are as artificial as your hillbilly tycoons."

Frank's crass psychoanalysis hit me wrong. "I love the woman. I'd give up everything I have for her. It's not about my pride."

"No doubt you've already done that. Tell you what; write her a check and see what happens. If she keeps it, you don't want her. If she don't take it, you're not getting her back anyway. You've done that girl a world of hurt. You won't get absolution, not from me anyways. Don't make that an issue. You reap what you sow, and I'd say you're suffering a mighty bad crop failure."

"I can't let her walk off from me. I have to make it right."

Frank thought about it and said, "Sure as hell can't help you out with that, but I will warn ya; makin' it right for her may be makin' it wrong for yourself. Give it time, son.. Not sayin' you'll ever get over it, but you'll just have to come down outa that tree you've backed yourself up."

CHAPTER FIFTY-ONE

My depression took hold the following day when Megan's attorney delivered a protection order to my attorney. I spent the week doing anything I could think of to get Megan's attention. Her parents hung up on me, so I wrote letters to them. Hell, I even sat out in the parking lot just so I could get a glimpse of her. I was pushing the envelope of my court order, and I got a visit by a police detective warning me to stop the letters, calls, and to stop stalking her. The old Owen could get by with that stunt because the old Owen walked about the streets in cargo pants, never being noticed, even by the likes of Jolene; and like Jolene, Megan wasn't going to offer me a refill.

With a four-day hangover, I'd left the hermitage in cargo pants, slinking away from my shame like a thief in the night. Like any other vagrant, my movement went unnoticed, and I was back in the vast anonymity of my previous life ...before I was struck with lottery rage. I drove aimlessly toward Briley Parkway, and about dawn, found myself near the airport.

Motel 6 is a good motel company, and they provide friendly and professional staff. Take away the frills; the accommodations covered the basics I had experienced at the Hermitage, but without the sticker price. I was on a weekly rate because I wasn't sure how long I would be in Nashville.

I reverted back to my not-so-healthy fast food diet, and was in my cargo pants lifestyle again. Shaving and bathing was too much of an effort.

My old P.O. Box had bag loads of solicitations waiting to be picked up. Hopelessly upside down, I took all the damn bags to the motel and sifted through the garbage, praying that Megan sent me a letter. Megan didn't, but Betty did.

Dear Owen,

My need of you and my thoughtlessness has brought great sorrow to you. If I had known how our affair would have turned out, I would never have done what I did. I wrote Megan a letter, explaining that it was entirely my fault. I don't expect her forgiveness of me, but I hope she forgives you.

I blame myself for your father's death. I cannot expect your forgiveness and wouldn't deserve it. It is a heavy grief that is mine to carry forever. I am not sure what I will do once I can bring myself to raise my head, but I promise that I will not be a bother to you from this day forward. I cry often, and the tears are for what I did to you. My tears stain my soul.

I knew I could love you, and I was overcome with temptations. A fleeting moment of happiness was broken by the impossibility of our situation, and there is no amount of regret left in my being. There are no more knights to come to my rescue. I will always be chained to the memories of love lost. I will always love you, Owen. Always.

If there is a single prayer to be heard, I pray that you reconcile with Megan.

Goodbye,
Betty.

So there it was, Betty was always going to love me, and I was always going to hate her, and Megan was always going to hate both of us. THE END. That's the way it was supposed to end, but it didn't.

Betty had enclosed a DVD. She and others on the cruise had entered a talent contest, and they recorded their winning performance. They named the band after our table setting in the dining room, 'Table Fifty Seven.' Frank and Erin were in it, and old Sam and Pearle produced it. I played the DVD, then played it again…and again. Betty put on a very hot performance. She was wearing the sexy dress that I bought her, and she was singing so beautifully that it brought tears to my eyes. I was so soothed by her voice, I forgot I was supposed to hate her, which added another layer of sadness to my dismal existence.

Motel 6 has a direct line to the FBI in the event that the 'most wanted' criminal is a guest. I know this because Joyce showed up. She had a reason to be there to let me know what's going on, and I kept telling her I was *waaay* beyond giving a shit.

Joyce wasn't a very good cop. Cops don't give pep talks to witnesses or suspects in a crime they're working on. But then again, she might have been working on me. Whatever her motives were, she didn't let me far off the leash. In fact, she was pushing me to just get over Megan and move on. It became a source of contention between us as I was constantly asking her about Megan and she constantly ignored my every ruse to get a glimmer of information out of her.

It was actually very nice of Joyce to check in on me every few days to make sure I wasn't in the tub with a razor blade. I always had a rum and coke for her, as she would often unwind her day with me. She didn't have to, but that's Joyce and still is. You can't believe what one human touch can do. The only reason I didn't kill myself was because of Joyce. I was sick of disappointing people, and if I killed myself, Joyce would have been pissed off. I had one other totally fucked up excuse for not jumping off the Cumberland Bridge. I was sure Megan wouldn't be there to watch me jump.

I did my shopping at Goodwill and Dollar General, like I had always done. With a week or two of facial hair, a Napa Auto Parts ball cap, and wearing a wife-beater- t-shirt, I could circulate with my old crowd. I was in charge of my schedule again, which is to say I missed all my appointments, didn't answer calls, and became decidedly anti-social.

I spent the remainder of July in a lethargic holding pattern, not moving forward nor backwards. I quit visiting Frank altogether because he warned me that the park was full of media trash looking to make sport of me. It was just Joyce and me, sharing a not so happy, happy hour in my hotel room. She took me fishing a couple of times and she let me whine on endlessly. She's a cop and couldn't help herself from trying to get inside of my head. It almost ended our friendship, but I always looked forward to her visits and forgave her bad bedside manner.

CHAPTER FIFTY-TWO

With Megan no longer running my schedule, Jerry took over as my truant officer. I had business with the bank, my attorney, my errant wife, and recently, a new attorney, Pat Jarrett. If I was ever going to leave Nashville and start over, I had to get shit done because the people I hired to do it were sucking me dry. I split the difference and bought decent business attire, shaved, and made myself sidewalk presentable. It was time to take matters into my own hands.

My bus ticket to a new start in life was tied to a series of court appearances, and the backlog on the docket would take years. I couldn't see myself stuck in Nashville with a dismal existence revolving around court dates.

My other reason was more immediate. If Carole Anne Fletcher was my daughter, what would a nine-year-old feel about a father who had abandoned her? How could I make that right? There was a bitter anger swelling within me. When I won the lottery, Carole's home in Colorado should have been my first stop rather than my dad's house. My lottery rage had yet another source of raw fuel to feed upon.

Jerry was my other friend who was on a righteous harangue when it came to me. He was solidly in Megan's camp and I could hardly blame him. I called Jerry at his office and asked if he had time to see me. Jerry's voice was jovial until he recognized mine.

He was short with me. "Hey listen, Owen, meet me at the Wild Horse Saloon after work. I need to catch you up on what's going on."

Maybe I did have a friend on planet earth. Jerry and I met up and ordered drinks. Jerry said, "Let's get business out of the way first. Your old lawyer is a crook. What was your opinion of Pat Jarrett? You want to know something? Kenny Scales is *waay* more flaming than I am."

"Do you two have the same manicurist or something?"

Jerry ignored me whenever I lit my joke lantern about gay people. He could makes jokes, but I couldn't. "Your little spending spree is just now catching up to us, and it's an itemized trail of lavish splurging that would make a pharaoh blush. Do you have any idea how hard it is to justify your high-dollar tryst with your dad's girlfriend? Follow that up with five-star accommodations here in Nashville and the freakin' Hope diamond engagement ring you bought for Megan." He shook his head in bewilderment. "I think I can mitigate most of it with the court, allowing that you were providing special services to the FBI in a major crime development. You'll still have to pay for it."

"I returned the pricey diamond I bought for Megan. I couldn't stand having it around me anymore. Shultz, who has a fine eye for stones, said the rock was a piece of gravel and offered me a stone quarry price. I told him I thought it was stolen, and I'd rather turn it over to the cops. Shultz didn't have a problem refunding my money at that point."

Jerry laughed. "Next time, buy something a little more modest. I see you checked out of the Hermitage. Where are you hanging your hat now?

"It's none of your business where I'm staying." He'd ratted me out to the feds and I still had a slight lack of trust because of it.

"Hiding out from Fox? He knows about your park hide-out. Now onto other matters, did you really fuck you father's girlfriend?"

"Who told you that? Nobody really knows for sure. Jerry, it's not what you think. You would have to know this woman. She has this overpowering sensuality, and I found a weak moment."

"Owen, spare me the details. So did you pork her or what?

"It was a brief affair. It's why I jumped ship in Martinique. The woman was just too irresistible. I put a stop to it."

"I'm Jerry. Don't be lying to me."

"Have I ever lied to you?"

"Yes, but we won't go into that. Fuck you for what you did to Megan. You brutalized that woman. Her mind is at the animal shelter waiting to be put down. That was fuckin' low, really fuckin' low. Nobody deserves what you did to her. Geez, you were fuckin' your future step-mom?" Jerry wasn't a bedside kind of friend.

"My dad dumped her in my lap."

"What was that? The 'lap' part I get. Screwing her I don't get."

I defended myself, saying, "He didn't have the balls to tell her goodbye. The bastard wanted me to tell her."

"This Betty, she must be something, huh?"

"Don't you watch TV?"

"It got pulled before I could see it, but I heard about it from you know who. Megan said she's a cow."

"She's not a cow."

Jerry began typing on his keyboard. He found an internet link to the newscast showcasing my début. Jerry's eyes bulged, but not for the reason I was expecting. "I *know* her," he gushed. "She's *here* in Nashville. That's Betty? Wow! I can understand how you got yourself into trouble."

"What do you mean you know her?" Where did you see her?"

"At the bank. She was at the service desk, and she opened a new account. You can't miss that red hair. She goes by the name of Elizabeth Stiles."

"How do you know?"

"Shit, she put in an application for a job in the PR department and I hired her on the spot."

"You what?"

His head bounced up and down enthusiastically. "She fits our brand. She's quiet, stays to herself, and isn't threatening to our other PR babes. I'm not firing her just because she had a real lapse of judgment by getting in the rack with you."

"I don't need this shit. She'll start stalking me. I can feel it in my bones. I'm done with her after what she did to...Megan and me."

"Megan told me about it. I guess you fucked Betty over too? Owen, what do you want? Get over yourself and move on."

"What I want is Megan."

"That's a tall order, sport. I'm afraid you did yourself in there. I'll put feelers out for you, but don't expect any sympathy from me."

"I don't, and don't put out any feelers. Megan doesn't deserve a jerk like me."

"You won't get any argument from me. What are you going to do now?"

"Avoid Betty and finish up my business in Nashville. After that, I don't know where I'll go. I just need to get away from my own train wreck."

CHAPTER FIFTY-THREE

I decided I needed a meeting of the ways and/or or a parting of the same, depending on what my Attorney, Patrick Jarrett, could come up with. I met with him and the cushion under my ass had barely settled when he said, "Owen, I've been vicariously following your cases through Jerry, the media, and word of mouth. I don't have a lot of questions. I need to get a handle on where you reside with this horseshit; then we can agree on a plan of action." He didn't waste a lot of hot air with idle chatter.

I was bewildered with where to begin, and I sputtered out my tale of woe. He stopped me halfway through my diatribe.

"Owen, you settle with these characters and we'll have more paper on our desk than the news stand on Fifth Street. You knock a beer glass over, and the owner will sue you for destroying his business. I shit you not; you'll become an easy mark for every shit-bag with some concocted complaint."

This guy was talking my style. Ole Owen was tired of taking it on the chin, and I was ready for a street brawl if it came to that.

He leaned back in his cheap fake leather man-chair with a smirk on his face. "The two dopes with the oral agreement complaint? I'm not even going to take calls from their attorneys. The Tarzan suit is going to get a response from me in the form of a countersuit claiming theft of artistic properties and for past royalties due to you from sales of Shylock's entire revenue stream. This business with your wife is a different matter. Your attorney should have demanded a hearing on the matter and forced the attorney filing the petition to refile. If in fact, Carole Anne is your daughter, I would expect you would want to do what is morally and legally right by her."

"My assets have been frozen. Can we do anything about that?"

Pat laughed. "I have to ask myself how that happened? You can't just walk into a courthouse, tell the judge that your neighbor promised to give you his car and expect the judge to impound the vehicle. You got hijacked, buddy. I'm going to appeal that as my first order of business because there isn't a thread of credible material evidence to substantiate the order.

"How long is all of this going to take?"

"It just depends on how much their attorneys can milk out of their clients. Why do you care?"

"I'm anxious to get the hell out of town."

"You worried about Fox?" He did a quick squinting eyeball run over me. "Yeah, thought so. Look, there's a criminal implication under his tail feathers. He's bluffing. How would it look if he didn't sue you? I'll need to make nice with the FBI agent running your case. They'll dictate how we handle Fox." He shrugged. "Can't be helped. We don't want to be on the wrong side of that. Anything else?"

"I'm pretty sure the DNA test is positive. If it is, I want that to be the first order of business."

"You might want to do yourself a favor. See if you can talk to Bonnie. What does she want out of all of this? We know what her attorney wants. You might wait until the DNA tests come back before you do anything. In the meantime, unbuckle your seat belt and feel free to roam about the countryside."

I thought our conference had concluded and rose to leave, but he waved me to my seat. "We have another matter that you need to think about. The FBI has done a thorough investigation of Elizabeth Style's background. They've found that your father's involvement with her is rather lengthy. Do you know anything about this?"

Yes I did, but I didn't want to tip my hand. I asked, "Why is that important?"

"Miss Styles is vague about it, only admitting that she resided near your father's duty stations his entire career. Why? Why would she be vague?"

I was angry. "What's your point?"

Look, Owen. The FBI isn't out to destroy your family name, but if there is linkage to find out who was pulling Roxanne's strings and why, the feds could wrap the case up quietly. Have you been in communication with Miss Styles?"

"That would be a bad idea." I said half-heartedly.

He nodded thoughtfully "From what I gather from Joyce, you are probably the only person who can get her to cooperate."

"What if I don't want to?"

"Alvin Fox will get by with murdering your father and stealing your money." Pat took another fifteen minutes explaining Betty's innocence and Alvin's complicity. He was wasting his breath because I knew it and pretended not to. I had no interest in solving Boot's murder, because it wasn't murder at all. He killed himself to protect the young girl he raped decades ago. My lottery rage blocked a shameful history of my past.

Jerry set up the meeting. I was nervous and conflicted about seeing Betty. I was alone in the conference room running a variety of opening statements through my head. Not one of them had a hint of forgiveness in them. I paced back and forth conjuring her image in my mind, remembering intimate moments with her. I felt cheated. When she entered the room, I felt a jolt that electrified every nerve in my body. I could not utter a single word, not even a hello.

She was impeccably attired in a business suit that partially hid her feminine attributes. She had changed the color, style, and length of her hair, but there was no mistaking her beautiful face. I wilted.

She was completely surprised and when recognition hit her, she stumbled, dropped her purse and turned for the door. Then she stopped, composed herself, and turned to face me. I saw waves of different emotions slide across her face as we simply stared at each other. She sat in the most available conference room chair at the opposite end of the table. She was first to speak. "Did you get my letter?" she asked.

I nodded.

Her voice became shaky as she said, "I can't begin to tell you how sorry I am. I struggle, Owen. Everyday. I really do. I can't forgive myself for what I did to you."

"Neither can I. But that's not what brings us together. The FBI chick hounding both of us wants to find out who was pulling Roxanne's strings and it's her belief that Alvin Fox is the culprit. She thinks he began a mining expedition the day I won the lottery and happened onto Roxanne Thomas. The story you told me didn't include Roxanne, but if the rest of it is true, then Roxanne's motives aren't hard to explain."

The end of September came along, taking its sweet time. I was ready for a change of seasons. Patrick Jarrett discovered that Kenny Scales had pigeon-holed my DNA test, and as my new attorney requisitioned the results; I was in fact Carole Anne Fletcher's biological father. Then he went to work straightening out my marital status. He found the original filing, complete with two party signatures. Apposing counsel wanted to file a new complaint and thus claim my lottery winnings as marital assets, but Pat got a judgment based on the original filing. Bonnie was now officially my ex-wife, and Carole Anne was officially my new daughter. I was a dad and ex-husband. Now what?

There was an awareness I didn't expect. I felt elation about it all and at the same time, a heavy weight placed around my neck. I was no longer on this planet alone, and I'd leave this planet with the spark of my soul flickering down the generations. Life, or my concept of it, contracted, and there just wasn't enough of it left. I had a long journey ahead of me.

I had a dozen pictures in my head. I was a father, teacher, friend, counselor, Indian chief, wizard, and jester. I imagined myself to be all these, but I didn't fit into any of the pictures I conjured. I'd change that. Yes, I would. I might even win Bonnie back. That's how optimistic I was, and I couldn't wait to leave the Cumberland River Bridge in my rear view mirror.

I rolled out of the Motel 6 before dawn and stayed behind the wheel until well after the sun went down. I stopped in Limon, Colorado for the night, and I thought about calling Bonnie to let her know I was on my way to meet Carole Anne.

Pat advised me to survey the landscape first. For all I knew I would be unwelcome vermin and Bonnie's big burly live-in lover would throw my ass off the mountain. His advice echoed through my mind. "Meet your daughter on neutral ground when and if Bonnie will allow it. Take your time with it."

I rolled into Aspen the next afternoon. It hadn't changed, nor had the people. I was planning on an extended stay, so I had to find a property manager to set me up with a condo lease. I picked Pruitt Management out of the hat. I told the receptionist what I was looking for. She smiled and said, "Bonnie Fletcher is our leasing agent, and she's with a client at the moment. Please have a seat and fill out the questionnaire. Who should I say you are?"

Aspen was a small town, but the coincidence threw me sideways. I wasn't up to an impromptu run-in with my ex-wife. I got cold feet and said, "I forgot to lock my truck. I'll be right back." I saw Bonnie's business card and swiped it off the counter. That was close, but I did save some research time. I had her cell number and her e-mail address. Her smiling face on the card hadn't changed that much in ten years. For a second, I felt my heart flutter. What was I thinking? This was the woman who left me ten years ago without a word. She also over-nighted her divorce decree two days ago. To be honest, I was scared to death.

It didn't take me long to find a nice condo to camp out in. It felt awkward being in anything but temporary lodging or my RV. Had it been almost ten years since I left these mountains? I had a great view out of my window. The mountain air cleansed my head, and I felt right at home in no time.

I couldn't help myself. I wanted to see what my daughter looked like, so I checked the local phone book to see if Bonnie was listed. There it was: 114 Birch Glen Rd., two doors up from the crappy shack that I used to call home. Most of the neighborhood had been rentals for temporary workers with six people crammed into cigarette box crash pads. The Birch Glen goat trail was always littered with old heaps too rusted to run. Bonnie's house was in serious need of repair, as in demolish it and start from scratch. I recalled that most of the residents were borderline criminals, who partied late and loud, got drunk often, and pissed off the porch. The neighborhood was home to dope peddlers and prostitutes. This was not the kind of neighborhood I wanted my child to be raised in.

I drove slowly by the house, noting the vehicles parked out front. There was a turn-around half a block up, and I parked my truck to observe the house. I didn't have long to wait. An early model Civic, blowing smoke, struggled to a stop and parked. Bonnie jumped out and so did this magnificent child. They were busy unloading groceries, as I ogled over my little girl. I was too far away to get a real good look at her, but I had half an idea what I would have looked like had I been born a girl. You don't have any idea what that moment was like to me. In the space of a few minutes, I saw the replica of me disappear with a sack full of groceries into the shack she called home. My head exploded as if I was there at her birth, nine years too late. The missing years were a forgotten happiness I could never get back. I will tell you this, being mortal is an everlasting lust to have your soul married to the ages with offspring, a continuance into a future existence. I saw that future of my life in the nine-year-old girl who danced into her sorry house. I had a reason to leave the Cumberland River Bridge after all.

In a week's time, I learned the two spent a lot of time together and always by themselves. There was no man living in the house, at least not at the moment. I will have to hand it to Bonnie; Carole Anne was always well groomed and wore clean clothes. She behaved well in public, smiled, and laughed often.

Did I really want to dive head long into this? It was better than jumping off the Cumberland River Bridge. It was time to take a different leap. I dialed her number.

"Bonnie Fletcher." The voice on the other end of the connection was the same one immortalized in my memories.

"Bonnie, it's Owen. Could we have a civil conversation?"

There was a very long pause. "It's always been civil, Owen, and that was the problem, wasn't it? On the advice of my attorney, I shouldn't be speaking to you."

"On the advice of my attorney, I need to start taking care of my daughter, and that's worth talking about."

"It is, and I'll let my attorney talk for me."

"He's a rather long-winded fellow and not very competent. He has a tendency to stretch things out, like nine years getting you your divorce. This could really drag on, and I don't want that, do you?" I said.

"The only reason I didn't send the papers to be filed was because I wanted Carole to have a father on paper and a last name that she could claim as her own. That's it, Owen."

"I'm fine with that, and I'm not going to ask you why you left me, but I ached for a long time."

"Liar."

"Where were we?" I said. "You know I'm asking for liberal visitation rights. That could be very difficult for you to dispute."

"Owen, I don't want you anywhere near Carole, ever!"

"When she grows up she's going to come looking for me."

"You're bluffing. You don't want anything to do with children. I know you, and you're an emotional lightweight. You don't have the guts to provide any of the heavy lifting in a relationship."

"People change."

"Ha! What do you want, Owen?"

"I want to know what you want out of this, and we can cut the crap and take care of our child like responsible adults."

"That's a lot coming from your mouth. When did you grow up?"

"Just recently. Come on, Bonnie, what's it going to cost you? We can meet, talk it over, and take care of Carole's future."

"Wait. Did I hear you say meet? Where are you?"

"I'm in Aspen. I want you to think about it and call me at this number. We could meet on neutral ground. I won't call you back or bother you, but I'm not leaving until I hear back from you. I think you'll be interested in what I have to say. Call me." I hung up, not giving her a chance to say no.

CHAPTER FIFTY-FOUR

I got the call from Bonnie the following morning. I crossed my fingers.

"Owen, you're right about my attorney. He *is* a long-winded bastard. He said that if I talked to you, it could have an impact on the outcome of the case. I'm going out on a limb here. Let's meet for lunch at the Cloverleaf Cafe. The only thing we're going to talk about is Carole."

Bonnie was sitting alone at a secluded table. It was clear she didn't recognize me as I approached. She hadn't changed much. She still had that athletic figure. The wind and sun had put crows' feet around her eyes, but otherwise Bonnie was still a pretty woman.

"Bonnie?"

She stiffened and her head snapped as recognition set in. "Owen?"

I gave her my famous Owen smile. She put her hand over her mouth and laughed. "My God, what happened to you? I've never seen you in anything but jeans or cargo pants. What's with the dress pants and the shirt that actually has a collar? What happened to you signature pony tail?"

I chuckled. "I got a million dollar hair cut. Can I sit down?"

"Sure. Let's have lunch before we get down to business—no…I changed my mind, let's get down to business first, and if I still have an appetite, we can have lunch." Bonnie had ice in her eyes and frost on her breath. We'd needed bullet proof glass and a set of bars between us if we intended to have a conversation.

The table she'd picked was by a window, half frosted over where the sun had yet to melt. Warm beams created a natural masterpiece of crystalline etchings on plain glass. Our wall between wintery weather was as paper-thin, as our marriage had been. She had a nice view of downtown traffic, and since her eyes couldn't meet mine, that's where they wandered.

She looked stunning, and to think this woman had been my wife until a few days ago. We sized each other up, while I jockeyed with a wrought iron chair. If I could read her mind, I thought she might have been thinking the same thoughts I was having. "I was married to this man for ten years? God, what was I thinking?" To amplify the unstated, she moved her chair an inch or two away from me as I seated myself.

"Down to business then," I said. "How do you want this to turn out? What is it that will satisfy you, and what do you want for Carole?" I was reciting from a script that Pat had prepared for me.

"I need to get Carole off Birch Glen Road and into a decent school. You know what it's like during the season over there. My car is just a puff away from disintegrating. The work is seasonal out here, and I need to make sure I have enough income to see that she grows up without want. I want her to be a little girl with friends to play with. I worry that she's not happy with what I can provide for her. She's a little trooper, Owen. I want her to have enough put aside for her to get any education she'll need to get her started in life. That's about it."

"I agree to all of it. Let's move on to step two. I have a prepared offer that my attorney wrote up, so let's get to the details. You give me a figure, and I'll tell you if it meets the offer. We'll start off with monthly child support."

"Owen, are you playing games with me?"

"Come on, Bonnie, tell me what you want, we can check off on the items we can agree on, and we'll compromise on the issues not checked off. So let's get this over with."

"I want it to be enough to get us through the slow seasons, and this season is going to be a slow one. I'd settle for thirty-five hundred a month, but I'd like four thousand. That's not asking too much, is it?"

I had to smile. I knew four grand was about twice her take home pay. I looked at the agreement and told her we were at six thousand. The ice in her eyes began to thaw. I mentioned back child support and she hissed at me. I could see a bitter pill being swallowed along with pride, "We got this far without you. I don't need blood money."

"Come off it. I don't want to have to revisit this again should you change your mind."

"We need a new car," she said. "Twenty-five-thousand could get us into something decent, and we could call that compensation for back child support." I could see a lump in her throat as the pride slid its way down to the core of her soul. I nodded approvingly, and said, "We're making progress." I pursed my lips and squinted miserly at her. "We offered eight hundred thousand."

Bonnie's head was like a swan's dipping at something invisible. I watched her blink a couple of times and shake her head in disbelief. "I didn't hear you correctly. You said eight-hundred thousand, but you meant eight thousand."

I shook my head. "No, put a calculator to it and take seventy-two thousand in annual child support times ten. Pat thought it would be best to round the number up."

Her hand flew to her mouth, then her chest, and back to her mouth. "Say that again? My attorney said I shouldn't expect to win anything in back child support because I left you without saying a word about being pregnant."

I wasn't going to tell her that her attorney was shaking us down for that amount. Obviously the dick-weed was not keeping his client in the loop. "That's on you, Bonnie. I did say eight-hundred-thousand dollars. Carole didn't get a choice in the matter, did she? I didn't get a choice in the matter either, did I? I suppose if either one of us had a choice at the time, we'd still be sitting here, talking about a whole lot less. Funny how life works when you're not there to screw things up."

"Oh ...Owen. I don't know what to say. I really don't. I never expected you to pay anything for my choice to raise her on my own."

"No, but your attorney does. Tell you what, put it into a growth investment fund and set it aside for Carole."

"I'm having trouble believing the words coming from Owen Fletcher." Her head turned toward the ceiling and she began to sway slightly. I put my hand to her shoulder to steady her. She recoiled and quickly grabbed the table with both hands.

In truth, Owen Fletcher had trouble believing what was coming out of his mouth too. As disgusting as it sounds, there is always a price to pay for sins, and I had enough money to pick up the tab for both of us. Then I mentioned a medical and dental plan for the family.

Her eyes widened and she took a gulp of water, "Crap, I never thought of that. You want me on that plan too?"

"Hell yes, what good are you to her if you're lame and sick all the time?"

"You've put a lot of thought into this. Where did this all come from? This is *not* like you." Bonnie was a tough woman who didn't cry on the outside. It's one of the reasons I had no idea that our marriage was in trouble. When I saw a ribbon of moisture forming on her lower lids, I knew that I had gotten to her.

Then I blasted her. "Now we come to alimony and/or maintenance. I'm going to come straight out with this. Not one dime. It's the principle of the thing, Bonnie. You walked out on me. It's called default by abandonment, so don't even think about crossing swords with me on the issue."

"We're *not* talking about me. We're talking about Carole."

The water works dried up and there was frost back on her windshield. I wanted to get on the pulpit and list all the reasons why we'd cross out that part of the agreement. Pat had advised me to stay away from past grievances or things could turn south in a hurry. After taking a breath, I brought up college and told her that a fund would be set aside for four years of college fees plus a living allowance, with the caveat that if she failed to go, or dropped out, she would lose the scholarship. Carole's education was serious business with me, and for once, Bonnie was in lock step with me.

We were down to the last few items. I explained that I would set aside a two million dollar trust that neither Bonnie nor I could touch, and it would be Carole's on her twenty-fourth birthday.

The last item was the most crucial. I told her I was *not* going to ask for visitation, which had Bonnie weaving in her chair again.

She had a wry look on her face. She glanced sideways and squinted her eyes. "I saw this coming. What's the catch? It looks like you're buying your way out of fatherhood here. That's it? Show up, shower your cash around and then around the bend you go? We did without you for this long, and we sure as hell don't need you from here on. What do you want, Owen?"

"There is a catch. I *will* meet my daughter, at least once. She will always have my phone number, my address, and knowledge of me as her father. You can deny me visitation, but one day Carole will come find me. When she does, you don't want her to hate you for keeping us apart."

"You bastard. I left you so she wouldn't know who you are. You're a bum and a loser. You belong on Glen Birch Road." She snorted with indignation. "Men like you don't have feet to fit into a father's shoes."

"I need to prove to you that I *am* worthy of the right to see my own child and become a *real* father to her. So here's the deal. I'm staying on in Aspen. I won't bother you or Carole, but the visitation agreement will read 'discretionary by the terms of the custodial parent.' It's something I'm leaving entirely in your hands." I extended my hands across the table to hers, but she snatched hers back as if I had hammered her fingers.

"Is that all written in the agreement?" She warily asked.

"It is."

"That gives you a license to stalk us. I won't put up with that."

"There's nothing you can do about the instinctive paternal desire of a man to protect his child. I promise you'll never see me."

"Damn you. Why can't you do what you've always *instinctively* done and run away from your responsibilities? If I even think you're stalking us, I'll get a protection order against you."

"Bonnie, I didn't come here to get your permission. All I want is the chance to have a reason to be alive. You owe me a lifeline since you're the one who threw me overboard."

"Don't lie to me. You didn't even know I was gone."

"Yes, I did. I've lived in an RV for the last ten years, and I've woken up every morning thinking I'd come find you."

"Why didn't you?"

"I didn't deserve you, or to frame it another way, you didn't deserve me. I don't have a lot to show for the last ten years."

Her voice hardened. "Now you think you do? You win the lottery and that makes you somebody? Wake up, Owen. You were somebody when I married you, and that would have been enough if you'd have let me be somebody to you. Some things have changed since I walked out on you. I *am* somebody now. I'm the mother of an awesome little girl. She pointed her finger at me menacingly, and all but snarled, "You're *somebody* I never want in my life again."

She'd made her point, so I'd make mine. "This isn't about you or me. We don't count, and let's stay on the subject about our daughter."

She raised her eyebrows and looked at me with suspicious wonderment. An uneasy silence descended around both of us. We were about done talking, and she seemed reflective of what was at issue. I could tell she was struggling with indecision.

"What's the matter, Bonnie?"

"It's not what I was expecting. You've caught me off guard ... way off guard."

"What were you expecting?'

"A settlement and a check. Something impersonal, like always. I didn't expect to see you, and I definitely didn't expect *this*. The words coming out of you seem real, almost sincere." She laughed, and spread her hands in a magnanimous teasing gesture. "This is Owen Fletcher? I don't even recognize you. The words of concern don't belong to you. I'm having a hard time with this. Sorry, I just don't trust my eyes or your words."

I shrugged to show my contempt for her doubting me and to send her a message that I didn't care what *she* could or could not accept. "Tell me yes and it's done. My attorney will present the agreement to your attorney while we have lunch." I said it in a take it or leave it tone.

She looked as curious as much as she looked wary. "What changed you?"

"I got my emotional elevator kicked through the roof, and I grew a conscience."

"I'm going to say..." She had to blink back tears. "Yes."

I threw her a set of keys, and she asked what the keys were for. I told her it was a bonus for saying yes, and I had a new SUV with all the trimmings parked out front. That made her thrilled with me, and I thought I saw the frost and ice begin to melt away.

"What are these other keys?"

It's the keys to Carole's new home. We'll go for a ride after lunch, and if you like it, we can close on it Friday."

Most people would think I was being overly generous with my bank account, but actually, I got off light. Pat told me that after going through the whole rigmarole of a protracted and expensive lawsuit, this settlement was a bargain basement fire sale without the price of the enmity that would be inflicted on both parties. Bonnie could go about her business, and I could go about mine, whatever that may be. We could both put our gears in neutral and be responsible parents. Pat made sure the settlement was about Carole and not Bonnie, which was logical and the decent thing to do.

Overall, it was a win-win-win settlement, and I should have felt at peace. I didn't. All I had accomplished was to remove one of the roadblocks of my lottery-induced rage. I still had a donut hole in my brain.

There I sat, in the Cloverleaf Cafe, with my estranged ex-wife, who was no longer gloriously pissed off at me. We still had a ten-year gorge of empty space to fill in and a happy kid who hadn't a single clue about me. I could roll boulders into the gulf into the next millennium and never build a footpath to the other side. There are some losses in life that can't be fixed. Just for the hell of it, I decided to throw a pebble in that direction and see what developed.

Munching on spinach salad, Bonnie and I talked openly about the settlement, and she was curious about the house that I'd picked out.

"You know me, Bonnie. It's a fixer-upper. I work for cheap, and I can put a new roof on it before the snow flies"

"Stop it. There you go wise-cracking again. Can't you ever just answer a simple question?"

"Made you smile, didn't I?"

"Yes, but you didn't answer the question. I was just asking because I want to know what kind of neighborhood my child is going to live in."

"You mean, our child. Relax. Owen has stepped up to the plate."

That's the difference between me and Bonnie. Unfixable. We talked back and forth until the check came, and I asked, "Can I drive your car?"

"No, I want to get there sometime today. Cars in the car wash move faster than you do."

I gave her a tour of her new SUV. She liked it. The color, leather seats, walnut console, and the four-wheel drive. I could see the beam of happiness on her face, and it felt good to know I'd put it there, even if it was only temporary.

"Thanks, Owen. I could never buy anything like this."

"I don't want my daughter seen driving around in a cracker-assed heap."

She wanted to know where we were going. I told her, and up into the mountains we went.

She said, "At least we're headed in the right direction. There are some amazing townhouses and condos at Bent Pines."

"Take the next left."

Her head swiveled and a confused frown crossed her face. "That's the wrong direction. There isn't a property up that road that lists under a million dollars."

"Then we're headed in the right direction."

Bonnie hit the brakes and stopped the car. She looked at me with shocked disbelief. "There is only one listing up here. It's a seventy-seven hundred square foot chalet, and it's listed at one-point-nine *million* dollars."

"That would be the one. Do you want to see it or not?"

Suddenly, Bonnie was crying and laughing at the same time. She kept stealing glances at me. "There's got to be a catch. What is it? I might have been born at night, but not last night."

"Yes, there is. You might have to use four-wheel drive to get back and forth during heavy snowstorms. Now drive. I want to get there sometime today."

Shaking her head in disbelief, she finally drove up the mountain to a large chalet-style home. She unlocked the door and we toured the house together. Every room had a view. Whoever said money *couldn't* buy happiness is spot on…but you can buy happiness for someone else. Her eyes were as wide as the grin on her face. Bonnie danced through all the rooms several times. Back and forth she went like a fox marking its territory. Finally, she walked out onto the deck, mumbling to herself. "Everything we own can fit in the master bathroom. I can get Carole a puppy. Owen, how am I going to afford the utilities?" So it went. Note, that at no time did she ever mention a space for me, not even when we were in the four car garage. So be it.

For the first time since I sat down at the Cloverleaf Café with her, I finally got a proper smile out of her. I walked out on the deck to look at the view with her. "Had enough, Bonnie?"

"Oh, Owen, I'm not sure we can afford something so grand. I haven't figured it out just yet, but the mortgage will put a big dent in our living allowance."

"What mortgage? It goes in Carole's name, free and clear."

She screamed as if I had thrown her off the deck and down the mountain. This time she did fall down. Her face sunk into both hands, weeping like a new widow. I left her alone and let the emotions she was experiencing overwhelm her. I was sure there were sorrowful ones mixed with the elated ones. I should know because that's what I was experiencing. She took her time getting to her feet and braced herself on the deck rail. She whispered, "I could kiss you."

"Yes, but you won't, and I'd like to negotiate a better deal than that. I'll settle for a hand shake."

That's exactly what I got.

We got into Bonnie's new SUV and started back down the mountain. "What's next?" she asked.

"Tomorrow I can have my attack dog meet yours, and we can put them back in their cages. Then we close on the house Friday. How does that sound?"

"I'm talking about you."

"Me, I've got a condo leased over in Bent Pines. I'm going to extend the lease for the season, and if I haven't met my daughter by then, I'll bug out and let you raise Carole."

"I can't promise you anything, but you're off to a good start. I remember Nashville, and I don't want Carole exposed to that or your don't-give-a-shit lifestyle."

"Does our meeting today look like 'don't-give-a-shit' to you?"

Bonnie was a cautious woman, some would say hard. She gave me the answer I was expecting. "I knew you were going to have to do something for Carole, no matter what, and I am impressed by what you've done, but that doesn't mean your feet fit into a real father's shoes."

"Carole is the last living person holding me on this planet, and if I'm going to live here, I have to put every part of me into accepting fatherhood, and it scares me. I don't want to fail."

"Something really bad happened to you, didn't it? What was it? I've never heard you say *anything* like what you've been saying today."

I nodded, but my eyes couldn't meet hers. "Yeah, something really bad did happen to me. I won the lottery. I remember when it was easy being me, but now I struggle with it … would you mind dropping me off in Bent Pines?"

CHAPTER FIFTY-FIVE

There are only so many tears you can devote to loneliness and forlorn loss of hope. I was over budget in that department, and I left it all in Nashville. Even Megan slipped off the viewfinder as Carole was a pleasant face to see in my active conscience. I found myself studying young children and their habits as I walked around town. My Carole set the bar. She was prettier, better behaved, and more intelligent than any on earth. I found myself in the children's department in stores and asking the clerks what was in fashion for nine-year-olds these days. I had a whole new world to discover. I was happy, surprised, and off balance as I gained knowledge of the concerns of parents. I passed a shoe store and saw a pair of shoes on a shelf that looked like goofy dad shoes. One of these days, I'd buy them and put them on for Bonnie.

Aspen was an entertainment town, and as I breathed in the mountain air I felt a longing for the music I'd been a part of. I could see myself doing gigs in the afternoon, entertaining tourists coming off the ski slopes. As much as it appealed to me, it wasn't a healthy occupation for a solid fatherly image. At the end of the evenings, I'd make my way home after listening to the new generation of lounge music. I was disappointed by the current sound, echoing dully through the streets.

I began digging out old music and rearranging it to a more upscale quality. I sat in my condo, listening to old songs on the stereo and devouring an ungodly and unhealthy ration of liquor. I watched Betty's CD of Table Fifty-Seven over and over, which didn't help. Then I'd awaken the next morning, or was it afternoon, and knew I had to snap out of it. Becoming a sobbing drunk and washed-up musician was not the image I wanted Carole to have of me. I was going to have to do something about it.

During my roam through nostalgia I ran across a guy that played in my band years ago. He was at a happy hour gig, strumming old worn out tunes that dated him. The tourist couldn't give a shit whether he strummed or not, so we talked. I called Butt Crack.

"Hey, Butt Crack, this is Owen."

"Hey, Owen, what's up?"

"Do you have anything solid put together for the season?"

"Same old shit. Stanley and Jimmy are supposed to meet up later this week."

"I have something I want to run by you. I'll load up on cold beer, and you can stop by my place around seven."

"I don't know, man. I'm a worn out old dog with too many fleas to scratch as it is. I don't want any new tricks to learn."

"You're going to love this!"

"Okay, but skip the beer. I quit drinking."

Pat Jarrett called me with the good news. He told me that Bonnie's attorney nearly jumped out of the fifth story window of his office when he showed him the agreement. He said, "I told him I would hold the window open for him so he wouldn't break any glass on the way down."

Pat laughed. "The fucker had the balls to conference with his client with me sitting in the room. He read her chapter and verse, then presented a fantasy settlement. He was all over the place, making you the biggest jerk on the planet."

I said, "That was her opinion when I talked to her."

"I reminded both of them that opinions and law don't always coincide, and if we were going to have a discussion about opinions, I'd shoot them an itemized set of questions calling Mrs. Fletcher's character into question. Then I asked if she was willing to have that on a public record."

"Pat, we agreed we'd not use that card. It would hurt Carole in the long run." That pisses me off. "What were you thinking?"

"I'm an attorney, my job is to bluff. My job is to make her attorney look like a cheap suit, which is what I did. I appealed to her maternal logic and how sensitive you were to her concerns for your daughter. Predictably, her attorney made it all about the money. When we got to the custody and visitation issues, he had an elaborate scheme to share custody and had a stringent visitation agreement. That did it. She snapped and we had our settlement."

"Are you sure? I haven't heard from her."

"You will. Her attorney gave her the low story on your connection with the Fort Benning massacre. You going to be okay with the settlement?"

"Yeah, I had hopes that what happened wouldn't be brought up. It'll certainly prejudice her feeling about me seeing Carole."

"Maybe not. If it comes up, just tell the truth. Okay, I have to get to work. Let me know how you're doing."

Bonnie called right after that. She told me we had a deal and she wasn't backing out, but her attorney had told her something that scared her, and she wanted to ask me about it.

I said, "It's all over the Columbus, Georgia newspapers. You can read about it on the Internet. I don't want to talk about it."

"We'll talk later. See you Friday."

I knew I had only a second before she put the phone down. It wasn't the best time to tell her my plans, and I didn't want her hearing it from anyone else, so I jumped right in. "Bonnie, I'm thinking about starting up a band to have something to do."

"Geez, Owen, not again."

"I'm just doing the arrangements. I'm not going to be in the band. I just want to try out a few ideas."

"Whatever." Her long sigh was a disappointed confirmation that I was a junkie making excuses for a fucked-up lifestyle.

Still, I argued my case. "I need a hobby. I'm just trying to find something to fill in an empty hole."

"I remember how you do hobbies. It became an obsession that caused you to leave these mountains. We both know how that worked out."

"It's just a hobby."

" Sure it is." Sarcasm and bitterness filled the air long after she hung up.

CHAPTER FIFTY-SIX

Butt Crack stopped by and he was impressed with my digs. He said, "Never once did I see a grand piano sittin' in the parlor of a ski lodge. When did you start thumpin' ivory?"

"It's easier to score music on a piano."

He wasn't done looking the place over as he continued to follow our conversation. "I suppose it beats a flat top and post-it notes. Man, you have some kinda gig going on or what? This place looks like a recording studio."

"I have neighbors so I keep the volume turned down."

His head was in the air, checking out the fixtures. "You must've turned the volume up somewhere along the line 'cause this ain't no roadie shack. No siree, I'd say Owen Fletcher hit the mother lode."

"You still staying over on Glen Birch Road?"

"Yep, like always. Wow, this is some duck blind you got here. Did you switch gears or something?"

"Yeah, I hit the lottery."

He didn't believe me and said, "If you're moving traffic, I'm out the door and don't want to know you're in town. I quit doing that shit a long time ago."

"That's good, Butt Crack."

"The name's Phil. Phil Thorpe. Disrespect me one more time, and I'll shove eighty-eight keys up your ass one at a time."

"Sorry, I didn't know you by any other name." I could tell he was uncomfortable and ready to bolt, so I said, "Can I get you something, soda, juice, milk?"

I sat him down with a glass of milk and played him the DVD of Table Fifty-Seven in their stride. He sat there saying, "damn, that's hot," repeatedly.

"What do you think, Phil?"

He didn't offer a comment.

"Well, what did you think?"

"Play it again. This time I want to listen to the music. That broad is hand-job hot."

I played it two more times for him. When I finished, he asked, "Who did the arrangement? It was fuckin' awesome."

"She did."

"You didn't?"

I shook my head and he said, "Now we have something to talk about. The red head, where is she?"

"Unavailable."

"What about the brunette?"

"Unavailable."

"I'm not going to ask. I gotta say I'm seeing genius at work here. She took a lot of liberties with some awesome Goldies and really turned up the heat. What I like is how the arrangement still resonates with the original song, but goes into outer-space with the lyrics …like a favorite song with new clothes on it."

"I want to replicate that sound. I've been re-mastering works to fit her vocal range. Maybe we could try it out on the mountain and see if it flies."

Phil looked at me as if I had a screw loose. "Didn't you say the redhead and the brunette are unavailable? You have some kind of plan to get them back?"

"No. We'll audition. I want you to see what I've been working on. I've got a Hall and Oates that I remastered. Take a look at it."

"You're joking. Why not Bing Crosby and 'White Christmas'?" He looked at the sheets I had scribbled on and scratched his head. "'Private Eyes' is lame, dude, even when it was a new release."

I went to the piano and began banging out the chorus. When I finished I said, "The chorus has too much ginger bread in it, too much harmony and not enough pitch. You sing the lyrics over the chorus like I wrote it."

We got through it and I looked at Phil. He was looking straight at me, blinking his eyes. "We crucified that song," he said. Phil dropped his sheet music and turned for the door.

"Where are you going?" I shouted after him.

"I've got to get my guitar out of the car. We've got a lot of work to do if we're going to headline that crappy song."

"Does that mean you liked it?"

"It means you're a damned genius. I loved it."

We tinkered with it until we were satisfied we had a pretty good song to showcase. Phil nodded toward the DVD and said, "Play that one more time." When it finished, he sneered and shook his head. "If we mean business, we need to get the redhead back."

"That's out of the question. We'll branch out and audition someone with her range." I asked him if he knew of anyone. There weren't that many female vocalists who made the circuit. The real hot ones usually ended up in a family way or out of the business for one reason or other. I told Phil that "hot" was not that important. We needed a vocalist, and we would work around hot. Off the top of his head, he couldn't think of anyone.

He hit his head with his palm. "Wait. Just a sec. Jimmy Hernandez hooked up with a gal last season who sometimes sat in with us. She needs a push, but she has the range of the brunette. The only problem is Jimmy. You know how he is. He's seasonal and so are his women. I'll call him and see if they're still together."

We needed to put flyers out for auditions, and I asked Phil to come up with something.

"How about 'vocalist needed, voice is important, ugly doesn't matter.'"

We were in the hunt for a female vocalist with Betty's pipes.

I spent the rest of the week renting a rehearsal hall and took a trip to Denver to purchase some audio equipment we would need. Phil stayed busy passing flyers around. The first audition was a complete bust, so we'd have to canvass Denver and all points in between if we were going to get a lead female vocalist.

In the meantime, I had business to attend to. I met Bonnie at the title office on Friday, and as promised, she had her own set of keys by midmorning. Business was done. Carole had a new home, so what more was there to say? Bonnie had been subdued and quiet through the transaction. We didn't even shake hands and I turned to leave. She stopped me at the door.

"You got a minute?"

"Sure."

"I read what happened to you. I'm sorry. I read between the lines, and that was really low, but it wasn't about the money they stole, was it?"

"No. It was about the woman I loved, and she isn't speaking to me either."

"If you'd learn to start talking to the people who love you, you'd discover a whole new world. She broke your heart, didn't she? That must have been a first for you."

"No. you own that title, but yeah, I got my heart broken. Megan's moved on. It's going to take awhile for me to get over it."

"I read the local gossip. This Megan, you're better off without her. I was talking about the other woman, the one you spent a million dollars on."

She had a knowing smile on her face, and it infuriated me. Before I could say a word, she said, "Call me sometime. I want to talk to you about Carole. How's the band coming? Good luck with that."

My mind side-stepped her comment about the band and went straight to the important point. "You mean that? I want you to tell me all about her."

"Let's have lunch later next week."

CHAPTER FIFTY-SEVEN

We were into our tenth Denver audition and we weren't even close. There was a natty hippie chic whom we put off until last. Phil knew about her. He said she was a street artist with a volatile temper and a thousand-horsepower bad attitude. Aside from being crazy to the point of institutionalization, she could make a train take a dirt road. Her mousy brown hair was in dreadlocks, and she had more body piercings than General Custer after the Indians got done with him. Dark eyeliner, like Egyptian queen Cleopatra, was smeared on her face, and I could barely see the color of her eyes. She got to her feet, dressed in a combination of buckskins and burlap. Butch to the extreme, she stared me down with a contemptuous sneer, sending attitude vibes at the speed of light.

"What's your name, honey?"

"Jennifer."

"Do you go by Jenny?"

She spit on the floor and said, "Didn't I just tell you Jennifer?"

Jesus, I was facing a Calamity Jane on steroids ready for a shoot-out. She had two wolf tattoos on both arms. Their fangs were jumping out at me and I was about to end the audition right then and there, but I played the DVD anyway.

After viewing it, Jennifer said, "Whoever did the rearrangements did a freakin' majestic awesome job. Give me a shot, Mister. This shit is right up my alley."

"The redhead did the arrangement," I said.

"No fucking way! I want to meet that broad some fuckin' day."

Phil gave me a what-the-hell shrug, and I said, "Give it a shot."

I'll tell you how that went. Jennifer parked the notes right where they needed to be first time. It wasn't as polished as Betty's performance, but it was close. I looked at Phil and he raised his eyebrows, then I gave her the tough one—Abba's "Waterloo," where Betty had arranged two distinct vocal ranges. Jennifer put the lights out. She understood why Betty arranged the song the way she did. She held the notes exactly the way I wanted them, and she finished with a wry grin.

I had a decision to make, and I needed to have a frank conversation with Jennifer before I made it. "You saw the performance of the redhead," I said.

"Yeah, fuckin' amazing."

"This is the deal, Jennifer, that woman had never sung a note in public in her life. She put that performance on with twelve days of practice. I drive down the road very fast and you have to keep up. I don't put up with bad attitudes, tantrums, or sulking. This is a job that requires a lot of work."

"I can do that, Mister."

"You can start by losing the attitude. If you can't be civil, pretend."

"Tell me I got the gig, and I'll be Little Bo Peep. Swear to God."

There was just one more item that wasn't going to work, but I pitched it anyway. "You're going to need a complete makeover, and I mean complete. We need to get you as close to the redhead as possible." I nodded at the tattoos and said. "I don't suppose there's anything we can do about those but to cover them up.

I expected Jennifer to walk off. Instead, she let out a long sigh and said, "Geez, I was hoping you'd say that. I'm so sick of these dreadlocks and this nappy outfit, I could scream." She started taking the piercings off and I was waiting for an explanation.

"Mister, the only way to make real street money is by being an outlandish freak, the freakier the better. Ordinary, well-dressed street artists don't make squat. You have to look like you need the money in the worst way. That's the way it works." She spit on her forearm and began rubbing vigorously. "See, they come off. Underneath, I'm freakin' Mona Lisa, and you don't mark-up Mona Lisa with permanent ink."

I told her she had the job and to catch up to us in Aspen as soon as she could.

She froze. "Hey, how am I supposed to get to Aspen? Wait five and I'll go with you." She scampered off before we could utter a word. I looked at Phil and he looked at me. We both shared the same reservation.

"No way, Owen, I've got a full house with Stanley on his way. Jimmie and Bobbie need a room to themselves, and I think Julian will want to bunk up until he finds his own crib."

I said, "She's not staying with me. Period. End of subject."

"Just until we get a little money coming in. Come on, Owen, you know how it works."

I did, and I gave up that lifestyle a long time ago. "You're the band manager, figure something out."

"That girl ...Owen! You can't be that inhumane. We'll build her a cage on the porch."

"Shit ...I'll get her a place of her own," I growled.

"That's a lot of green to spring for, especially if we don't know if she'll work out."

I didn't care. There was something about that rag-bag girl that I had a hunch about.

We were busy through the weekend. Jennifer cleaned up nicely...sorta. We still had some work in that department. After losing the burlap rags and the nappy hairdo, Jennifer seemed much smaller in stature. Her teeth need to be bleached if she was going to open her mouth on stage. Other than that, her face, which was now visible to the naked eye, was quite attractive. She still exuded her pissed off ghetto attitude in a mean-assed butch kinda way. That would have to change too.

We went into practice and I pushed Jennifer. At least I was doing something. Riding herd on our diva was a fulltime job.

CHAPTER FIFTY-EIGHT

I met up with Bonnie at the Cloverleaf on Wednesday. She told me how life had suddenly changed, and it had been so fast she'd hardly drawn breath yet. Much of the strain in her face the last time I had seen her was gone. I pretended to share her happiness, and I couldn't shut her up. She reached into her purse, removed an envelope, and handed it to me. "I thought you'd like to have this," she said.

I opened the envelope to find Carole's school picture in it. The picture of Carole Anne Fletcher was a multi-million dollar photo, worth every penny. I studied it. It was me. She had that charming Fletcher signature smile. Her hazel eyes danced in my face, and she had my complexion.

I was choked up. She had my thick hair that was cutely bobbed. "Tell me about her, Bonnie. Don't leave anything out."

"She's too much like you. Nothing bothers her, and she doesn't have a shy bone in her body. She's always singing, and she has your gift for music. The first thing I'm doing is buying her a piano and lessons to go with."

"I'm for hire."

Bonnie rolled her eyes.

We forgot the time as we talked. I was drinking it all in, every small detail, no matter how small. I wanted to know her habits. Her likes and dislikes, her achievements, moods, fears, and all of her little girl dreams. Bonnie was surprised each time I'd interrupt her to elaborate on something she took as a casual statement. She looked at her watch. In a hurried voice she said, "I need to go. I have to pick Carole up at school. Owen, you really act like you care. How's the band coming along?

"It keeps me busy. It's a work in progress." An idea struck me. "We're putting on a promotional concert at the Snowmass Mall two weeks from Saturday. I'd like Carole to be in the audience."

"I thought you weren't in the band."

"I'd make an exception just this one time. Come on, Bonnie; give her a sneak preview of her papa."

"That's not the way I want her to meet her father. I detest that whole scene. We got all that on Glenn Birch Road, and the place is filling up with seasonals. God, I'm glad we're out of there."

"So much for that idea," I said.

"Come up with something better."

Jimmy Hernandez; his girlfriend, Bobbie; and Stanley got into town. They settled into Bonnie's old shack on Glen Birch. Jimmy was lead guitar, Stanley was a whiz on the key board, and we had a drummer and base player already signed on and up to speed. The big question mark was Bobbie.

Bobbie was a tall reed of mystic good looks. She was right off the reservation and very shy. Her speaking voice was low and quiet, and I wasn't sure about her. She was nervous and too shy to even sing in front of us, but Jennifer took over. "Let's do this together. See that back wall? We're going to paint it with our voices. Use those stomach muscles like you're giving birth." The results were not what I was expecting from such a waif creature. After a few run-throughs, Phil and I both saw the possibilities.

I showed everyone the theme of the band. After they reviewed Betty's DVD, there were smiles on every face. They all knew we were on to something, and I had to chase them off at the end of the night.

We went into practice early the next day. We spent most of the morning bringing Bobbie along, and Jennifer took her under her wing. I had to say this about Trophy, the name of our new band; these veterans were dead serious about music. Even when we went into break, they collaborated to workout individual flaws. I could see that Phil had a steady hand on the band, and I backed away to work on more material. It was rewarding to watch them bond, form relationships, and begin a music family. The days flew by, and we had a finished product ready for the public. The only question was whether the public was ready for us.

I talked to Bonnie a couple of times before our public debut. Everything was fine on the home front, Bonnie's home front anyway. I really didn't give a shit about mine. Bonnie said Carole was upside down in her new home. It took a lot of convincing to get it through her head that they actually lived there. Carole was a chip off the old block, and she worried that there was just too much space to put anything. Bonnie laughed as she told me that Carole's favorite activity was moving the furniture around everyday after school.

I asked when I was going to meet my daughter. She stiffed me both times. It was about my occupation, such as it was. I explained that I was just background noise. Phil managed the band and it was on autopilot.

She said, "You're incredibly talented, Owen. It's not fair of me to make you give up the only thing you're good at, but you understand why I can't let Carole be around musicians and road trash."

That pissed me off, and I said, "Then why did you move her to Glenn Birch Road and live in the middle of it for the last ten years? We made it off Glenn Birch Road and made it to Nashville, remember? Don't make me feel dirty, Bonnie. I didn't put Carole back here. You did because you can't put up your skis. When are you going to figure out that you lost the title to Miss Snow Queen a long time ago?"

I forgot how many times I tried to apologize for blowing up. Bonnie didn't take my calls, and I wasn't going to leave messages for Carole to overhear.

Saturday came and I was excited to be launching my killer band. We were supposed to set up in the outdoor pavilion, but we got a treat from the mall manager. He moved us indoors to the conference center. We were setting up when who walks in but Jennifer. I had argued with her about her shoddy makeover, and I'd given her an open check book to do something about it. She did, and what a transformation. Her tomboy persona was, well, gone. She wore an elegant black dress that was runway hot, and she filled it out. Phil and I both did a double take and he said, "Now that's what I'm talking about."

She walked up to us looking like a real diva, and she whispered in my ear, "I'm not as hot as the redhead, but I'm damned close."

The public was beginning to filter in. There were maybe forty people in the center when it was our time to debut. It was a disappointing beginning for Trophy. Let me rephrase that, it was a dismal start for Trophy. I decided to waive the flowery introductory crap or else we'd loose half of the audience. I said to the band "Let's get out there and get to the business end." We received a lack-luster reception. The applause was more or less an inquisitive invitation. The faces of those that were in seats were unenthused and I sensed restlessness.

Right there in the front row was a little girl clapping. My Carole. We took the stage and I gave her a heart sign. Here we go.

We started with Alicia bridges' "I Love the Night Life." Standing in front of me was a child trying to sing along, going wild and totally out of control. That was my Carole: *my* daughter, my bridge to life. The auditorium was beginning to draw a crowd, but my whole focus was on that little sand bag shaking her little butt and gettin' the rhythm. Bonnie had to rein her in a few times.

We had a lot of things working for us. Jennifer talked to everyone like family, and she had an immediate niche-following without singing a single note. Bobbie's shy quality created a curiosity. When she belted out her song, people looked at each other with mystification, never expecting such a strong vocal performance. Phil was completely at ease, as if he was the inventor of music, while Jimmy crooned to a certain crowd of young ladies. Stanley was Stanley. He was comical, as he was lost in his own world as master of the keyboard. We didn't let up for an entire hour, and we got what we came for. I gave the audience a new sound, a classic look, and tons of personality.

We were about to wrap it up when Phil surprised me and called me front stage. "Get out here, Owen. Let's see if you still have the stuff rock stars are made of."

I was as nervous as a new groom standing in the back of the church. I could really blow this. I turned to the band and said, "We didn't rehearse this, but my daughter is out there, and I want to close with 'Babe I Love You' by Styx."

Jennifer said, "I don't even have to guess which one is your little girl. Sure thing, Owen. We've got your back."

Jimmy gave me his microphone, and I spoke into the mike. "This song goes out by request to Carole Fletcher." I saw Bonnie gasp. I want to tell you, there's no harmony that resonated better than that little voice singing back at me as I sang her favorite song. I went to the edge of the stage and put my mike to her face and let her sing a part of the chorus. That was the first time I had a live performance with my daughter, and she had no idea who I was. You never forget moments like that.

We finished to a strong standing ovation, and I went around and introduced everyone but myself. Our new fans were leaving, and Phil was talking it up with entertainment managers interested in taking us on. I let Phil handle it because there were two members of the audience who hadn't moved. Bonnie motioned for me to take a seat with them. My heart leaped out of my chest, and I didn't bother to take the stairs. In seconds, I was sitting next to my child, anticipating what was to come. Carole turned her cute little head and said, "You're really good, Mister." I saw Bonnie's expression which meant, "Let me handle this."

"What did I tell you this week about your daddy?" Bonnie asked.

"You said daddy didn't drown in the ocean." What kind of story had Bonnie told that child?

"What else did I tell you?"

"You said daddy was captured by pirates." Good job Bonnie.

"And?"

"You said daddy escaped from the pirates who had captured him, and he was coming to see me. I don't believe you, Mama!" I saw her little jaw start to tremble.

Bonnie had concocted a fish tale to prepare Carole for this meeting. Little girls didn't need to deal with adult problems, and I was glad that Bonnie handled it the way she did. I was going to have to study up on pirates.

"Carole, I told you that daddy had a surprise for you didn't I?"

Carole knew something was coming. "Yessss ...?"

"This nice man is your daddy, and he put this concert on just for you!"

Carole looked like she had just been stung with a cattle prod. Bonnie and I were smiling, looking at a little girl whose head was on a swivel, looking back and forth at her parents in shocked disbelief. Carole started to cry and so did I.

"Are you really my daddy?" she said with a look of intense hope.

I felt my throat constrict, as I fought to keep my tears in check. "Yes, I am, and I thought of you everyday those mean old pirates had me chained up."

"Is that true, or are you just making that up?" Carole was a wise ass, just like me.

"Yes, it is."

She put her fingers on my face, probing as though I might be wearing a mask. She had a hungry look in her eyes, then they flew open with gleeful recognition. "You look a lot like me! You really are my daddy!" That little sprite was in my arms so fast, and small fingers were clasped around my neck.

Bonnie said, "Carole, you keep asking me why we have a new house, a new car, and lots of nice things. Your daddy didn't only escape from the pirates, he took all their treasure chests with him, and he wants to share some of it with you."

"Daddy, did you buy Mommy and me a new house? Mommy makes a lot of stuff up."

"Yes, I did." Bonnie didn't have to do that. She told me later she didn't want Carole growing up thinking that I'd deserted her.

The members of Trophy were touched. They'd put their heads together and had their own idea of how to mark a special moment for my daughter and me. They invited Carole and me to the stage to sing a song.

Bonnie was instantly in her feathers, glaring at me. "Owen, I don't want Carole around those kind of people."

We declined the invitation.

My reunion with Carole went smashingly well I thought. Bonnie didn't and she told me straight off that I was forbidden from seeing her again if I ever took her around my music crowd. Carole was just too young, and she needed time to be a little girl. I could deal with that...she was probably right.

CHAPTER FIFTY-NINE

My visitations were restricted to weekends that were supervised by Bonnie. Carole and I hit it off so well that Carole ignored her mother most of the time she was with me. I had to correct her and tell her to mind her mother. Carole badgered me constantly about the band, and I kept telling her no. She told her mother that when she grew up, she was going to be just like Jennifer.

Bonnie didn't have to work anymore, but her love of snow skiing was in her blood as much as music was in mine. She was a paramedic on the ski patrol and coached competitive skiing. Sometimes she took Carole up on the mountain with her. They left me in the dust, so I always waited for them in the lodge.

One afternoon, I got a call from Bonnie. "Owen, I'm stuck on the mountain. Can you pick Carole up from school?"

I jumped at the chance. I went to the school, and Carole couldn't wait to introduce her pirate father to her friends. Afterwards, we went to my condo. I thought it would be a good idea to cook a meal for the family. Carole also thought it would be a wonderful idea, and she took off to the kitchen. It wasn't long before I heard her laughing. Marching into the den, she put her hands on her hips and stomped her foot. "Daddy, we need to go shopping. There's nothing but junk food in the cabinets."

After filling two carts full of nutritious food, we went back to the condo and set to work making a meal. Carole taught me how to make a salad from scratch, while she put a roast in the oven with peeled potatoes and carrots. My daughter would teach me how to cook, whether I was willing or not.

Bonnie showed up after dark and a hard day on the mountain. She was delighted to see that Chef Owen and Chef Carole had a happy time cooking together. My privileges with Carole opened up, and it became a regular habit for us to cook dinner together. One night a week became two. Eventually, I got a key to Bonnie's house so that I could babysit Carole after school. Why is it that happiness accelerates the speed which you go through life? If I was any happier, I'd be dead in a week.

We weren't exactly a family, and Bonnie and I were smart enough not to go there, but we became good friends. Bonnie had a new boyfriend who was taking up a lot of her time. He was a new doctor at the community hospital. Daniel was a nice guy, and I thought that maybe this romance would take. I was fine with it because it gave me more time with Carole.

During one of Bonnie's date nights, Carole and I sat at the piano, and I started banging away. Little fingers began repeating what I had just played, and we were caught up in a new passion, which we kept to ourselves. By Christmas, Carole could play holiday music that was exceptional for a child her age, and I went to her school to listen to her play in front of her peers. Proud dad for sure, and pissed off mother for sure.

"Owen, what did I tell you about this?"

"You didn't say a thing about me teaching her to play the piano. She's really good, isn't she?"

"Just the piano. Don't even think about taking her around the band."

"I've kept my promise. I'm trying to be a good dad."

"Yes, you have, and you need to take a break from it. You need to find a woman in your life. Get out and date."

"I can't. I haven't got past Megan."

"I never thought you had the depth of soul to hurt for more than ten minutes."

"It took me ten years to get over you." I knew how to shut Bonnie up.

Winter zipped along. Phil and the gang played to a full house every night. I played to a full house every other night. During my interludes, I'd check in with my Nashville friends. I was really checking up on Megan, trying to explore the possibility of an opening to make an apology of some sorts to Megan.

Jerry and Megan ran in the same circle, and he derailed my inquiries by throwing me another woman to think about. He said, "You know Elizabeth is working in our public relations department. She's damned good at what she does. This might piss you off, but she's become a good friend. We talk about you a lot. I wish you'd give her a break and stop hating her for something that wasn't her fault."

"I don't want to hear about that woman. What about Megan? How does she feel about me?"

"That dog won't hunt…ever. The less said about her, the better. Elizabeth would like to hear from you."

I was quick with my response. "Jerry, don't make Betty a fault line in our friendship."

Pissing off Jerry was always ill advised since he never had much control over his mouth. "You need to speak with your attorney and the FBI chick, because neither one says a word to me about *your* scandal. You don't live here, but Elizabeth does and you burned her at the stake."

There was something Jerry wasn't telling his old pal. He was decidedly taking sides with Betty and putting distance between Megan and himself. Truthfully, I was worried how Megan was coping. I could only guess how hard it would be to show her face in our old social circle. I asked Jerry if she was getting out, if she was still being harassed, and how she faced the humiliation of Betty's betrayal.

Jerry snorted, then laughed. "Did you ever hear the story how Libby Custer made a career promoting General George Custer's false legacy? Megan basks in the sympathy of a woman supremely wronged and she's made herself a celebrity spinning the scandal. Your old friend Stevie Sievers props up her saga and has a lot to say about you in your younger days. They're quite a pair."

"Are you saying she's dating Stevie?" It came as a shock to me. Stevie doesn't date. He plays with dolls and hangs around toy stores. I didn't believe Jerry and said so.

He snorted again and said, "That's the rumor. As a known associate of yours, our mutual friends clam up in my presence. Ask agent Houseman or Pat Jarrett."

One thing about Jerry, He didn't pass on rumors without substantive proof. He's a tight lipped banker.

"What aren't you telling me?" I asked with a tone of deep resentment.

Jerry was done. He said, "All I can tell you is both of their bank statements share the same address. Figure it out for yourself." He hung up on me.

I slammed the phone down for only a second. I dialed Joyce. She had to know and I wanted to find out what she knew—and when.

Joyce was less than cordial when the subject came to Megan. As per usual, Joyce thought Megan and Fox conspired from the very beginning. She also believed that the partnership was flawed because Fox was only partially successful siphoning a few million dollars on his elaborate scam, where as Megan saw a means to get it all by marrying me...Well—half if she divorced me, or all of it if she were widowed. "You want my theory?" She asked.

"No. I want the truth."

"Megan became star struck when you introduced her to Stevie. It was obvious that you weren't going anywhere in the celebrity circuit. Fox played his hand and sabotaged her plans to marry into money, but more importantly into society. In doing so, it ended their partnership leaving her to put distance between Fox, you, and the whole sordid debacle. She played the 'wronged-woman' card to the hilt but what the general public didn't know and you apparently didn't either, she had been having a tryst with your buddy, Stevie, before your engagement blew up in your face."

Naturally I was in total denial. I got tired of her rant and said, "Joyce, you're making this personal and I know how you feel about Megan. When did you learn about Megan and Stevie?"

"I wouldn't be talking to you now if you are interfering with my investigation into a conspiracy to commit murder. Megan is and has been a suspect from day one. It broke my heart to watch what happened to you and I couldn't say shit to you."

"Why are you just now getting around to telling me?"

"Because you're too fucking obsessed and you're dicking around and asking too many questions that's going to impact my investigation."

Her voice lowered and I knew she was going to lie to me. "Megan's relationship with Fox leaked bubbles from the very beginning. Fox is a manipulator of imperial rank. He provides the gas and the matches, but when the fire starts, he's nowhere to be found. I don't think she had any idea where Fox was headed, but she was in too deep because she understood one fact; Fox was insulated behind her and she had been manipulated into committing several felonies on his behalf. It turned into murder. I believe we'll find that Fox had everything to do with your ambush at Lawson's farm. Megan leaked the details. Why, I don't know."

"You've known this all this time and didn't tell me?"

"Look, Owen, something has changed in the investigation. Have you talked to Jerry?"

I was snippy with her. "Jerry is all taken in with Betty's bullshit. He hinted there was a rumor."

"Did he tell you that your old pal Stevie eloped with Megan two weeks ago?"

How was I supposed to respond to that? I didn't say anything because there was nothing in my mind but fierce anger.

She said, "You can stop beating yourself up over Megan. It's out in the open, but not in a transparent manner. Megan and Stevie started shacking up a week after they met. They used your room at the Hermitage while you were off being Farmer Brown. I had a tail on her as I suspected her intentions."

I was in denial and blew up, "You've always been suspicious of her. You're making this up. You don't know what went on in the hotel. They have tight security there and Alvin Fox would have been notified."

"Didn't need to notify Fox or have you forgotten? Your room was wired and if you're smart enough to figure this out, Fox has incriminating evidence on Megan, which means he isn't done with you yet. My source didn't come from our field agent or Fox."

I felt violated. "You mean to tell me you were recording what went on in my suite? How dare you. Did you have a warrant? I don't believe this. Jesus, I need to call Patrick." I was crushed by her blatant accusation and I directed my anger upon Joyce. "You're lying. You're jealous of her, aren't you?"

"On a personal level, maybe, but on a professional level I want her behind bars. Do you remember when you had Peggy pick up a few things you forgot while she was shopping in Nashville. She came by the hotel and caught them by surprise. It got ugly and loud."

"That was a long time before I asked Megan to marry me."

"I'm only guessing, but that may be the reason Megan eloped with your buddy. My take away from Peggy is Megan has a history of multiple suitors at the same time. They feel bad with what happened to you, if that's any consolation."

"Who else knows about this?"

"Just the housekeeping staff that cleaned up after her. We've talked to them."

The line was quiet as I jammed up my brain trying to think of anything further to say. "I wish you had told me a long time ago."

"You were leaving town, and it was a struggle for all of us to get you out of here in one piece. We all agreed. Me, Pat, Walt, and Peggy— all of us, except Jerry."

"Why not tell Jerry?"

"He's still a person of interest in the bank fraud case, besides, his loyalty to you is...commendable. You'd been through enough."

She changed the subject. "Pat tells me you're a champion father. One of these days, I'll take a vacation and come see your family." We talked about Carole, Bonnie, the band, and my new passion, fatherhood.

We closed on a good note, like the note you hear when a patient flat lines. It would take awhile to clear the clutter of faulty notions and to tear down the ivory tower I had built around Megan. Megan had complete control of my life and the full extent of it was scary. Her ambitions got out ahead of her while mine lagged in the wake of her duplicity. Being perfectly honest, I think Megan loved the vision of who she wanted me to become. She was fooling herself if she thought I'd be anything other than the vagabond she met at the lottery office.

CHAPTER SIXTY

February blew by, and we were on to March and the height of ski season. We had more than an abundant snow fall. The slopes were crazy with skiers on spring break. Bonnie and her crew went about the mountain inspecting conditions and closing off access to dangerous areas. Between keeping herd on exuberant kids with a death wish and patching up those who came close to fulfilling it, Bonnie spent more time on the mountain, giving me even more time with Carole.

Carole started inserting vocals with her piano playing, and I coached her. One day she asked me if we could write a song for her mother.

After we had worked on it for a couple of weeks, Carole couldn't wait to debut it for her mother.

It was a Saturday afternoon, and we were polishing the song for Carole to play and sing her mother's song when Bonnie got home from the mountain. We took a stretch. I fixed us two glasses of juice, and we walked to the glass partition overlooking the valley below. Carole put her little arm around my waist. "I love you, Daddy. Do you think Mommy will like my song?"

"It's going to take her breath away, kiddo."

"Do you think Jennifer will like it?"

"Jennifer will steal it if you're not careful."

"Do you think it's that good?"

It was better than I let on. 'Bonnie's Song' would have to sit on the shelf for a few more years, or I would be in real hot water with the boss of both of us. I said, "What good is it to write a song to your mother if you don't intend for it to belong to her?"

Carole removed her arm from my waist and pointed. "Look there, Daddy, an avalanche."

I could see snow roiling from behind a peak in the distance. The avalanche was huge. A globe of white hung over the site. Swirls of snow raged within the dome. Carole and I stood there viewing the massive beauty of nature's destructive power. In all my years I hadn't seen anything quite like it. It was in a far off distance. Father and daughter were mesmerized by the sheer magnitude of it, never suspecting it would touch us.

The phone rang an hour later. The voice was panicked. I looked at Carole who was still spellbound by the avalanche. The caller's words were garbled with grief, but I immediately understood the meaning of the call. We were being summoned to the emergency aid center at the resort.

We arrived to a vigil of the relatives of the members of the ski patrol. Most of the personnel knew Carole very well and when they saw her, they began weeping. We were taken into a room, and the tragic event of the day was revealed to us. Bonnie, and two of her teammates, had gone into the back bowl to retrieve stranded skiers who had slid by the barriers. The avalanche caught the rescue party and buried it. Bonnie was among the missing. Hope was not lost, and they were doing everything possible to rescue the victims.

The pall set in and each hour that went by was another layer of granite on my shoulders. I had a little girl who wouldn't give up hope. We waited into the night for any word of survivors.

Carole slept in fits on the floor of the emergency center, waiting for word. We spent the night in the center, and in the morning, I caught Carole nibbling on a donut and drinking a cup of coffee, trying to talk the rescue team into taking her to the site.

We stayed with the other relatives trying to prop each other up with a faint whisper of hope. It was late in the afternoon when the first body bag came down. It was like sitting at a table with a revolver on the table that had one bullet in it, and I would spin the cylinder, put the barrel to my head, and pull the trigger. With each body bag that followed, I put another bullet in the chamber. Our body bag came down just before four o'clock. Bonnie was gone. Carole had lost an amazing mother, and I, a good friend. We had witnessed the grief of other relatives of victims with horror, and now it was our turn.

Daniel, Bonnie's love, was a basket case as he came down the mountain.

Carole went screaming from the center across the open snow, and stopped below the ski lift line of holiday skiers, and she screamed at them, over and over. "I fucking hate you bastards, all of you!" There she was giving everyone riding the lift the finger, venting her rage. Daniel and I joined her, took up her chant, and gave the world our fingers. We didn't stop until the last set of skiis passed overhead. We hugged each other, fell to the snow and cried until we were given sedatives and taken home.

Bonnie's house was being bombarded by well-intentioned mourners who had known her most of her adult life. It was all too much for a young child. Phil came to the house and hustled us out. Jennifer was with him, and they took the two of us to my place. Phil said, "Owen, I'm here to take care of things. You take care of Carole. Jennifer will stay with you. I'll handle everything here at the house."

Jennifer was stroking Carole's locks and singing softly to her. Carole, drugged out of her everlasting mind, was sleeping in fits of jerks and starts. Asleep and under sedation, the poor child cried and convulsed without stop. I was helpless. At that moment, I wanted God to come down from heaven so I could get between him and my little girl.

I had experienced a close and personal loss of someone close to me. The feelings hit me like a truckload. As an adult, I had an understanding of what a tragedy was about, or thought I did, but this was much different. Carole was too young for such a calamity to be settled upon her fragile mind. I was, for once, having pain that was not of my making and not owned by me. My pain was for my child who was now motherless. I wanted us to leave and run away, like I had so many other times. A child was mixed up in this awful tragedy, and she didn't deserve for me to fall apart on her. I was, to my knowledge, the only thing left for Carole to cling onto. I had to buck up and be strong enough for the both of us. That was a new role for Owen.

I was up at four, making coffee, when Jennifer came out and said she could use a cup. I thanked her profusely. Jennifer said, "Oh, I've been there. I lost both of my parents, and I was just a year or two older than Carole is. I had a night just like this one, and you know what? All I had was my uncle, and I would crawl into his bed every night, wanting to hurt someone for taking my parents away. Do you mind if I sleep over until this crisis is over?"

"Jennifer, you've done enough. Go home and get some rest." I was curious that she asked to stay over. I didn't want her help or God's help. She was mine and nothing was going to break our bond.

"Go home. I'll snuggle up with her, so when she wakes, I'll be there."

Jennifer frowned. "You can't be doing that."

"Jennifer. My daughter needs me."

"Yeah I know, but not in that way. My uncle felt exactly like you feel. You know what I did, Owen? When the child protective services began asking innocent questions, I accused my uncle of molesting me."

"Jennifer, your implication is revolting to me."

"Just listen, Owen. By suggestion and my own desire to strike out, I made that story up. My uncle is the kindest man in the word. I wanted to wound someone for my loss. Do you get it? I need to be here."

I was shocked and it showed.

"Owen, someone had to be responsible for my pain, and that person was the one closest to me. It was all fabricated, but I began to believe it myself. My story of abuse was so tight, I had the CPS believing it. Eventually, I was taken from my uncle's house and put into foster care."

"Geez, Jennifer. You're scaring me."

"I hope so. As many times as I've tried, the dear man has never spoken to me since. I'm here to make sure that doesn't happen to you and Carole."

I was seeing a soft side to this explosive woman, and that was welcomed. I needed help.

"Jennifer, I don't know what I would do without you. I don't even know where to start."

"We're just going to have to take our time with this. We need to keep her medicated for a while, but that's going to have to stop somewhere along the line. The sooner the better because it could turn her into a drug dependant teenager, like what happened to me."

Bonnie's memorial service was an elegant affair. I made sure of that. Phil had made all the arrangements. One could hardly get into the church for all the flowers. Bonnie, God bless her, had touched the hearts of all who knew her. The memorial was well attended, followed by the final act of taking Bonnie's ashes to be scattered at her favorite site with the best panorama of the mountains. We were met by an honor guard of the ski patrol. There was just Daniel, Jennifer, and me to escort Carole to the site. I stood there on that cold and windy spot, hoping that the elements would bring Bonnie's spirit home to rest in our hearts. I prayed for it, but she never came. The words of the pastor were faded whispers from another world. At last, the moment to send Bonnie home came, and Carole stood singing the song we wrote to her mother, as the pastor cast Bonnie's ashes to everlasting obscurity. The child's overpowering voice was strong and echoed to the valleys below, sending a chill to the spine of all who could hear. Carole finished the song and collapsed. Jennifer was there to catch her but no one was there to catch me.

I was now a single father with another woman full of rage on my hands. Thank God Jennifer had forewarned what to expect, and thank God she was there to keep a disaster from happening. Carole would sneak into my bed at all hours of the night like a sick torn lover, and Jennifer was there to yank her back to her own bed. At three in the morning, we would hear her on the piano, singing her mother's song, and at other times watching my DVD of Betty. We went through a month of the unexpected from Carole, and she wasn't getting any better.

Jennifer had a PHD in street psychology. She came to me six weeks into our mourning period and sat me down. As yet nothing was working. I had a sleep-deprived diva, singing laments at all hours of the night and day.

"You need to take Carole away from here. She feels that she's in a tomb with her mother. She hates the mountains that she looks out on every day. She hates the people who go up that mountain, and she hates you for making her look at her anguish every day. As much as I hate to say this, Bonnie forced her daughter to endure hardships so that Bonnie got her will and freedom in these mountains. When you look at it, it was a selfish thing to do."

"Don't talk like that, Jennifer. Bonnie was a good mother."

"Did I say she wasn't? Look, Carole's waking hours are consumed in hatred of this place. The only thing that soothes her is her obsession with your DVD of Betty. She watches it six or seven times a day. Give her some slack. She needs music in her life."

"I promised Bonnie."

"Fuck that, Owen. Neither you, nor Bonnie, can hold that child from her passion. One day she'll explode, and you'll find her with a guitar, wearing dreadlocks, singing in a subway tunnel, doing drugs out the ass. Is that what you want?"

"Is that what happened to you?"

"Yeah, fucking straight that's how it happened, and I'd give anything to walk it backwards. Give her a leash, and play it out a little bit at a time. Bring her to practice this afternoon."

For the next month, we showed up for every practice. Carole took to Stanley, and he let her play the keyboard to a couple of tunes that weren't too difficult. It seemed to break the spell. Carole was back in school, her strong will was back, and she was determined to catch up with her classmates. Her teachers were superb and gave her extra tutoring. We weren't out of the woods, but I could see daylight.

CHAPTER SIXTY-ONE

One afternoon, I was reading a cookbook. Cooking is an art form, and I was on my way to becoming an abstract artist. Our kitchen looked like a Picasso when I was tampering with fresh ingredients that were supposed to be edible. The doorbell rang, and there stood the entire band in a festive mood. They barged in without asking. "What's going on, Phil?"

"We fucking did it, sport. We actually did it."

"Did what?"

"Nashville, sport! We're going to Nashville for a recording of our first album, and you aren't going to believe this. If that works out, we're going to front for Jackhammer on their next concert tour."

I was happy as hell for them, but what did that have to do with me? Jennifer grabbed me by the collar, threw me on the floor, and sat on me. "You're coming with us, or I'll kick your ass all the fuckin' way to Nashville. You're going to manage and direct us, and I won't take no for an answer." See what I mean about Jennifer? Her exuberance can take on a violent form.

"Nashville is a long way from here," I said with a dubious lilt.

"Unless you want my stump grinding boot up your ass, you better say, yes Jennifer, and come along nicely."

"Let me think about it. Carole has to finish the school year."

"I'm not letting you off the floor unless you promise. You can catch up to us in Nashville, later. Now promise."

"Under one condition. No travel. I'm a stay-at-home dad."

Carole was leaping with joy at the news, and she put all her energy towards finishing school. She celebrated her tenth birthday, playing a piano concert for her school chums at our house. For ten, she could hammer the keys. I kept myself busy, closing the house up and shipping our things to Nashville. Before I knew it, we were sailing across the Cumberland River Bridge, the same bridge that I had so many sad thoughts about. It was as if a cycle had been completed. Bonnie had left me in this town. Megan had tossed me out the window, and Betty, well I guess you could say I tossed her over the bridge. I felt trepidations about crossing that bridge one more time.

We checked into the Hermitage until I could find the real estate I was looking for.

Never take a ten-year-old to the Mecca of their dreams and expect them to behave. We had been in Nashville the sum total of one day before my little spook discovered the sound of music drifting up from Second Street. She knew better than to ask, so she did what every kid would do. She hatched a plan to sneak off and check out the music scene on her own.

My darling angel was down Church Street and in the first bar while I was busy reviewing sound tracks. It was after three before I decided to intrude on her solitude and when I found her gone, I sounded the alarm. I had every employee of the hotel scouring the hotel for her. The doorman admitted she'd pulled a fast one. "She said she was waiting for her grandpa and when she burst through the door, she grabbed hold of a kindly gentleman's hand and began talking a mile a minute; he didn't think anything of it."

I didn't even have to ask which direction she went. I bloody well knew. I quickly began my search and yeah, there was a cute kid taking in the free music venues up and down Second Street. She used the same ruse she pulled on the doorman. I pub crawled all the way to the Wild Horse where I caught up to her.

Up Second Street we went, and I was babbling the whole time and all but dragged her toward the hotel. I got tackled by a kid and his dad. They thought I was abducting her because they had seen her with other people during the afternoon. These two good samaritans would not let me go unless I could prove who I was. They escorted us to the hotel and waited until they received satisfactory verification. That's Nashville for you.

I put her in her room, slammed the door, and said I was calling the FBI. That's exactly who I did call. Joyce was snickering while I tried to get some parental advice out of her. She said, "You want to bring her down, and I'll book her? Don't make a big deal about it. When you cool down, turn the tables on her and tell her how much trouble she could have gotten you into."

I poured myself a drink, sat on the couch, and wondered what kind of discipline I'd meet out. This was my first timeout when it came to heavy confrontation with a ten-year-old kid. I couldn't let something like that slide, could I? What would Bonnie do? God I missed her.

I heard the warble of a child's voice coming from the next room. She must've been upset and crying, knowing she'd been very bad. I tiptoed to the door and opened it an inch to check on her. Poor kid. She was lying on her bed with her face in a pillow… laughing. I was so pissed off I couldn't see straight. I pulled the door closed, leaned against it, thought about it, and…laughed.

I had to get Carole out of downtown Nashville before she started any bar fights. Jerry had already smoothed the way by connecting me with an agent friend of his. I was hooking up with Jerry, his agent, and Pat Jarrett at the Capitol Bar and Grille later that evening. I didn't want to leave Carole alone in her suite, but I didn't want to take her around Jerry and his pals either.

Jerry said over the phone, "Come on, Owen, I want to meet your little girl."

"Jerry, the words that come out of your mouth can melt church bells. I'll bring her, but you have to tone it down."

"Fuck you. I work in a bank, remember? I'll have my very best banker's face on."

"That should scare her. Make sure you tell Pat the same goes for him."

I told Carole about my friends, but not everything, and told her they were dying to meet her. Carole, who'd never met a stranger, was eager.

Jerry and his realtor friend showed up about the same time as Pat. Pat had agent Houseman with him. We met, and introductions were made. I have never seen grown men go so ape shit over a ten-year-old. Thank God Joyce showed up. She added an odd mix that made Carole curious.

Joyce said, "I heard you had quite a day. Did you enjoy the music venue?"

Carole said, "Yes, I did. There was this one group, called Diablo Locos, who's pianist played 'slide' boogie.' The instrumentals were to die for. I also liked—"

"Enough, Carole." I said.

"Yes, sir."

Joyce couldn't help herself and laughed. "Make sure you take your daddy with you. He could get into a lot of trouble with the law."

"Oh, I know who you are! You're the arrest lady at the FBI, who will put me in jail if I run off without daddy. You don't look wicked at all. You just need to eat better and get well."

Carole dazzled them with her smile and charmed them with her little pretend adult behavior. She was flirting, and I would have to put a stop to that.

Jerry asked Carole what she was going to do when she grew up. "Mr. Davis, I'm going to be a diva, and I'm not going to wait until I get grown up."

That provoked a spirited laugh from the grownups, which irked Carole. "I play the piano, and I'm quite good at it," she said in protest.

Jerry looked at her and egged her on by saying, "There's a piano in the lobby. Would you play Mr. Davis a song?" I rolled my eyes at Jerry.

"Can I, Daddy?"

It pissed me off that Jerry had called Carole out. "Do it, honey."

We made our way out to the lobby, and with the permission of the desk manager, Carole got her little butt behind the grand piano and started off by hammering down on "Rockin Pneumonia." People walking through the lobby stopped, backed up to see my little girl attacking the keys, not believing what they were witnessing. She had an audience. Just to prove she was not a one trick pony, she dove into "Nothin From Nothin," and piped out the song with her immature voice dead on. I'd give her performance a ten, but I was her dad. She stood arrow straight and said, "That was by Billy Preston, who started his musical career at the age of ten. Thank you for listening." She bowed to enthusiastic applause.

Carole took her cue from me and excused herself to go to her room to watch TV. I went with her to settle her in for the evening and then back to the grille to catch up on old times. When I sat at the table, Pat said, "I'm in love with your daughter."

"We all are," Jerry said. "For a tiny little voice, she took on a tiger of a song, and she was all about business. Wow! Chip off the old block."

I talked to Jerry's realtor friend about property and set up a house hunting tour for the following day. The man left for another appointment. Pat brought me up to date on my legal issues, which I had forgotten all about. Jolene and Hajji's cases were both dropped. My problems with Tarzan was about to be wrapped up. Not only had Tarzan dropped the original complaint, but they were going to have to pay me royalties on the materials I wrote and they used. Pat was holding Joyce's hand the whole time which was a surprise at several levels.

Jerry knew the music business and wanted to talk about the new buzz in town. "You have no idea what you've got, Owen. When I played the demo after Bonnie sent it to me, I played it in the car, and it was like silk and lightening at the same time—

"What did you just say?"

"I said it was smooth and smoking hot."

"Did you say, Bonnie sent you the demo?"

"Yeah, how did you think Clayton Phillips got it? I thought you knew. Old Clayton went bonkers, and you should have seen his dour old puss light up. That doesn't happen very often."

Not even believing what I had heard I asked again, "Wait, our Bonnie sent you the Demo. Not in a million years, Jerry. Bonnie hated the music business. Are you absolutely sure?"

"Hell yes, I'm sure. She sent a letter, and I think she talked to Clayton …just before the accident. You'd have to ask him about it, but I think she told him that you planned on leaving Colorado at the end of the season ….Did I say something wrong. You don't look so good."

I was transported out of the room, and I was ten years in the past, sitting with Bonnie in our beat-up Jeep Cherokee, singing our away across Kansas and Missouri to our new home in Nashville. What I would have given for her to have been with us on our second trip. If only she had told me.

CHAPTER SIXTY-TWO

It might sound like I spoiled my daughter, but I let her come with me to pick out our house. It wasn't exactly a *house* we picked out. It was a two-hundred-forty acre horse farm with a pond, woods to play in, pastures, a horse stable, and solitude. The farm backed up to a valley just off the Natchez-Trace Parkway, not far from Franklin, Tennessee. Our neighbors were deer and wild critters. Officially, it was known as Miller's Hollow, but Carole named it Spooky Hollow.

The main house was a mansion with enough square footage to build a recording studio, which was the first thing I'd do. The previous owner was a country star who needed to downsize after a bitter divorce settlement. It was idyllic for what we needed. Carole could be a little girl, and I could work from home. Nashville was just a short commute up the road. We settled in quickly.

That summer, Carole spent most of her time outside with the horse that I bought for her. She needed the companionship. Often, I would see her riding Filbert around the property, singing songs to him. She marked her territory and named her little retreats in the forest that surrounded the property. She'd leave me post-it notes in the tack room to let me know where she and Filbert would be hanging out. I didn't need the notes because I could hear her singing halfway to Franklin.

I went to work with the band. Their new album was due for release around Christmas. They had spent most of the summer fronting for Jackhammer and creating a niche following. I was writing new material and remastering old songs for them.

I adopted the habit of setting a kitchen timer on my work station, least I became too preoccupied with work. I'd take a midmorning break with Carole and check to make sure that she did her chores. Sometimes that break took up the whole afternoon. There was always plenty to do on a horse farm, and Carole quickly became the ramrod.

One hot July morning, I made up a gallon of ice tea to take down to the barn. I went to the stables, expecting to find Carole grooming Filbert. It was quiet and dark. All I could hear was the sound of barn swallows. No Carole. No post-it note. Hide and seek time.

Then I heard the stomping hooves of a horse. Filbert couldn't kill an ant if he stepped on it. Then I heard a snort. Not a Filbert snort. Then a giggle. A Carole-giggle coming from the silage bin.

"Carole! Carole, what's going on? Come down outta there."

My hearing wasn't playing tricks on me, but my eyes were. The dark head and mane of a magnificent animal poked out of a dark stall. The eyes were the same loving eyes of my old friend, Traitor. His head bucked with delight and excitement as I walked near him.

"What the hell?" I said, completely dumbfounded. "Where did you come from, boy?" I didn't need an answer and my arms went around his neck. I could hear little hands clapping as I had a reunion with my faithful best friend.

Walt Marsh came hand in hand with Carole from their hiding place. He wore a wry smile, and Carole a possum grin.

Walt said, "Traitor is a man killer. Damned near killed my new son-in-law." He spat when he said it. "You've ruined that horse, and I was either going to have to put him down or give him to you. What's it going to be?"

I couldn't find a single word in the galaxy to say what I was thinking. I simply nodded.

"Welcome to the neighborhood. What made you buy this place?" He bent down to look at Carole. "See that ridge yonder? My place starts the next ridge over, about six miles as the crow flies. I got grandkids about your age under foot all the time."

"Walt, can we talk in private?" I asked.

"Saturday. Could use your help getting in the second cutting. You up for some of Peggy's fried catfish?"

"Walt …"

"I know what you're thinking. Megan and her sissy husband don't come around for family gatherings, and it's just as well."

I detected bitterness in his voice, which needed to be talked about, but not in front of Carole. He patted Carole between the shoulder blades and said to her "Get your daddy up early 'cause there's lots of work needin' done. Filbert may not know the way, but Traitor does. See you on Saturday."

"You can depend on us, Mr. Marsh. We won't waste a bit of daylight," She chirped.

He cackled and winked at her. He turned and walked off. We heard his voice boom, "Takes the steady hand of a good woman to run a spread like this. You're a lucky man, Owen Fletcher." He laughed again and disappeared from sight.

CHAPTER SIXTY-THREE

By September, my studio was finished, and I could get some real work done. Carole was off to school and making a rash of friends.

Personally, I found contentment with my life as a father, songwriter, and band manager. Contentment did not fill every empty space in my soul. I had grown used to an inner sadness, which was hard to keep from Carole. She supposed it was our common bond, but it was more than losing Bonnie. Mine was a debris field that started in the Waffle House where I discovered I'd won the lottery. Sometimes I'd go a full week without having a lottery rage moment. I was getting better.

Jennifer was always dragging in luscious women for me to meet. She nagged at me constantly to get out. Invariable, nothing stuck. It wasn't due to a lack of interest. The women I met all had sunshine lives, good looks, nice educations, and some interesting careers, but none had the depth to fill the shallow end of my heart. If I had been in the market for a soulmate, someone to share my life experiences with, I'd have to burrow my way to the gates of hell to find her. When I did, she wouldn't be the type of woman I'd want around my daughter.

Admittedly my experience with women was a circular path of utter confusion, naïveté, and more recently, suspicious of motives that brought me to a lonely destination. In my younger days, when I was broke and living by the sewer lid, I had no problem attracting women but I didn't have the steam to warm a cold heart. I was cavalier about it all. Now that I had it all, I had no one to share my life with. To be perfectly honest, I got back what I dished out.

Now that I was rich and could afford to purchase a reasonable facsimile of a loving relationship I discovered I was two dimensional. Owen Fletcher and his bank account were inseparable and it was always an issue. Whether I didn't conform to expectations of a wealthy bachelor of good breeding, or being too simple and undeserving of my station in life, the women underfoot had ambitions...theirs and mine. I concluded it would take a lifetime and millions of bucks to sort out, so I opted out. Megan had given me that tour. It hurt and a year into it, I was just getting over it. She really is a bitch.

My selective memory takes me back to a small sliver of exaltation. My affair with Betty was nothing less. I was certain I had found my eternal partner in life, but her secret indiscretions left her no doubt that we were forbidden anything longer than fourteen days. In parting she ripped every fiber of my comprehension of who I was, who my mother was, and what my father had become. Time had not dislodged a satanic hatred of her. Our sensational public exposure is a humiliating stain that is still talked about and thrown in my face.

What Betty and I share in common is the criminal history of an evil man and her silence about it causes me to hate her even more. I have a fear of her. I shudder to think if the motives of Roxanne Thomas's murder rampage were discovered. There was an FBI investigator probing close to the truth. Joyce Houseman was unrelenting in trying to make me slip up during her interrogations. To Betty's credit, she has kept her promise to remain silent about all of it. The truth would only hurt the living. The victims were dead, except one.

I talked to Pat Jarrett about it. He said, "Agent Houseman needs a witness to corroborate that Alvin Fox had manipulated a deranged drug addict to get revenge upon her abusers. Without Betty's testimony all Joyce has is hearsay. Why Betty is tight lipped is beyond me. She *is* a victim." He shrugged his shoulders.

I gladly volunteered my opinion. "If she says a word she'll go to prison."

"For what?"

"I don't know. Extortion. Perjury. Withholding incriminating evidence." I ticked off a number of offenses that collected in my head.

"You really don't get it, Owen. Her silence means she's protecting someone. Joyce seems to think it's you."

"Bullshit, Pat," I said indignantly.

Pat frowned at me and said, "Alvin Fox has buried all the evidence. It's only a matter of time before he gets around to Miss Styles. You really need to speak with her."

I agonized over speaking with Betty for a week. It took me that long to construct my opening sentence. Jerry was only too happy to set up a meeting in one of the conference rooms at the bank.

Here is how a paranoid mind works. I didn't think Betty had anything to do with Roxanne's murder, but I thought the reason she was still above ground was because she and Alvin had colluded to steal five million of the bank's money. I wouldn't let go of the slightest implications condemning her even though I knew better. In fact I was safeguarding my wounded pride with false propositions. I knew she was innocent of the rumors spread about her but I wasn't ready to forgive her because she had taken away from me the ground beneath me. The decades behind me were empty because of her.

I wasn't prepared when the door opened and she stepped into my line of sight. My heart stopped beating and a flood of familiarity washed over me. Betty was beautiful—breathtaking. I recalled how her demure deportment had a soothing effect upon me. I think I gasped and she noticed me sitting at the head of the conference table. She dropped her purse and tripped slightly. She lowered her eyes and fetched her purse and as she rose, she headed for the door murmuring something under her breath.

I blurted out, "Betty, we need to talk."

She stalled and turned about reluctantly. With her eyes lowered, she said, "Owen…Please. I'm so sorry…You surprised me."

"We need to talk."

"It's been so long…I don't know what to say. All that comes to mind is to apologize…for everything."

"This is not about forgiveness, Betty. It's about Boots. It's about Roxanne. It's about Alvin Fox." There was no kindness in my voice. "You made a confession to me. Turns out it's true."

"Owen, I was ambushed. Tricked. You did that. I would never have—."

"You did anyway. Whose idea was that? Fox?"

Tears danced in her eyes and I wasn't moved, or so I tried to pretend. She said, "I have learned that Fox had no intention of keeping the truth from you but it was a set-up, which made me a convenient patsy. You could blame me. I make no excuses for myself."

"It worked—because I do blame you."

"What do you want, Owen?"

"I want you to sit down with Agent Houseman and tell her exactly what transpired."

Her head whipped up unexpectedly. Her voice was soft but strong. "I will not do that. Why would you want me to?"

I had my line memorized because I expected the question. "Justice Betty. Justice for Roxanne, justice for my mom, justice for all of Boots' victims and lastly, justice for his and Mike's murder. You are the link to Alvin Fox."

She shook her head and looked me in the eye. "I can't. I have done enough damage to the Fletcher family. I made a promise to Boots."

"You owe him nothing. What's wrong with you?"

"I owe you. I promised you. I will not drag your name through the mud."

I was quick. "Or are you afraid for your own reputation?"

"Where have you been for the last eighteen months?" She smirked and said, "I've done my best to put distance behind me and our affair. I changed my name, let my hair grow out, and changed my appearance, but you won't believe how many times I'm recognized as "that woman."

I shrugged as if I wasn't particularly interested.

She said, "A post-mortem conviction of your father won't stick to Alvin Fox, but it will stick to you and your brothers. I love you too much."

I scoffed at the notion, turned my face away and said, "So you said, but you had an expiration date and to be fair you warned me. I was just too stupid to believe you in the first place."

"Owen, I'm content to have been loved by you. What we shared between us was a gift from God and I pray for redemption everyday. Forgiveness is too much to ask for—."

"Yes it is."

She nodded a couple times then looked away. She stood, gained her composure and said, "I know how this works, Owen. I've lived the lie all my life and I can tell you it's better this way.

I will not betray you of your legacy." She turned sharply and walked away with all the dignity she could muster.

Depending on my mood there wasn't a day after that without me thinking of Betty. Not one, and sometimes several times a day. I would alternately relish in her humiliation and then recall how much I loved her while she took care of Lawson and Tammy on the farm. There was a block of time that I cherished, a few weeks of pure happiness. God had put Betty on this earth specifically for me. As weird as this may sound, I hated my father for stealing the innocence of the young girl meant for me. He ruined God's plan.

At the other end of the spectrum I accumulated all the sordid accounts of the destruction of the lives of young girls and found that Betty and my mother, by their silence, abetted Boots' perverted habits. But what did I know about the terror, manipulation, and mind twist of a violated teen? All the sick pieces of that episode were beyond my comprehension. At the end of the day, Roxanne killed the beast that tormented her and that was justice.

At the end of *my* day, I concluded that Betty was right. What we had between us was a flick of flame smothered by darkness, never to be rekindled. Water under the bridge. Stop obsessing and move on. But the sun comes up in the morning and I'd visit dark passages from my distant and not so distant past, which, by the way, would never have come to me had I not won the lottery.

CHAPTER SIXTY-FOUR

In December, I received some good news from Jennifer and Phil. They were getting married on Christmas day. Good for them. I had a twinge of jealousy, knowing I'd probably never get to that happy plateau. Phil and Jennifer had more news. "Trophy was getting a spot concert at Opryland, a two week holiday gig. Jennifer had yet another surprise for me. "Owen, we're going to showcase 'Advice on Vice,' and we need you there to perform it. It's going to be the album leader. We need you to do the cameo publicity in front of it."

"Definitely no. I don't perform. That's the deal."

"It's just an industry insider gig to get some excitement brewing. It's local and just for two weeks. One song, your song, what can it hurt?"

Whether I liked it or not, my notoriety created a stir. Some good, and some not so good. Whatever...tragic figures always have a following, no matter if they're on their way up or on their way down. I had to concede to Jennifer's request. I pouted, rolled my eyes, and shrugged my shoulders.

"You'll do it then?"

"One condition. There will be no soundtrack."

"Deal dude!" She gave me a knuckle buckle and said, "Just one more thing. Opening night is a by-invitation-only performance for all the moguls in town and a few showboats. It's our Christmas present to Carole. You okay with that?"

"You're up to something, Jennifer. I don't want Carole anywhere near the stage. You got that?"

"Whatever you say, Owen."

The night of the concert was upon us and Carole was freaking out because I never took her to live performances of the band, which was another promise to Bonnie that I was about to break. Carole bounced in the car before we even got to the parking lot. Why did I have the vague idea that she knew more about what was in the making than I did? She was getting out of hand, and I had to give her a stern lecture about manners, ladylike conduct, and public deportment. It was a waste of breath, so I left her with a serious admonishment. "You act up once and you'll spend the rest of the evening here in the parking lot. Are we clear about that?"

"I'll be good Daddy. I'll make you proud."

That should have been a tip-off right there.

The auditorium for our private bash had seating for 800, about 799 more than I deserved or wanted. Clayton Phillips.... music mogul, owner of several labels, Vice Chairman of the Tennessee Music Academy of Performing Arts, and total prick.... met me at the door. "Owen Fletcher, as I live and breathe, we're glad to have you back."

Did he slap my back? Clayton Phillips kicked my ass out the door the first go around. A thought passed through my mind. I should have waited in the parking lot until it was all over. But it was a surprise for Carole, and more to the point, a public relations stunt for Trophy. I'd muddle through.

"Lead the way, Mr. Phillips."

It was a packed house. There was a spotlight on me as I made my way toward the front of the auditorium. Clayton's plastic teeth and plastic smile dazzled in the light. I was baffled by the standing ovation I received. I'm sure I looked like a prisoner from the Tower of London on his walk to the executioner's block. Little Carole had a firm grasp of my hand, so I was going to be just fine. She waved and smiled, and I gave her a reminder grip to knock it off.

A second spotlight lit up a special seating section on the stage. When I recognized the faces, I stopped dead in my tracks. Jerry was there. Frank sat next to him. Peggy and Walt were a comforting sight. I abso-freakin'-lutely lost it when I saw my two brothers, Lawson and Ron standing, clapping. What the hell was going on? I could hear Ron's unique laugh above the din of applause. Lawson was nodding his head approvingly. How did Jennifer pull this off? The last I saw of either of them was at Dad's funeral. I didn't have time to absorb the oddity of it all.

What was Stevie Sievers doing in my box seats? Seated next to him was Megan. She couldn't lift her head, and I couldn't move my feet. My brain was in total disarray. I looked elsewhere to save us both an embarrassing moment. And when I did, I saw the entire crew of the table fifty-seven band in living flesh. Carole spotted Betty the same time I did.

"Oh daddy it's her! It's her." Carole was doing a lindy hop while I was a flag pole and my face was at half mast. I had no idea that a forgiving heart manifests a physical sensation. Pieces of concrete turned to dust and my limbs ached with desire. Sorrow dripped like melting snow on a spring day leaving a void to be filled with unrestrained joy.

The shock of seeing Betty caused a wave of uncertainty within me. I saw her beautiful eyes dart between me and Carole. She was fearful what our reaction would be as she twisted in her chair and looked as though she would take flight at the slightest hint of rejection. I had to fix that. I bent and whispered into Carole's ear and she catapulted across the stage. I intently looked at Betty as my little muffin stomped right up to her idol, put out her hand and said, "My name is Carole Fletcher, and I know everything about you. My daddy and I both love you. We watch your video all the time. Thank you for coming Miss Betty."

Betty tried very hard to disguise her reaction, but I saw her light up. A smile curled upon her lips and her eyes danced with delight. When her arms spread, a little girl swamped her. The audience are country folks and that kind of scene brings out the hankies. Betty looked over Carole's head and I didn't miss the invitation to join Carole.

What was I to do? I'd gotten through the forgiven part as I recalled, but if I took one step in her direction who knew how that would turn out? I tentatively took a step and Carole said, "Hurry up, Daddy. We don't have all night."

Jennifer was at the podium and she was in the spotlight. "Find a seat Owen, and buckle up. We're getting' ready to tear your house down."

She already did. My entire history was sitting in that box. What the hell was Jennifer thinking? Half my guests I could hug. The other half I wanted to garrote. My FBI gal- pal sharply prodded me. My clan was on their feet applauding as I looked at familiar faces and was confused by their expressions. I went up on the stage and a woman met me half way. It was Tammy, Lawson's girlfriend. I was stunned by the medical miracle because the doctors had assured me that walking wasn't in the cards for her. We hugged and kissed, then she escorted me to a seat in the special box. She whispered in my ear, "Lawson's really sorry, please don't make it hard on him. He didn't know."

"Know what, Tammy?"

"We love you for what you did for us. Look at me, Owen." She didn't answer the question.

I couldn't because I knew she was crying. I looked at Lawson, and he gave me that Fletcher smile and a thumbs up. That was good enough for me.

So there I was, face to face with Betty. There are times we're sandwiched between what we expect of ourselves, what we perceive others expect of us; and what we intend, want, and desire doesn't have a speaking part. Pride is a rude fellow and often speaks out of turn, which is what I did. Betty was expecting a polite hug and I stiffly said, "What are you doing here?"

My words stung her and she recoiled, blinked her eyes and hung her head. "I knew it was a bad idea. I'm sorry, Owen." She looked around, embarrassed and she seemed to be looking for an exit.

Carole was only ten, but she was wise beyond her years and had a decent lock on the situation of two adults acting like children. I take that back, one adult acting like a child. She grabbed my arm, pulled it around Betty's waist and hugged both of us tightly. Once flesh touched flesh, the radiant scent of her hit my senses, and my lips brushed up against hers, it was a galactic bonding of two souls coming together in our own universe.

Jennifer's voice brought us back to the mother planet.

"Hey, you two. These people came to see a concert. You can talk later."

We sat down, and Little Britches tugged my sleeve persistently. "Look, Daddy." She pointed to a huge screen with a velvet backdrop, the AMA logo and words that read, THE TENNESSEE MUSIC ACADEMY CLELEBRATES OWEN FLETCHER. If Jennifer had planned a celebrity roast, when it was over, I'd roast her, slowly...very slowly.

Clayton took to the podium, and I was curious what kind of back flip the bastard planned to talk his way out of what he did to me. He was always a good bullshit artist, and as he held his arms out to embrace his audience, it was perfectly clear that this event would be no exception. I snagged a look at Pat Jarrett, and he lipped, "This is going to be good."

Clayton began. "Owen Fletcher's first trip to Nashville was with the original members of Shylock, some twelve years ago. As we all know, Shylock set the standard and raised the bar in the country-rock genre. The genius of that success is the envy of every artist in the industry. What we didn't know, and we've recently discovered, is that Owen Fletcher was the inspiration of what followed."

That was bullshit. I wrote the music, arranged it, and performed it. He droned on and back-pedaled for another five minutes. Stevie and I were being honored for fifteen top hits that Shylock massacred, but made a ton of bucks off. I wrote seven, Stevie wrote three, and the other five were collaborative pieces by both of us. Slick Clayton didn't strip the awards from Shylock. He more or less stapled Stevie and I on the tail end ...as in oops.

I'm not a politician, but Pat Jarrett was. We had just won a huge lawsuit and a non-disclosed chunk of change that I still can't talk about. Pat wanted some form of public recognition and political payback. I actually didn't enjoy the crow feathers that Clayton Phillips was spitting out. I was busy synchronizing brain waves between Betty and me. Just so you know, Carole's brainwaves were interrupting every chance she got.

Now that Clayton got that out of his system, Stevie and his bitch could get the hell out of my box seats. I turned to look at them. Stevie gave me a wink, and Megan still couldn't look at me. So far, that part of Owen Fletcher Night was dismal, boring, and disappointing.

Clayton, sly bastard that he was, switched gears. "Tonight, I'm wearing two hats. As the president and CEO, it is my honor to sign the genius of Owen Fletcher's latest inspiration to Emblem

Studios. It is the marriage of the past with the innovative creativity of a giant in our industry. I think you'll find that he's made selected classics as timeless as Bach or Beethoven. Ladies and gentlemen, celebrate Owen Fletcher." He directed his attention to me like he was one of the wise men at the birth of Jesus. "Owen?"

Owen-what? What was Owen supposed to do? Go home was a good idea. I stood and made a few humble bows, then sat my ass back down. Clayton, never wanting to be upstaged, took my impromptu speaking part away from me—and a good thing too. He said to my polite standing ovation, "Enjoy the evening and I'll turn the podium over to the master of ceremonies, Miss Jennifer Barkley, lead singer of the sensational Trophy Band Company."

That lit the sky rocket sitting next to me, and I had to put a hand on her wiggles. There were a series of new images on the screen, and the audience slow-rolled a round of laughter. The photos were of a street musician wearing dread locks, burlap and leather, face painted like a Parisian harlot, and enough studs stuck to her body to hold up the Golden Gate Bridge. The woman in the pictures was making the most hideous faces. I had to laugh. This event was going to hell in a hurry, and I was beginning to like it.

With microphone in hand, she came charging across the stage dressed like a hot new diva in town. Her backless, ankle-length gown sizzled. Jennifer did a runway waltz to tease the audience. Then she opened by pointing at the screen. "What do you think? I clean up pretty good, don't you think?" She walked about, flirting with her fans. "Yup, that was me before Owen ran me through the car wash." She made a few more comedic lines about me. Then she turned to me and said softly, "Thank you, Owen. I love you."

The stage lights came up, and she and Trophy went to work, rocking the house with a Marvin Gaye classic. I had run three vocals through the arrangement, and halfway through I could see I had made a hit with the seasoned artists in the room. Jennifer and Bobbie worked it and made every note spark, while Phil delivered the goods. The audience was standing before they even finished.

Jennifer said, "I could sing Marvin Gaye all night long, but this is Owen's night, and do I ever have a surprise for him." She paused and looked directly at me and Carole. "This all started with an amateur contest on a cruise ship. The screen showed slides of the group on the ship. Jennifer narrated with a humorous spin.

"Table Fifty-Seven got us through some pretty tough times and was the inspiration Owen provided to us. He made us sit and listen to this amateur demo over and over again. The young lady sitting next to Owen still can't get enough of Table Fifty-Seven. The demo and the people in it are her anchor, right honey?"

Carole's head bounced up and down.

Anyone who knew much about me could make the connection without Jennifer going into it. Jennifer walked over to our seats and asked, "Carole would you like to introduce Table Fifty-Seven?"

Carole's hand shot to cover her mouth, and her hazel eyes were swimming pools of surprise. Mine were filled with shock. Jennifer gave me a 'would you get off your ass' look. That's all it took to get Carole up out of her seat. What the hell? I was right behind her.

Jennifer began bringing Table Fifty-Seven out on the stage, while the demo played as background music. Carole walked right up to old Sam and put her hand out. "Mr. Sam, I'm Carole Fletcher. Daddy says you're a cracker-jack manager." Sam smile proudly as Carole did a little curtsy. "Miss Pearle, I'm pleased to meet you. I learned a lot about playing slide piano just by listening to you on the demo tape you gave my daddy."

Pearle was smitten immediately but confused. She covered nicely. Pearle bent down to hug my little girl, and that provoked "ahhs" from the audience. Nothing bashful about my Carole, and so far, she was showing good manners until she asked Sam if they really lived on a cruise ship and if he threw his medicine overboard every morning.

She came to Jack and Erin, and Carole stole the show when she said, "Miss Erin, can I give you some advice?" I didn't know what to expect and rolled my eyes. Erin and the audience giggled. She bent down to hear what a wise ten-year-old would have to say. Carole said in a hushed voice, "You should hire Mr. Sam to be your agent."

Jennifer said to the audience, "I swear, this is not scripted. She gets it from her dad."

Disaster hit when Sandy and Irene came on stage. Carole greeted them politely and made small talk, then she asked, "How are the book sales doing?"

Irene indignantly asked, "What book sales?"

"Daddy said you were Bible thumpers, trying to sell books on the boat. I hope you made enough money to pay for everything."

There was an implosion in the auditorium. Peals of laughter ricocheted off the walls. I wilted to the size of a flea from embarrassment. Carole looked at me, confused. "I'm trying to be good, Daddy. Did I say something wrong?"

The problem was, I told her something wrong, so it bit me on the ass and I found myself saying to Irene, "It's hard to explain things to children."

Sometimes it's hard for children to explain things to their parents. When it came to Betty's turn to be introduced, Carole said, "This is Miss Betty. A long time ago I asked my mommy if it's okay for a girl to have a bestest, best friend that she didn't know about. I told her about you and she said it was okay and you've been my bestest, best friend ever since. Is that okay with you?"

I could feel the tension rise from the audience as they awaited Betty's response.

"Carole, darling. I could use a bestest, best friend right about now. Have you asked your daddy if it's okay?"

It was quiet, but not pin-dropping quiet, as I could hear sniffles and the clearing of throats in the crowd.

Carole said, "He's a daddy and there's just some secrets between us girls."

Betty's imploring eyes locked on mine. She held Carole at arms' length. Then she smiled at me and softly said to Carole, "Miss Jennifer tells me you can rock the house with every song we performed on the cruise. Can you help us out?" Carole's butt was bouncing, her legs were flexing like a sprinter waiting for the starter's pistol to go off. She looked at me for permission. I looked at Jennifer, and she gave me a head nod. Against my better judgment, I said, "Show Miss Pearle what you've got."

Pearle walked over and took her hand. "Thanks, Owen; my old fingers need a rest. Come along, child; let's make some believers out of these monkeys."

Bonnie would kill me for this if she were here. I prayed for forgiveness. Then the music began with "Change the World," by Eric Clapton. Little Miss Flash had an unsteady start, but Betty's singing put Carole right back in the grove. The performance was wild. If eardrums were made out of glass, the audience would all have hearing problems tomorrow. Rich, vibrant, and up into the bleachers it went with the rattle of piano keys chasing it.

Lawson was pulling and tugging on me throughout the whole song. Tammy was gripping my hand, and I was frozen with awe. The audience was over-the-top screaming at the end of it. Who would have ever thought a classic Clapton tune could be rearranged and still remain a Clapton original? Betty took on "Show Me the Way" and three more classics, followed by Abba's "Waterloo." What a way to end a performance, but Betty wasn't finished.

She softly stroked Carole locks and said, “We don’t have to, but would you like to sing ‘Bonnie’s Song’?” Carole looked over at me for the longest moment with an expressionless face. I didn’t want to influence the moment, and I stared back at her. We had a conversation without saying a word to each other.

She said, “My daddy helped me write this song for my mommy. I sing it every day. Would it be okay if Daddy sang it with me, Miss Betty?”

How do you say no to that? Lawson had to help me up. Betty touched me gently and looked into my eyes. She whispered, “I love you.” She guided me to the piano bench, and I sat next to my daughter. Carole squeezed my hand, gave me a hard hug and said, “Let’s blow them away for Mama’s sake.”

“Bonnie’s Song” was not a lamented sonnet. It was a fast paced, bluesy song that you would sing in the backseat while going on vacation, type of song …with silliness to it. There was a place in the song for anyone to join in if they felt like it. It could go on forever like ‘Row, Row, Your Boat.’ You could speed it up or slow it down and it was full of places for impromptu musical interruptions. It fit the slide style of piano genre that fit Carole’s style of playing.

We kicked it off, and Table Fifty-Seven joined in. We did the first refrain without singing, so the audience could get an inner pulse going. Then Carole kicked in with the lyrics. She stretched her ten-year-old pipes to the adult level and grabbed notes I didn’t know she had in her body. Then Betty joined in, followed by me. Jack and Erin came onboard. I looked out into the audience and saw laughing and weeping at the same time. Carole’s face was red, and sweat beads formed on her little brow. She was having the time of her life, and she was putting on a performance. She closed her eyes, looked to heaven and sang the last refrain solo.

When we finished, there wasn’t a dry eye in the house. The auditorium was dead silent. Tammy got to her feet and started a slow clap. Old Sam and Ethel were next up, and I didn’t think they could clap any faster. Then it caught on, and the clapping intensified and then quickened, followed by yells. Carole gave me a hard hug, hopped off the bench, and flew into Betty's arms. What was this all about? I looked out at Jennifer, and she gave me the gesture, 'would you do something?' I joined Betty and my daughter with hugs and kisses. Had I missed something?

Yes, I had and it dawned on me. Carole and I had both been infatuated with Betty, but at different levels. Carole saw in Betty a part of her mother, lively and vibrant, which soothed her anguish and calmed her. To a ten-year-old, Betty was like an elixir and a far off fairytale princess. She was a fictional model of whom Carole would one day emulate.

I never saw it, but Jennifer did. Jennifer, smart minx that she was, killed two birds with one stone. Jennifer brought Betty to life for Carole, if only for one shining moment. However, Jennifer was much more devious than that.

This was not working out to be Owen Fletcher Night at the Grand Ole Opry. This was a full-blown personal intervention that I didn't see coming. Hell, I was a full grown man, and I should've been able to figure that out on my own. I could see there was a mutual admiration society going on between my daughter and my ex-lover. That didn't even sound right in the same sentence. I had been intercepted and sandbagged by three women. There I was frozen in time with three sets of adoring eyes on me.

Jennifer took Carole to the ladies room so Betty and I had a brief moment to talk. We both started at the same time; stopped, and did it again. "You go first," I said.

She shook her head. "I swear this is not my idea. You can blame Jerry and Jennifer."

"It went really well, so let's skip that part. What do you want from me?"

"A long time ago we agreed that you and I had an expiration date. It's coming up on two years soon. There hasn't been a day that I haven't thought about it. Oh, I don't know what I want to say. I'm afraid to say anything—Have you given any thought to us maybe…never mind."

"What? Maybe picking up where we left off? Until an hour ago it never crossed my mind." I wasn't about to tell her that for the last two years I woke up everyday plotting ways to murder her. "Where we left off was where we both wanted to cancel that expiration date and start a life together. Remember that? So let's be smart about this and finish that conversation first."

"What? I don't understand. I hurt you badly. I have a lot to prove to you before you can stop hating me."

"Being angry isn't the half of it. You owe me the heart you took from me. I want it back."

"But…?"

"Here comes Carole. We don't need to be talking this way in front of her."

Jennifer asked, "Does this child come with a leash?"

I picked Carole up and instead of her arms wrapping around my neck, they went for Betty. She took Carole from me and they hugged for dear life. Betty looked at me with curious humility. I think she was as surprised as I was and felt completely out of place. She cupped Carole's chin and said, "Honey, your dad and I have a concert to finish. We'll talk later."

"Promise?"

"I promise."

I had a concert to finish, but did I hear her say we had a concert to finish? The spotlight went center stage where Phil and Jennifer stood like they were posing for wedding pictures. In a way they were. Carole and I returned to our seats to await Jennifer's next surprise, and it wasn't long in coming.

Country folks like a good happy ending to a family story, and Phil was telling his. "Somewhere between dreadlocks and silk gowns, I figured out that the woman standing next to me had wrapped me up tighter than bailed cotton. I'd spent a week working up the courage and trying to find the right words to ask her to marry me."

Jennifer said, "Phil had found the courage, but if he was going to find the words, I'd be waiting into the next century. So I said, December 25th … and he just looked at me." She made a face that made the audience laugh.

Phil said, "I hadn't popped the question, but Jennifer flew past that necessity. We'll be tying the knot on Christmas Day."

There was polite applause as they kissed. Jennifer smiled and resumed her homily. "Music is the only family I've had since I was fourteen. I'm an impetuous kinda gal, and when I get something in my head, I just go for it and usually get what I go for. I got family planning in my head, and I got a little ahead of myself. I'll be leaving the Trophy Band for the foreseeable future…but I'll be back."

Phil smiled proudly and said, "That leaves us looking for a replacement, and we thought tonight would be as good a time as any to showcase the powerful voice that started all of this. Miss Elizabeth Stiles has agreed to finish out the season provided she can convince this august gathering…Can I see a show of hands for volunteers to judge her performance?"

All hands went into the air and Jennifer said, "I told you, Phil, these people all have day jobs. Elisabeth's got this." The spotlight shone on Betty. She smiled and waved.

Phil acted like a county judge and announced, "Miss Stiles, are you ready to rock this room?"

My little girl stood up and yelled, "Go for it, Betty!" That wasn't in the script either and got snickers from the audience. It was a put up deal, and I pulled Carole back to her seat next to me.

"But, Daddy, she wants to be in our band." She hopped back up and yelled again. An inch of defiance could not be overlooked. I wasn't talking about my daughter. I was talking about Jennifer.

The spotlight followed Betty to stage center, and I followed Jennifer stage left.

"You and I are going to have a one-on-one. I have half a mind to fire you."

"Cool, Owen. I quit. Thanks to you, I got knocked up by the most wonderful man on this planet. I'm going to have something that you and God gave me…a family I've never had. Now that's better than fuckin' music. I'll take that, and you and I can be stay-at-home parents."

"What's Betty doing taking your place?"

"I've brought the complete drama of your life into one room. You're the nicest, most fucked-up moron I have ever met. When Owen Fletcher leaves tonight, his fucking lottery rage will be resolve for all time."

"What's going on, Jennifer?"

"Jesus, Owen, you are so guilt ridden over Carole's life that you don't have one for yourself. Do you think nobody notices? You are the poster child of the broken-hearted, dude. You lost Bonnie and we know what that cost you. You lost Megan because of your fucked-up dad. The sorriest loser in all this is Betty and you can fix that. How many times have we all watched that DVD of her? We all see in your face how you feel about her. You *and* Carole! The two of you are both in the tank in love with her. You can't trick us, Owen."

"Who made the decision to put her in the band?"

Jennifer rolled her eyes. "The decision was unanimous. Your vote doesn't count, but Carole's does. Look at her, Owen. Look at your daughter. Do you see that? Look at Betty. Love at first sight, brother. You've got one shot to fix it. What's it going to be? And don't shrug your shoulders at me. Get this fixed …tonight …or I'll chain-drag your ass to the Cumberland Bridge and hang you myself."

Jennifer's lips were drawn tighter than piano wire, and both of her fists were balled up. She was street mean and ready for a brawl.

"It gets fixed …tonight," I said.

"Good. Let's join your fan club and enjoy the show."

Jennifer and I swished quietly back to our seats. Carole was on her feet pointing at Betty, yelling, "Betty's in my daddy's band!" Carole crawled up into Jennifer's lap, gushing over Betty. "Isn't she beautiful?"

Jennifer said, "Yes she is, in more ways than you'll ever know."

Carole barely whispered, "I just love her sooo much."

"So does your daddy. He just has to rediscover why he loves her sooo much." Jennifer gave me her gunfighter glare, warning me not to even blink.

The concert continued with Betty pushing the envelope of her beautiful voice. She was singing to me and my baby, as if we belonged to her. Halfway through the concert, I realized someone had to fix Owen and his obsessive lottery rage.

At the end of her last song, Betty spoke into the mic and stared straight in my soul. "I need a little help here. Our hit single, 'Advice on Vice' was written many years ago by Owen Fletcher. Owen, would you mind coming up here and give us a hand?"

I looked around the arena and saw expectations on the faces of the entire inner circle who I realized were there for me, nodding for me to go on stage.

I asked Jimmy for his guitar and then turned to Betty. "We have to get through this concert, you and me. Then we'll have a concert of our own."

I heard her breath catch, a moment before words spilled out from her on a rush of air. "You mean that, Owen?"

"You went to a lot of trouble to get me here. I was wondering when you'd get around to taking ownership of me. Honey, we've got a lot riding on this song, you up to it?"

"I've been practicing the song ever since I heard you and Stevie belt it out at Blue Notes."

I did a double take and said, "That long ago?"

She had a cocked smile and was about to say something when Phil said, "Come on you two, let's get our work done first."

Musically, we fit. Betty was very flirty with me, which put another way; she was damned sexy carrying her part of the song. Halfway through it, I could tell that our audience was over the moon with Trophy's debut single. When we finished, we got more than we came for from our peers in the audience.

Clayton Phillips knew he had a hit on his hands. He came on stage to grandstand, and he wormed an encore from Betty and me.

I saw her look at Carole. Her eyes held so much joy, as her fingers brushed my cheek. "Do you remember our first song together?"

I smiled. "In the dining room with Pearle and Sam, "Over the Rainbow.'"

"Let's do it for Carole."

We went to the box seat and sang it for her. Little girls cry at the drop of the hat, and that's not what we got out of her. She stood up and sang the chorus with us. When we finished, sly old Clayton was waving his wand about. This time, the audience asked for the encore.

Clayton blared out. "One more, Owen. One for old time's sake, then we'll go to the mezzanine for champagne."

We exchanged glances and consulted with our backup. We finished with Celine Dion's, "I Will Always Love You,' which were coincidentally the last words of Betty's letter to me. There she stood with me, lost forever in my passion for music. I saw it in her face. We sang it as though we had something to prove to each other. We hugged and kissed with the spotlight on us.

On impulse, I whispered into her ear and Betty fainted dead away. This time I was there to catch her, and I would be there to break her fall for the rest of her life. My little ten-year-old leaped across the stage. “Daddy, what happened to Betty? Is she hurt?”

“I smiled at Carole and said, “She’s in shock. She’ll be fine in a minute.”

“What did you say to her? You weren’t mean, were you?”

“No, honey, I asked her to marry me.”

Her eyes bugged out and her hand went to her mouth. “Really? Did you?”

“Yes, I did.”

I had Carole hugging me and pounding her fists on my back. “Daddy, what did she say?”

“I’m not sure, but I think she said yes.”

EPILOGUE

This is a good place to end this story, but there is just too much more to tell. Betty and I married on Christmas Day, as did Phil and Jennifer. Carole got to be flower girl twice in one day. Jennifer and Phil produced a fine baby boy, and they named their first born after me. Owen Thorpe is a bit like his mother and no better house broken than Traitor.

Trophy went on the road, and Betty went with them. So did Carole and I, when the opportunity presented itself. I made it easy, as I used the royalty check from Shylock to buy their private jet. Thanks to Pat Jarrett, Shylock would be buying gas for my jet for a long time to come. Speaking of Pat, he married Joyce Houseman, my FBI girlfriend. Joyce is a normal person after she put on some weight … well, almost normal.

Carole was right about one thing. She didn't wait to be grown-up to become a superstar. She and Betty cut the title to "Bonnie's Song," and, it became an instant hit. People on vacation or on a road trip will be singing "Bonnie's Song" long after I'm gone.

I'm successful with my career as a producer and manager of new and popular talents. I make a good living staying at home. This might sound strange, but after getting jump-started with my lottery winnings, I haven't touched a cent of it since. I get statements from Jerry, and I treat them like junk mail.

As for Jerry, when you think about it, he was crudely the last person who I thought would turn out to be a pure winged butterfly. I'm not his best pal and never wanted to be. We'll let it go at that, but none the less, he was the only person who saw me through the fun and exciting ordeal of winning the fucking Tennessee State Lottery. We hang out with him and his significant other from time to time.

I've been thinking about cutting a check for Hajji and Jolene, but Pat keeps telling me not to. Hajji, the goofy, greedy bastard he is, was given enough money for selling me the ticket to buy three more liquor stores, and staffed them with Iranians. Now Jolene is a different matter. She doesn't waitress anymore, which is a good thing. She became a doctor at Webster Community Hospital after receiving a full and anonymous scholarship to Vanderbilt School of Medicine.

We see Jack, Erin, and the twins a couple times a year. Old Ethel died on a long cruise, and Sam picked up a new girlfriend to cruise the globe.

Alvin Fox is still running cheap scams on lottery winners. He'll get caught one of these days. Bad things happen to bad people, but the world doesn't work that way. If I was going to fix my lottery rage permanently, I needed to put Alvin Fox in the same hidden place with all my other ghosts. Just so you know, if I ever see Alvin Fox in a crosswalk, I'll run three red lights to run over that fucker.

Lawson and Tammy finally got married after all these years, and then divorced six months later. But they're still together, go figure. We see them a couple times a year when Betty and I can get away to Indiana. He bought meaner dogs, and I could write a book about his latest conspiracy theories.

Megan and I patched up our differences …socially. She's a jealous bitch and hits on me when our spouses aren't around. Eventually, she'll fast forward her way out of her marriage to Stevie, but in the meantime, his life is reduced to being the lonely pussy he's always been. Poor guy is like a train set making laps around Megan's Christmas tree.

Walt and I bust our asses helping each other out on our farms, like good neighbors are supposed to do. Peggy keeps us well fed, and she's given up talking about her fucked-up daughter.

Traitor and I get out by ourselves to talk about things.

So what was the lottery rage all about? It was about Owen Fletcher getting sized up for an expensive emotional make-over. I care deeply about my country, my family, and my many friends. I love music, my life, my way of thinking. I have endured the pain and suffering that is part of living. I actually belong to the human race. The pain of life is unavoidable, and so is the reward of happiness on this side of it if you take the time to soak it in.

It has occurred to me that earth is actually hell. When you fuck up in heaven, God sends you here to learn how to be worthy of heaven. Bonnie was a quick learner, and that's why she rollerblades with the angels in heaven. Boots, on the other hand, will be here for several lifetimes, maybe forever. If I hadn't won the lottery, I would probably end up stuck here until I did win. Figure the odds on that and how many lifetimes it would take to earn roller blades to skate with Bonnie? I'm not in a hurry to make that trip as I am having too much joy on this short journey, and when it's all over, I won't be back. I still buy lottery tickets ..just in case.

AUTHOR BIOGRAPHY

Retired US Air Force officer and airline pilot Robert Lance is an active businessman and the former CEO of a communications corporation. In addition to *Lottery Rage,* he is the author of *Mischief Island, Caesar's Cat,* and *The Shadow Spy.*

Lance holds a graduate degree in Russian studies and regularly contributes to academic societies specializing in his areas of expertise. He is a member of the Association of Former Intelligence Officers, Veterans of Foreign Wars, the RAF Club, and International Thrill Writers.

Active in the "war bird" community, Lance is an avid traveler who constantly seeks new experiences and adventures.